LYNN ABBEY
THE
FORGE OF
VIRTUE

POPULAR LIBRARY

An Imprint of Warner Books, Inc.

A Time Warner Company

POPULAR LIBRARY EDITION

Popular Library®, the fanciful P design, and Questar® are registered
trademarks of Warner Books, Inc.

Cover design by Don Puckey
Cover illustration by Janny Wurtz

Popular Library books are published by
Warner Books, Inc.
666 Fifth Avenue
New York, N.Y. 10103

A Time Warner Company

Printed in the United States of America

First Printing: January, 1991

10 9 8 7 6 5 4 3 2 1

"You A Coward, Boy?" The Brigand Taunted.

The tip of Jordan's bastard sword quivered slightly, drawing the brigand's attention, but not his attack. Jordan's bluffs were not as well honed as his other fighting skills.

A moment had passed. Drum and the gypsies were losing ground to the remaining brigands. Jordan's sides and back had begun to feel naked. Shield or no shield, he had to attack.

The brigand blinked, and Jordan lunged, with his left side leading, against the iron shield boss. He batted the brigand's sword aside with his own, then tried to reverse it for a killing thrust. Jordan did not feel the tip meet resistance as it should, yet the brigand toppled backward, taking Jordan with him.

Jordan succumbed to panic. He knew his awkward stab couldn't have pierced the brigand's mail and he knew even better that there was no worse place to be in a fight than belly-down. But the brigand wasn't struggling at all. Jordan watched with disbelief as dark blood spurted through his enemy's lips . . .

THE FORGE OF VIRTUE

One

The lords and ladies of Britannia had been arriving at Hawksnest all month. Every spare room in the villa was already occupied and the most illustrious guests weren't expected until just before the feast. Two huge tents filled the paddock: shelter for the extra servants and retainers. Everyone would be comfortable—so long as the weather didn't turn to rain.

Erwald Ironhawk, normally an even-tempered man, scurried from the hall, down to the kitchen, up to the solar, and back again, shouting orders to shadows and servants alike. His wife, Lady Barbara, followed at a discreet distance, soothing the ruffled feathers and setting things to right.

"This shall pass," she said to herself and the red-faced butler. "He'll be himself again once the feast is served. By this time next week, we'll be laughing at ourselves."

The butler pursed his lips skeptically.

Barbara shrugged. "There's no way we can get wine

from Trinsic by midnight. It's not as if we could send an ox-cart out to the hill to wait until the moon gate appears —so don't worry about it, Alfwin. When the time comes, send up our own good wine. If my lord notices—which I very much doubt—tell him you did so on my authority."

"Yes, my lady."

Alfwin sped along the atrium walkway to the stairs that would take him down to his precious wine butts. Lady Barbara watched him go, then stared at the place where he had been, wondering if the vast estate of Hawksnest would, indeed, survive tonight's feast. Her eyes watered; she was looking straight at the red-orange disk of the setting sun. As if to confirm her worst suspicion, the clang of the campanile-tower tocsin echoed against the white marble walls of the atrium.

The lookout had sighted the first of the Companions riding out of the forest—and here she was, still in a house-gown! The wave of panic Lady Barbara had resisted heroically these last ten days crested above her. Companions were arriving; the sun was setting. Her husband's villa—her villa actually, the land was passed through her family line; her lord was simply the eldest son of a wealthy paladin merchant of Trinsic—was hosting the springtide Conclave of the Peers of the Virtue.

Scooping up an armful of skirt, Barbara, Lady Iron-hawk—born mistress of Hawksnest, dutiful mother of two sons, and sober wife these last twenty years—ran to her tiring room like a hare fleeing the hounds.

She was herself a Virtue Peer having received enlightenment at the shrine of Spirituality before the dawn of her eighteenth birthday, but she had not taken her quest further despite her father's urging. The shrine of Spirituality—one of the eight virtues revealed by Britannia's legendary Avatar—lay beyond the plane of the temporal world. It was equally far from everywhere; she had not needed to travel the length and breadth of the land to visit it—merely enter the nearby moon gate at midnight.

Her husband, whom she had not known at the time, had received enlightenment from the shrines of Honor, Justice, Valor, and Honesty before assaying the midnight venture to Spirituality's shrine. Each Peer charted his, or her, own course along the paths of Virtue. Erwald got as far as Spirituality, and not beyond it.

No Britannian had yet duplicated the Avatar's quest.

The Companions, the guests of honor at any Peerage Conclave, completed the quest with the Avatar, but they—like the nameless Avatar himself—were not Britannians. Though men and women of mortal flesh, the Companions seemed not to age and were said to come from a place beyond the spheres and stars about which they never spoke.

"My lady, I thought you'd never get here. Hurry, there's still time for your bath. The water's all sweet and steaming," said Agatha as she embraced Lady Barbara, loosening the laces of her gown as she did.

Barbara's embrace was simpler and, perhaps, more sincere: she hadn't known her own mother. Despite the residence of an honored and well-paid healer, Lady Adelaise had died hours after giving birth to her only child. The magic of Britannia could work miracles, but it could not rewrite destiny. Adelaise had been destined to die at the age of twenty. Agatha, a suntanned farmer from one of the outlying estate cottages, had been destined to nurse and raise her overlord's daughter instead of her own, stillborn son.

"This way, my lady."

House servants, trained by Agatha's steady hand, collected Barbara's discarded gown as she stepped out of it. A well-run estate depended on such delicate dialogue: Barbara, Erwald, their children, Jordan and Darrel, and a double-handful of equally privileged retainers created the disorder which, in turn, provided respectable employment for many times their number of servants. The luxuries of their tables and tiring rooms supported the plainer, yet comfortable, life available elsewhere within the villa, and, to a lesser extent, in the dozens of outlying cottages.

The estate of Hawksnest revolved around Erwald Lord Ironhawk and his extended family as the world of Britannia revolved around the sun.

One girl held the light brown tresses of Lady Barbara's hair away from the water while another scrubbed her back. The estate's mistress had only to sit on the submerged stool where she worried whether the Hawksnest vintage truly was as fine as those her husband's family traded at Trinsic. She glanced at the window, foolishly fearing that Erwald, bathing in his own tiring room on the opposite side of the atrium, could see the doubts rising from her head. Doubly foolish: Thoughts were private in Britannia; no mage was powerful enough to pierce the protective curtain of the human spirit. More immediately, her husband put his faith in calendars, not weather. He had not given the order to remove the leaded glass of winter from the villa's windows: Nothing at all could be seen clearly through them.

Agatha held up a linen drying sheet in which she wrapped her lady as she emerged from the bath, clipping it tight with a jeweled broach. The entourage reentered the tiring room proper. Barbara sat on another stool. The woman who artfully arranged Barbara's hair was, like the lady herself, born and raised on the estate. The scented creams massaged into her neck were, likewise, products of their own gardens and apothecary. The linen had been grown here, retted here, dyed here, and woven on the loom that dominated the solar above her bedroom. Except for Lady Barbara's jewelry and the embroidered silk girdle Agatha adjusted carefully around her waist and hips, everything had been produced from start to finish at Hawksnest.

"Is my husband dressed?" Lady Barbara asked, slipping her hands through the slashed arms-eyes of the formal blue surcote that would protect her bleached linen gown from the rigors of a six-hour banquet.

Agatha nodded. "Yes, my lady, his buskins are laced and he awaits you in the atrium."

Servants knew exactly what was happening anywhere on the vast estate. Their knowledge was utterly independent of magic. Nothing moved, nothing broke, no one laughed or cried, but a servant saw it and shared the observation with a comrade. After a lifetime among them, the lord and lady of the estate seldom noticed their ever-waiting audience. The audience, however, never forgot the play.

"And my children?"

Agatha shot a glance past her lady's shoulder; a grimace spread over her face. "Darrel's got himself filthy already. They're bathing him in the kitchen. Hugh's been looking for Jordan all afternoon and can't find him."

Wrinkles appeared on Lady Barbara's forehead; for a moment she looked every one of her thirty-seven years. She was used to the mayhem that followed her younger son, Darrel, throughout the villa. She didn't like it, but she was used to it. Jordan's misbehavior was atypical of him, and all the more puzzling. She thought it had something to do with tonight's feast—she hadn't noticed it before the preparations reached a fever pitch at the beginning of the month—but Jordan was eighteen and there could be a hundred explanations for his disappearance.

"Althea?" Lady Barbara seized on the simplest of those hundred explanations.

Althea had lived at Hawksnest nearly her whole life. Lord

Erwald brought her and her older brother, Balthan, back from a similar Conclave more than ten years ago. Their father was a Virtue Peer who, Erwald said, received only the enlightenment of Honor before abandoning his Quest. Simon the Wanderer, as he called himself, supported his family for a time in Trinsic, city of Honor and Lord Erwald's mercantile family. As the years passed in frustration, Simon lost his glimmer of enlightenment. Eventually—or so Erwald said—he put out as a common seaman on an eastbound merchant-explorer that never returned to port. Lady Barbara judged it more likely that Althea and Balthan's father had drowned himself in wine at one of Trinsic's less than reputable taverns.

The Peerage didn't have much to say about those who fell away from Virtue's path. Their egalitarian philosophy proposed that the Avatar's quest was accessible to anyone, provided they were ceaseless in their striving and knew their spirit's strength. Compassion and Sacrifice were virtues as well, and the Peers, as individuals, stood by each other, offering as much help as the sufferer would freely take. But a man like Simon the Wanderer shattered from the inside out and there was no saving him.

So Erwald Ironhawk saved his peer's children instead. He brought them to Hawksnest where his servants tended to their well-being and he undertook to chart their course through life. Neither child was particularly challenging in that regard. Balthan displayed a talent for magic from the start. He taught himself the spells of linear magic: handfire, hearthfire, dust-be-gone, stir-the-pot—spells so simple they lacked proper names. But when Balthan set a waxed, knotted thread in the chicken coop and the poor birds scratched all day in sun-wise circles, Erwald sent him straight to the arcane Lyceum south of the city of Moonglow.

Lady Barbara suspected Althea's talent for magic was

greater than her brother's, but Althea was as shy and quiet as her brother was outspoken. She was devoted to the daily life of the estate. Althea's skills freed Lady Barbara from many of her traditional duties, thereby giving her abundant time to fret about the children.

Now that Althea was no longer a gawky child, Lord Erwald was starting to think about her dowry and his Peerage friends with spare sons. Barbara said nothing—her usual course when her lord husband was hip-deep in his schemes. Jordan wasn't blind and neither, for all her dutiful timidity, was Althea. The servants had seen the two of them together more than once. Of course, they'd seen Althea with that young blacksmith, Drumon, much more often; and Jordan preferred the company of his Valorian stallion to any mere man or woman.

The campanile tocsin clanged double-time, disrupting the thoughts of everyone in the villa. The heavy, padded surcote was not a soft house-gown to be tossed over one arm while she ran like a barefoot farmer. Agatha took the straps worked into the garment's hem and followed her lady down the stairs at a stately walk.

"My lady," Erwald gave the greeting an intimacy no servant would have imagined or dared.

They hugged and kissed while their separate entourages frowned at the damage such an embrace did to their clothes, then Erwald took the hem straps from his wife's maidservant. He held Barbara's left hand in his right and brought the straps behind his back in his left. The dark blue brocaded fabric of her surcote perfectly matched that of his dalmatic. No one could mistake that they were the lord and lady of this estate, nor that they were bedecked for one of their society's most formal occasions.

The tocsin ceased its clanging.

"Let us greet our guests," Lord Ironhawk suggested.

"Gard tells me it is Lady Gwenneth and her husband, Iolo Arbelest, Bard and Companion."

As if there might be another Iolo Arbelest who was neither a bard nor Lord British's boon Companion.

Throughout the many years that Lord British ruled his eponymous land, he actively discouraged his people from honoring him or his Companions overmuch. He was ruler by circumstance, not by right or birth, or so he said; likewise his Companions. It was a measure of the love, and awe, the people had for him that they respected his wishes. They erected no statues in his honor. They called him *lord,* as they called all men of wealth and position, not sire, highness, or majesty.

"Julia slipped in without anyone recognizing her. Geoffrey's been sighted from the tower—" Erwald ticked off the best-known names in the land, names that were almost invariably not given to anyone's children because the Companions, like Lord British himself, lived unchanging from one generation of Peers to the next. "Save for Shamino and Blackthorn, I think they'll all be here."

Lady Barbara moved in step with her husband. "Blackthorn's not coming? He always—"

She swallowed her words, but not before they cast their pall over them both. Barely four months had passed since court-heralds had raced pell-mell through the land bearing the unthinkable tidings that Lord British and all those with him had failed to return as planned from an expedition into the newly discovered caverns deep in Spiritwood forest. The realm was well-ordered and secure; it had not plunged into chaos. It was, instead, suspended in disbelief. No one stepped into the void Lord British left behind, but Lord Blackthorn, a Companion whose talents lay in administration rather than adventure, took upon himself those many

insignificant but essential things that could not be left un-
done.

"I forgot," Lady Barbara apologized. She missed a step
at her husband's side trying to recompose her face into a
radiant smile.

Erwald squeezed her hand. "We all forget," he assured
her. "Lord British meant that we should not grow dependent
on him. Perhaps he knew that some day he would leave—
perhaps just *vanish* into the Underworld as he seems to have
done. Blackthorn's a good man. He'll be a good overlord."

There was little conviction in Erwald Ironhawk's voice.
Blackthorn was a good man; all the Companions were good
men and women, as were the Peers. The simple laws and
philosophy of Britannia inclined most citizens toward good-
ness. A good man, however, was not necessarily a good
leader, nor a good ruler. Already, in ways that were difficult
to put into words, Lord Blackthorn demonstrated a certain
dogmatic adherence to Lord British's precepts that ran
counter to their spirit.

The Peers of Hawksnest looked at and beyond each other.
Life was pleasant on their estate and elsewhere in Britannia,
the product of five generations of peaceful prosperity. They
inherited a world unchanged from their parents' hands and
had blissfully expected to pass the same to their children.
Lord British's disappearance had, so far, changed nothing
in their day-to-day lives, but the future they had once embraced with confidence they now confronted with anxiety.

"Don't think about it," Erwald advised his wife as her
brow wrinkled. "So long as we Peers adhere to the virtues
of the Avatar, our lives, and the lives of those around us,
will be secure."

Lady Barbara closed her eyes. She took a long, deep
breath and regained the facade of serenity that was expected

of her. Extending her arms to an angle that was both elegant and uncomfortable, she reopened her eyes. "Our guests are waiting."

The feast hall dominated the marble villa. Its walls rose twice as high as the surrounding atriums. The copper-gilt slopes of its roof formed a pyramid that blazed in the sun when it was, as it had recently been, polished. A ring of long tables, open in the middle and along the arc closest to the kitchen, nearly filled the hall. Every man, woman, and child of Hawksnest could be comfortably fed and entertained in the hall, but the Virtue Peers, though fewer in number than the residents of the estate, could hardly be seated cheek-by-jowl on common benches. Chairs of all sizes and descriptions, many of them brought great distances by their owners, studded the ring of tables like jewels in a crown.

The Virtue Peers were without internal ranks. There was one high chair, directly opposite the opening in the circle, and it was always empty, waiting for the Avatar who never came. The rest were set in the straw. A total stranger, standing where Lord Ironhawk stood in the east gallery overlooking the hall, might think the glittering men and women entering through the high doors in the south wall were simply picking the most convenient seat. Such a stranger would be wrong.

A veritable war of furniture had been fought in this hall these last ten days as retainers shuffled chair-suites from one part of the circular table to another. Erwald noted several significant changes in the last hour alone, but mostly he noticed that his own suite of five gilded, cushioned chairs —each surmounted with a rampant hawk of iron—remained precisely where they belonged: a quarter-turn, sun-wise, from the Avatar's empty dais.

Althea appeared at the western end of the gallery wearing a gown and surcote whose simpler brocade and embroidery proclaimed her lower position in the household. In point of fact, the girl had no need of ornament. She could have come to the feast in a threadbare house-gown straight from her herb garden, and not one in ten would have noticed. Her hair blazed more radiant than the feast-hall roof; her eyes were large and a deep, clear green.

In Erwald's private opinion, his ward was too pretty for her own good. Every Peer he knew was watching her. She was bright and winsome—everything a young woman should be, especially in the eyes of a man who had no daughters of his own. He'd set aside a handsome dowry for her, for all that it would be paid in gold, not land. He'd half a mind to start the negotiations this very night. He knew at least four Peers with sons of the proper age. If Lord Ironhawk could not imagine letting her choose her own husband, neither did he plan to marry her off to a man of his own age, or a boy half of hers.

Althea was not alone. Two young women who understood that they held their position at Lady Barbara's pleasure, not Althea's, accompanied her, as did a still-damp Darrel in a tunic as green as his father's dalmatic was blue.

"I'll have that lad whipped 'til he thinks twice about running through the mud in new clothes," Lord Ironhawk muttered, scarcely noticing that his second son was already walking slump-shouldered and staring at the planks beneath his feet.

"It won't do any good, my lord," Barbara said reasonably, if not sympathetically. "Boys are like that, sometimes. He means no harm. He's already afraid of you. He'll turn mean and hateful if you break him to your will."

"He's got to learn."

Lady Barbara shook her head but said nothing. She held out her hand for Darrel to kiss, the proper greeting from a lord's son to his lady mother. The boy brushed her hand aside, thrusting his arms through the slashing of her surcote to give her a desperate hug. Barbara gave silent thanks that he was freshly scrubbed, then stroked his hair.

"Come, hold your mother's other hand while we enter the hall." She unwound him from her waist.

"Wife," her lord husband protested, "this is not done—"

Barbara squared her shoulders. "Has Blackthorn started issuing laws all of a sudden?"

She nodded at Althea who merged into the family's tail with her attendants. Trumpets sounded as they descended the final stairway.

"Where's Jordan?" Erwald Ironhawk demanded, craning his neck around. "Where's my son and heir?"

But no one paid him any attention.

Two

Jordan Hawson, heir to the vast estate of Hawksnest and eager to prove himself a virtuous man, flattened against the floor of the west gallery above the villa's feast hall. A knothole in the planks revealed the Lord Ironhawk greeting the Virtue Peers, flanked by his lady wife, his beautiful ward, and his youngest son. The guests might attribute Erwald's slight flush to excitement or pride, but Jordan was Erwald's son, not his guest; he knew better.

"He'll have me whipped bloody . . . He'll do it himself."

The young man rolled onto his back and covered his eyes The dark blue brocade dalmatic he was not wearing burned clearly in his imagination. All month he had promised himself that if he could not attend the feast as his father's Nominee, he would not attend it as a silent ornament in his father's entourage.

"It's not like I'm some soft merchant's son," Jordan muttered, striving to rekindle the anger that the sight of his father's face had doused. "I'm good with my sword, and *he* knows it; he's even admitted it. I've trained the Valorian—he didn't think I could, but I did. I'm *ready*. Lewis Widebridge won't be eighteen for another six months. His parents are Nominating him tonight, and he's nowhere near as ready as I am."

The argument hadn't worked with Erwald, and now it failed to work with Jordan himself. The young man no longer needed his father's presence to hear, and be defeated by, the echo of his unchanging words. Eighteen was too young, no matter how many other fathers and mothers thought differently. Erwald Ironhawk began his Virtue Quest at the shrine of Justice when he was twenty-five and, by all the unchanging powers of the universe, that's when he'd Nominate his sons and where he'd send them. End of discussion.

Unable to recover his indignation, Jordan lapsed at once into recriminations that were too shameful for spoken words.

I'm not ready—not really. If I was ready, I'd just put on a white robe and Nominate myself. I'd beseech the Peers for the mantra of Valor. If I was truly ready I wouldn't need to have my father's blessing.

Stashing his new dalmatic in the garde-robe and then hiding in the gallery were, perhaps, not the acts of a mature and virtuous Peer, but Jordan would have been far more foolish to commence his Quest without Erwald Ironhawk's blessing. He owned nothing in his own name except his Valorian stallion, his sword, and a gilt goblet given to him by his grandmother on her deathbed; everything else was entailed to the estate.

When Lord British decreed that every citizen had the right to retrace the Avatar's path of enlightenment and virtue, he did not intend for his realm to become a land of perpetual pilgrimage. Instruction might be free at the strongholds of

Truth, Love, and Courage, but bed and board were not. The Peers provided mantras, not transportation to the remote shrines. The Virtue Quest was as expensive as it was dangerous.

With his parents' blessing and endowment, Jordan would lead his own entourage; without it he'd have to sell his sword-skill to someone like Lewis Widebridge. Faced with that choice, wisdom dictated that Jordan bend to his parents' wishes. More accurately, to his father's wishes, as he'd long since found the keys to his mother's heart and her privy coffer, which, though much deeper than his, was not deep enough to send him around the shrines of Britannia in a style befitting his rank or in the order of his own choosing.

Seven more years of memorizing unbelievably dull treatises on moral philosophy. Seven more years of practice with his sword, with a bow, with the Valorian—who might well be spavined or winded by the time the Quest began. Seven more years of waiting—a lifetime when viewed from the age of eighteen.

"I just wish he'd listen to me: I'm *ready*."

Jordan repeated himself several times before the horns began a different fanfare and he was drawn back to the knothole.

Colin the Steady, Brother of the Silver Serpent, Lord of Sunrise Keep, and the only man alive to receive enlightenment at seven of the eight shrines (Humility, the knight's downfall, remained beyond his grasp), came forward to give the convocation address. Jordan had heard all the doughty exploits that earned him the sobriquet Colin the Steady, but Lord Colin was past seventy now, and steady was the last word an eighteen-year-old would use to describe him.

"Peers of the Avatar's Virtue—good folk of Britannia, gathered at a turning point in our history—"

Jordan closed his eyes; Colin's voice creaked like a barn door.

"—Lord British is gone from us. Our captain no longer stands on the bridge of his ship guiding us through the storm with his wisdom. The common folk of Britannia look to us, who have trod partway on the Avatar's Infinite Path, to guide them. We must consider our example—"

Disdain split Jordan's lips with a groan. He opened his eyes and stared through the knothole, praying that he hadn't given himself away. He hadn't. His mother and father and all the other overdressed Peers were mesmerized by the old man's words. Jordan wasn't surprised; as he saw things, there was nothing the Virtue Peers enjoyed more than *considering*. They would consider something forever and never quite get around to *doing* anything about it.

The simple truth was that as much as he wanted to begin his Virtue quest, Jordan didn't want to wind up like his father or any of the other broadbeamed narrowminded Peers. He wasn't interested in axioms, principles, or virtue. His only interest in Hawksnest was the style in which it could support him. His dream was to slay a dragon in single combat and his quest was a means to *that* end, not his father's staid notion of enlightenment.

"Weren't you ever young?" he asked the knothole as he'd asked his father many times before. "What about Valor? Where's the Valor in managing an estate? Where is the Glory?"

Glory's not a virtue. Forget glory if you seek enlightenment. End of another hundred or so discussions.

Colin hadn't finished the convocation. ". . . Lord British led without leading. His laws gave our citizens freedom to choose. Lord British gave us harmony, not conformity. Now we must consider: Can we sustain harmony without Lord British, or do we need conformity?"

Jordan noted, with no small satisfaction, that the Peers were beginning to look bored. Even his father, that would-be paragon of virtue, seemed more interested in the clot of food-bearing servants in the kitchen passage than another of Lord Colin's lengthy considerations. His mother had that eager look she got when her thoughts were far away from the conversation, but Althea—Althea, whom he'd invited to join him in his contrariness—actually seemed to be listening to every word. She was nodding and frowning as if the old man's speech meant something to her personally.

"—Those of you, my fellow Peers, dwelling peacefully on your estates, do not slip into complacency—"

The young man made a fist and pounded the floor. *Slip* —his father hadn't slipped, he'd dug a hole and *jumped* into complacency.

"—Consider, if you will, how your lives will change if the guilds of the cities can no longer train your artisans, if you can no longer exchange your produce for hard goods when or where or with whomever you please. What if our brothers and sisters on magic's path found their freedom constrained?"

Jordan wasn't surprised to see Althea's eyes widen on that remark. She had a brother on magic's path—not that Balthan didn't need a little constraint now and again. The brilliant and ambitious mage didn't spend much time at Hawksnest anymore, but when he did, he and Jordan were sure to be at loggerheads through most of the visit. Althea was the only one who actually liked her brother, and even she admitted that he could be unforgivably caustic. She could well imagine the trouble Balthan would bring down on himself—if Colin wasn't talking to hear himself talk.

Jordan looked away from his family for a moment. The other Peers were every bit as bored. His friend Lewis was actually paring his fingernails with a dagger. But the Companions scattered around the table were grim as the young man had never before seen them. He couldn't see below Iolo's shoulders, but he'd swear the bard had a knife in his hands—and he wasn't cleaning his nails with it.

"—So long as Lord British sat on his throne we knew what evil was, and what it was not. Where shone the light of Britannia, evil withered and the Path of the Avatar was as wide as it was incorruptible. Lord British was our tocsin. Now who shall sound the alarm?"

Colin the Steady paused once again for dramatic effect. His chest swelled as he prepared to utter the answer everyone expected, but he waited an instant too long. The tocsin of Hawksnest, a man-sized disk of bronze hung in the campanile tower, startled everyone with an unceasing clamor.

Jordan rolled over. Through the breezeway columns below the eaves he saw what none beneath him at the tables could see: the tocsin swaying and flashing in the moonlight. A silhouetted watchman relayed a message with his torch. A circle, two rapid dips, a northerly arc—meaning that a moon gate had opened unexpectedly to the north; two riders were seen galloping through, headed for the villa proper. Jordan scrabbled to the stairs, keeping his hips low and hoping that no one would notice the light when he opened the door. He didn't know who'd ridden through, but, since only a magician of the highest rank could compel a gate to open against its moon phase, their coming must be important.

He collided with the under-watchman on his way to the stable. "How far?"

"Not far," the youth answered without stopping. "We saw the flash."

Jordan veered away from the stable. There'd be no time to saddle his Valorian to ride out and meet them. Under the best of circumstances, it took a quarter hour and the help of two grooms to get the steel-grey animal under saddle, and the grooms were undoubtedly feasting with their own peers in the paddock tents. He ran toward the foregate. The gate-porch was empty. There was no one but himself to grapple with the heavy beam.

" 'Ware the gate! We come from Britain City with an urgent message. Will you open the gate for us?" An unfamiliar voice boomed from the farside of the gate.

"I'm trying," Jordan shouted, finally getting his arms around the great log. Normally it took four of his father's men to lift the rough-hewn beam out of its brackets each morning, but, spurred by a determination to hear the message before anyone else, Jordan hauled it over the angled iron. He staggered a good ten steps before regaining his balance. Then the beam fell through his numbed arms. It bounced in the gravel before coming to rest a thumb's width from his toes. Jordan imagined the injury he'd so narrowly avoided, and was unable to move.

" 'Ware the gate! We must speak to the Companions. Our message is most urgent!"

The same man's voice as before, and still unfamiliar in Jordan's ears. With his gut and heart pounding against each other, he managed to slowly open the gate. Something dark and sinuous brushed his hand. Flat, glistening teeth clashed against metal, barely missing the young man's arm.

"Have a care around him, boy, he's nasty with strangers."

Another Valorian—Jordan berated himself inwardly for not expecting that. He knew their temper intimately and tried to prove it by grasping the reins just below the horse's chin as he did with his own stallion. The animal settled down at once.

"You know how to handle Valorians—good." The man tossed the knotted reins at Jordan as he dismounted. "Help me with the lady."

Jordan rubbed his cheek where the leather stung him. He didn't think he hit his groom in the head each time he dismounted, but perhaps his groom was simply better at dodging than he had been. The stranger assumed command so completely and naturally that Jordan was convinced he was a Peer of his father's accomplishment or higher. There weren't many such men; Jordan should have been able to recognize him.

The stranger made a steel-plated fist; his mail coif framed a sneer. "Stop staring, boy—didn't you hear me tell you to hold the lady's mount?"

Thus demoted to the rank of stableboy, Jordan hurried to do as he was told. The lady on the other Valorian clearly needed assistance. Her blazing staff, resting in a stirrup, supported her rather than the other way around. Yet its light fell almost entirely on the ground in front of the horses; only a small amount escaped the constraint of the Vas Flam spell to illuminate her face. Her eyes were closed and though magically created light tended to distort color, Jordan knew she was very pale.

"Is she ill? Is that what brought you?" he asked, forgetting that he was merely a servant.

"Does Lord Ironhawk suffer arrogance in his desmene?"

The stranger's voice had an edge better suited to hardened steel. Jordan would have feared for his front teeth, but the stranger's hands were fully occupied getting the magician from her horse to her feet. She let go of the staff; its light blazed in all directions, momentarily blinding Jordan. He recovered, only to find himself once again in the withering disapproval of her companion.

"Which way to the hall?"

"This way," the glower deepened, and Jordan remembered his manners, "*my lord.*" He started up the path leading both horses and the guests.

"See that you walk them cool before you feed them or let them drink. And wash them as well. Check their hooves. The bay stumbled a while back. I think she might have thrown a shoe . . . at least it's lost a nail. The dun gets a mash of grain and oil before you give him hay. He'll chew wood, so put him in a corner box with an iron crib—I assume Ironhawk has one?"

Jordan nodded. A plowhorse could be loosed in a paddock without a second thought, but Valorians were almost as renowned for their quirkiness as their speed and endurance. Jordan's animal not only chewed his stall to kindling, he would work himself into a sweated frenzy without a dog to keep him company in his stall.

The gentleman was midway through his instructions for the care of his saddle when the lady interrupted, "I can't believe he demanded the words of power." They were the first words she'd uttered since coming through the gate.

Each of the eight members of the Great Council of Magicians was the keeper of a single ancient dungeon and the spell-word that kept it sealed. The words of power were, in some ways, similar to the eight mantras of virtue guarded by the Peerage. But unlike the mantras, which were meant to be revealed, the words of power were Britannia's most closely guarded official secrets. No one, except Lord British and the Avatar, knew all eight.

Jordan tried not to be obvious as he listened for the gentleman's response.

"And I can't believe they were so bullheaded as to refuse to surrender them."

"The Eight have wisdom that must not be put into words; they have reasons for everything. They'd never be 'bull-headed.' "

The gentleman snorted derisively. "I'll give them reasons." But to Jordan's dismay the lady magician hushed him before he could recite his list.

They entered the foregarth where Jordan bumped into the under-watchman. Lord Erwald and Lady Barbara were surrounded by their fellow Peers at the top of the steps. Jordan had reconsidered coming between them and the travellers. He brought the Valorians to a halt and kept his face in their shadow. The gentleman made a disdainful sound with his teeth.

"Are you the only lad on watch tonight?" he asked, and, not waiting for an answer, began shedding his armor. He shoved his gauntlets under Jordan's arms, then bent deeply from the hips, allowing both his coif and hauberk to slide noisily to the ground. Jordan expected to be told to pick them up, but the gentleman did that himself, depositing the rank and heavy garments across Jordan's shoulders.

Now Jordan recognized him. "My lord DuPre," he whispered.

The paladin and Companion winced, as if hearing his name through a servant's lips stung his ears. When he spoke again, it was not to acknowledge a young man's awe. "I'll be leaving with the dawn. There won't be time to wash the mail in sand and vinegar. Grease it, then, but lightly. Use beeswax, if your armorer's got it, but on no account use anything heavier than chicken grease." He turned away and took the magician's hand lightly in his own. "Are you ready, Meraise?" he asked, using the lady's name for the first time.

Jordan watched them cross the foregarth. Lord DuPre embraced his father about the shoulders and kissed the hand of both his mother and Althea. The Companion was all grace and courtesy where it counted, and nothing counted with a night-duty stableboy. The heir of Hawksnest wished, for a moment, he'd worn the padded brocade his father commissioned for him. But, no, stubbornness kept him in a comfortable tunic and trousers so loose they might well belong to two other men. In the moonlight he looked like a servant, and so he had been treated.

There was a lesson to be learned, and he'd have plenty of time to learn it. Between the horses and the armor, Jordan would be lucky if he got to the feast before midnight.

He was, in fact, very lucky. The retainers feasting in the paddock tents were no less curious about the alarm than their mistresses and masters. When word reached them that a Companion and a magician had arrived unescorted, Hawksnest's conscientious servants came straight to the stable where they were surprised to see the young lord with his arms wet to the elbows rinsing the sweat from a dun stallion's hindquarters.

Jordan knew every facet of the care of a knight's horse and armor. He could—if he absolutely had to—remove a broken shoe, then shape and nail a fresh one in its place, though neither he nor the unfortunate horse would enjoy the ordeal. Lord Erwald Ironhawk made certain his sons were well-taught, then allowed them to remain inexperienced.

The grooms did not protest that they could do all that Jordan struggled to do both quicker and better. They did not have to. Once Jordan realized they were hovering in the doorway, he repeated Lord DuPre's instructions word for word and retreated to his rooms in the villa where his slashed suede breeches and padded brocade dalmatic were waiting for him.

"My father?" the young man asked as loyal Hugh adjusted the young master's belt. "What will he say when he sees me?"

"He'll greet you as any noble father greets his son, my lord."

"But is he angry?"

"I think he has forgotten, my lord. The message Companion DuPre and the magician Meraise have brought from Britannia is most serious. All is in an uproar. The lady-mistress has not called to the kitchen for another course since they arrived."

"What *is* the message?" Jordan wrested away from his body-servant's ministrations and made the final adjustments to his appearance himself.

"I do not know, my lord," Hugh said, bowing from the waist.

Another time, Jordan would have pressed for the truth. Hugh was as great a gossip as the head cook or butler. He was also obsessed by propriety and appearance. It took hours of argument and bribery to wheedle the family secrets out of him—hours which, at that moment, Jordan did not have.

He acknowledged the bow with a nod as he passed through the door. Hugh was right about the uproar. Jordan could hear the Peers shouting long before he descended the stairs from the family quarters to the public rooms. He eased through the doors without anyone seeming to notice and was working his way along the walls toward the noisiest corner when Althea rushed up to him.

"The Great Council of Magicians is disbanded. Lord Blackthorn demanded the words of power and they dissolved themselves rather than violate their oaths—" Jordan's eyes widened; for an instant he envisioned gory puddles in the throne room, but it seemed the magicians had taken a somewhat less drastic stance. "Lord Blackthorn swore they're all traitors and that he'll go to the Codex, if he has to, to open the dungeons. They've all gone into hiding and Lord Blackthorn has outlawed them. Outlawed! Oh, Jordan, think what this means.''

The young man thought it meant that DuPre was right, the magicians were being bullheaded. Lord Blackthorn was the man Lord British chose to sit as the kingdom's Protector in his stead. ''If Lord Blackthorn thinks opening the dungeons will bring Lord British back, then the Great Council should honor him.''

Althea tossed her head in exasperation; all Jordan noticed was the glint of candlelight reflected in her hair. He forgave her for not joining him in his rebellion, and it was only with some difficulty that he heard what she was saying.

''. . . It's not the *magicians* I'm worried about. It's not even Lord British. It's Balthan. You know what he's like. He doesn't have any sense at all when it comes to these things. There's no telling what he'd do or say.''

''Why should he do or say anything, Althea? He's not a member of the Great Council, is he—did I miss another of his ambitious conquests?''

''He's amanuensis to Felespar, and Felespar *is* a member of the Great Council. Can you imagine what would happen if Lord Blackthorn's men burst in on them and tried to force Felespar to surrender his word?''

Jordan let his immediate response go unspoken. Balthan's loyalty was whisper-weak, but he'd rise ferociously to any challenge of right or position. If Felespar resisted Lord Blackthorn, Balthan wouldn't hesitate to get between them. Jordan's heart began pounding—he'd held his breath unconsciously and let it out with a sigh. ''Maybe they got into hiding—''

''My brother run away?'' Althea arched a pale copper eyebrow over an emerald eye.

If he were going to continue this conversation sensibly,

Jordan realized he'd have to look *beyond* Althea rather than *at* her. "Well, if Felespar wanted to go, Balthan would go with him, wouldn't he? He'd do what the old man told him to do, wouldn't he?"

Althea saw Jordan's gaze wandering away from her and heard the vagueness in his words. She was angry for a moment, then she understood. If it were Jordan or his father in Felespar's place, Balthan would be contrary for contrariness' sake. She thought it might be different between Balthan and Felespar, because Felespar was a magician and not a Peer, as their father had been, but she couldn't be certain. "He has not written to me since last fall—before Lord British vanished. Balthan is my brother, my only living kin. I love him, but I do not know him . . ."

Jordan was no longer listening. Althea followed his line of sight: He was looking across the hall where Iolo the Bard and Lord DuPre were engaged in a very heated discussion. It was unheard of to see Companion arguing in public. She couldn't hear them through the din of other conversations in the hall, but she could read a few of the words their lips formed: Blackthorn, British, damned fool, and magician, among others.

"Of course—they were there," Althea exclaimed, recapturing all of Jordan's attention. "Lord DuPre was there! He rescued Lady Meraise and brought her straight here. He's certain to know what's happened to each of the Council mages. Once we know what has happened to Felespar, we can safely guess what's happened to my brother. All we have to do is ask." She lifted up on her toes to kiss Jordan demurely on the cheek. "Thank you, Jordan. I wasn't thinking clearly. I didn't know what to do until I saw where you were looking."

Jordan muttered something inane. Since his recent discovery that Althea had become a woman, with all that implied to his imagination, he could no longer think of her as his little sister. He found these outbursts of sisterly affection sufficiently uncomfortable that he'd agree to anything—even interrupting Lord DuPre in midtirade—to get out of them.

Fortunately, interrupting the two snarling Companions was easier said than done. From twenty feet away, it was clear that they were continuing a long, painful, and very private discussion. When Jordan did not speak up, Althea, who under normal circumstances would never think of addressing a man from a different estate without a proper introduction, blinded herself to her own actions and took a step forward. Jordan caught her arm and held her close to his side.

"*Look!*" he hissed, indicating the half-dozen Peers who were doing just that.

Regardless of their rank, the men and women of Britannia chose to believe that Lord British and his circle of Companions were different not because of their apparent agelessness, but because of their harmony—as if strife among family and friends were the ultimate cause of mortality. The sight of Iolo's inflamed cheeks and DuPre's knotted brow was more disillusioning than Lord British's unexplained absence. It almost—but not quite—overcame the substance of their dispute.

Neither Companion liked, or trusted, the man Lord British appointed to sit on his throne during his underground adventure. They could have ended their disagreement there, without regard to the roots or consequences of their judgement, but it was not in the nature of either man to leave any issue unexamined. Iolo was inclined to ask the root questions: had Blackthorn changed; had he changed since Lord British's disappearance; how was he changing?

"It's not what he did yesterday or the day before that troubles me, DuPre, or what he'll do tomorrow. It's the *pattern* I'm worried about. I don't think he knows it himself but something's pulling him to one side over the other—and it's not concern for our lord."

The paladin ground his teeth together and stared at the ceiling. "All the more reason to listen to him, I say. He knows what he's doing. Look—British wants to go exploring the fresh Spiritwood caverns. None of us thinks it's a good idea, but we let him go because he's British—what was 'pulling' him, tell me that if you can, Iolo. So, now he's gone, and we've got to find him, or at least find out what happened to him—and Shamino can't find his trail once it gets out of that first cavern. Something *very* strange is going on—maybe it is 'pulling' Blackthorn—but so far, I think it's pulling him in the right direction. The dungeons are the key to the Underground: They've got to be reopened."

"I'm not saying they shouldn't be reopened—it's the how of it, DuPre. It's the fact that Blackthorn's feet get heavier each step he takes. He didn't ask the council to reopen the dungeons—he didn't ask any one of us to go a-dungeoning. What he asked for was the words of power. Doesn't that tell you something?"

"It tells me that you're no different from those damn-fool magicians. You're living in the past."

Jordan had experienced enough futile arguments with his father to recognize when one coil of the endless spiral was complete and the next about to begin. He saw Meraise, alone and ignored, sipping a glass of wine in one of his father's chairs.

"Let's ask *her*." He tugged Althea's arm until she saw what he had in mind, then she led the way.

Althea fell to her knees more to be seen than from respect. "My lady? May I ask you a question most dear to me?"

The hollow-eyed magician, a woman a few years older than Lady Barbara and clearly on the brink of exhaustion, nodded slowly.

"My brother, Balthan, he sometimes calls himself Wanderson after our father, is amanuensis to Mage Felespar of the Council—"

Awareness glinted in Meraise's eyes. She didn't recognize Balthan by either of his names but, of course, she knew Felespar. "Taken," she whispered on drawn breath. "Tortured!" she added on the exhale. "*Tortured!*"

Althea's boldness deserted her. She covered her mouth with her fingers and cast a horrified glance toward Jordan. The young man didn't know what to say. Torture was unheard of—the word survived as a relic of the Dark Ages before Britannia's unification—yet the sound of Meraise's words confirmed the truth of them. "Killed?"

"No, not killed, I think." Meraise looked up. Incredibly, Jordan's foolish question served to lift her out of her stupor. "He did not give *him* what *he* wanted." Her voice grew stronger as she recalled the Council mage's courage. "They will not let him die." She watched something neither Jordan nor Althea could see.

None could deny the strength of a mage's mind or will, nor that they were more vulnerable to madness. Jordan moistened his lips and chose his next words with greater care.

"There was a man with him? A young man—about my age, but shorter, darker, not as strong. His amanuensis—"

Meraise shook her head. "He is alone. His fingers are

bent and bleeding, but he will not give them what they want . . .''

Jordan cupped his hand around Althea's ear. "It's no use. She's as far gone as last week's fish."

Althea gasped at the vulgarity, but she didn't argue. "Meraise says Felespar's alone. Does that mean Balthan escaped . . . or that they've killed him already?" she murmured, echoing the magician's ominous "they."

For a moment Jordan thought both women were drifting into madness, then Althea snapped back to the tangible world.

"I know what I can do. I can find out if he's dead or if he escaped."

Her nails dug into Jordan's wrist; she did not notice him wince. Perhaps all women should be taught wrestling and swordwork—along with the restraint that went with such mastery. As gentle and delicate as Althea seemed to be, she had no notion of her own strength and led him painfully from the feast hall.

Three

Jordan had no idea where Althea was taking him, but he hardly expected to be led to her bedroom. He would have balked and risked a bloody forearm had he known that was her destination—no sense seeking his father's wrath on two counts. But Althea had only recently been allotted a room of her own and Jordan had not troubled to find it. Moreover, had she not closed the door with an unmistakable air of ownership, he would have guessed it was but a common drudge's, not hers.

The wrought-iron cot was far simpler than his curtain bed of carved wood. The linen was clean, tight, but thoroughly patched. A bouquet of dried flowers—broken and faded by winter—stood in a crude earthen vase beside the wash bowl.

Another inane question burst from his lips: "Does my lord father—I mean, do *we* treat you well?"

Althea laughed—a musical sound that virtually guaranteed he would embarrass himself again. "Of course *you* do. What more could I want from a room?"

A glazed window, Jordan thought—and snared that thought before he uttered it, only to be brought down by the next. "Everything's so plain. There's nothing here to say it's your room at all, and not some drudge's. Agatha—"

"Oh, Agatha. She's always cadging favors from Lady Barbara." Althea's voice was light and frivolous. She paused to open a plain wood casket. When she spoke again her tone was somber. "I don't want to be like that. If I were—then I would feel like a drudge or a ward on charity . . ."

Jordan considered ripping his tongue out and stomping on it a few times to teach it better manners. Althea *was* a charity ward, and everything he said held a mirror to her poverty and her father's disgrace. He'd begun a garbled apology when Althea snapped her fingers. A spark flashed, and the oil lamp sizzled to life.

Having suffered through Balthan's boastful displays of talent and learning more often than he cared to recall, Jordan was generally repelled by magic rather than dazzled by it. Althea's small spells were different, partly because anything Althea did fascinated him, and partly because the meager spells of linear magic were genuinely useful. How nice not to have to grope blindly for tinder and flint but to simply *snap* up a spark. Of course, it wasn't that easy; it wasn't something Jordan could do at all. Not that he hadn't tried often enough, when he was certain no one—especially and specifically Balthan—was looking. Jordan tried magic almost as often as Balthan tried to teach himself how to use a sword—and with roughly the same success.

Even linear magic required reagents as well as discipline and talent. Althea was never without her little hoard of herbs and oils. Sweet-smelling reagents, unlike the eight noisome reagents of the high magic Balthan went to Moonglow to learn. When Jordan thought of Balthan, he thought of the stable-garth on a steamy summer day, or the sheep-pen when the flock was freshly sheared and dipped. When he thought of Althea, he thought about riding the Valorian through fields of ripening hay and the rose arbor in the moonlight.

With a shudder his Valorian stallion might envy, Jordan shook *those* thoughts from his mind and fixed his attention on the cloth-wrapped, heavy object Althea removed from her casket as she spoke.

"He said he didn't want to craft it for me, but he was so proud of making the spell—it's a spell of the third circle, he says, and he's only confirmed to the second. It's very unusual for a mage to discover a spell above his circle—"

Jordan heard himself thinking that Balthan was, at the very least, unusual, and found himself drifting back to that accursedly romantic rose arbor, but just before he was reduced to the desperate act of kicking himself in the shin, Althea undid the silk knots. A truly remarkable globe appeared in her lap.

"What *is* that?"

Althea held it out on the palm of her hand. Jordan shied from its unnatural beauty. Rainbow colors twined in translucent ribbons, shifting constantly without tangling or ending. And at the center of the globe, imperfectly seen through the changing patterns, was a lump the size of a man's thumb from knuckle to nail—a lump with stubs that might be arms and legs.

"That's not real, is it? It's not some wee *demon* you've got in there?"

"No," she replied, crooning as she might for an infant. Since he would not hold it for her, Althea set it again in her lap. "It's a talisman." She laughed again—this time the sound was forced and reminded Jordan of the look on his brother Darrel's face when their lord father commanded him to mount a Valorian: part privilege, part excitement, and a great dollop of terror.

"*Kal Wis Por Mani*," Althea murmured, rubbing a few drops of amber oil over the glass. "*Kal Wis Por Mani*— that means Invoke Knowledge of the Movement of Life. The ho-mun-cu-lus"—she spoke the unfamiliar word her brother taught her with the same murmuring intonation she used for the syllables of high magic themselves—"the ho- mun-cu-lus is a part of him. Balthan made it with parings of his own flesh and nails, with a lock of his own hair, and with a drop of his own blood drawn out from his heart."

Jordan rubbed his chest unconsciously and craned his neck to watch. The talisman glistened in the lamplight. He did not want to come any closer to the burgeoning magic than he already was. A warrior—and Jordan imagined him- self to be such a worthy—drew more blood over the course of his life than any mage, and never wanted to draw his own.

"Will you hold the lamp for me?"

He would—but he wouldn't like it. He sat catty-corner on the bed. Althea's knees touched him when she dangled the globe above the flame from a filament so fine it was almost invisible. All she thought about was her brother, while all Jordan thought about were the consequences if his father should come bursting through the door.

"You're not holding it steady."

"Sorry."

Jordan willed his shoulders and arms to relax, as he would if he held a sword in his hand. He practiced swordwork nearly every day with unbated weapons in the Hawksnest arena. The chance that he would be fatally wounded any morning was, surely, no greater than the chance that his father would find him here on Althea's bed. If he could face the chance of death each day, then he should be able get the image of his father roaring through that doorway out of his mind.

"It's working!"

Worry became impossible. The amber oil steamed and separated. A drop fell onto the lamp, which sputtered and seemed to burn brighter than before. But perhaps it was not the lamp burning brighter, perhaps the talisman itself had become luminous. The shifting patterns in the oil surrounding the patchwork poppet were reflected onto the globe's surface where they moved faster.

A Peer's son knew the magic of light spells, gouts of flame to roast a man in his armor, and the numbing touch of a healer stanching blood or mending flesh. Magic was power, raw and dangerous, but this—this shimmering globe no larger than his fist, pulsing with gentle brilliance—this was *magic*, and it held the young man transfixed.

The homunculus began to move. One moment it was a crude and shrivelled root, the next it was Balthan himself: quick and furtive, glancing over its shoulder, unhappy to be interrupted. It seemed to grin, and Jordan caught himself grinning back. He always forgot Balthan's smile. It was a smile to make a demon nervous. When he wanted to, the darkhaired mage could charm a snake out of its skin.

There had been good times between the brawls: Days spent swimming in the mill pond and fishing in the race. Midnight expeditions to the kitchen in search of honey cake. That rainy day when the two of them got trapped in the ruins beneath the hypocaust, and the countless times they went back in search of mystery and treasure. Balthan was a little bit older—a year, maybe two—no one knew for certain. Simon the Wanderer claimed he had forgotten when or where his children were born, and their mother's name.

Watching the homunculus bob in the globe, Jordan recalled Balthan saying how Simon used to take him and Althea into some dark tavern, sit them on the bar, then tell them to sing while he drank their pittance. Althea still sang, different songs, of course, but just as beautifully. Balthan never did; a ballad or carol invariably fired his smouldering rage.

It's a shame, Erwald Ironhawk would mutter to his family after banishing Balthan from a midwinter songfest. Jordan hadn't understood; now, suddenly, he did. Lord Erwald might have softened from the Iron Hawk of his questing days, but he was no broken drunkard.

"Jordan?"

The young man blinked and wrested his thoughts from the past. His ears told him Althea was brittle with fear. His eyes told him why: A jagged sliver of sooty darkness cut through the globe. It did not shift as the translucent color ribbons shifted, but was as steady as a dagger's blade. The ribbons slowly reformed around it, never touching it.

"What does it mean? Is he . . . ?"

Althea couldn't answer. Her hand trembled and the talisman began to swing through the flame. Jordan thought he noticed something. He shifted the lamp to his left hand and caught the globe in his right. The glass was hot, but not enough to burn his weapon-callused fingers. The luminous oil vapors vanished once his flesh touched them, but the ribbons inside the globe lingered, coiling around the inanimate homunculus, keeping it away from the slash of darkness.

"He's not. It doesn't touch him. The lightning . . . darkning doesn't touch him." Jordan turned the talisman so the frightened girl could see what he had seen.

The filament slipped from Althea's finger. She clasped her hands together as relief sent tears down her cheeks. "Thank all the stars in the heavens—thank *you*, Jordie, for knowing."

Jordan set the lamp on the floor and replaced the talisman very, very carefully on its wrapping cloth. The slash faded as the fluid around the homunculus cooled. Jordan didn't know much about magic—the Avatar was a magician but His quest and philosophy were not at all arcane. Still, the young man suspected the darkning would not disappear altogether. Gingerly he rotated the globe so the shrivelled figure would drift down and away from the shadow.

He cleared his throat. "May I assume it has not done this before?"

Althea dried her tears on the pointed sleeves of her gown. "I've only used it once since Balthan made it for me. It didn't, then. But he said it wouldn't last forever, and couldn't be used very often. He tried to explain why." She shook her head and blotted her eyes. "I couldn't make sense of half of what he said. I don't think he knew himself quite how it worked. Maybe it just gets dark like that. Maybe it's what I should have expected . . . ?" Althea's voice rose. She looked like a little girl.

Patting her hand and nodding, Jordan tried to find that particular tone of voice adults used to calm children. "I'm sure that's all it is. Knowing Balthan he's probably found a dozen different and better oils to put inside a talisman since he made this one."

It didn't work. Althea brightened, then sagged forward, wrapping her arms over her breasts where Jordan would not consider pursuing them.

"Something's wrong, Jordie—terribly wrong. He's in trouble. He's desperate."

Jordan retrieved the talisman. The translucent ribbons

shifted as the glass and oil shifted, but not of their own energy as they had before. They were no longer evenly distributed through the fluid, but formed an imperfect barrier between the faint darkning and the now-lifeless homunculus. Without thinking, Jordan gave the globe a quick quarter-turn. The ribbons and the darkning rearranged themselves as he expected, but the homunculus moved differently—against the motion, a signpost rather than a weather vane.

"Where was Balthan last?"

"Yew . . . I think. I don't know. He could be anywhere. Felespar kept a house in Yew; that's where I wrote to him, but his letters—when he sent them—could come from anywhere."

Jordan closed his eyes before she finished talking. He wasn't a mage, and this room had no windows, so he had to reconstruct the corners between here and the feast hall in his mind. If his reckoning was right, Balthan's homunculus pointed about north-northeast while Yew was almost due north of Hawksnest.

The darkning slash could be manipulated: up or down, north or south, and everything in between. The homunculus always pointed north-northeast, although the more Jordan rotated the globe the longer the little figure took to reach that orientation. Britain City was north-northeast. Lord DuPre and the lady-mage Meraise came in haste from Britain City.

"I think we should go back to the feast hall and tell my father," he said with a long, unhappy sigh. "There's more—"

Althea snatched the globe from his hands, secreting it swiftly in its cloth. "No." She hurried to stow it safely deep within her wooden casket. "No. We won't tell Lord Ironhawk anything."

"That *thing*, that homunculus-whatever-you-called-it,

pointed to Britain City. You think Balthan's in trouble. Now we know Felespar's in trouble, and we know that Meraise and DuPre left Britain City because of that trouble. Maybe it doesn't mean anything, Althea—but I don't think we can take the chance.''

''We'll have to.'' She flattened herself against the door. ''I won't let you tell your father. He mustn't know about the talisman. Balthan said so.''

This was the sort of stubbornness Jordan associated with Balthan, not his sister. ''So Balthan gets angry with you—''

''Jor-*die*!''

The enchantment was broken. Jordan hadn't been Jordie, at least in his own mind, for years. He tolerated the nickname when his mother used it, and he'd ignored it a few moments earlier because Althea had been the one slipping back into the habits of childhood, but hearing it shrill and drawled in a woman's nagging voice brushed Jordan's fur the wrong way. He rose from the bed.

''The only way that *thing* of yours is going to help your brother is if we take it to the hall right now while the Companions, Peers, and that magician Meraise are here.''

Althea shook her head left and right, stopping when she saw her casket on the table. Abandoning the door, she dashed to protect the globe. ''We can't,'' she insisted. ''We don't know who can be trusted and who can't be.''

''Who under my father's roof cannot be trusted?!''

''I don't know! I don't know those people. I don't know what they'll think. Maybe they'll think Balthan's to blame for what happened to Felespar.''

The thought had crossed Jordan's mind; he let it remain unspoken. ''All right, maybe I was wrong. Maybe we shouldn't announce it to everyone. But my lord father, surely, and Iolo the Bard. We can wait—''

Althea was already shaking her head. "Maybe I was wrong to trust you. I can't tell anyone until I know more for certain."

"What more can you learn? Do you have an oil to make that poppet talk? No—I didn't think so. I don't think he's going to send us a letter. You won't come to the bottom of this from Hawksnest."

Althea had devoted her life to obedience and inconspic-uousness; her will was strong, but untested. She wilted under Jordan's examination, but refused to admit defeat. "Then I shall have to leave Hawksnest as my brother did."

"Balthan left with a full purse and a passage to Moon-glow. Be reasonable, Althea. I'm trying to help you, and Balthan. Finding out what has happened to him will be like a . . ." Jordan smiled as the words unfolded in his mind. "Like a *quest*." And suddenly there were a host of pos-sibilities begging for his examination.

"No, not a quest." Althea rocked the casket in her arms. "No matter how desperate he is, my brother would die before he let himself be helped by a Peer. You should know that. He's never forgotten; he blames them for our father. He always said we could have been a family if father had not been seduced by a Peer's foolish Virtue Quest."

An hour or more passed before Jordan found the right words to reassure Althea that what he had in mind was sufficiently different from a Peer's Virtue Quest. A gong with a much sweeter voice than the tocsin proclaimed mid-night when Lewis and the others would be Nominated for their Quests. Jordan heard the sound and thought only of the hours remaining until dawn. The oil lamp sputtered out. Althea began to yawn.

"Yes—I see it now. You are right, Jordie, it's the only way. We'll leave at dawn—tomorrow's dawn, not today's.

I'll need that much time to get ready. Most of your lord father's guests won't be leaving until then, anyway. Who will notice two more travelling through the gate if we draw our hoods up tight?''

''You'll see, Althea, it's not just the only way—it's the best way. Dawn tomorrow, then.'' Jordan made his way across the unlit room. ''And, just in case, it's probably best we're not seen together during the day today. I'm probably going to sleep until midday, anyway, and then I'll be busy in the stables.''

''You swear you won't speak to Lord Ironhawk, or anyone else? This is our quest, ours alone to rescue Balthan from whatever mischief he's fallen into.''

''I swear it,'' Jordan said, closing the door behind him.

He lied to her, and felt no guilt as he retraced his steps. Lord Ironhawk *had* to be told, as did the other Peers, the Companions, and the magician Meraise. Even if Balthan were as innocent as a newborn babe, the darkning slash in Althea's globe could not be ignored, and certainly could not be left to the young and inexperienced to unravel. So Jordan lied, or thought he did. He weighed the words he'd use to explain the situation until he reached the corridor dividing the way to his rooms from the way to the feast hall.

No matter how he tried, Jordan couldn't think of a speech that would gain him membership in the rescue party. They would, in the end, be more likely to take Althea, since the talisman belonged to her. There was no way they'd take a green youth who hadn't been Nominated for his Virtue Quest. So, he hadn't lied, at least about talking to his father, but he still lied.

Jordan lifted his door as he opened it, keeping weight off the notoriously loud hinges. Hugh snored undisturbed in the antechamber and did not wake as Jordan painstakingly gathered his sturdiest tunic, his riding leathers, and his second-best buskins. His sword and his mail shirt, neither of which could be quietly moved, were in the armory beside the stable and presented a different, but hardly insurmountable, problem.

No, the greatest challenge was getting his Valorian under saddle and out of his stall without awakening the entire world, and in that Jordan got help from an unexpected corner. Lord DuPre's duncolored stallion was in the next stall, and the older, larger horse took Jordan's as a rival who needed trouncing. The dun whistled and planted kick after solid kick into the walls of Lord Ironhawk's stable. There was little chance the thick planks would give way, but no one explained that to Fugatore. The four-year-old stallion quivered in the farthest corner of his stall; he reacted to the appearance of his master and his tack with uncommon affection.

Even so, the cocks had crowed more than once and there was a pale glow on the eastern horizon before Jordan led the Valorian from the stable and gave its girth-band one final check.

"You never give up, do you, Fugatore?"

The Valorian snorted as the wide leather strap was cinched snug against his ribs. Jordan led the animal along the wall, behind the villa's outbuildings. He had a moment of fear when the hen-byre door swung open just ahead of them, but the drudge was more concerned with the fresh eggs in her apron than in what might be happening behind her shoulder.

Jordan got another boon from fate: The gate beam lay in the gravel exactly where he'd dropped it, and the gate-porch was as deserted as it had been then. Lord Ironhawk would be furious when he found that the gates had been open all night, but Jordan wasn't about to tell him. He led Fugatore, whose shoulders were higher than his, to the mounting block, and, mindful of the extra weight of his sword and mail, hoisted himself into the saddle.

Four

⌒⌒⌒

*J*ordan kept Fugatore on a tight rein as they made their
way through the foregate settlement. The windows here
had sharper eyes than anywhere else in the estate, because the people of the foregate owed nothing more than
land-rent to Hawksnest. Some of the tall, narrow houses
were as old as the villa itself and built from the same fine-
grained stone. Some of the families had dwelt in the foregate
for generations. A few of them were wealthy by any standard
with stout iron locks on their high doors and colored glass
in their windows. The private quarters would, however, be
cramped and dark despite the jewel-like windows. The artisans of the foregate were frugal; their houses completely
filled their rented land with nothing left for atriums or even
kitchen gardens.

In all of Hawksnest, the foregate was the only place where
Jordan's father was called Lord Ironhawk by courtesy, not
right. Guild law prevailed here, and the artisans stood firmly

by all those peculiarities of custom that freed them from the traditional obligations of tenant and landlord. Each craft—blacksmith, wheelwright, fuller, potter, and all the others—had its own far-flung guild and customs. In the cities they might be rivals, but on Britannia's isolated estates, they made common cause.

Lord British did not look kindly on Britannia's tendency to split into classes. His entire reign was a testament to one enlightened man's battle on behalf of equality and opportunity. And, as there were few citizens who did not love their monarch and fewer still who did not respect him, Lord British kept it possible for individuals to choose their own destiny. He could not, however, keep them from choosing tradition.

Jordan, guiding Fugatore along the single, twisted street, knew his foregate neighbors well, but not closely. He was not tempted to lift a loaf of steaming bread from the slab beside the baker's oven, nor take a handful of hard apples from the unguarded barrel beside the wheelwright's door. He was grateful that the foregate community, like his own within the villa walls, was slow to rise this morning—and irritated at the same time.

"When there's a feast to be had, there's no difference between a carpenter and a plowman; but when the harvest's late and there are storm clouds building on the horizon, there's no guildsman who knows how to use a scythe or drive a team," the young man muttered, guiding Fugatore around a heap of straw in front of the tanner's house. "And we must give each of them an abatement for the value of their dung and the privilege of spreading it on our fields."

A shutter slammed. Jordan swiveled in the saddle, an eyeblink too late to see which of the many windows had shut . . . or opened. He couldn't see a face, but that didn't mean he wasn't watched. He kept his thoughts to himself until entering the broad trampled area before the arched bridge over the stream that provided water for both the foregate and the villa. The water was high, as it usually was this time of the year, and running fast. Fugatore's ears pricked toward the sound; he began to tremble and chomp the smooth bit between his teeth. Had another horse, even an ox or donkey, preceded him across the sturdy wood-and-stone bridge, the young Valorian would have followed placidly, but crossing alone was another matter. His silver-grey shoulders turned a sweaty charcoal color; he danced sideways until he bumped into the drainage stones and scared himself from another direction.

Jordan pounded the colt's ribs with his heels and slapped the sweat-foamed neck with the knotted ends of the reins. The Valorian tossed his head and bolted, his single-minded fear of the bridge instantly replaced by a determination to run without regard to direction or footing. Jordan was ready and brought Fugatore under control on the far side of the bridge.

"Now—that wasn't so bad, was it?" Jordan reassured the blowing animal. "Maybe next time you'll go over with your eyes *open*?" he continued in the same placating tone, thinking that it would be a long journey indeed if they had to go through this every time they came to a bridge or gate.

An irregular star of paths led away from the bridge. The most-travelled went north and south; either route joined the old Paladin's Road between Trinsic and Britain City after meandering among the hamlets, assarts, and cottages of the vast Hawksnest estate. Jordan chose a rutted, easterly track that showed signs of recent use. Cutting across field and forest—and coincidentally past the moon gate whose secrets he did not yet know—would take him beyond the ken of the campanile tower before anyone in the villa suspected he was gone, and bring him to the Paladin's Road before noon.

Jordan loosened his grip on Fugatore's reins. He wouldn't have minded if the horse had bolted again, or at least picked up his feet in a canter, but the colt was well-bred if not well-mannered. He had a Valorian's instinct for a long journey and settled into the ground-eating walk that made him worth every gold crown Erwald Ironhawk had spent on him.

To the young man's thinking, the most dangerous part of the entire journey was behind him: The campanile tocsin had not roused his father from a wine-fogged sleep. The path ahead of him was quiet and empty—or it should have been. Jordan was startled to see two figures trudging past the crest of the moon-gate hill. Shielding his eyes from the morning sun, he leaned forward to get a sharper view. That was all the encouragement Fugatore needed.

If the ancient Valorian breed excelled only at a walk, they would have become the companion of itinerant pedlars, not the darlings of Britannia's Peerage. But those hind-quarters that were so loose and fluid at an amble could stiffen for an explosive, bone-rattling gallop. Jordan grabbed the pommel and barely kept his seat as Fugatore charged across the meadow.

The hikers were nearly hidden by baskets strapped to their shoulders. One was much larger than the other; his basket sprouted several objects, one of which might be a double-bit axe. The other wore a cloak that dragged on the ground and was probably the woodsman's son—or so Jordan believed until they heard Fugatore's hoofbeats behind them and turned around. A shock of sunset-amber hair surrounded the short hiker's face—and proclaimed her identity.

"Althea!" Jordan shouted. He did not recognize the person with her. "Althea . . . Whoa!"

Fugatore came to a stiff-legged halt some distance beyond Althea and her companion and became immediately aware of the dewy grass tickling his belly. He was prancing and tossing his head, but Jordan finally got a good look at the second hiker's face.

"Drumon!" Jordan coughed with disbelief. "What are *you* doing here?"

The frantic voice of the young man's conscience warned him that he was treading on dangerous ground with his accusations. Althea hadn't done anything he wasn't doing, and her reasons were undoubtedly better. But *Drumon!*—that great lout of a farrier from the foregate. Standing in front of a fire day after day, hammering iron between iron, had made the smith as strong and dense as the beasts he shod.

Drum angled his head, met Jordan's stare with impenetrable silence, then turned to Althea with a helpless expression on his whiskered face.

Jordan also looked at Althea. "You said you'd spend the day getting ready in your room . . ."

She flicked her hair behind her shoulder and faced Jordan squarely, without quite looking at him. "And you said you would do the same in the stable."

As his conscience warned, accusations weren't going to win Jordan's day. He tried an explanation instead. "I only did what was best . . . right. I had to."

"You had to lie to me!" Althea's cheeks were a few shades darker than her hair. "Telling me everything I should gather—as if you were actually going to wait for me. I should have guessed! Balthan was right. And I suppose you went and told your lord father, as well."

"I did not."

Althea trilled—a high-pitched sound common to women and caged birds, and one which men were wise to fear. "I don't believe you. Give me one good reason why I should believe you."

Jordan understood that he had no reasons she would consider acceptable. He was speechless despite his own gut belief that Althea, not he, was in the wrong. He was astonished when Drumon interceded on his behalf.

"In this, at least, I think Master Hawson tells the truth, my lady." The farrier paused for breath. Althea's eyes widened, then he continued. "He travels alone. If he'd told his father, half the Conclave would be thundering along after him. Lord Ironhawk wouldn't send his eldest son off alone—not when he won't even Nominate him to his first shrine. And he certainly wouldn't send him off without food or blankets."

The farrier's measured words stung Jordan to the quick. If they'd been less than the absolute truth, he'd have drawn his sword—he remembered to bring *that*. But they were the truth, and he felt foolish; he had forgotten food and blankets. Jordan focused on a lonely cloud behind the campanile tower. Homilies about the virtue of humility hovered in his mind's eye, closer than they'd ever been before but still beyond his grasp.

Althea was truly surprised to see Jordan—much more surprised than angry. After all, she'd made up *her* mind to leave this morning the moment he'd suggested waiting until tomorrow. She'd turned to Drumon because he was strong and tractable, and because she knew he was enough in love with her to abandon his livelihood. Still, she was from the villa, not the foregate. She saw her friend's eyes glaze; her anger vanished and was forgotten.

"I'm sorry," she said gently, sincerely, and thinking only of the humiliation he felt, not the acts which caused it. A maiden could not properly offer a man greater comfort, so without thinking, Althea reached out to stroke Fugatore's black velvet nose.

Jordan reacted when he realized what Althea was going to do. He closed one hand over Fugatore's reins and wrapped the knotted ends around the other. He locked his legs against the saddle leather and his heels into the stirrups. Jordan was ready, but it was a rare knight whose arms were stronger than a Valorian's neck, and he was not that man.

Drumon, the farrier, knew horses generally and Fugatore specifically. He would rather shoe an ox than a Valorian and was unconvinced that Fugatore would outgrow his skittishness. Either way, Drum wasn't intimidated by the colt's drawn-back lips or flattened ears; he simply made a fist and clouted the animal on the muzzle before Althea had an inkling of her danger.

Fugatore screamed and sank into his haunches. Jordan guided him along a wide circle before coming back to Althea and Drum. The frothing corners of the colt's mouth were bloodstained.

"Please go back to the villa," he pleaded with Althea. "I'll find your brother. I swear it. I give you my oath."

Althea shook her head. Her face was pale rather than flushed. "You can't, Jordie. You don't even know where he is. You can't find him without the talisman, and I can't give you that."

"I know he's somewhere north-northeast of here. I'll find him. I'll ask questions. Balthan's a memorable sort. He won't have disappeared without a trace."

Pulling her cloak-hood tight around her face, Althea put an end to the uncomfortable conversation by striding forward on the trail. Jordan held Fugatore in check until she passed.

Drumon didn't need to say aloud that he'd follow Althea to the Underworld and beyond; the set of his jaw and brow were eloquent enough. Nor did the farrier need words to express his thoughts about Jordan and his unruly horse when an abbreviated snort conveyed his opinion with absolute clarity. He gave the pair a final appraisal, then started after

Althea, his long legs narrowing the distance between them from the first step.

"I'm coming with you," Jordan shouted, cautiously letting out Fugatore's reins. "We can travel together."

"We can't," Althea insisted, walking backward for a moment.

The Valorian fought for the bit and Jordan had to rein him in again. She had a valid point: Fugatore sensed her fear and it drove him wild. But Althea wasn't referring to a temperamental horse.

"Lord Ironhawk will come looking for you, Jordan, when he realizes you've gone, and he'll find all of us. I don't want him to know—"

"You're his ward, Althea. My lord father would look for you, too—"

Althea shook her head vigorously. Fugatore replied with a challenging scream. He pawed through the grass and tried, despite spurs digging into his flanks, to rear. Jordan shouted that he could not hear what Althea was saying. In a misguided effort to be helpful, she came closer to him, and the Valorian. The farrier pulled Althea to safety while Jordan got another opportunity to display his skills of horsemanship. When he returned to the path, Althea and Drum were walking east without him.

Ironhawk's heir watched them with an irritation Fugatore might understand. Drumon had an axe, but he had a sword. They had food and blankets, but he had a purebred Valorian. Jordan was a warrior: a protector of the weak, meek, and peaceful. If he could not be the splendid, solitary hero, he should be leading this quest, and yet he found himself sawing at Fugatore's bloody mouth, struggling to hold the colt to the pace Althea set for him.

Twice more in that long, frustrating morning, Jordan

sought to convince Althea that she and Drum should return to the safety of Hawksnest. Both times he failed. Fugatore could not see Althea's face without becoming headstrong, and Althea staunchly refused to see Jordan's logic.

"I'm sorry," she insisted, though her tone and stance proclaimed the opposite, "but Balthan's my brother and he wouldn't want you or your lord father to rescue him—if he even needs rescuing. He might not be glad to see me."

Jordan seized the slender thread of doubt. "All right, what *will* you do if Balthan doesn't need rescuing and you think he does?"

But Althea could not be baited down improbable pathways. "I'll do whatever I have to do." She faced east again and resumed her steady, if slow, walking.

Fugatore struck out after her and Jordan was compelled to tighten the reins again. The sting of metal made the Valorian hold his head unnaturally high. Jordan patted a dark grey shoulder; Fugatore shied from his touch. Six months of training eroded in a single morning. That, more than anything else, made the young man's heart heavy. He stopped thinking about Althea and gave his attention to his frantic, confused horse.

Jordan hadn't forgotten everything in his rush to escape Hawksnest. He remembered a pair of boar-bristle brushes and a chamois square which made short work of the sweat drying in Fugatore's coat. Nor had Jordan forgotten the jar of sweet-balm to soothe the jagged nicks his spurs made in the colt's flanks. Nothing would soothe Fugatore's sore mouth except replacing his bridle with a halter, and that Jordan could not do unless he also conceded defeat and led the animal back to Hawksnest's stable.

The sun was nearing midheaven before Jordan was satisfied that his horse was calm enough to be ridden again. Fugatore seemed to agree—at least he didn't nip when Jordan lifted himself into the saddle. The eastbound trail was empty as far as Jordan's eye could follow it: across a narrow stream and past two stony hills before disappearing behind a third. They paused to drink from the stream. Jordan dug an old water-sack out of the saddlebag. It leaked along the seam, but there was a chance the leather would swell as it was saturated, so he filled and plugged it, and slung it over his shoulder. A cold trickle ran down his spine. It would be annoying later, but at that moment it felt very good. Remounting, Jordan let the Valorian set his own pace until they caught up with Drum and Althea, which they surely would before long.

Filling his belly with water served to remind Jordan exactly how long it had been since he'd eaten a good meal, and how unforgivably foolish he'd been to race away from the villa without visiting the food storerooms. The more he thought of the barrels of fruit and the wheels of soft, yellow cheese, the hungrier he got. When he got his first glimpse of Althea and Drum they were sitting beside the trail— undoubtedly enjoying their lunch. His stomach churned in protest.

Fugatore was hungry, too, and more interested in browsing through the grass than in tormenting Althea. Jordan bound the Valorian's ankles in sturdy hobbles and hoped getting himself something to eat would be as easy.

Drumon looked up from his meal. "Those purple flowers over there," he gestured with a broken loaf of liberally buttered bread, "crack-weed."

Jordan's shoulders fell. He should have noticed. The plant was notorious for colicking horses. Older animals usually knew from experience that the sweet-tasting leaves weren't worth the agony they caused later on. Fugatore was young, stable-raised, and headed straight for the fragrant flowers which, once Jordan's eye was attuned to them, bloomed in profusion through the dappled shade. Unhobbling the Valorian and leading him some distance down the path to a sunny patch where there were no purple flowers nor any other obvious noxious weed, Jordan prickled with the notion that his unwilling companions had chosen their rest spot deliberately to thwart him. Then Althea offered him a piece of bread and the suspicion was forgotten.

"Have we left Lord Ironhawk's desmene yet?" she asked, slathering cheese on the crust with her knife.

Jordan paused to scan the horizon. They were far from the moon-gate hill and the tower, but not yet beyond his family's estate. There were boundary pillars set at regular intervals along the invisible line separating Hawksnest from the rest of Britannia. As heir, Jordan was obligated to set eyes and hands on each one at least twice a year, fulfilling a tradition that was more superstition than magic. His father claimed he felt a difference in the air itself whenever he returned to, or left, his lands. Jordan knew where they were because he saw one of the man-high stones in the distance, not through some arcane perception.

"Not yet, but soon." He pointed to the sentinel standing off by itself.

"Does the ring truly protect Hawksnest from outsiders?"

Jordan tore into the bread and answered her between swallows. "No—it's the smell of civilization that keeps the headless ones and trolls away. They're smarter than mere beasts; they know what the smell of man means. The smell of iron and steel, anyway."

Lord British's benign leadership might have united Britannia and brought it safety from its enemies, but it did not follow that there were no dangers left in his realm. Britannia had its share of petty brigands and wolfshead outlaws; it also had creatures whose very existence and nature set them against mankind. The sword at Jordan's side was not a vain affectation. The shrine-to-shrine journey of Questing Peer was dangerous. More Peers abandoned their Quest after a desperate brawl with inhuman foes than failed to receive the enlightenment of a particular virtue.

Jordan received his first diminutive sword when he was five. Since then he practiced with the weapon nine days out of every ten in a sandy arena behind the villa. At eleven he graduated to a full-size blade. At fifteen he disarmed his father with a bated weapon. After that both he and his mentors used live steel. An assortment of scars on his chest, arms, and legs reminded Jordan of the mistakes he'd made when he thought he knew more than a swordmaster.

The young man knew how to defend himself, but he'd never fought for his life, or killed his opponent. Drumon might get lucky with that heavy double-bit axe he carried; he'd never be skilled with it as Jordan was with his sword. Nothing could shake Jordan's conviction that he was the only one who had the ability to protect them from whatever lay beyond Hawksnest's boundary ring.

The self-assigned responsibility made him swell with pride, and it made him shiver.

Jordan finished the bread and cheese without tasting them. His mood spread to Althea who seldom left Hawksnest since Lord Erwald Ironhawk had brought her and Balthan home with him from that Peerage Conclave many years ago. She stared silently at the boundary marker. A breeze lifted her hair and draped it across her face; she neither brushed it behind her shoulder nor looked away from the stone. When Jordan said it was time to be moving, she packed her basket with awkward, distracted movements.

Drum scowled at her and then at Jordan when the latter said he'd ride a bit ahead of them, but he did not object.

The stone pillar was hidden from sight by the time they crossed the invisible divide. Despite his assurances to Althea, Jordan strained his senses to distinguish the air of Hawksnest from the air of greater Britannia. The difference, if there was one, was too small for him to measure, unless he counted the prickling at the base of his neck—and he refused to count that, blaming it instead on his sweat-stiffened tunic.

Meadows gave way to scrubland which quickly gave way to the unnatural quiet of a pine forest. Rust-colored needles from seasons past obscured the seldom-used track and muffled the sound of Fugatore's iron-shod hooves. Birds sang in the thick branches high above their heads. Sunlight filtered to the ground in angled bands. Now and again something would crackle in the distance. They'd all stop and look toward the sound. Sometimes they saw a tiny dust cloud spiraling through the shafts of yellow light.

"A squirrel," Jordan would call from his vantage point on Fugatore's back, or "A rabbit" or "A weasel." His voice reassured Althea and Drum, but it was all pretense. Nothing he recognized moved through the forest debris and the itching between his shoulder blades had become a constant annoyance.

The light shafts struck the forest floor at deeper angles and in smaller numbers. The shadows were darker and broader. Jordan recalled that the season was spring and nights were cold and still much longer than the days. He hadn't planned to spend a night in the forest; he expected to be on the Paladin's Road and snug in a charterhouse inn by sunset. He hadn't planned to hold Fugatore to his slowest walk or wait five minutes out of ten for his companions to catch up with him again. Time and distance blurred in Jordan's mind. He worried that darkness would force them to stop for the night before they reached the relative safety of the Paladin's Road, and was elated when he saw rutted, bare ground intersecting their path.

"We've made it!" he shouted in the loudest voice any of them had dared since entering the forest.

The other two came running. Fugatore laid his ears back when he saw the young woman's flying hair, but he was too tired to lunge for Althea when the hem of her cloak brushed his flank. She stopped short in the middle of the road, looking from right to left and radiating disappointment.

"Where are we?"

Jordan took a firmer grip on the reins and brought Fugatore abreast of her. "We've reached the Old Paladin's Road from Trinsic to Britain City."

"But, where are we? Where can we stay for the night?"

Drumon slapped the Valorian's hindquarters to keep from surprising him. "She's exhausted," he whispered bluntly to Jordan. "Is there shelter near here?"

"Nothing closer than Hawksnest itself. There might be an abandoned assart a half-league south—but I'm not sure of the memory, and it's the wrong direction anyhow."

The farrier nodded with resignation and pointed to a clearing. "Any problems with that?"

"No water."

"I'll go looking for it."

"Fugatore."

"I'll take him with me."

Five

Night fell quickly on the forested road. Before Drum returned with water, the sunlight waned and the shadows filled with shades of purple and grey. Althea swept up a mound of pine needles and touched it with her hearthfire magic. The tinder flared and made the trees beyond the little bare-earth circle seem darker still. While Althea dribbled more needles on the fast-burning fire, Jordan stumbled through the shadows searching for firewood.

Althea yelped and scrambled to her feet when Jordan dumped his armload of branches into the clearing by the fire. Each apologized for frightening the other.

"I was listening so hard for Drum that I didn't hear you coming, Jordie."

Althea got down on her hands and knees to build the fire—and conceal the embarrassment burning her cheeks. Lord Ironhawk fed, clothed, and sheltered a score of retainers whose daily tasks included tending the hearthfires.

Althea helped the servants freely with her simple magic, but she didn't lay the kindling. She shoved one stick after another into the blaze without plan, and without concern for her long hair falling forward from her back.

Jordan caught a fall of amber as it swung toward the flames. "Here, let me do it," he said, gently pushing both Althea and her hair out of harm's way. His offer had no hidden meaning, but Althea flinched as if she'd been judged and found wanting at every shrine.

"I'm sorry I don't know how to build a campfire. I'm sorry I don't know anything at all. You think I'm a helpless and stupid woman. You think I should have stayed home and left this to men like you."

The branches Jordan was trying to balance against each other fell into the tinder with a shower of sparks. Jordan spat on his fingers, pulled them out, and began again. He didn't know much about dealing with women, but he knew better than to agree with Althea just then. He liked being called a man, too; it almost made up for the earlier Jordie. With more luck than skill—Jordan could count the number of times he'd made a fire from kindling on the fingers of one hand—he got the sticks propped against each other.

"You're just tired," he said, his hands hovering above the stick pyramid, ready to begin again. "You'll see. Tomorrow will be better."

Althea knew a false promise when she heard one. "How? Will Fugatore like me? Will my feet hurt less? Will it rain?"

Satisfied that his fire was not about to collapse, Jordan slapped the soot from his hands and gave Althea his full attention. "I don't know. I'm the one who left home without food, remember? Fugatore doesn't have to like you; he just has to get used to you and you to him. Then you can ride him, and your backside will hurt instead of your feet. And as for rain—we'll get wet until it stops. But you *are* tired and hungry—'' She almost looked too exhausted to eat. ''If you've got any food left, let's eat it and then you should get some sleep.''

''You're the one who's hungry.'' Althea smiled. ''You're always hungry. I can't imagine how you left Hawksnest without weighing yourself down with a barrel of food.''

Jordan scuffed the dirt with his knuckles. He couldn't answer that one. When he travelled to Trinsic with his father, they stopped early in the day to hunt game for the evening meal. Lord Ironhawk field-dressed his own kills— his son did the same—but bread, cheese, wine, everything that wasn't spit-roasted and eaten while still half-raw, simply appeared when they were ready for it.

''I've got parsnips for roasting and pepper-sausage,'' Althea said, unloading parcels from her basket. ''And a crusty pudding. I even took one of Agatha's mincemeat savories!'' She held up a wax-sealed crock for Jordan's appreciation.

The young man imagined he could eat everything Althea set down on her apron, including their parchment wrappings, when he heard a twig snap. He was on his feet with his sword drawn before his heart beat twice. Althea screamed, and so did Fugatore from the darkness beyond the firelight.

''Hammers and bells,'' Drum complained, seeing Jordan's sword and the gaping look of horror frozen on Althea's face. ''It's only me.''

Jordan fed the sword back into its scabbard, reflexively making certain that it could be drawn just as easily when he needed it again. ''We can't see out of the firelight and we can't take any chances. Call out when you see the fire. Let us know who you are and that you're all right. Don't leave us guessing.''

A pair of water-bags slid down Drum's thick arms. ''What about me? How will I know it's safe to make noise?''

"We're lit up like puppets in a shadow play," Jordan snapped as he pulled Fugatore's reins from the farrier's other hand.

"Now that's true enough. Doesn't either one of you know how to build a fire that won't burn itself out in an hour?"

The farrier did not waste time on an inferior fire, but built another one to his own liking on the other side of the clearing. Doubly ringed with stones and set in a shallow pit, Drum's blaze would stand against the wind, should it rise, and the rain, should it fall. Althea scrutinized his every move, questioning the position of each layer until the pyre was ready for her hearthfire magic. Jordan watched as well, but stayed loyally beside his humble hearth until it was reduced to embers.

Drum's fire was everything a campfire should be on a cold night: bright, warm, and aromatic from the pinewood and the slices of sausage Althea roasted in the flames. Jordan hesitated before joining them. He knew he should feel grateful for their food and fire, but what he felt was bitter rage.

"You've used up all the wood I gathered."

Althea flinched and Drum scowled, but neither said a word.

"I'll have to get some more. There's none left here in the clearing." Jordan was ashamed of himself, but shame alone couldn't keep him quiet. "Did you leave even one stick I could use as a torch?"

Drum prodded the fire with his toe until a single branch broke free with a shower of sparks; Althea misread the gesture and tried to placate Jordan by offering him the first slice of heated sausage.

"Have something to eat first, then I'll go with you with handfire so you can see."

Had he been alone with Althea or Drumon, Jordan might have risen to the occasion with an apology, but the words to appease them both eluded him, and so he did not try. Althea portioned the food fairly. She tried to be cheerful, but by the time she passed around the crusty pudding she was as sullen as her companions.

Neglected by everyone, the fire burned down.

"We should set our watches for the night," Jordan said, yawning.

Drum caught the yawn. He groaned and stretched before replying, "We can't be more than a league from Hawksnest. There haven't been brigands on this part of the Paladin's Road in years."

"Just because no one's been robbed or killed doesn't mean there haven't been brigands," Jordan retorted. "And I don't mean to give them an opportunity. If you're so tired, I'll take the whole night myself."

"I'll wager you'd be sleeping sound if you were by yourself and not trying to impress us—"

"No, Drum," Althea interrupted, "this time Jordan's right. There's no reason not to set up watches. If we were each alone, we'd have no choice but to sleep unguarded, but we're not each alone."

"All right, Jordan. See the Lazy Hunter over there? I'll wake you up when he touches the trees in the west. That should be about midnight."

"Looks right to me." Jordan shuffled to his feet.

"There are *three* of us. I can take a watch. I'll take the first watch. That bright star—I'll wake Jordie when it's halfway to the tree."

A bucket of cold water could not have tightened Jordan's shoulders faster than Althea's words. He peered through the darkness toward Drum. He could barely make out the farrier's profile; reading his expression was impossible. Jordan considered it against nature for a woman to stand watch while healthy men slept, but he'd made enough provocative remarks for one night. If Drum didn't object, he wouldn't tell Althea she was a woman and couldn't stand watch. Drum wasn't at all happy with Althea's offer, but saw no reason to draw attention to his opinion when Jordan had been so generous with his all evening.

The clearing was silent except for the distant hooting of an owl.

"It's settled then," Althea said, clapping crumbs from her hand as she stood up. "I'll take the first watch. What should I listen for?"

Jordan couldn't explain the difference between ordinary sounds and suspicious sounds. "Just listen—and don't be afraid to wake me if you don't like what you hear." Not that he'd be asleep. He could keep watch with his head propped against Fugatore's saddle as easily as he could sitting beside the dying fire. Or so Jordan told himself as he spread his cloak over a pine needle mattress. He wasn't that tired. He'd just close his eyes and listen . . .

"Jor-*die!*"

He began moving the moment he felt pressure on his arm, before his ears heard Althea's voice or his mind recognized it. His hands were around her throat by then. Jordan released her at once, then sat with his fist against his chest, unable to speak.

"Jordie? I think it's time for your watch. I'm not sure. The sky's cloudy now, and I can't see the stars, but I've been counting my heartbeats. I've counted to a thousand, ten times."

Jordan's heart pounded that many times since he'd opened his eyes. "I'm awake now," he assured her. "I'll take over."

"You're sure? I could stay up until it's time to wake Drum."

"No." Jordan sprang to his feet. "I'm fine. Let me

borrow your cloak. You can sleep there under mine against Fugatore's saddle. It's warmed up for you.''

"Oh—Fugatore's been restless, he keeps snorting and stamping his feet. I don't know what's wrong—I didn't think I should go near him.''

Jordan frowned as he tucked the thick wool under Althea's chin and lied when he told her the Valorian was probably dreaming. Horses had a keen sense for danger. He scratched the whorl of hair between the colt's eyes and tried to keep him quiet while he strained his own ears listening to the night sounds.

There were none—not even the faint sigh of a breeze in the pine trees. Clouds covered the patch of sky above the clearing, but they were no longer moving. The weather was changing, Jordan told himself. Probably it would rain tomorrow. The air was thick; it riled the horse, nothing more.

Fugatore rubbed his cheek against Jordan's arm, presenting another perennially itchy spot for soothing. When Jordan failed to do what Fugatore expected, the colt whinnied loud enough to wake the dead. Jordan tried to quiet the horse by squeezing his mouth shut. Fugatore thought it was a new game and butted Jordan out of the clearing.

Jordan tumbled backward over a tree root. He wound up sprawled on his back, unhurt and indignant. "Fu-ga—''

One sound cut through the noise of Fugatore pawing pine needles. It might have been a pinecone falling. It might have been the young man's imagination—but Fugatore quieted, too. Jordan stood cautiously and listened.

He heard it again—behind his right shoulder when it came from the left before. Two pinecones falling on a night when the air was absolutely still? The loudest sound in the forest was his pulse throbbing within his ears. Jordan gathered the borrowed cloak over his left arm and reached for his sword with his right. His fingers closed over the hilt. Better to be safe than sorry—

"*IRONHAWK!*"

Jordan leapt into the air as he shouted and came down facing the other way with his sword drawn. There were sounds in the clearing, now behind him, but more importantly, there were sounds in front of him. Grunts that recalled no animal the young man had ever hunted, and a stench that made him think of a freshly turned midden and tales his father told around the winter fires.

They mat their hair with bird droppings—the younger ones anyway. Female trolls like a mate who reeks.

They were on him before Jordan could fill his lungs for another warning. He whirled the cloak beside him, breaking the clasp at his neck and tangling at least one of the beasts in its folds. Jordan used his sword defensively, making swallowtail cuts in the night, until he had a parrying dagger ready in his left hand. Then he began to fight.

"*IRONHAWK!*"

Fugatore squealed, and a troll screamed. Hairy, clawed fingers brushed Jordan's cheek, barely missing his eye. He swung blind with both weapons. The dagger struck deep. Hot blood spurted over his hand.

"A torch!"

Jordan kicked the troll in the crotch; his dagger was free. He spun to the right, still night blind, and caught the attack that years of practice said would be waiting there. His dagger impaled a wooden club. The impact numbed his shoulder and compelled him to discard the knife. Putting both hands on the hilt, Jordan swung his sword like an axe. It bit deep into a troll's midsection. The stench was overwhelming.

"*IRONHAWK!*"

* * *

Althea awoke with the cold hand of terror twisting her gut. She couldn't identify the noises piercing the darkness, but the sum of them was desperate and mortal struggle. The shock and fear imprisoned her. If she did make a sound— if she did not even breathe—perhaps they would not find her. Then, like frost melting from glass in the morning sun, Althea imagined a brigand's hand over her mouth, his knife at her throat. She threw aside Jordan's cloak and bounded to her feet.

Better to die fighting than to risk capture.

She carried a knife, as did every Britannian old enough to cut meat from the common platter. It was a pretty trinket with a tassel dangling from its beaded hilt. It was better at cutting silk floss for embroidering than slicing meat, and no use at all as a weapon.

"IRONHAWK!"

Frantic as she was, Althea's mouthed a hasty benison thanking the nameless fates that the attack had come in Jordan's watch, not hers. There was a squeal and a scream. The first came from a horse, the second could not have come from a man's throat.

"A torch!"

A torch. The last shred of Althea's panic boiled away once she found a purpose. Her knife might be useless in a fight, but she had magic. Not Balthan's sort of magic, with its streaks of flame and numinous wisps of deadly poison, but magic all the same. Thrusting both hands into the pouch knotted through her belt, Althea coated her fingertips with greenwood ash. She left a trail of sparks behind her searching for the ashes of Drum's fire.

The linear spell of hearthfire worked best on dry tinder and volatile oils. Althea wasted precious time trying to make a wrist-thick branch burst into flame before noticing the half-dozen fires her magic had kindled in the pine needles. The closest one was nibbling at her skirt and more than enough to transform the branch into a torch.

"*IRONHAWK!*"

Althea raised the torch over her head. "I'm coming!" She ran toward Jordan's voice.

Drum woke up with the Ironhawk battle cry echoing inside his head. The notion that Jordan was playing a nasty trick on him lasted no more than the instant needed to reject it. The farrier knew trouble when he smelled it, even if he didn't know trolls. He lay still another moment, locating the sounds in the darkness, recalling exactly where his basket was and where the axe was within it. Then, untroubled by the faintest glimmer of panic, Drum retrieved the weapon and strode beyond the clearing to the sounds of conflict.

The farrier lacked a fighter's reflexes. When he heard a noise, Drum leaned toward it, unbalancing his whole body. He held the axe away from his shoulders, imagining that was how a trained fighter carried a weapon, and snagged it in branches he could not see. Though he brought no skill to combat, his innate strength and size made this lack not as great a disadvantage as it might have been.

Without forewarning, a club slammed against his back. Drum grunted, then he swung the axe. The problem wasn't finding an enemy, or hitting it—Drum was used to striking the same spot on the anvil time and time again with an iron mallet—the problem was getting the axe-head out of a corpse. Killing wasn't like shaping metal. The axe didn't bounce back for next stroke and anvils didn't moan.

When a tentative shake didn't free the weapon, Drum slid his left hand up the wooden haft and pushed the hairy thing off. Wondering what, under heaven, had attacked them, he hoisted his weapon to the same awkward position as before.

Althea brought the torch into the blackthorn scrub. The farrier counted seven half-grown trolls. His first thought was to defend Althea and leave Jordan to his own devices. But trolls were nocturnal beasts who feared fire; they weren't going near Althea. Drum reckoned he'd defend Jordan's back—from a healthy distance. The Peer's son cut a wide swathe with his bastard-sword.

The trolls were stronger than men. One against one, in a fair fight with bare hands or clubs, no man could hope to stand against any troll, even half-grown ones like these. But men seldom fought fairly. They armed themselves with tempered weapons and protected their backs with boiled leathers and steel. They fought in teams and beat the trolls back into the night.

The skirmish was over as suddenly as it had begun. The trolls dropped their crude weapons moments after Drum established his position behind Jordan. Their inhuman shrieks faded swiftly into silence. Jordan gasped and let the swordtip rest on the ground.

"They're gone." He wiped his forehead with his sleeve, and saw the blood congealing on his fingers. It wasn't his own—he hadn't been hurt—but it left him queasy all the same.

Althea ventured closer with the torch. She recoiled when the light revealed a hairy corpse. "What are they?"

Still dragging his sword beside him, Jordan snatched the torch from Althea's hands before its flames spread into the pine trees. "Trolls."

"Are you hurt?"

Jordan said nothing, unwilling to put his feelings into words. He'd spent the better part of his life waiting for the day when he would fight and kill an enemy. He'd been warned by his father and others that there would be no triumph, no exaltation; that his knees would knock louder after the danger was past than before. Not him, he'd swear: He was a fighter; he was a *man*. He'd never shrink from a battle. His nerve would never break. How much worse could a sword-struck corpse look than a wolf after the hounds finished with it?

He had the answer now, and it would stay with him the rest of his life.

"Jordie—are you all right? You're trembling."

Jordan cleared his mind with one last shudder. "I'm fine." He forced himself to clean his sword on the troll's shaggy legs.

That was more than Althea could bear. She staggered sideways, clutching her stomach.

Drum clapped a hand on Jordan's shoulder. If he felt Jordan flinch, he had the compassion not to mention it. "You did well by yourself."

"Who'd expect trolls on the Paladin's Road. Brigands, maybe—but *trolls!*"

The farrier shrugged. Brigands or trolls—they were much the same to him. "You were right to post a watch. I sleep like a stone." He released Jordan and combed his curly black hair with his fingers. His expression changed to one of abject misery. "She'd be dead if you hadn't been with us. No different than if I'd killed her myself."

Amid the swordwork, archery, hunting, horsemanship and those endless homilies on virtue, Erwald Ironhawk gave his sons a rudimentary understanding of a Peer's obligations as a leader of lesser men. It was wrong to let Drumon sink into despair, however selfishly satisfying it might feel. Jordan fed his long-hilted sword into the scabbard.

"You judge yourself too harshly, Drumon. Look at your

axe—the fight wasn't over before you got to it. You did what you were supposed to do: sleep while I kept watch, and wake up when I needed you."

"She said she might need protection along the way—but I wouldn't have set a watch. I sleep like a stone—"

"You knew I was watching, so you slept. If you thought you were the only one protecting Althea you would not have slept like a stone, I promise you."

"I didn't trust you, Jordan. I meant to stay awake all night—"

Althea screamed hysterically, sparing Jordan from a similar confession. Drumon dropped his axe to sweep her up in his arms as she ran near him, her cloak streaming behind her, while Jordan forgot his weariness and cleared his sword in a single one-handed move.

"What happened? What's wrong?" he demanded, positioning himself between Althea and whatever had frightened her.

The young woman sobbed incoherently. Jordan exchanged a worried glance with Drum, then, sword in one hand and torch in the other, went searching. The source lay in the blackthorns: a wounded troll. Its fingers were longer than a man's, its palm much broader, but still not big enough to cover the bleeding wound on its belly.

The other trolls were dark of skin, hair, and eyes. This one had sandy hair and eyes the clear blue color of a cloudless sky. It seemed more man than beast until it saw Jordan, then it found strength to snarl, revealing splayed teeth and a coal-black tongue.

Jordan retreated involuntarily as a sinewy arm stretched toward him. He saw the extruded guts, swallowed hard, and forced himself closer.

"There's one over here that's still breathing."

Althea's sobs got louder; Drum had to shout over them. "What do we do with it?"

Jordan didn't answer. The troll must know it was dying; it must know it was no longer a threat—yet it snarled, dug its fingers into the dirt, and dragged itself across the ground. The torn hemwork of a woman's apron hung around its shoulders. The brightly knotted fringe snagged on an up-thrust root. The creature pulled but failed to free itself. Sweat made a putrid paste of its warpaint. Its chest heaved, its arm twitched.

Something midway between mercy and morbid curiosity made Jordan lift the fringe with his swordtip. That was when he noticed the troll's necklace: a crude thong with irregular bits of crinkly leather strung between rough-textured nuts. A moment passed before something deep inside him snapped and shrieked: *ears . . . human ears!* Jordan closed his eyes and told himself that the other things were nothing more than hazelnuts. He lost all feeling between his churning stomach and his feet.

"Jordan! What's taking so long?"

Drum's voice seemed to come from a distant world. Jordan tried, and failed, to answer. Severed ears and much worse danced in his mind's eye; and they would not be banished. He was breathing but his lungs weren't working until the sword moved in his hand.

The sword hadn't moved by itself. The troll held the tip lightly against its throat. Trolls weren't supposed to have a language; this one was eloquent.

"What's wrong?" Drum asked, startling Jordan who had not heard him approach.

When Jordan recovered, the point of his sword rested against his leg and the troll's eyes were pleading with him. "I can't do it," he whispered.

"Can't do what?" Drum looked down at the troll without seeing its trophies or its eyes as Jordan saw them.

"I can't finish it."

The distraught young man jumped again when Althea appeared on his swordside. "Kill it!" she urged him. "Kill it!"

Jordan tried to find words that would explain both the horror and empathy he felt for the vanquished, dying troll.

"What are you waiting for?" Drum asked without rancor. "It's suffering. Put it out of its misery."

Jordan's tongue stuck to the roof of his mouth; he couldn't have told them, even if he had been able to find the words.

"For the love of virtue, Jordan—we're men, not beasts—"

Drum's words weren't the right words, but they were sufficient to break Jordan out of his stupor. After passing the torch to the farrier, Jordan took his sword in both hands and plunged it into the troll's breast.

Its spine arched. Its eyes opened one last time and remained open after Jordan withdrew the blade. He knelt to close them.

"Don't touch it!" Althea restrained him.

Jordan allowed himself to be led back to the clearing. Drum got the fire going brightly again. None of the three considered going back to sleep; none had anything to say either. Jordan shifted restlessly from one perch to another. No matter which way he turned, he was sure something was staring at him, but he did not go back to close the troll's eyes.

Six

*D*awn came without fanfare. Birds stayed on their night roosts as the sky changed from black to an angry, mottled grey. Gusts of wind whipped through the trees, warning the weary travellers that they'd find no shelter from the coming storm beneath them. While Althea sliced pepper-sausage, Drum scattered the ashes of their fires, and Jordan inspected Fugatore's hooves.

"Breakfast's ready!"

The bread was still fresh. The meat portions were hearty and Althea assured them that plenty of food remained in her basket. After tense, exhausting hours of silence, both men relaxed slightly.

"Must have been a hard winter in the mountains to drive trolls this far south," Jordan said before filling his mouth with bread and sausage.

"Is that where they come from?" Drum asked. "I thought

they came from the swamps. You know, trolls, water, and bridges—they go together.''

"The big males set up under bridges because of the rocks, not the water. They get a ready stock of their favorite weapon and easy shots at their favorite targets. When the Trinsic patrols hear about it, they'll come up the road in force. Nothing a cohort of paladins likes better than camping upwind of a bridge and baiting trolls all night. They're not really very smart—the trolls, that is.''

In repeating what he'd heard others say about the beasts, Jordan meant to be witty but he made Drum feel foolish for asking the question instead. The big farrier hunched over his food and would not be baited into saying another word.

"The ones last night didn't have rocks," Althea said softly just before the silence became unbearable. "I don't suppose it has anything to do with Balthan, do you?''

"Just a coincidence. A hard winter in the mountains. The females must've driven out the oldest of the youngsters.''

"They had clothes. I didn't think trolls wore clothes.''

"They weren't—" Jordan stopped himself from saying that the trolls weren't wearing clothes; they were displaying trophies. But that thought filled his own mind—especially the grisly necklace.

"Well, if you say so, Jordie.'' Althea shivered. "But I can't get rid of the feeling that they're still out there watching us. I keep thinking about Balthan, too.''

Jordan gulped the last of his breakfast and hurried off to finish grooming Fugatore without responding to Althea's worries. He had assumed he was the only one whose neck hairs had tingled all night, and was not relieved to hear Althea felt that way too. Under the ominous clouds, it was all too easy to make a connection between trolls and their rescue quest.

He looked up in time to see a flash of lightning, then

counted slowly until he heard thunder. If weather lore held, they had an hour before the storm would be overhead. When the distant rumbling faded, Jordan found there was another image haunting his thoughts: the strange darkning streak in the magic globe. It awakened the same eerie fascination the necklace did and was just as difficult to get out of his mind.

The only notion Jordan could conjure up to banish his deepening anxiety was an image of his father wearing a grim expression and mail shirt. Erwald Ironhawk's reaction to trolls infesting what he thought of as his part of the Paladin's Road—much less trolls who collected trophies from their victims—was predictable: He'd summon every paladin in Trinsic and half the Peers of Britannia to his war court and lead them on a troll-harrowing the like of which hadn't been seen in living memory.

But Lord Ironhawk would make time to confront his eldest son before he did anything else, and the easy prediction of his own punishment was enough to keep Jordan from turning back.

Jordan shoved his fingers between Fugatore's belly and the saddle girth. As always, the horse was holding his breath. Any other time Jordan would lead the colt in a tight circle or wait until the animal had to breathe naturally, but there was too much stewing in his mind for such compromise tactics. Jordan jabbed between the Valorian's ribs with his fist, then defended himself against Fugatore's teeth while he tightened the girth two notches with his other hand.

Fugatore stamped his near hind foot and shook his head vigorously, but he'd gotten no more sleep than the rest of them and, for once, didn't fight the inevitable. Jordan swung into the saddle just in time to see Althea struggling to lift her basket onto her shoulders.

"Give it here," he offered. "I'll tie it behind me."

The Valorian was ready to accept the bridle, the saddle,

the weight of a mail-shirted rider, and even the company of a wispy, fearful, nonrider as the price of returning to a cozy stall with a rack of hay and a bucket of oats—but he was not ready to accept a basket tickling his hindquarters. Fugatore executed a series of vicious leaps and kicks. Drum and Althea scrambled for cover while Jordan held on with his knees. He survived Fugatore's first two attempts to unseat him, but on the third he collided with the saddle-horn. His feet came out of the stirrups; the basket went sailing out of his hand.

The next thing Jordan knew he was flat on his back looking up at Althea.

"Are you all right?"

"Damn that animal—"

Jordan levered himself up on one elbow before thudding back to the ground. He wasn't seriously hurt—a few bruises, mostly to his pride and dignity—but he'd had the wind knocked out of him. Closing his eyes, Jordan waited for the dizziness to subside. Althea wiped the young man's forehead with her skirt hem. He opened his eyes and felt lightheaded for a completely different reason. She put her arm around him and helped him sit up.

"Are you certain you're not hurt?"

Before Jordan could answer, Drum appeared in front of him and pulled him to his feet. Fugatore was nosing through the pine needles, questing for his oats. Jordan grabbed the reins and led him to the basket which lay intact on the far side of the clearing.

"It's no use," Drum advised. "He's no packhorse. He'll never carry a creaking basket on his back."

"He'll do what I want him to do."

Jordan winced as he lifted the basket. His mail shirt probably saved his life during the battle with the trolls, but despite a quilted undertunic, it magnified the bruises he got hitting the ground. He considered stripping to the skin and asking Althea to rub some liniment into the swelling, but the thunder was getting louder so he put the thought out of his mind as he shoved the basket under Fugatore's nose.

"There—get a good smell of it. It's not anything that's going to hurt you . . . and it's going up on your back—"

The basket struck Fugatore's nose harder than Jordan meant it to, but the animal stood obediently. Jordan rested his head against the saddle, catching his breath and grateful that the horse was tall enough to hide him from his companions. Some of the welded rings must have snapped when he hit the ground. The broken ends pierced the quilting to his skin where a day's worth of dried sweat salted the wounds. He'd need more than liniment by nightfall. Biting his lips shut, Jordan climbed into the saddle.

"Let's go."

Drum walked between Fugatore and Althea. After the second or third time the farrier cuffed him on his tender mouth, the horse stopped trying to nip the girl and settled into his steady walk. Reason warned they couldn't outwalk the rolled clouds looming behind them, but hope made them try. Althea stretched out every stride in an effort to maintain a Valorian's pace until she set her foot down squarely on a sharp-edged stone and had to sit down immediately.

The storm chose that moment to splatter them with wind-driven raindrops.

"I'll catch up," Althea insisted bravely from the middle of the road. "My stocking's twisted. I just want to get it straight before the ground's too soaked to sit on." But she was massaging the ball of her foot, not loosening her shoes.

A few steps ahead of her Jordan and Drum exchanged knowing glances. They hadn't noticed her shoes before: soft suede slippers that protected neither her ankles nor the soles of her feet, unlike the sturdy buskins they both wore.* It was a miracle Althea had come this far without hurting herself.

Drum's glance jumped from Althea to Fugatore; Jordan shook his head. "If you and I both held the reins, maybe —but the moment one of us relaxes, he'll throw her off," he said too softly for Althea to hear.

"What, then?" Drum did not have to whisper. Wind swirled loudly through the trees. The raindrops fell thicker and faster.

"We'll have to get her a pair of boots."

"Where?"

Jordan sighed and listed slightly in the saddle. The broken links scratched his shoulder; he ignored them. "We'll go slow."

Drum scowled.

"You suggest something. What would you do? Imagine the two of you are out here together; I'm still back at Hawksnest wondering where Althea is. What would you do?"

The scowl deepened to a sneer but he said nothing.

"There! Right as rain and twice as ready," Althea announced, taking a step toward them. She was walking on the outer edge of her foot and didn't deceive either man with her forced cheeriness.

"We'll go slower now," Jordan said as the sky opened above them. "Tell us when you need to rest."

The storm pelted them from all directions. They each had circular cloaks made from felted wool, a material as waterproof as any fabric could be made without resorting to magic. Wind turned the cloaks into flapping sails; they were

---

*The women of a Peers intimate family, even wards on charity, seldom left the manicured grounds of their villas on foot.

quickly drenched to the skin. Jordan's mail shirt became a heavy, cold prison. Then lightning struck a nearby tree, deafening and terrifying each of them, including Fugatore, who planted his hooves in the mud and would not take another step.

Jordan dismounted, leaving his cloak behind to protect the valuable saddle and the even more valuable food in Althea's basket. "Shelter. We've got to get to shelter!" he shouted, pointing at the trees.

With the reins in one hand and Drum's cloak in the other, Jordan started into the forest. He got the horse moving but not Drum, who had never seen a tree explode and might never trust wood again. Jordan grabbed Althea instead; she came willingly and the farrier followed her.

Nothing would have pleased Jordan more than to see a cave mouth yawning up in front of them. It was not an altogether idle fantasy. Magic and natural forces riddled Britannia with caverns, some of which—the eight dungeons the Great Council sealed with magic words—descended to a dark and ancient Underworld. New sinkholes appeared each spring. Most such caves were shallow things better suited to hibernating animals than adventurers, although the one into which Lord British disappeared was an obvious exception.

Jordan hoped for one just tall enough, and deep enough, to shelter them until the storm stopped. The best he could find was a thicket of vine-draped trees whose leaves had unfurled. The thicket was already occupied by two red deer and their fawns which were more afraid of the storm than the intruders. Althea said the fawns were adorable; Jordan abandoned any thought of fresh meat for the stewpot.

Thunderstorms were not unusual for this part of Britannia, especially in the spring. Sometimes the sky turned an eerie shade of green and tornadoes roared across the land destroying everything in their paths. This storm was unexceptional and would scarcely disrupt the daily routine of the villa or foregate. It was different in the thicket without the security of stone walls and shuttered windows.

The air sizzled with another nearby lightning strike. Althea screamed and held her hands over her ears, but the worst was over. The sky slowly brightened, the wind died down, and although the rain did not stop it fell more gently. The does bounded separately from the thicket, taking their fawns with them.

Jordan slicked his hair out of his eyes. "Let's go."

"Is it safe?" Althea asked. She stood apart from Drum now, but made no move to follow Jordan.

"It's as safe as it's likely to get all day."

Drum adjusted his basket. In silhouette, with the cowl falling over his eyes and the basket rising above his shoulders, he was unrecognizable. He shook the excess water from his cloak and started walking.

When they returned to the Paladin's Road, Althea stripped off her flimsy, ruined slippers, vowing to continue barefoot despite the vigorous objections of her companions. Jordan had Drum lift her into Fugatore's saddle. The Valorian didn't throw her off immediately but his manner made it clear—especially to Althea—that he would the instant the reins were slack. Jordan swore that would never happen, but Drum helped her out of the saddle. He carried her until they came to a carved stone marker.

"White Flower Valley," Jordan announced, halting as he did.

The Valley estate was almost as large as Hawksnest. The Alaines lived in a villa every bit as fine as Erwald Ironhawk's. Jordan knew Sir John Alaine and his family as well as he knew any other Peerage clan; certainly better than he knew Drumon's family in the Hawksnest foregate. If they went down the narrow trail, they'd be at the villa by midday. There'd be warm food, dry clothes, and a soft bed for each of them—and a messenger headed cross-country to tell Hawksnest where the fledglings had come to roost. This misguided venture would come to an end no better than its beginning, and, if he was very lucky, Jordan figured he might get his father's Nomination to the Virtue Quest before he reached the unimaginable age of thirty.

Leaving Fugatore groundtied on the road, Jordan explained what awaited in White Flower Valley, but withheld his own preferences. Althea lifted her skirt and tiptoed delicately down the embankment. Her feet were corpse-white but not completely numb; she grimaced when she reached the squishy mud of the White Flower Track. Nonetheless she stood there, staring at the point, some two furlongs away, where the track vanished into the low-lying clouds.

Althea looked back at Jordan. Her hair fell in untidy ringlets, her lips were pale, her cheeks ruddy; by any measure she looked bedraggled and fragile. Jordan hoped she'd made the only sensible decision.

"Whatever you decide to do, Jordan, we'll do, too."

That was not quite what Jordan had in mind. "Leave me out of it," he snarled. "You know what lies ahead on the road, and you know what will happen when you get to White Flower Valley. You decide."

She shrugged and turned away from the valley. "I have decided. I've decided to do what you do. If you go to White Flower Valley, Drum and I will follow you. I still want very badly to rescue my brother, but I see now that there's no hope of doing it without you. Drum and I don't have the skills for this—" Althea silenced Jordan with the tilt of her chin. "Oh, I know you didn't bring food . . . but you wouldn't be starving—you'd have killed those fawns. And it's not just the trolls—though, by destiny's hand, they were enough—but the storm, too. You took charge; you're more like your father than you imagine.

"You're my leader—my lord. I hope you'll want to keep looking for Balthan, but I will follow you regardless."

Jordan kicked a pebble as hard as he could, then another, and another. "Truth to tell: my mind's divided."

"Because of me?" Althea asked, starting up the embankment. The wet gravel shifted—no great problem if she'd been wearing boots, but she wasn't. Jordan grabbed her arm before she fell. "Because of me." She answered her own question before he released her. "Would you keep going if I went down the track to White Flower? If Drum and I went?"

He walked away from her and stared at the sky. The cowl slipped onto his shoulders; rain splashed his face. "I don't know. We don't actually know that Balthan *needs* rescuing. If he does, he wouldn't want me doing it. My lord father and Sir John should both know about the trolls. The road touches their desmenes and we didn't kill them all. At least three got away. One troll is too many as far as Lord Ironhawk is concerned."

"You'd go back then, to Hawksnest over White Flower Valley?"

"I didn't say that."

Absently, Jordan scratched behind his ear, and became aware how matted his hair had become in a single day. His face felt like crosscut wood. Jordan had a moustache—he thought it made him look older and more dignified—but, at its best, his beard was a scraggly disgrace. He preferred to go clean-shaven. He'd remembered a bag of pumice soap, but the thought of mixing it with cold water sent a shiver down his back. Another reason to go to White Flower Valley, but hardly a sufficient one.

None of Jordan's reasons seemed sufficient one way or the other.

Fugatore raised his head. Neither Jordan nor Althea noticed, and Drumon chose to say nothing. The first lesson the Valorian colt had been taught, a full year before he became Jordan's birthday present, was not to move when his reins hung straight from his bridle to the ground—a thrown or injured rider didn't need a wandering mount—but Fugatore was a clever horse, and had learned that the reins moved when he tossed his head. He saw Drum watching him, but Drum wasn't the one he had to obey, so he shook the reins to the center of the road. His nostrils flared and his ears pricked forward. He pawed the ground and whickered.

When the Valorian was several paces up the road, Drum decided it was time to speak. "Something's coming."

Jordan snapped to attention, saw how far Fugatore had gotten, and went after him with a growl brewing in his throat—then he heard hoofbeats.

"Get back!" he commanded Althea and Drumon, pointing to the woods where he wanted them as he hurried Fugatore off the road.

Althea gathered her skirt, but hesitated at the steep embankment. "Why—what's wrong? Why can't we just stand on the edge—"

Jordan veered toward her; Fugatore, naturally, balked and Jordan's already sore shoulder suffered before he got his other arm around Althea's waist. They all skidded down the embankment. Althea jammed her toe and gave Jordan a punch in the kidney as she spun free of him.

"That wasn't—"

She stopped short. Jordan wore the same expression he'd had while fighting the trolls. His sword was half-out of its scabbard. Althea could discern the hoofbeats from the rain herself. The horses were galloping. She didn't see where that justified Jordan dragging her down the embankment—and she'd tell him so, as soon as the riders went by.

With the embankment in front of them, not even Drum could see what was coming much before it thundered past: two horses, one rider. Coal black coursers spewing clods from the road and sweat from their flanks as they ran. A rider in blued armor, with his visor down and a court-herald's pennant braced against his leg like a lance, headed south on the Old Paladin's Road. It was unlikely that he had seen them.

Jordan scrambled to the road as soon as it was clear. He seized a stone and hurled it after the rider. "You're killing them!" he shouted, snatching up another stone. "They're flesh and blood just like you!"

The rider was already out of sight. Jordan let the stone slip through his fingers. Sometimes the court-heralds came to Hawksnest, their second horse foundering beneath them as they entered the stable garth, their first left for dead somewhere behind them. By right of that red-and-black pennant, a court-herald could claim two horses from any lord's stable for the next leg of his journey. Not Valorians—Fugatore was safe—but any other horse. Sometimes they tossed a copy of their precious message at Lord Erwald's feet. Once they took a rouncy mare with a soft mouth and a gentle disposition. By the time Jordan got her back her mouth was scarred, her ribs were broken, and her legs were ruined. He never rode her again.

Jordan swore no message could be so important that sound horses were run to death to insure its delivery. On a grander scale, he knew he was wrong. Some messages were worth the lives of any number of horses, and their riders. He knew, as well, that good news never traveled so fast.

"Do you think he'll stop at Hawksnest?" Drum asked, leading Fugatore up the embankment to the road.

"Don't think so." Jordan took the reins and held the colt's head close against his chest. He scratched all those itchy places a horse could never reach. "He's still got a horse behind him. He won't stop at Hawksnest unless there's a copy for my lord father—and if Ironhawk's on the roster, Alaine would have been, too."

"Lord Erwald's still got guests from Conclave."

Jordan was about to counter that messengers for the Conclave would use the moon gate, as DuPre and the magician Meraise had done. Then he thought about the message those two carried and said nothing. Lord Blackthorn might not have any court-heralds left who were also magicians of sufficient rank to compel the moon gates. He might have guards at the gates to catch any magician who tried to use them.

Another reason to go back to Hawksnest? Yes. A sufficient reason? Not by itself, but taken with all the others— finally, yes. He faced his companions.

"We're going home."

"No." Althea's voice was strange. Her eyes focused on something Jordan could not see. "No—it's too late."

"Althea—" Jordan started toward her, only to find Drum's huge hand pressed against his chest.

"Althea . . . my lady?" Drum reached out to her.

She trembled and was herself again, or nearly herself. "Didn't you feel it?" she asked. "It was like the air grew heavy and cold behind him. It is the message he carries."

"*Al-the-a.*" Jordan sidestepped Drum's hand. "You said you'd follow where I led."

"The talisman—let me see the globe. Get it . . . please."

Jordan untied her basket from Fugatore's back because it was so unlike Althea to behave this way and because once she planted the seed in his mind, he thought he must have felt something cold and heavy in the rider's wake. Why else had he thrown a stone at a court-herald? Interfering with such a man in the course of his duties was one of Britannia's few capital offenses.

He found the pouch by the shape of the objects it held.

"It *has* gotten darker," Althea said with some satisfaction. "And it aligns with the herald."

The talisman rested on her hand, half-in, half-out of the pouch. She was standing under a tree on a rainy day. "Of course it looks darker," Jordan said as he took the sphere from her. He moved too quickly for Althea to have a chance of stopping him. He held it up against the brightest sector of the sky. The darkning was there, a streak of soot in the honey-colored oil. It didn't point anywhere, but, to Jordan's consternation, the homunculus righted itself. The sun wasn't shining; the rain cast no shadows, but Jordan knew in his heart that the stubby arm pointed north-northeast. He returned the globe to Althea.

"You saw?"

Jordan yanked his fingers through his tangled hair. "What difference does it make? You swear by the honor of your ancestors"—he knew it was a bad choice of oath as soon as he said it—"that you'll do what I tell you to do from now on?"

Althea let the globe fall to the bottom of the pouch. She clasped her hands together and held them out for Jordan to hold in formal oath-sealing. "I swear it, lord."

She wasn't lying, but Jordan suspected a sworn oath didn't mean as much to her as it would to him. Still, that wasn't the reason he didn't take Althea's hands between his: She was still holding the pouch and he wanted no part of any oath that might—however irrationally or arcanely—touch either the darkning or Balthan Wanderson.

"I swear it, lord." Althea repeated, shaking her hands and the pouch suspended from them at him.

And rather than explain why he wouldn't take her oath, Jordan wrapped his hands over hers. "So it is sworn," he said quickly. Then, taking advantage of her position, he lifted Althea up and deposited her on Fugatore's back.

"Jordie! Get me down. He doesn't like me! He'll throw me—you said so yourself!"

Jordan's smile was broad and his voice was soft as velvet. "You said you'd do what I told you to do. I'm telling you to hold onto the saddle-horn and keep quiet. Fugatore won't throw you; I won't let him. I told you that before, and you wouldn't listen. I'm telling you again and you will. We're going to Paws. We're going to get you a decent pair of boots." He noticed Althea's bare legs dangling between the hem of her cloak and the stirrups. "And we're going to get you a pair of leggings. Make sure you've got smooth cloth between you and the saddle."

Althea hurriedly tucked her skirt around her legs then grabbed the saddle-horn as Fugatore started walking. Neither she nor Jordan thought to ask Drum for his advice or opinion, which was as the farrier preferred it. He adjusted the straps of his basket and the cowl of his cloak, then fell in quietly some five paces behind Fugatore.

Seven

*T*he travellers were beyond discomfort when the sun would have been highest in the sky—had they been able to see it. Such warmth as the hidden star could provide turned the rain into a fine mist that penetrated the oiled wool of their cloaks. As the day waned, the temperature fell and the rain returned. When they reached a crossroad signpost the sky was charcoal again, whether with another storm or the coming of night they neither knew nor cared.

"Britain City, straight on," Althea read aloud for Drum's benefit. Letters were not a part of a farrier's education. "Paws, east."

Jordan's thoughts were as numb as his feet. His shoulder, unfortunately, remained exquisitely sensitive. It throbbed and burned whenever Fugatore twisted his neck around to nip at Althea's knees, which he'd done countless times and did again while they stood at the crossroad.

"Give it up, Fuge," he pleaded.

Limpid eyes blinked at him; a wet, velvet nose butted him gently. The colt couldn't give up. It could not understand why Jordan walked and Althea rode. It could not understand that it must behave even though her hands had the strength of straw and her smell was maddening. Fugatore was not willful, not disobedient; he was simply a horse, not a man.

"How long 'til we rest?" Althea asked. She'd done exactly what Jordan told her to do, but her legs were chafed raw. Every step the horse took jarred her spine. Move with him, Jordan said; she was too tired for that and was moved by him instead.

"An hour, if the light holds." He got his legs moving. "If it doesn't storm again."

Fugatore set the pace. They were on the road to Paws. Drumon stood by the signpost. Althea groaned as she reached for Jordan's shoulder.

"We're going the wrong way," she protested.

"We're going to Paws."

Althea released him. A stray tear escaped her eyes as she straightened up. She blotted it with her sleeve, leaving her face damper than it was before.

Paws was not the sort of place a young woman of good birth went if she valued her reputation. It was famous for its fairs, where anything imaginable could be bought or sold, and which ran one week out of every month. It was also famous for its citizens, who smuggled everything conceivable every day of the year, by land and by sea. At that particular moment, however, Althea was willing to surrender her reputation for a bed, a bath, and a bowl of hot, steaming stew. Her reputation was all she had to offer; she had no money of her own. She had her spindle and needle—the implements by which an honest woman might earn her keep—but she was too weary to use them.

Surely Jordan, in whom she'd placed her trust and her brother's rescue, considered that they'd need a silver piece or two to purchase comfort for all of them at a decent inn —if such could be found in Paws. Surely there was nothing to worry about . . .

"I don't care who your lord and mighty father is, I ain't never seen him and I ain't never seen you. You could be Lord Brit himself in disguise and you wouldn't get no food here, nor bed, without giving me three pence first." The innkeeper was a gravel-voiced man with belligerence carved in his coarse face. "Now—have you got the pence, or not? This ain't no tick house."

Jordan was dumfounded. He identified himself as Erwald Lord Ironhawk's son. He'd offered to seal their debts with the Ironhawk crest. He'd showed the innkeeper the signet ring worn on the second finger of his right hand. All to no avail.

"These is hard times. Ain't nothing what it seems anymore. Maybe you be Lord Ironhawk's son. Maybe you gave him the grinning barber on the highway instead. It's no time to be trusting *your* honest virtue. I be doing it all up and square: you pay or you go someplace else—where the keeper's soft in the head."

They'd already been to the only other hostelry in Paws. Rooms were scarce with the monthly fair rising in the fields beyond the village.

"You wouldn't care where or how I got my silver but you balk at an honest signet. I tell you: Lord Erwald Ironhawk will honor his mark even if I wasn't his son—even if I'd slit Jordan Hawson's throat just as you accuse me of doing."

"You admit it, then—"

Jordan pounded the bar with his fist. "Honor and Justice—is this some flea's inquisition!"

A curious pall fell over the public room of the inn. Jordan hadn't mean to shout so loudly, but heated arguments could hardly be uncommon in a place where men kept their swords on the table beside them while they ate.

"Ain't no Inquisition," the innkeeper said with considerable dignity. "Ain't no Inquisition. We're all just common, law-abiding folk doing our best in these here times. We don't ask no questions. No questions at all. I burnt up my ticks because I didn't want to ask no questions nor answer them either. I deal in copper and silver now, 'cause metal ain't sticky and coin don't remember."

Fear entered the room, and danger. Jordan's education honed his perception of these enemies. He'd have to be a fool to ignore what his senses told him. Jordan was not a fool, but neither did he understand why he must now move with sublime caution. In swordwork, standing flatfooted was an often fatal mistake, yet Jordan stood that way because he did not know what else to do.

Drum, the farrier, stepped into the breach. He placed a line of copper coins on the bar, nine in all. "Three pence each for room for the night and a seat at the board."

The innkeeper eyed Jordan, the coins, and Drum in rapid succession. His gaze came to rest finally on the coins. "That's one room for all three of you," he said as he swept the coins into his apron.

Drum felt a tug at his elbow: Althea registering protest over the accommodations. Women of gentle breeding did not often seek lodgings in public hostelries for the simple reasons that if they had a room to themselves their reputations were vulnerable to outsiders, and if they shared a room to protect them from outsiders, they were vulnerable to their own retainers. It was not, however, Althea's reputation that was uppermost in the farrier's mind; he knew she was safe with him, even if he wasn't completely certain of Jordan Hawson.

Foregate raised and guild trained, Drum understood the uses of minted metal. His world was very similar to the innkeeper's. "One room will be fine. We have a horse— we'll tend him ourselves. How much for a stall in your stable, and feed? Mind you, we leave the dung—"

"Pence and a half-pence."

"And a pole by the hearth to hang out our cloaks?"

"Another pence."

"Two for the stall, the feed, and the pole." Drum produced two more coins from his fist, not revealing the number he continued to hold or the size of the purse beneath his cloak.

The innkeeper examined the new coins carefully. They bore a tolerable likeness of Lord British with his scepter and his crown on the face and the irregular star of the Codex Insignia on the obverse. There were an extra two dots on the Codex: the seal of the Trinsic mint where Hawksnest did most of its hard trade. Once again the innkeeper studied his guests.

"You'd bear witness for him?" he asked Drum. "You're in this together? What do you claim to be?"

Drum shoved his forearm between them. "I am a farrier," he said, displaying the faded guildmark of his apprenticeship and the somewhat redder one of his journeyman passage.

"Can you shoe an ox?"

"If you have the forge, the iron—and the ox."

The innkeeper tapped the last two coins with his fingers. "You can have these back after he's shod."

It was as good as bargain as they were likely to get on

a rainy night in an unfamiliar town. Drum nodded his consent and requested that their meal be brought to their room before leading Althea up the stairs. Jordan went off by himself to see to Fugatore's stabling.

The room was tiny. Along the outer wall the eaves were too low for Althea to stand up straight and Drum couldn't take a step from the door without cocking his head. A cold brazier sat in a sand-box in the corner. It would remain cold; Drum had not bargained for charcoal to feed it. The roof was nearly watertight, but the drafts were too strong for the lamp when they hung it from a hook in the beam. Althea fumbled at her waist for a pinch of greenwood ash to rekindle it. She snapped her fingers through the ash to make a spark.

"Did you notice how the keeper reacted when Jordie said *inquisition*?" The young woman sought refuge in conversation—anything to tear her attention away from the room's sole piece of furniture: a four-man bed with a distressingly lumpy mattress. "It was as if Jordie was talking about one thing, and he heard another. And not anything pleasant— I'll wager. Maybe it's me and my worries for Balthan, but I'm starting to feel that there's something very wrong and Balthan's only a small part of it. We've got to keep going, but, well, trolls aren't the only danger I fear we're going to face. That's why I cadged Jordie there at White Flower Valley. You understand, don't you?"

Drum was not a Peer's son who blurted his way through nervousness. Moreover the adoration he felt for Lord Ironhawk's beautiful ward tangled his tongue deep in his throat. The best he could manage was a grunt.

"You think I was wrong? I know you and Jordan Hawson don't get along and he thinks there's no rain so long as he's not wet. But sometimes it doesn't hurt to have a Peer's manners—"

A second grunt as Drum wrenched off his buskins.

Althea's voice became very small. "I—I thought he'd have brought money. I should have known better. Father never handled money either; he made Balthan settle the accounts wherever we went. He said they couldn't do anything to a boy, but, mostly, he just reckoned copper coins beneath him, somehow. And we almost never had any silver . . ."

The farrier stretched every way he could. Joints and tendons popped. He sighed with relief and leaned against the door. "Well, I don't have much silver either. I don't begrudge him bringing us here, but I hadn't figured on inns every other night—"

A knock on the door put an end to Drum's speech. He wasn't going to talk to Erwald Ironhawk's son about money—that was too much like talking to Lord Ironhawk himself. But it was the serving girl with a kettle and bowls, not Jordan. The smell of sausage simmering in cabbage filled the room, replacing any thought or conversation.

They were each eating their second bowl when Jordan came through the door. He sniffed the air appreciatively, but shook his head when Althea offered to fill the third bowl. Leaving his buskins beside Drum's slightly larger ones, he climbed over the bed and crouched beside the brazier. Althea was about to apologize for the lack of charcoal when, without warning, the mail shirt descended noisily over Jordan's head and shoulders to the floor. The young man shuddered and remained as he was, with his knuckles buried in the steel links.

"Are you all right?"

Jordan sank to his knees with a groan. "I feel like a shipwrecked sailor touching his feet to the sand."

He straightened the mail as best he could; then, after rummaging through with the saddle bags, he began kneading a dark greasy substance through the metal. A few moments passed before the drafts remixed the air and the scents of sausage and cabbage were replaced by something less appetizing.

"What is *that*?" Althea wrinkled her nose and tried to wave the odor away with her hand.

"Boar grease," Jordan replied, the tightness in his voice indicating that he was not immune to the smell.

Althea flapped both hands vigorously before giving up. "Rancid grease, you mean! For mercy's sake, *stop!*"

Jordan grabbed the shirt by its leather-bound neck. He examined the bent and broken links at the shoulder. Drum could probably fix them, if the farrier had the right tools available. If Jordan could bring himself to ask . . . and *pay*. The steel slithered back to the floor and he began greasing the front. "Can't *not* do it. If I had a sand bag and sour wine-vinegar I could clean it properly, but I'd still have to grease it up. It'll rust stiff by morning if I don't."

Horror dawned in Althea's face. "That thing's going to be in here with us all night—smelling like *that*? No, Jordie, you can't be serious."

He struck his head standing up. "None of us smells very good. We'll survive." After closing the foul-smelling sack he wiped his hands on his leggings and reached for the bowl Althea no longer offered him.

"How can you bear to eat, smelling like that?"

"I remind myself that I'm hungry." He took the bowl himself, but ate in exile on the opposite side of the room.

The lamp sputtered. Althea tried hearthfire; the oil was gone; sparks were useless. She made a handfire, but the nimbus around her hand was not as bright as a flame and far more tiring than the finger-snap of hearthfire.

"I've got to sleep," she said, surprising neither of the men.

There was one blanket folded on the mattress: a ratty piece of worsted cloth not fit for rags at Hawksnest. Travellers ordinarily brought their own linen to an inn. The inn wasn't Hawksnest and Althea wasn't an ordinary traveller. She shook the cloth out, grimaced at the holes, and curled up beneath it, extinguishing her handfire as she did.

"I'll sleep in front of the door," Drum said.

The ropes holding the bed together creaked as Jordan stretched out on them. "I trust the latch, but have it your way." Althea was already asleep, and Jordan was close enough to dreaming himself that he did not hear Drum's reply—if he replied at all.

Althea suffered a moment of terrified disorientation when she awoke alone in the room she scarcely remembered. She sat bolt-upright and regretted it. Her back had stiffened while she slept without moving on the sagging bed. She couldn't feel her legs at all, and knew that boded ill for standing and walking. The merest thought of riding made her thighs throb. Jordan and Drum would have to understand that there was no way she could sit on Fugatore's back that day.

They probably understood before she did. That explained why they left her in the room to sleep. Althea threw her legs over the edge. She was stiff and sore as she'd never been before, but she wasn't an invalid and she wouldn't have her companions treating her like one.

Her slippers dried exactly as she crumbled them. The first one cracked as she tried to straighten the suede. A gash appeared along the sole. She left the other where it lay. With a wide-tooth bone comb she attacked her weather-beaten hair. Althea's arms weren't as sore as the rest of her, but they were sore enough by the time she'd gotten rid of the tangles. She made a single braid and left it hanging. Then, shamed by her halting walk, she left the room.

The public room of the inn was empty and dark. A slave did drudge work in the kitchen and would not answer when Althea spoke to her. For a moment Althea was anxious, then a deep bellow brought her confidence back. The sun was out and the inn yard was crowded as Drum did battle with an unhappy ox. The beast lay on its side, a snubbing rope drawn through its nose-ring to a post and three of its legs bound together, while the farrier fitted a ruddy iron half-shoe to the hoof of the fourth. Althea noted that the other hooves were unshod; Drum would be busy the rest of the morning. She looked for Jordan, but neither he nor Fugatore was anywhere to be found.

He had not reappeared before noon when Drum untied the snub. With pincers and hammer gripped in hand, the farrier sought out the innkeeper, who wisely returned the two pence. Althea followed Drum to the horse-trough where he immersed his head and shoulders before untying his shirt-sleeves from his waist.

"Where's Jordan?" she asked.

Drum shrugged the shirt smooth around his neck. "He woke me up at dawn when he left. Wouldn't say where he was going, except that he'd repay me for the room before supper. Figure he went out to the fair. Maybe he hopes there'll be a dice pit going. His kind only knows two ways to gather coins: tax it out of the rest of us or game it up."

"Fugatore's gone, too."

Drum cocked his head in surprise. "Is he now? I hadn't thought the man had it in him . . . Well, that's his affair. You need shoes."

The few local shops were shuttered and labelled with arrows directing clients to the fair, north of the village. Althea took one look at the churned mud masquerading as a road and lost heart.

"If I had shoes, they'd be ruined," she complained.

But Drum hoisted her onto his shoulders like a child and carried her to the fair, where a thick layer of sand kept the mud to a minimum. The fairgrounds were as crowded as the Hawksnest foregate and as large as the villa. A few of the merchants maintained permanent stalls, but most hawked their goods from carts, tents, and blankets. When they weren't shouting for customers, they were screaming at each other. Entertainers roamed everywhere, each with a cup and a cry.

Bedazzled, Althea watched a midget in particolored hose stride by on stilts taller than her head. Drum's fingers slipped from her hand. She stopped walking and stared at the melange of color and movement. A wizened gnome of a paste-jeweller, who knew estate-quality cloaks and clients when he saw them, hustled up to lure her with his gauds and baubles.

"An emerald to match your eyes?"

He dandled the deep green bird's-egg before Althea. Sunlight sparkled on its facets and drew her attention away from everything else. It couldn't be real. Lady Barbara had a tiny emerald pendant which was—or so she said—worth more than all her other jewelry combined. Instinctively, Althea knew a decrepit little man with grease-stains on his cap wouldn't be the owner or seller of a stone many times larger than Lady Barbara's.

"Pretty?" the merchant asked.

"Pretty," she agreed and started to follow him when strong, familiar hands closed around her shoulders.

"Buy a gaud for the lady?" the merchant asked, his voice growing faint as he absorbed Drum's size.

Drum had nothing to say to the merchant. He took Althea's wrist firmly and led her away. "Don't let go of me again. Don't go wandering off. We find a cobbler and then we go back to the inn."

"We must look for Jordan," Althea countered, seizing any excuse to remain in this wondrous place.

They found a handful of cobblers before Drum chose the one with whom he would bargain. Althea wanted a lady's kidskin boot, but it was Drum's copper on the barrelhead so she got a scaled-down version of the tongue-and-lace buskins he wore.

"My feet feel like the stomp in a butter-churn."

"Do you still want to look for Jordan, or go back to the inn and see if he returns to us?"

A dark, frightened glance escaped Althea's eyes—until that moment she had not considered that Jordan might have abandoned them. Searching her memories, she could not recall if she'd seen the mail shirt draped over the brazier. "We'll look for him," she said quickly.

They did, well into the afternoon. They wandered quickly through the knot of clothmen selling uncut bolts and used garments, where Althea suggested he might be. And they wandered more slowly outside the livestock pens, especially the roped-off arena where the horses displayed their strength and gaits to prospective buyers. Drum inquired about Valorians and was shown all manner of animals from serviceable rouncies to carthorses with rheumy eyes and sparse coats, but no Valorians.

Finally, when her new, heavy buskins caused her more pain than her bare feet had the day before, Althea conceded defeat.

"He's not here. He's gone. We may as well leave."

Drum was ready to leave the fair, the inn, and the village; Althea begged another night in a bed with a roof over her head—and more time to get used to the buskins. The farrier would bargain with merchants and argue with Jordan, but he wouldn't challenge Althea in anything. He paid for another night's lodging while Althea labored up the stairs.

She winced at each step until she opened the door and smelled Jordan's mail shirt, then her feet no longer hurt.

They waited for him on the bench in the stableyard where Drum shod the ox earlier, but neither of them noticed Jordan when he came through the gate. They were looking for a tall, grey horse and its rider, not a man riding a mule with a pony following along behind him.

"It took longer than I thought it would," Jordan apologized, recognizing his companions before they recognized him.

The answer was obvious, but Althea asked anyway: "What happened—where's Fugatore?"

"I tried to sell him at the fair—but no one could offer half of what he was worth. So I asked who held the land beyond Paws and went there instead."

"You *sold* Fugatore?"

Jordan frowned as he dismounted from the mule. "I loaned Fugatore to Baron Hrothgar of Malamunsted, to stand at stud. He loaned me this mule and pony, and a purse of silver enough to see us to Britain City and then some. If I return everything by the end of next month, Fugatore's mine again, and the baron has mares in Valorian foal as usufruct."

"And if you don't return everything?" Althea asked softly without meeting Jordan's eyes.

"Baron Hrothgar owns a Valorian stallion he's too fat to ride and I have—I have whatever I have left."

Althea embraced him. "I know how much he meant to you. I'm so sorry."

"Don't be." Jordan shrugged free of her as he spoke. "I did it for you. You can ride the pony easily. The children had her as a pet; she'll wriggle under the blankets with you if you're not careful—or so they told me. The mule can carry Drum or me and most of our supplies.

"How much do I owe you: five, seven—" Jordan spotted Althea's boots sitting where she shed them "—one silver piece or two?"

Drum got up and wiped his hands on his thighs. "One silver piece is more than enough. I entertained the other guests while I took care of the innkeeper's ox." Money was a large part of virtue among tradesmen everywhere. The farrier would take what he was owed, and be honest about the rest. "I've paid tonight's lodgings for two—Althea and me. You're still owing your share." He behaved with honor and honesty; he absorbed Jordan's glower without a flinch.

"I said I'd be back."

Jordan placed a coin firmly in the farrier's palm. Althea caught a glimpse of the purse tied to his belt as he fished out another. It was larger than the one Drum wore, and, it seemed, filled with silver rather than copper. With a little caution, a fist of silver could see three people anywhere on the mainland and get them home as well—where Jordan could beg his father for another purse to redeem his pledge. Althea felt guilty and relieved at the same time.

"I'll need a second stall tonight—see to it, will you, Drum? You're so good dealing with thieves and smugglers." Jordan turned sharply on his heel and stalked to the stable leading the animals, leaving Althea and Drum to avoid each other's eyes.

The three ate supper downstairs with the inn's other guests. The conversation of strangers was easier to take than any words they might exchange among themselves. Lord Blackthorn's ultimatum to the Great Council of Magicians was common knowledge, with most of those in the room ready to support the regent whether they understood his motives or not.

"Lord British was different," a somberly dressed merchant summed up at the end of his meal. "But now he's gone. We need a strong man on the throne—a man who knows his own mind and is not afraid to act when he has to. The Peerage gentry, the magicians, and all that ilk—let them complain. It's not them that make Britannia great. They fear for their privilege and complain about the new laws that make all men equal. I say—let them complain. It's high time for a little more equality in Britannia, and Blackthorn's the man who'll get it for us.''

Jordan's appetite vanished. His clothes and his manners marked him as the only member of the loudly berated Peerage in the room. "Lord Blackthorn's feet are heavy," he said, parroting Iolo Arbalest's words from the Hawksnest Conclave. "You'll find them planted on your necks before long." His chair overturned as he stood up. He righted it noisily and left.

Althea came upstairs a little bit later. She could hear the scraping of a whetstone against steel through the door and knocked before she entered. "Jordan? May I join you?"

The scraping stopped. The door swung open.

"Until three nights ago Blackthorn was a name—another Companion, a man I'd try to impress if I got the chance." Jordan resumed his seat on the bedframe and continued honing the edge of his sword. "Merchants were men who bought our surpluses and sold us whatever we couldn't produce ourselves. And tradesmen—"

Althea could tell he was thinking of a particular tradesman. She sat down beside him wrapping her feet in the hem of her skirt and her arms around her knees.

"Now I don't know what to think," Jordan said after a long hesitation. "It's like everything's being stood on its head, and me along with it."

"I've felt that when I touched Balthan's globe and when the court-herald passed us on the road," she whispered.

"The shadow in the globe is *real* and he's trapped in the midst of it."

Jordan turned the sword and began working on the other side. "Then we don't have a wisp's chance in sunlight of rescuing your brother."

The blade was several hours past sharp when Drum burst through the door. He was breathing heavily and shut the door with his body as if someone had chased him up the stairs.

"We've got to leave."

"What now?" Jordan asked without looking up.

"I didn't want to come upstairs after everything that had happened. I had to think about what you said, and what the others were saying after you left. I went out for a walk— I walked clear around the village. Nothing helped so I was coming back to confront you—"

The whetstone paused midstroke; Jordan Hawson, Erwald Ironhawk's heir, looked up. His expression as sharp as his steel. But Drum went on without noticing.

"I took a shortcut through the stableyard. That one merchant—the one all dressed in black—he was there too, and talking to someone. I couldn't tell you why, but my heart near stopped beating with fear and I couldn't take another step. I was just standing there when they saw me. They didn't say anything I could hear, then there was a flash—like your handfire, Althea, but so bright it blinded me. I thought I was going to die—"

"But you didn't," Jordan interjected.

"When my eyes cleared they were gone, and the fear with them."

"One of them was a magician," Althea asserted, though she knew of no light spell that could cause the effects Drum described. "A powerful and independent one."

The farrier nodded. "I thought so too—but why would *that* merchant be talking secretlike to a magician? And it came to me that I didn't want to stay around to find out."

Jordan slammed the sword into its scabbard. "For once, Drumon, I'm inclined to agree with you."

Eight

The three left Paws with all the stealth and subtlety they could manage between them. Jordan's trek to Malamunsted provided him with enough knowledge to avoid the road that had brought them to the fair-village and lead them over fields and scrubland until they rejoined the Old Paladin's Road a half-day's journey north of the crossroad. There were no signs of pursuit. Those travellers they encountered seemed innocent enough. Innocent, at least, of interest in other wayfarers.

Jordan shook his head in puzzlement as another merchant wagon rolled past toward Trinsic with its doors bracketed and its curtains drawn. "Not even a fare thee well," he grumbled as he urged the mule up the steep embankment to the road. "Has all Britannia gone tight-lipped and surly?"

"We're hardly paragons of courtesy," Althea temporized, "keeping to ourselves as we do."

"We gave them the right of way and the driver didn't

even doff his cap or lower his whip—just kept his face pointed straight ahead. I tell you, it's harder *not* to look someone in the eye than to greet him politely.''

Althea smiled and shook her head. Her pony followed the mule without any urging. As Baron Hrothgar promised, the pony was even-tempered and an excellent mount for an inexperienced rider. Indeed, the pony was oblivious to her rider and everything else except the progress of the mule in front of her. Althea might sway from side to side in futile pursuit of comfort; her skirt or cloak might catch the breeze and flap against the animal's hindquarters; her hands might move as much as a bee in a field of clover—nothing disturbed the pony. The beast had a mouth that was equal parts iron and rubber and a sloppy walk that was the antithesis of Fugatore's smooth gait.

Privately, Althea thought she understood the merchants' sullen expressions; travelling was not the adventure she imagined it to be and she knew why those who could avoid it usually did. The sharp spasms of her first days in the saddle had passed; now three days' journey beyond Paws, she ached all over and no one place in particular. She dreamed of sleeping in her own bed and eating meat that was neither half-raw nor cooked beyond recognition. Bathing was unthinkable. Althea had washed her shift and hose the first night after their flight from Paws at the campsite Jordan found beside a deep, swift stream. But wriggling into the still-damp linen the next morning was an experience the young woman did not care to repeat.

Drum took the journey in stride. Like Althea's pony, the farrier seemed unaffected by the changes around him. His beard was already full. His leather garments were sweat-stained and singed from the forge fire before they left Hawksnest. One night—or six nights—of wearing them while he slept did not change their appearance. Drum voiced a rare dissent when Jordan offered to walk while Drum rode the mule. The farrier neither wanted or needed to sit on any beast's back. And since Drum appeared capable of walking faster and further than Althea's pony, Jordan conceded the matter without argument.

Only Jordan thrived on their emerging routine. No stream was too shallow or cold for his morning bath. He fell asleep the moment he closed his eyes after his watch and had the temerity to spring to his feet in the morning. After a charcoal-maker demanded five pence for a scrawny rabbit to put in their evening stewpot, Jordan fashioned a crude spear from his boot-knife and a stick, then terrorized the underbrush for game.

"There's nothing so cheap as a Peer with his pence," Drum muttered when Jordan called a midafternoon rest and disappeared on the trail of a wood-pig. "Like as not, we're here for the night. Let one of us call a halt and he's full or reasons to get going again, but let him see tracks or fewmets and here we sit 'til the Ironhawk hunter returns."

"Maybe he'll get lucky. He said the fewmets were fresh. If he does bring down a wood-pig we'll have enough meat for two or three days," Althea said as she stretched her arms and legs.

"And how will we cook that much meat, Althea? Will he ask me, all polite and courteous, to forge him a rack and spit?"

Althea walked to the edge of the clearing without answering. Jordan and Drum had been scrupulously polite to each other since leaving Paws. Althea wished they'd both be a bit more polite with her.

She carried the pouch containing Balthan's homunculus globe, but did not dare open it. Sometimes it seemed that the only thing her companions had in common was an aversion to magic in general and her brother's magic in particular. As a result, Althea did not let them know that she examined the globe by handfire each night during her watch. She'd rubbed it with the bitter oil only once since leaving Hawksnest: The oil was an integral part of the Kal Wis Por Mani spell; when it was gone, darkning or no, the homunculus would no longer respond. She could not waste precious drops each time she felt anxious.

The previous night Althea had been more than anxious. She had been dreaming about Balthan when Drum woke her for the watch: He lay like a corpse on a bier with darkning shadows flickering around him. The sight of Drum silhouetted in firelight had expelled the other details of the dream from Althea's mind, but left the dread behind. She waited until the farrier's snores were even, then she removed the globe and the tiny vial of oil from the pouch. Her hands trembled when she opened the vial. It was easy to shake a few drops onto the globe, but difficult to reinsert the stopper. She closed her eyes and exhaled deeply, starving her lungs in a failing effort to calm herself. Her fingers jittered with a mind of their own when she rubbed the oil over the globe. She recited the spell-words in a breathless whisper:

"*Kal Wis . . . Por Mani. Kal Wis . . . Por Mani.*"

Althea lifted the homunculus globe into the firelight. The slick glass was too much for her trembling fingertips. It hit the ground with a soft thud and rolled into the ashes.

The knuckles of Althea's right hand showed four red gashes where she'd bitten herself to keep from screaming. Her eyes saw that the globe was undamaged, but the heart-stopping panic, once begun, must run its course. The power of the spell dwindled before she laid the talisman securely in folds of her skirt. Bits of charcoal ash and dirt obscured the iridescent movement within the globe. The homunculus still pointed north-northeast as it had before, but it was cramped into the lower hemisphere. Its stubby feet appeared to touch the inner surface of the glass. Its head was no more than a hair's breadth from the darkning which seemed, itself, to have split in thirds like the grasping talons of an evil bird.

An hour, maybe longer, passed before Althea could trust herself to wipe the glass with her cloak. The spell was completely exhausted by then. The homunculus pointed no-where and everywhere as she cleaned the sphere. She was bone-cold through the rest of her watch and the cold had lingered within her throughout the day.

With the afternoon sun falling warmly on her face, Althea desperately wanted to examine the talisman again. She hoped against hope that the darkning talons were a trick of the fire-light or dirt, that Balthan's homunculus floated free. She fondled the smooth object within the pouch but did not with-draw it. There was too much to lose, too little to gain, she told herself grimly. Her evening-star wishes should not be squandered on the artificial homunculus but on her real brother, wherever he might be. Althea vowed she would do whatever she could—whatever was necessary—to reach him in time, and returned the pouch to the saddlebag, unopened.

Thereafter Althea kept the peace between Drum and Jor-dan, and kept them moving north-northeast toward Britain City. They were ten days out of Hawksnest, some two days short of Britain City at their current pace, when Jordan spotted smoke rising beyond the next bend in the road and reined the mule to a stop. Both Drum and Althea recognized the expression on his face when he beckoned them forward.

"Trouble," he confirmed their suspicions in a whisper, cocking his head toward the smoke. "Take the animals and lie low off the road here. I'll scout ahead." He dismounted and gave the mule's reins to Drum.

The farrier squinted at the dark grey plume that thickened while he watched. "What do you think it is? A cookfire that's gotten out of hand? A brushfire?"

Jordan shrugged. "Either or both, but I'm not taking any chances."

"I'll come with you."

"No—stay with Althea. I won't be long."

He walked along the road about a furlong before disappearing down the embankment. By then Drum and Althea were in the woods off the opposite side of the road. Jordan was as good as his word, returning in less than a quarter-hour. It seemed much longer to Drum and Althea, who broke cover to greet him as he ran back along the road. There were still furrows of concern on Jordan's face, but he made no particular effort to be quiet coming down the embankment.

"What was it? Nothing serious, I hope?" Althea asked.

"Brigands and gypsies. I didn't venture close enough to see everything. I'd guess the gypsies had problems with their wagon and stopped to fix it. The wagon was on its side, I think, before they were attacked. Their horse was loose and now they're trapped."

"Gypsies?" Drum asked. There were tinkers as well as farriers in the smithguild, but no gypsies. The itinerant folk did their metal-mending without a guildmark. Some of them were as good as any guildmaster, but most were not, and a journeyman like Drum was sworn to destroy their tools when he had the chance.

Althea looked from Jordan to Drum and back again. "What do we do?" she asked, not certain how she, herself, would answer if the question were put to her.

"The wolfsheads have them at their mercy. The gypsies are strong and tough, but no match for armed brigands. They've got one bound already on a wagon wheel; they mean to burn his secrets out, I wager. The women—" he grimaced. "I could hear screams behind the wagon. There were children, too; I couldn't count how many."

"How many bandits?" Drum asked.

"Five that I could see. At least one behind the wagon, maybe more. I didn't see a guard; I doubt they've set one. They know their trade: good weapons, good armor. If I had a bow and could take a few out before they spotted me—" Jordan shook his head. He didn't have a bow.

"What do we do?" Althea repeated.

"Well, they'll see us if we ride by on the road. We can stay put here and hope they're in a hurry . . . and hope they're headed south. They probably are, else they would have found us first, but maybe their lair is on this stretch of the road. We can creep along in the woods, behind the embankment until we get past them, but then we'll have to watch our backs like eagles until we reach Britain City day after tomorrow."

"I take it you don't think it's safe to leave well enough alone," Drum said drily. "You'd risk your life, and ours, for a passel of gypsies."

Jordan's back straightened. He stood as tall as the farrier, though he was considerably slighter of build. "I hold no more love of gypsies than you do," he snapped. "They're not welcome at Hawksnest while my father holds it, and they won't be when I do. But, by the Eight, the Three and the One, my fingers itch. The brigands have boiled the blazons off their armor, but not completely enough for me: That band made a cohort pact with a Peer for his Virtue Quest. The Avatar knows what's happened to their Peer. Like as not they killed him first."

"Like as not, he's their leader," Drum corrected softly.

There was murder in Jordan's eyes when he looked at, and past, the farrier. No man or woman had ever duplicated the Avatar's completed Quest, which meant that they all failed somewhere along the way. Most Peers understood the paradox of seeking perfection without the chance of attaining it, but there were always a few who did not. Of those, most were like Simon the Wanderer: shattered men who were no danger to the rest of Britannia. But some embraced their failure as a dark virtue and embarked on a wolfshead life of anarchy and destruction.

"All the more reason to give them a sword's justice."

Drum shook his head. "You're truly thinking of making a fool's quest of this. It's one against five or more—you said so yourself. What do you hope to prove?"

Jordan had no answer.

"Isn't there some other way we could help those poor people?" Althea asked, unwilling to let Jordan sacrifice himself on what Drum rightly called a fool's quest. "What if we wait until nightfall?"

"We could wait. They'll have finished with the women by then, and whatever wine they found. We might be able to slit the bandits' throats while they sleep, but I doubt it would help those 'poor people.' "

Althea shrank from the look Jordan gave her. "We can't help you," she said weakly. "It's five against one. It's you or the gypsies. My brother or the gypsies. I—I guess there's nothing, really, that we *can* do for them."

The ugliness faded from Jordan's face. He seemed more himself when he spoke again. "The odds are bad, but not impossible. That kind doesn't like a fair fight any more than an even fight. The sight of Drum here with his axe might be enough to send them running over the horizon. And if you came around through the smoke to free that gypsy man they've got on the wheel—if he's still alive."

"It's still a fool's quest," Drum muttered as he loosened

the straps holding the basket against his back. "Like as not, the gypsies'll show their thanks by robbing us blind."

"There's no pleasing you, is there, Drumon the Farrier?" Jordan cast the parting shot of the discussion as he went to retrieve the mule and pony from the break where they'd been hidden. "Just hold your axe, look mean, stay out of my way, and everything will turn out all right."

Jordan led the animals away when they were close enough to hear the shouts and screams of conflict. He tucked the empty sword-scabbard beneath the mule's blanket and re-moved leather and mail coifs from his saddle bags before hobbling the pony; the mule could be trusted to stay put. His cheeks were flushed with excitement when he returned and revealed his tactical plan to his small, woefully inex-perienced cohort.

Althea tucked her long skirt through her belt. She ex-changed her delicate ladies' knife for Jordan's razor-sharp boot-knife. She bit her lips to keep them from betraying her fear, and could only nod when Jordan asked if she was ready to make her way around through the smoke to the other side of the gypsy camp where the one man was bound on the wheel.

When Althea was gone, Jordan confined his hair within the smaller leather coif before donning the protective mail which he secured beneath his chin and laced through grom-mets around the neck of his mail shirt. Drum watched with faint amusement; the farrier's preparations were complete the moment he picked up the axe.

"If anything happens to her because of this, you'd better hope you're dead first."

Jordan nodded and then scurried to the verge of the gypsy camp to await Althea's signal. He'd told her to flash the knife blade in the sun. He'd neglected to remind her to stay crouched to the ground as she did; it hadn't occurred to him that anyone would stand up under the circumstances. The sight of Althea's red-gold hair rising in the opposite verge was signal enough. Jordan shouted his family's war cry and bounded into the camp with his sword sweeping before him like a scythe.

No one—not even the gypsies—noticed Althea.

The war cry gave Jordan a one-moment advantage during which he hacked through the shoulder of one bandit and plunged his sword deep into the belly of another. There were men whose speed was great enough to eliminate three opponents before their war cry faded, but two was nothing an inexperienced warrior need be ashamed of. Jordan heard steel sliding free around him. He leapt over the corpse of the gut-struck outlaw and, with both hands on the hilt, struck his guard stance.

Time flowed like syrup the night the trolls attacked; it sizzled like lightning once the wolfshead cohort recovered from their initial surprise. Jordan could not pick his targets nor place his sword strokes with any delicacy; he could not think at all—but that was precisely the way Erwald Iron-hawk trained his sons. Thought was just another enemy in a free-brawling melee. Instinct and reflex were allies. In the Hawksnest arena each day's practice ended with blindfold drills.

Jordan was good, there was no doubt of that; Drum nearly lost an arm while momentarily awed by his companion's deadly skill. But the brigands were good, too. As Jordan predicted, Drum's size and obvious strength made the outlaws cautious and gave the farrier the fraction of a second he needed to use his axe as a quarter-staff, fending off a murderous cut. And the gypsy Althea freed needed no urging to join the battle. Huddled by the wheel, with her knuckles pressed against her lips, Althea saw that the sides were evenly matched. The outcome rested on a single contest: Jordan and the raven-haired wolfshead chieftain.

The heir of Hawksnest swallowed hard and adjusted his grip on the bastard-sword. The headlong rush of time slowed. Jordan felt the acid burning in his arms and shoulders, and in his right leg. He could not feel his left leg; it supported him, it moved as he willed it to move, but it did not belong to him. As time jelled, Jordan looked down. There was a great tear in his breeches. Pulpy blood congealed in the cloth. He saw the mottled red and purple of his sinews. Jordan saw, but did not feel: The wound belonged to his leg and his leg did not belong to him. He blinked and forgot what he had seen.

The brigand chief held a convex shield with a smooth iron boss in his right hand and a sword that was some two handspans shorter than Jordan's in his left. He kept his body aligned behind the shield. Jordan could see his hazel eyes peering over the nailed rim, but nothing more of his face. The brigand held his sword above and a bit behind his head, inviting Jordan to attack but not attacking himself.

Jordan shifted to a one-handed grip on the bastard-sword and settled into a moderate crouch, proving to himself, and the brigand, that the wound on his thigh was ugly but not yet serious.

"Come on, boy—what are you waiting for?"

Jordan showed his teeth when he smiled and refused to be baited into an attack. Lord Erwald disdained shields, even a strengthened bashing shield such as the brigand carried. *What are you there for?* Ironhawk would say whenever Jordan asked to be taught shieldwork, *fighting or sitting? A shield makes a man sloppy and impatient. You find yourself facing a shield, son, make him waddle to you.*

Lord Ironhawk's advice where weapons were involved was usually sound. Jordan held himself at the limit of the brigand's sword reach, which was well within the reach of his own sword, and refused to attack. The brigand feinted a second time with his shield; Jordan neither retreated nor flinched.

"You a coward, boy?" the brigand taunted.

The tip of Jordan's bastard-sword quivered slightly, drawing the brigand's attention, but not his attack. Jordan's bluffs were not as well-honed as his other fighting skills.

A moment had passed. Drum and the gypsies were losing ground to the remaining brigands. Jordan's sides and back had begun to feel naked. Shield or no shield, he had to attack. Most men filled their lungs before their war cry, but not a man trained at Hawksnest. Jordan's second shout was not as long or loud as his first, but it was just as unexpected. The brigand blinked and Jordan lunged, his left side leading, against the iron shield boss. He batted the brigand's sword aside with his own, then tried to reverse it for a killing thrust. It was not the ideal use of the bastard-sword, whose total length was necessarily greater than the fighter's arm. Jordan did not feel the tip meet resistance as it should, yet the brigand toppled backward, taking Jordan with him.

Jordan succumbed to panic. He knew his awkward stab couldn't have pierced the brigand's mail and he knew even better that there was no worse place to be in a fight than belly-down. The second-worst place was belly-up with your enemy on top of you. By rights the brigand, who was in that position, should have been as desperate as Jordan to get back on his feet. But the brigand wasn't struggling at all. Jordan watched with disbelief as dark blood spurted through his enemy's lips.

It made no sense and fed Jordan's panic. Luck abandoned him; his mail shirt was caught on the decorative nails of the shield. Rocking frantically to free himself, Jordan broke the cardinal rule of combat: He let go of his weapon to use both fists for leverage. His mind's eye showed a dagger aimed between his ribs. Jordan's lungs went rigid with anticipation, then, finally the shirt and the shield separated and he rolled onto his back, groping with instantly redirected panic for the sword hilt.

There was nothing between Jordan and the distant sun except a few streaky clouds. No dagger, no outlaw, but Jordan remained in the grip of panic until he found his sword and raised himself onto one knee.

The brigands were scrambling up the road embankment, the gypsies and Drum in pursuit. Althea was coming toward him. She looked frightened, and then feeling returned to Jordan's left leg, expelling all else from his thoughts. Color drained from the outer world, the inner one seethed with angry reds. Everything lurched and began to spin crazily.

"I will not faint," Jordan commanded himself weakly.

The sword slipped through his fingers; he did not hear it strike the ground. He tried to balance himself with his arms; his head sank forward until his cheekbone rested on his right knee. The spinning stopped for a moment, then Jordan could not feel his hands and was powerless to keep himself from flopping over like a thunderstruck cow.

"It's only a flesh wound. Nothing . . ."

Jordan didn't shame himself. Althea knelt beside him before his strength gave out completely. Unmindful of the brigand's blood clinging to Jordan's coif and mail shirt, Althea embraced him and held him upright until he purged himself of shock and panic. Jordan took two deep, shuddering breaths. He could feel his hands, one in the dirt, the other crushed in the folds of Althea's skirt. He could feel the wound in his leg for what it was: a nasty graze that peeled back his flesh without severing any ligaments. It would hurt like living fire and leave an impressive scar, but it would heal so long as he kept it clean. He could not remember, and would never remember, how he'd gotten it.

Jordan was more comfortable with his wound than he was with the location of his right hand.

"I'm all right now," he insisted, disentangling himself as quickly as he could. His sword made a tolerable crutch to get him back on his feet. "It's just a graze. It looks worse than it feels."

The last was an outright lie. Jordan very nearly collapsed again when he put his full weight on the injured leg. He was clinging to the sword when Drum returned with the gypsy men, without any outlaw prisoners.

"That looks bad," the farrier said.

"It's not as bad as it looks," Jordan replied, tapping his last strength to stand without aid.

Drum shook his head. He saw a fair assortment of injuries at the forge. "It'll need burning to crust it over. Can you do it?"

At that moment Jordan recognized that there was no way he was going to be able to hold red-hot metal against the injury for the requisite ten-count—especially as the graze was wider than his palm and therefore much wider than any knife blade or sword. He'd have to sear it at least twice before the work was done. "Maybe later. A few hours won't harm me."

The farrier had something else he needed, but did not particularly want, to say. He scuffed his toe in the dirt and spoke to the furrow. "You're a master with the sword, Jordan Hawson. You were outnumbered and surrounded when you charged into the middle of them. I thought you were a fool but five men tried their best to kill you, and only one could touch you. I never thought there was art to killing. I thought it was just hack and hack until only one man stood. You showed me otherwise.''

Jordan smiled uncomfortably—he was abandoning the idea that there was an art to killing just as Drum seemed to be embracing it. "What about the rest—I saw you chasing them.''

"They got to their horses," Drum answered apologetically. "We couldn't catch them. They went north on the road. I guess we better be careful, right?''

Jordan shook his head. "They'll lie low for a while. We got their leader.'' He looked down. The brigand was stone dead, but Jordan didn't believe he'd killed him. "Drum—give me a hand here, will you?''

The farrier stood beside him. "What? Do you recognize him from the Conclaves?''

Jordan sighed. It was foolish to expect an isolated compliment to signal a change in the big man's attitude. "No—I've never seen him before. Just kick him over for me. I'd do it myself but I don't kick too well at the moment.''

Drum used his hands rather than his boots to turn the brigand over. He sprang away as if he'd released a snake the moment the corpse's back was in the sun. Jordan sucked his teeth and swore. He'd been right: He hadn't killed the man.

The broken, crushed fletching of a timely arrow remained on the ground where the brigand fell.

Nine

eers of Britannia hunted with bows and arrows; they did not fight with them. Insofar as Erwald Lord Ironhawk understood the Avatar's virtues of valor and Honor, neither could exist in the heart of a warrior who killed from a distance or, even worse, from behind. Jordan, Ironhawk's son, would have used the bow against the brigands strictly to even the odds in the subsequent, honorable swordfight. On the other hand, the Peers of Britannia spent much more time hunting than they did fighting. Jordan examined the crushed fletching with a knowledgeable eye.

Whoever made the arrow that killed the brigand leader, assuming that the fletcher was also the archer, made arrows that were both beautiful and accurate. The vanes had been carefully cut. Three of them were edged with a red dye; the fourth with blue which, Jordan discovered, left a slightly different texture on the feathers. It was a novel idea that he'd share with his father: If the blue vanes were placed consistently around the shaft, the archer, reaching into the quiver, would know the alignment of the arrowhead the moment he selected his arrow.

"Must've been one of the gypsies. One who ran when he saw they were outnumbered," Drum said, staring at the broken arrow without seeing half of what Jordan saw.

Jordan forced himself to consider the possibility; he was prejudiced against gypsies and readily convinced himself that they preferred the bow to a more virtuous weapon. But the puzzle pieces would not join. The arrow was made by someone who lived by the bow, by someone with tremendous patience and confidence; these were not the traits anyone associated with gypsy wanderers.

"I'd like to meet the gypsy who could make this shot. Get our mule and pony; we're not going to linger anywhere near that archer if I can help it."

Drum didn't question Jordan's reasoning when he liked the conclusion. Dust rose from the dirt beneath his heels as he headed off. Limping badly and grinding the sword into the ground with every step, Jordan showed the fletching to each of the gypsies, women as well as men. They swore there were no archers among them. Two of the women made the finger-sign against misfortune when Jordan explained where he'd gotten it.

"Put it back with him," a long-faced woman with charcoal-rimmed eyes and reddened lips commanded. "It is his death. He will come looking for it."

Gypsies believed things about death and fate any other Britannian would dismiss as superstition, and they believed them with fervor. The gypsy woman snatched the broken shaft from Jordan's hand. She hurled it across the camp at the corpses, then she spat in their direction.

"Dig a hole and put them all in it." Her sweeping gesture included the brigand leader and the two men Jordan had killed in the first moments of the fight. "Fire is too good for them!"

Jordan staggered back from her. It was said—though like so much else with the gypsies, never proven—that they burned their dead on open pyres and carried the ashes of their revered relatives in secret compartments within their wagons. The rest of Britannia buried their dead in unadorned graves. Jordan helped to dig the graves of his grandparents: that was an honor. But digging the grave of men he'd killed or who meant to kill him: that was something else. He might have been tempted to leave them as they'd left the trolls.

The young man's attention was diverted from distasteful decisions when an old woman clambered onto the doorframe of the overturned wagon. She was stooped over at the shoulders and waist. Wispy tufts of snow-white hair escaped her bright, patterned kerchief. Wrinkles covered her face so completely that her features nearly disappeared. The gypsy woman who would bury the brigands rather than dignify their deaths with immolation hurried to lift the crone from the doorframe to the ground.

The women jabbered in their own language. Jordan realized that despite her fragile appearance, the crone held the power in this gypsy family. Men, women, and children sorted themselves into fire beaters, wagon fixers, horse groomers, and cooks—except for the long-faced woman who helped the crone hobble closer to Jordan.

"We're in your debt," the old woman said in a strong, clear voice that belied her physical appearance. "We would give you something in return."

The words to say there was nothing in a gypsy wagon that he or his companions would ever want swam in Jordan's throat. He swallowed them whole when he got a good look into the crone's sharp birdlike eyes. "It was all virtue to come to your aid, you owe us nothing," he mumbled instead.

The crone was not deceived by Jordan's hasty dissembling. "Nothing living is *all* virtue."

Her voice seemed to come from another place and time. It weakened Jordan's knees, and firmed his resolve to leave the place as quickly as possible.

"We follow the Avatar's Path—"

"You follow another path," the crone corrected. "You seek a man."

At home, in Hawksnest, Jordan knew that no one could foresee the future or read the thoughts in another mind. Here in the unfamiliar gypsy camp he was less certain. Drawn into the depths of the crone's eyes, Jordan's thoughts swung inexorably to Balthan. It was as if the arrogant young magician were right beside him, and it was only with the greatest difficulty that he wrenched his thoughts back to the dust and smoke of the camp.

"We seek the man who shot the arrow that saved my life. If he is in your family, let me thank him and there will be nothing owing between us."

"What makes you think the archer was a *man*?"

Jordan's knees filled with water. He dug the swordtip into the ground to keep himself upright. Meaningless syllables leaked out of his mouth. The crone cackled.

"When a man's crimes equal the measure of his destiny —it is his time to die. If it needs a sword to bring his death, a sword is provided. If it needs an arrow, the arrow is provided. But if the sword fails, surely the arrow will suffice?" The crone showed her teeth—both of them—when she grinned.

Jordan looked at the ground but the old woman's grotesque smile stayed with him and seemed to hover inches above his toes. He shook his head to rid himself of the image and the logic that preceded it. He looked right and left for a sign of brilliant red-gold hair. Althea would know what to say; she would not be overwhelmed by a frail woman whose hunched shoulders were no higher than the middle of his chest. But every head he could see was covered with a kerchief or dark hair.

"Al-thea . . ." Jordan's voice was as shaky as his knees. It warbled and cracked the way it had when he was thirteen. He turned around completely and tried again. "Al—?"

The figure emerging from the smoke was not Althea. Jordan didn't know who it was. The hood flopped forward, and the cloak revealed nothing. At first, remembering what the crone had said, he was not sure it was a man, but surely no woman had a hand like the one holding the stout long-bow. And surely no woman could shoot such a bow when Jordan could see he would need all his strength to draw it and have none left for a smooth release.

"My l—"

Jordan's voice cracked; this time the failure saved him from embarrassment. The archer revealed himself. His long hair was the color of the smoke behind him. His face was lean, weathered, and, unlike the gypsy crone's, ageless instead of ancient. His eyes were also grey—so light they seemed to shine like silver. His beard was a shade midway between his hair and his eyes, and like the rest of him it was supple and narrow.

"Shamino?" Jordan whispered, then coughed and tried again: "Lord Shamino, Companion of the Avatar and Lord British."

There was a wry smile on the archer's face as he crossed the camp with long easy strides. This was a man who could walk beside a Valorian until the horse was tired. "You were right the first time."

But Jordan Hawson could not bring himself to speak so familiarly to such a man nor to take his outstretched hand in the friendship of equals. Shamino withdrew his hand.

"You needed an inch less sword or an inch more arm— and as it seemed you'd not grow a hair's breadth before the brigand had his sleeve knife between your ribs, I thought it best to intercede. I didn't want you dead before we had a chance to talk."

Jordan gulped air. His knees were solid, but he still felt dizzy. He remembered knocking the brigand's sword aside; he didn't remember him dropping the sword or releasing a spring-loaded weapon into its place. But Shamino didn't lie. Shamino had more secrets than any man. Lord British, himself, said Shamino was a man of unsolved mysteries— but he'd never been caught in a lie. Jordan wiped the clammy sweat from his hand before offering it to the archer.

"I—I owe you my life. I never saw the knife. I knew I was in trouble, but I never saw the sleeve knife. I didn't even guess he wore one."

"It was his day to die, not yours, Jordan Hawson. Be glad of it, don't dwell on it."

Jordan nodded. The ranger's advice was sound, not dissimilar from the advice Jordan gave to Drum after they fought the trolls. It wasn't advice that halted Jordan's downward spiral into melancholy but the echo of his own name.

He knows me. He knows my name. He's been following us— Half-formed questions assumed the pattern of an answer. "My lord father sent you after us . . ."

The air between the two men chilled. Jordan ceased pumping the ranger's hand. Their eyes met; Shamino's held denial and disappointment.

"You know my name. You said you were following us. Why—if not because my lord father sent you?"

Shamino did not speak. He blinked slowly, without

changing his expression. Jordan was the one who looked away.

Yet, what else could it be, Jordan asked himself. Why else would a Companion be there to save his life if his lord father had not begged Britannia's greatest tracker to find him? A contrary thought formed on Jordan's next breath: Find and *follow?*—when find and bring my son back at the end of a dog's tether would be much more like the Erwald Ironhawk that Jordan knew. But if Lord Erwald hadn't set Shamino on his trail, who had?

"I don't understand—and why would you wait until there was a knife pointing between my ribs? Why not announce yourself when we came upon the gypsies ourselves? I would have done everything different if you'd been with us—" A possibility as swift and straight as Shamino's arrows penetrated Jordan's groping thoughts. "You meant to see what I would do. Ordeal and challenge! Before each Virtue's Shrine comes ordeal and challenge! My father sent you to take my measure before he Nominates me and I receive my first mantra—"

Jordan's voice rose. His thoughts were translated into words without hesitation or wisdom. After a moment, Shamino frowned and shook his head.

"This has nothing to do with your father or the shrines of Virtue."

"But why follow us? Why know my name?"

"I know your name because I have heard your companions use it often enough and loudly," Shamino said curtly.

The young man's thigh began to throb. He looked down. The wound bled freely; his leg was stained bright red past his knee. It could no longer be ignored. "I don't know what's wrong with me. I've been cut before, but I don't think I can stand any longer. I think I better sit down while I can."

Jordan tried to walk and found he could not. He glanced at Shamino, a puzzled expression on his face.

"You've lost more blood than you think," the veteran archer explained, tucking his arm beneath Jordan's sagging left elbow. "You're going into shock. Don't fight it so hard; there's no shame to it."

A wave of relief crested over Jordan. He closed his eyes and surrendered. The throbbing pain in his thigh vanished and so did everything else. He was grateful for the moment's respite, but when he opened his eyes he was lying in a nest of blankets and the sun was a great orange ball hovering over the western horizon.

A woman Jordan had never seen before leaned over him. "He's awake!" she shouted.

Before the young man had time to panic, familiar faces appeared: Althea and Drum—both looking worried. Shamino appeared as did the gypsy crone, who seemed neither worried nor surprised. Jordan remembered his injury. There was a cool tingling in his thigh but none of the throbbing he remembered and none of the burning agony he would expect if they'd cauterized it while he was unconscious.

"My leg!" Jordan screamed, sitting up and throwing the blankets desperately aside.

Shamino clapped a restraining hand on Jordan's shoulder. "Easy there, lad. Nothing's wrong. The little grandmother's taken good care of you."

Jordan uncovered the bleached linen bandage. He saw his leg extending beyond it. His toes wiggled when he made them, as did his kneecap. He sank onto his back again and weakly returned the crone's gap-toothed smile.

He looked at Althea. "How long—"

"A good night's sleep and you'll feel like new," Althea assured him before the question was complete.

"—was I out?"

"Most of the afternoon," Drum responded. "You gave us a good scare, I'll hand you that."

Jordan sat up again. He looked beyond the circle of faces. The wildfire was completely out; a cookfire blazed beneath a cast-iron pot. The gypsy wagon sat properly on its garish painted wheels. The mule and pony were tied and eating beside the gypsies' horse. There was no sign of the brigands or their graves. Jordan dismissed his own question out of hand; there were other things of greater concern.

"Why were you following us?" Jordan directed his question to the ranger, but he watched Althea and the crone for their reaction. The gypsy's expression did not change. Althea pressed her lips together; she looked anxious and unhappy, but not surprised. Jordan suppressed a sigh.

"I was looking for Lord British," Shamino began, taking possession of Jordan's undivided attention.

The ranger usually shunned any gathering where the clothing was uncomfortable, the oratory interminable, and the food drowned in thick sauces with fanciful names, but he had come to the Peerage Conclave at Hawksnest. He'd disguised himself as a retainer and mingled with the common men and women who ate with less ceremony in the paddocks. Ordinary folk, Shamino explained, were forthright with their feelings and suspicions.

"You came to my father's villa to spy on his guests?" Jordan asked with a similar forthrightness.

"In a manner of speaking, I did," Lord British's oldest Companion confessed. "You've heard it all by now yourselves. Iolo says you were in the audience when he and DuPre staged their argument—"

" 'Staged their argument' . . . ?"

Shamino nodded. "We've all sensed it: a darkening of virtue. British sensed it first. He traced it to Spiritwood and a newborn sulphurous river—the Maelstrom river whose source he meant to find, and cleanse.'' The ranger paused and shook his head, remembering. "It was not so strong then. None of us guessed; British least of all. Now he is gone, and evil—yes, *evil*—settles on the world like ashes. And I sift the ashes—''

"I told him our quest has nothing to do with his. We're looking for my brother, not Lord British," Althea interjected.

Jordan cocked his headed at Althea, appraising her outburst, wondering if she'd shown Balthan's homunculus to Shamino or she'd meant to keep it hidden. Then Jordan saw the gypsy cook tasting her stew and all other concerns drained from his mind. He was famished. His stomach had contracted to a hard, unhappy knot. Jordan's mouth flooded and he knew the crone had used magic to mend his leg. His fast-healing body was a fire burning fast on tinder. He'd eat like a horse until its normal balance was restored. He'd eat the horse—shoes, saddle, and all—if nothing else was passed his way, and soon.

"Food," he croaked, succumbing to the imperatives magical healing left within him. "Get me food!" He'd thrashed out of the blankets again and was attempting to rise to his feet. "I've got to eat."

The crone fastened her bony fingers on Jordan's shoulder. "Your bowl's coming." She retained resonance with the magic working within Jordan. When she shoved, he toppled backward. "Be patient."

Jordan tried; the effort cost him any semblance of tact. "Have you shown him the talisman?" he demanded, and when Althea's scowl was the only answer he got, Jordan commanded her to bring it out.

Althea masked her rage with silence. She distrusted the old archer from the moment she looked into his silvery eyes. All afternoon she'd stayed clear of Shamino and when that was impossible—because he seemed determined to question her—she'd answered him with carefully chosen words, not caring how poorly the Companion thought of her, so long as he did not guess her secrets. Then Jordan gave them away for nothing. Once the talisman was mentioned, there was no more hiding it. Her onetime friend could not have left her more shamed and defenseless if he'd stripped her naked with his own hands.

"You're wrong," she hissed, then ran to do his bidding.

"The shadow takes the weakest first," Shamino said sadly, "but the innocent are not far behind."

Althea would not give the talisman to the ranger with her own hands. She held the heavy pouch over Jordan's lap and let it fall. It was an accident that it struck the bandages and made him wince: a very satisfying accident. She met Shamino's frown with a smile.

Balancing the oil-filled sphere on his fingertips, the Companion examined it in the sunlight. The homunculus drifted aimlessly below the sooty darkning streaks. "Did you make this?" Althea's reply was inaudible; he asked again.

"My brother, Balthan Wanderson, made it for me last autumn." Althea's voice reflected the anger she could no longer conceal. "It was between us, so I might know how he fared. Balthan is *all* the family I have," she stared at Jordan, lest he misunderstand her meaning. "He was aman-uensis to the great magician, Felespar. When I learned what happened to Felespar, I feared for him. My brother is hot-tempered."

"I can imagine," Shamino said drily, continuing to ex-amine the globe.

"Whatever has happened to my brother it is no more his fault"—Althea paused to moisten her lips—"no more Bal-than's fault than Lord British's disappearance is his."

The look Althea received from Shamino was all she feared it would be.

"I did not say it was," the ranger averred. "Mistakes are made with the best of intentions—no blame or fault attaches to anyone—but mistakes are made, nonetheless."

"But you seek to rescue your friend—just as I seek to rescue my brother."

Shamino returned the globe to its pouch. He held it out for Althea to take. "I seek him, yes; but rescue? Dear Lady Althea—I cannot think of rescuing him until I have found him. I want very much to rescue him, but the shadow corrupts—surely you sense that. What if rescue is possible, but not wise?"

Althea snatched the pouch. "Balthan is my brother and I *will* rescue him if I can." She looped the thongs around her belt and pulled them tight. "Will you stop me?"

Both Drum and Jordan whispered her name reproachfully, but the ranger did not hesitate to respond to Althea's final question.

"My lady, I know all the magicians of the Great Council, and I know Felespar's amanuensis. I will not stop you . . . I offer you my help instead."

Jordan sat straight up, his hunger pangs forgotten. A Companion of Lord British, the best tracker the world had ever known, offering to help them! Balthan was as good as found, and his own future never looked better. Then Althea spoke:

"Our paths go in different directions, my lord. You seek your friend, Lord British. I seek my brother. I do not pretend that Balthan is entirely worthy. His troubles have always been of his own making, and I do not doubt that they are this time as well. Your offer is generous and virtuous, but I cannot accept it. Lord British needs you. I beg you—leave my brother, Balthan, to us."

"Althea!" Jordan rose between them, balancing precariously on his good leg. "Remember the court-herald riding by? Remember what you said—how the ho—"

"I was mistaken," Althea snapped. "You said so yourself. In my wildest dreams I never thought my brother crossed fates with *Lord British*!"

Jordan turned to Shamino. "A court-herald rode by us, hell-bent for Trinsic. I cursed him for galloping his horse to certain death. I don't know what came over me: *I actually threw a stone at a court-herald*! Then Althea said the court-herald cast a shadow—"

"Jordan! No! Don't shame me. I was wrong. I—I was afraid you'd turn back."

In desperation, Jordan looked to Drum for support, but the farrier was staring at the sky, pointedly ignoring everything else. Jordan's shoulders sagged. His healing leg began to throb. "You weren't wrong," he said softly to Althea. "Think of it: A Companion of Lord British is offering to help us find your brother."

Althea looked straight through Jordan. Shamino kept him from falling as he lowered himself to the blankets in defeat.

"The lady knows her own mind," the ranger said as he released Jordan's hand. "Do not argue with her."

Twin weaknesses of hunger and pain addled Jordan's thoughts. "But if we could help you find Lord British. Our paths crossed; you followed us. If there's a chance . . . ?"

The ranger shook his head. "Not for a chance, Jordan Hawson. There is too much at risk for chances. The shadow I follow has a nature of its own. What it cannot corrupt it repels. It grows stronger in the presence of doubt and falsehood, and more difficult to track. I did not reveal myself at first because following you, as you followed a shadow, seemed surer than following the shadow itself. That was

my mistake: There is no easy way with evil that does not
become corrupted by evil.

"I take my leave of you now, before the shadow grows
so dark we all lose our way."

Shamino raised his hood and left the camp.

Ten

Shamino was absorbed by the forest before he had gone ten strides into it. His forestry skills were only slightly less than magical, but Jordan lost interest in Lord British's Companion before he lost sight of him. Shifting breezes had brought him another whiff of the simmering stewpot.

"He was disappointed in us," Drum mused. "He couldn't beg, and we wouldn't offer, so he left."

Groaning for effect, and from the healcraft imperative gnawing in his stomach, Jordan stretched out on his blankets, covering his eyes. Erwald Ironhawk was both rich enough, and prudent enough, to keep a well-supplied apothecary's cabinet. Through his many years of martial education, Jordan sipped the bitter tinctures of healcraft more times than he, or his father, cared to count. He knew all healcraft brought hunger, but the aftermath of the crone's healcraft was worse than anything he'd experienced at Hawksnest. A voracious beast threatened to take control of his body—especially his mouth. Jordan used every trick of discipline and denial he'd learned in the practice arena to beat it back before he could reply to Drum.

"Why didn't *you* say something? I gave you the chance, and you just stood there, dumb as a tree."

"It was not my place to say anything and it was too late by then. Lord Shamino was right. We four couldn't possibly travel together *after* he'd seen Balthan's talisman—and the idea that the four of us should travel together didn't exist before you forced Althea to reveal that she had it. If any of us had suggested it the moment we saw him . . . anytime at all during the afternoon . . ." Drum's voice trailed off. He did not mean to share his conclusion—if he had one— with Jordan.

The ravening beast growled. The young man rolled on his side. The ache in his thigh was nothing compared to the imperative in his gut. He gasped and forced his body to lie flat and be patient. "You're one of us," he said through clenched teeth. "You could have said something. Offer an opinion before the fact, rather than a complaint after it. I wasn't going to argue with you."

"It was not my place," Drum repeated, as if the matter should be as clear to a Peer's son as it was to him.

Jordan groaned again. He sat up in time to see Althea approaching. Her scowl was as dark as any storm cloud, but that mattered less to Jordan and his gut-dwelling beast than the steaming bowl she carried. She thumped it down in Jordan's lap. Hot gravy dribbled onto his bandages. He sopped it up with his sleeve before it stained the linen, then sucked the gravy out the cloth while he waited for the spoon Althea had tucked into her belt.

"The crone says to eat all you need. Lord Shamino provided the meat." She slapped the spoon into the bowl. "We won't eat until you're finished."

A tattered remnant of his intelligence informed Jordan that Althea was upset. But the beast had taken firm control of his actions, and it had no need of intelligence. He crammed his mouth with meat that was too hot to chew and burned like naphtha when he swallowed it whole. Tears streamed from Jordan's eyes, but the beast was momentarily stunned and he could speak in a raspy whisper.

"What about you, Althea—do you think that Shamino was disappointed that we didn't invite him to join us? Or is that what you wanted all along?" Not, perhaps, the gentlest or wisest way to raise a delicate subject, Jordan conceded to himself as he eyed another chunk of meat—but the best he could do under the circumstances.

Althea braced her fists against her hips. "I'm not talking to you."

Jordan turned away from her. He closed his eyes and clapped his empty hand tightly over his mouth. He willed himself not to giggle; he might well have commanded the sun not to rise for all the good it did. Recklessness swelled irresistibly within him. There wasn't a drop of wine or beer in the stew; the beast in his gut was drunk on food and Jordan was along for the ride.

"You're a disgrace!"

Jordan couldn't defend himself. He could barely keep the bowl from turning over in his lap. Althea turned hard on her heel, raising a cloud of dust. Jordan let go of the spoon and his lips. He clutched the rim with both hands as whoops of uncontrollable laughter echoed through the camp. His face was streaked with tears when he looked up at Drum.

"I don't think she wants to travel with us anymore."

"I'll go with Althea. You can rot in the fires of Hythloth for all I care."

Jordan tried to say he wasn't himself, but the thought got tangled in a hiccup that struck his heart like a knife. When the blinding pain subsided, the beast was in control again and the young man's world was no larger than the steaming bowl.

Jordan surrendered to the healcraft imperative. His spoon rose and fell mindlessly, shovelling the contents of two brimming bowls into his mouth before the beast was sated. He was scrubbing the inside of the bowl with his thumb when the imperative consumed itself. He was once again aware of who he was and what he was doing.

Appalled by his gluttony, Jordan thrust the bowl away. His stomach was distended: a lead weight pinning him to the blankets. Jordan hauled himself onto one knee. Shoulders sagging and hands resting limply on the blankets, he waited for the nausea to pass before he staggered into the bushes. He felt weak but almost human when he returned. The gypsy crone stood on the edge of the blankets examining the empty stew bowl by lamplight.

"You did well," she said approvingly. "Come here. Sit down. I want to see the wound now that you've eaten."

Jordan stayed where he was. His body was weak, but his will was his own again. "The wound was nothing. You changed me into a beast. I drove my companions away. I'd drive you away, too, if I had the strength."

The crone grabbed Jordan's wrist and twisted it; he landed hard on the blankets. "But you don't," she reminded him. "Men like those wolfsheads—they whet their blades on dung. The poison was already in your blood when I put the poultice on your leg. You—with your fine sword and mail shirt—have you ever *seen* a man die of blood poisoning?"

Clammy sweat bloomed on Jordan's face and in the palms of his hands. . . . Before his mind's eye Jordan saw a little girl, not a man but the cook's daughter, step on a rusty nail while exploring the forbidden pantry and concealed her injury from everyone until it was too late for anything in the apothecary cabinet. Lamed animals found swift mercy at the edge of sharp knife, but the little girl lay a week in agony before death claimed her.

Jordan straightened his leg without additional urging, and allowed the old woman to examine the wound. It was tender; he yelped when she prodded it with a twig, but the ache and the heat were gone.

"It will scar," she announced, probing a different part of the healing wound. "I'm no Lyceum mage who lets her patients pretend something never happened. But, come tomorrow morning, you'll be strong enough for a day's walking. You'll be in Britain City by nightfall."

"Who knows?" Jordan sighed, wondering what he would have to do to patch things up with Althea and Drum, or if he should.

The crone screwed her head around. She jabbed her twig into the hollow beneath Jordan's chin. "*I* know."

Gypsies claimed a number of arcane skills that could not be defended by natural or magical philosophies. They used cards, crystals, incense, and vials of colored oils to illustrate their self-proclaimed prophecies. There were many, Peers among them, who believed in the gypsies' powers, but not Jordan. He closed his hand over hers and pushed the twig away.

"You healed me, and I'm grateful. I have some silver, if you want more—go down this road past Paws until you come to the marker for Hawksnest estate and tell my father I owe you, but don't play games with me. Anyone could guess that all eight Virtues direct me to travel with Althea and Drum regardless of whether it's what any of us wants.''

The crone straightened her back. The weight of her years lifted from her shoulders. "Do you dare to play a game with *my* cards? Come into my wagon if you think all my knowledge is guesses and spying.''

Echoes of healcraft recklessness lingered in Jordan. He countered the gypsy's smile with a grin of his own. "I dare.''

"Will you invite your friends to play with us?''

Jordan's grin broadened to reveal his even teeth. "Why should I do anything—you already know everything that's going to happen, right?''

"The cards—Jordan Hawson, son of Erwald Ironhawk and Barbara Jormsdattir, heir of Hawksnest—the cards tell me. I listen and they tell me who—*what*—you are.''

"I just told you to go south to Hawksnest where my father would pay my debts—half of Britannia could mark my name from that. Any gossip could, and you have the look of a gossip.''

The crone threw her head back, cackling merrily. "If pride were a virtue, you'd be Avatar on its strength alone!''

A frisson rippled slowly down Jordan's spine, but he already knew he was too proud. This wasn't the first time pride brought him to the brink and left him no choice but to jump. His leg didn't bother him. He reached the wagon door ahead of the crone and bowed courteously as he opened it for her. If he didn't have wisdom to stay out of trouble, he'd at least be stylish on his way to the scaffold.

The air inside the wagon was thick with dust and the cloying scent of countless aromatics. Jordan's first thought was that the old woman was trying to poison him with the vapors—then he remembered that the wagon had been on its side when he first saw it. One whole wall was dark and shiny from the spill.

"It is good that summer is coming and we can sleep outside," the crone agreed when she saw where his eyes had wandered.

"Maybe we could play our game outside—"

"The cards could be removed from the wagon, but not the table."

She pointed at a round table which Jordan had, in the dim light and dust, mistaken for a bed.

"May we remove the cloth?" he asked, smiling once again and reaching for the fringed and patterned material.

The gypsy returned the smile. "You may."

Jordan whisked it off with a flourish, and lost a measure of his confidence when he looked down at the wood. The tabletop was as thick as a man's hand from fingertips to wrist and cut from the cross-section of a single tree. The circles and lines of the Codex Insignia—a visual interpretation of the wisdom underlying the eightfold path to Virtue —had been burned into the wood. Jordan knew, without quite knowing how, that generations had passed since the tree was cut and the pattern etched into the wood. He swallowed hard and bravely traced his finger along Honor's path.

Against all expectation, the groove behind Jordan's finger glowed with a faint silvery light. He sat down heavily on a three-legged stool.

"Not there," the crone objected. "There." She pointed to another stool further around the table. "Leave room for your friends."

Jordan told himself, as he moved from one stool to the other, that the woman was a gypsy—an *old* gypsy who knew all the tricks of her clan's craft. She was a charlatan, not a magician, and there was no guessing what she had learned from Althea and Drum during the long afternoon while he lay unconscious. Even the glowing Insignia could be a trick prepared in advance. If he believed her table glowed through some arcane power, then he might believe the rest of her babbling prophecies. But Jordan's armor of skepticism had been badly dented and he was unconvinced by his own arguments.

The crone placed a small silk-wrapped package in the center of the carved Insignia. With a practiced flourish she undid the tasselled cords, revealing a deck of cards which she began to shuffle.

Jordan's education was the best his father's wealth and prestige could buy. Bruma Hage, a one-eyed woman with a pirate's tattoo on her cheek, spent two winters at Hawksnest teaching Jordan the rules of every game she knew—and, more importantly, the ways in which the rules were broken. Jordan learned about shaved dice and plugged dice. He saw how a deck of cards could be stacked in the shuffle or in the deal. Before she left Bruma swore to Jordan that he'd be safe at any gaming table so long as he remained sober.

The crone's knobby fingers made the cards dance in ways Bruma Hage never showed him. When the gypsy squared the deck and shoved it across the table, the young man's hands remained in his lap.

Obviously, pirates didn't gamble with gypsies.

"What game are we playing?" he asked at last.

"The Avatar's game—cut the cards."

Jordan reached for the deck. "And the stakes?"

"Visions of the past and future."

"Right." He split the cards quickly and left the two piles where the crone would have to stretch to retrieve them. Then he deliberately leaned back on the stool and laced his fingers behind his neck.

She dealt the first card facedown and placed it over the

circle of Spirituality at the center of the Codex Insignia. The next three were for the Principles of Truth, Love, and Courage. Jordan lost his composure and balance. The faceup cards were like none he'd ever seen before. Neither court trumps nor pips, they were crudely painted vignettes. The card closest to Jordan, in the circle of Truth, showed an armored knight confronting a merchant in what appeared to be the merchant's home; a child cowered behind the chimney where neither man could see her.

"What kind of cards are these? What are the values? Which is highest, lowest . . . ?"

The crone snickered. She began laying cards on the six worldly virtues, represented by the angles of the Insignia Honesty, Honor, Valor, Sacrifice, Compassion, and Justice. Then she took the card at the bottom of the deck—the card which been just above Jordan's cut—and held it aside.

"What is it that stands apart from all other virtues, that touches no principle directly, yet encompasses them all—"

"Humility," Jordan interrupted. He knew the Avatar's catechism forward and back—if this were the game the crone had planned for him, he could play with confidence. "What every serf is born with; what every Peer must strive to attain. To hold water without a cup. To see the moons while the sun shines—"

Jordan was himself interrupted as the wagon rocked on its axles and the door opened.

"Jordie! I thought you'd left." Althea halted just inside the door, leaving Drum to stand half-in and half-out of the wagon.

A gusty draft swirled through the wagon. The lamp sputtered and nearly died, but the cards on the table didn't move at all. Jordan didn't notice the lamp or the cards. He watched emotions parading across Althea's face, trying to guess which ones were sincere and which were not.

"Sit down. Join us. We've saved two places, one for each of you."

Althea moved to the stool beside Jordan. "You knew we were coming?"

Jordan rolled his eyes and sighed dramatically. "Don't bother, Althea. I'm not impressed and I'm not fooled."

"About what?" Althea caught her balance a handspan above the stool and sank no further. "What's going on here? Maybe I should leave."

The wagon shook when Drum slammed the door. He couldn't stand up straight and loomed behind Althea like a vengeful guardian. "Do we sit or leave?"

"There are two of you," the old woman purred. "Each of you must decide for yourselves alone."

Satisfaction surged briefly through Jordan's veins, then the gypsy flipped Humility's card over: A young knight confronted a flaming dragon with nothing more than his bare hands. Jordan paid no attention to Althea scooting her stool closer to the table.

"Should we start over?" Jordan asked, hoping the answer was yes.

The crone affected not to hear him. She drummed her fingers on the wood, studying the eleven cards with fierce concentration. She picked up the card of Sacrifice and dragged it along Virtue's straight path to Compassion. Althea swallowed a shriek when the etched channel between the two cards glowed briefly with silvery light. The gypsy made other pairings; she turned the cards of Truth and Courage facedown and put the doomed knight of Humility in Courage's circle. Then she began dealing again.

If there were rules to the gypsy game, Jordan could not

perceive them. The crone dealt, and then she regrouped the cards, sometimes retrieving cards previously covered. The only card she never touched was the facedown card of Spirituality at the center of the Insignia. At first the channel between two cards glowed when they were paired, but in later rounds the glimmer might appear in another part of the etching or it might not appear at all.

Finally all the cards were facedown and there was only one card left in the crone's hand.

"Have you been paying attention? Do you know where your cards lie?" she asked with a lopsided smile.

Jordan fidgeted on his stool. "Would it matter?"

"No," she conceded, placing the card not in the center of the Insignia, where Jordan suspected it would go, but outside the circle where Humility's cards lay in an untidy heap.

The entire pattern shimmered to life. Pulses of pale color shot along the straight paths, other pulses chased each other on the circular tracks. An image rose above the facedown card at the center: a youth girded in the finest armor, his sword raised high above his head.

Jordan leaned forward until his forehead almost touched the shimmering planes and spheres. The gypsy woman said nothing; she didn't need to. The image began to move. An allegory unfolded before his mind's eye:

The shining youth was everything Jordan wished to be: a paragon of skill and virtue, ready to give battle for the right and just causes. A man born to lead other men, trained to lead, eager to lead. A man of confidence who treated all men and women as his equals, asking nothing of them that he would not ask of himself. His virtue was secure, his motives were pure; he tested both at every opportunity.

He was the epitome of the Avatar: radiant with potential, waiting for the right moment to reveal himself.

Jordan made a fist. It rose and fell slowly beside him, never striking the wooden table. His eyes opened wide. His mouth tightened in a silent scream. The allegory reached its climax. The shining youth rose to the challenge. He did everything right. And he was vanquished. His followers were vanquished as well. All that he cherished was blackened and trampled.

Jordan's lips formed the word "pride." He thought if he treated everyone equally, if he sincerely believed anyone could do what he could do, then he had defeated pride. But all he'd done was deceive and delude those who followed him. He was isolated behind a facade of false camaraderie.

"Who are my peers? Where are they?" Jordan whispered as the etched Insignia dimmed and the allegorical image faded. He sat down on his stool, unaware that he'd spoken aloud.

"How can you hope to find them," the gypsy countered, "when you never stop striving long enough to know them?"

Jordan squeezed the answers to the gypsy's question and his own in a knot as hard and heavy as the finest steel blade, then he buried the steel in his heart. Nothing, no one—not even his own ears—must ever hear those bitter words. He was Jordan Hawson, heir of Hawksnest, and the ideals his father laid before him were no less exacting than the virtues of an irrelevant Avatar. To win his father's approval, Jordan must rise above his companions: The rough equality of peers was a failure by Erwald Ironhawk's measure. Jordan could not afford a failure.

Althea took Jordan's cold, clenched fist and held it in her lap. "I do not think much of your game, madam," she said, meeting the thrust of the gypsy's sharp eyes and countering it with righteous indignation.

"He calls it a game," the old woman muttered as she gathered the cards. "I do not."

"What do you call it?"

"Destiny's window. A view of the path to come . . . if nothing changes. For those who dare to open their eyes, it is possibility, nothing more."

The crone could shuffle the cards without looking at them, and stare between Althea and Drum so that each would swear she stared at them. When the deck was squared the old woman set it in easy reach of either. She arched an eyebrow in silent challenge.

"You first." Althea looked at Drum, whose expression did not change as he cut the cards into unequal piles.

"My destiny was sealed with the smithguild's journeyman iron. I'm content; I ask nothing more than what I've fairly earned."

Althea had not seen the gypsy deal out Jordan's cards. Jordan fought both sides of an internal, civil war and did not notice that the farrier's pattern was different from his own until it was almost complete. None of Drum's cards lay faceup, none had been shifted along the straight virtue lines. The etching was dark and dead when the crone peeked at the last card in her hand.

"Perfect balance can exist in no man," she said to the farrier. "As one foot must lead the other, where would you place your last card?"

"Honesty," Drum said without hesitation. "The honest tradesman has no enemies."

With a little smile, the crone laid the card faceup on the appropriate pile.

That's Drum, all right, Jordan thought, rousing from his acid misery. *Selling the finest cloth while his own tunic is a patchwork of grease stains and tatters*.

Drum did not notice the painted-on patches. He saw a man who prospered in his trade, whose wares were the best, whose stout money-chest was chained to the wall and protected with three good locks. When the etching began at last to glow silver, the farrier watched without the least apprehension: Fortune came to the man who plied his trade with honesty.

The merchant's image rose out of the card, the walls of his shop, the countertop on which he displayed his wares, and his rich Peerage customer as well. Jordan expected that coins would be exchanged, the cloth would be cut to the agreed-upon yardage and the images would smile contentedly. He was surprised when the image remained frozen: surprised and then relieved. If he could not see the movement of Drum's vignette, then neither Drum nor Althea had seen the ignominy of his. There were so many little, shameful secrets hidden behind Jordan's heart that he sincerely believed he'd never notice another one. Blood flowed into Jordan's fingers, relaxing his fist. With patronizing strokes, Jordan freed his hand from Althea's and settled back to watch the farrier's reactions.

For Drumon's eyes alone, the merchant completed that one transaction which symbolized a lifetime of scrupulously honest dealing. He asked favors of no one, and expected none in return. A family appeared— and the only question Drum asked of the future was not answered: He could not see the wife's face; the color of her hair was hidden beneath a matron's modest veil. Still, their translucent images displayed the respect an honest man was due; Drum was satisfied with his view through destiny's window.

The table's silver glow reflected off the farrier's smug grin; Jordan's jaw dropped.

"What has *he* got to be so happy about? A journeyman farrier the rest of his life—he won't seek the master's mark because there's no one to tell him exactly what his masterpiece must be. Not student, not teacher—but doing the same journeyman's work the rest of his life!" The three-legged stool scraped across the plank floor. "A pox on your cards, old woman. If that's a *man's* destiny—I'd sooner be a sheep!"

The way to the door was clear behind the crone. Jordan got to his feet and chose the other way behind Althea and Drum.

"Sit down!" the crone snarled.

After a moment, Jordan did—but not because of her command. The merchant's image stood alone atop the cards of Honesty. His wealthy customer was gone, his goods, and his shop. He covered his face with his hands and dropped to his knees. He withered and shrank like a candle before the flame. Drum's eyes showed white all around; he braced his palms against the table edge, but could not move away.

Jordan was vindicated. "So—the honest sheep is shorn with the r—"

Both women hissed at him. The wagon was quiet as the image flickered, collapsing into itself until it was no more than dust whisked away by the draft.

"No one came," Drum murmured. "Was he hated so much?" he asked the crone. "He'd harmed no one. He did his work honestly and asked for nothing he had not earned. Did he die at the end?"

The gypsy had gathered the cards and was shuffling them. "At the end it no longer mattered."

"He owed no man and no man owed him—ever. Surely that counted for something?"

"How shall one count what does not exist?"

Drum emptied his lungs and said no more. The crone halted with cards split in her hands. Her eyes met Althea's, daring the young woman to speak.

Althea accepted the dare. "I think your cards show the worst that might happen if we do not learn from our mistakes. I know that I've made many mistakes and will make many more. I would not refuse a chance to learn from my mistakes before I make them.'' The young woman kept her voice even and her hands folded in her lap.

"So young, and yet so wise,'' the crone said to the cards, her tone contradicting her words. "What could *I* show her?'' She put the cards in the center of table and quickly mimicked Althea's pose. "You may lay them out yourself.''

"I don't know how.''

"There is no right way, no wrong way. Place them where you will. Learn from your mistakes.''

Althea gritted her teeth and reached for the cards, until Jordan covered them with his own hand.

"You dealt them out for Drum and me, why not Althea? Why must she be asked to do something we were not challenged to do?''

"It's all right, Jordie.'' Althea pulled most of the cards from beneath Jordan's hand.

Jordan sprang back. "I was trying to spare you—'' he explained.

"I've watched how it was with both you and Drum. I'm ready.'' She squared the cards Jordan had covered into a second deck. "That will be my cut.'' She glanced up at the gypsy, whose face was exquisitely without expression. "It *is* my cut. And the card that's uppermost goes facedown over Spirituality.'' She placed the card. "And the next goes to Compassion, because that's a mother's most important virtue. She cannot comfort her children—''

The card Althea held in her hand showed nothing of Compassion, mothers, or children. A grotesque, many-fingered hand manipulated a puppet which held another puppet which, in turn, held yet another puppet, and so on until the puppet drawings were diminishing dots. The card had not appeared faceup for either Jordan or Drum, and unlike the other cards, seemed unconnected with the eight virtues or the three Principles of Truth, Love, and Courage.

Althea let the card fall from her hand. It fluttered in the constant draft and came to rest on the table without touching any straight line or circle. She quickly covered it with a facedown card and placed the next on Compassion. Althea continued around the angles and circles from there without hesitation or explanation, placing all the succeeding cards facedown. With two cards thus removed from the regular sequence, however, she came up short with only one card to place on Honesty or Justice and none to hold in reserve.

"I made my mistake first off," Althea complained, dropping the card facedown on neither virtue, adding it instead to the one covering the puppets. "It won't work at all."

But, of course, it did—slowly at first, more slowly than it had for Drum. Ebbing and flowing with silver pulses, the power of the gypsy's cards sought a pattern beyond the etched channels of the tabletop. The shimmering grew brighter, swifter until the channels could no longer contain them. The crone jumped with the rest of them when, with a single brilliant pulse, the silvery light suffused the entire table with an eerie glow.

No cards lay faceup; no images rose before their eyes or in Althea's mind. She spread her arms, prepared to sweep through the shifty light, gathering each and every card into a single, jumbled pile.

"I said it wouldn't work—"

Althea's disdain turned suddenly to shock. Her eyes were wide open, and her mouth. The swirling drafts stopped abruptly. The deep sleeves of Althea's gown draped limply from her arms; the candles on the shelves burned without flickering. The young woman's fingers wriggled, casting shadows into the silver light which formed spiral eddies of pale color. A look of intense concentration formed on Althea's face: brows tightly furrowed, lips pursed, and the tip of her tongue emerging between them. She controlled the colors, and through their movement struggled to contain the darkness emerging between them.

The gypsy crone was intrigued by this unprecedented use of her scrying table, but, then, she did not recognize the jagged streak dividing the pools of color. Jordan and Drum knew better. They looked up at the same time, confirming each other's suspicions with worried glances. The darkness was more than an absence of the color or light. It filled the channels of the etching; it flowed around and swallowed the facedown cards. It divided, and, despite Althea's best efforts, the whorls of color reversed their flow, becoming smaller and dimmer.

Jordan seized a candle holder from the shelf behind the gypsy. He slammed it down in the inky sludge creeping to the table edge between himself and Althea. The darkness was burning cold and thick like honey. It numbed his wrist and lapped at the candle. Jordan grabbed the other two candles on the shelf and placed them beside the first, never thinking that if—when—the stream extinguished them, the entire wagon would plunge into darkness.

"Not that way," Drum exclaimed as the first candle guttered. Before Jordan could ask the inevitable question, the farrier lunged for Althea. "Got to get her out of here!"

Jordan understood. He vaulted over the table, throwing the patterns into chaos, knocking the candles aside, opening the door for Drum and his human burden just as the light vanished.

Eleven

nce on the ground outside the wagon, Althea clung to Drum. She gasped for air between long, whimpering sobs and was oblivious to the gypsies gawking at her. Her memory of the moments after she placed the last of the cards on the scrying table was blurred, but a few startlingly clear visions lingered, and these transfixed her with their nightmarishness: Balthan disappearing headfirst into the maw of a winged serpent; Drum swept away in a foul, viscous flood; Jordan pierced front to back by a flaming greatsword—and herself trapped in an endless spiderweb.

"It wasn't real. None of it was real," Drum assured her. "You said so yourself. A window, not a door. Mistakes you don't have to make."

Drum's words were gentle but Althea could not bear the thought of any mistakes, made or unmade. She pounded his forearm while she hid her face in the coarse wool of his vest. The farrier stroked her hair helplessly.

Jordan remained in the wagon. He wouldn't leave until the old woman was outside and the old woman wouldn't leave. Whatever dark power Althea awakened had been shattered when Drum hustled her into the clear night air. The danger that had the gypsy crone shrieking came from the candles Jordan knocked over in his headlong dash for the door. The hot wax clotted on the aged wood, but it ignited each card it touched. Flames were scattered across the table. They leapt to the crone's sleeve when she flailed at them.

Grabbing the crumpled tablecloth, Jordan whirled it around the old woman's arm and pointed her toward the door. The crone was light as a cat, nearly as agile, and twice as tenacious.

"Get out!"

Jordan hit her harder than he'd intended. She bounced against the wall and fell to the floor; she didn't try to get up.

"I don't deserve this!" the young man shouted for the benefit of any arcane presence which might linger in the wagon, then pulled the tablecloth from the crone's limp arm. He smothered the flames.

"Be careful, you Peer's-son fool. You destroy my cards and my table!"

The crone beat Jordan's head and shoulders with a lath she'd found on the floor. The wood couldn't hurt Jordan through his mail shirt, no matter how hard the crone swung it, and she swung it with all her might. But there was always the chance she'd get lucky and jab into his eye. Ducking and dodging with every step, Jordan backpedaled for the open door.

She put everything she had into one final *whack* as Jordan ducked under the lintel. The lath splintered on his protected shoulders. His feet missed the rickety ladder entirely. He stumbled, and landed belly-up on the ground. When he opened his eyes he was staring into a huddle of hostile, suspicious faces—none more hostile or suspicious than Drum's.

"Listen to her!" Drum complained. "Do something before she curses all of us."

Jordan did not rise. His thigh was throbbing again and he thought—hoped—they might think twice before mobbing a man lying helpless on the ground.

"Look at these! Ruined. *Ruined*. And none like them in this world or the next!" the crone ranted.

The mob parted. A withered, knobby hand thrust a fan of charred, broken cards before his face.

Jordan stared and rejected everything he could think of saying. With the crone's increasingly picturesque curses ringing in his ears, Jordan tried to imagine what his father would do or say in a similar circumstance. His mind remained empty; Erwald Ironhawk would never sink to these depths. Jordan swore to himself that if he ever saw a gypsy wagon again—attacked by trolls or brigands, on fire or wallowed in the mud—he'd keep going.

"May the great toes of your clumsy oaf's feet curl up to strangle you while you sleep. May your destiny close its eye and fall into an endless midden—"

"Beldame," Jordan used the term normally reserved for the proprietress of an exceptionally seedy brothel, "beldame—if they're irreplaceable, we can't replace them. We can only leave—"

A flicker of movement caught Jordan's eye: Drum shaking his head and creasing his lips with an exaggerated frown.

"We'll leave when the sun rises. We'll keep apart until then."

He got slowly to his feet. The healing wound ached like a rotten tooth. At least it wasn't bleeding. He couldn't walk but staggered across the camp, following Drum who seemed to have forgotten him.

Althea sat hunched over with her back to the world and her shoulders still shaking with sob-spasms. None of Jordan's many tutors told him how to deal with a crying woman. He balanced on his good leg and waited for her to notice him. When she did, Jordan scarcely recognized her. Travel had been hard on all of them—they all needed baths and a thorough grooming—but Althea was the most bedraggled. Wisps of broken hair framed her sun-blotched face and escaped from every plaiting. Tears and rubbing turned her eyes an angry red. Bruised circles of exhaustion beneath them completed the portrait of her misery.

"It's all my fault," she said with an unladylike sniff. "Me, my brother, and my brother's talisman—in that order. If it wasn't for me, none of this would be happening. You've been wounded. The gypsies have cursed all of us. I'm leading you to your doom and death—"

Notwithstanding the virtues of Humility and Compassion, and simple commonsense caution, Jordan was obliged to disagree. "We agreed that *I* was leading. Not wisely, perhaps. Certainly not well—but *I'm* leading—"

"No, you're not. You're doing everything to please me. You and Drum both. *I* know it, because *I'm* making it happen. The card showed me everything: The darkning shadow controls Balthan; he controls me; and I control you."

Indignation overcame Jordan's aching thigh. He stood firmly on both legs with his arms folded over his mail shirt. "No one *controls* me. I'm no puppet on a string. I do what I want." The words were strong coming from Jordan's throat, but weak in his ears. How many times since that fateful moment when she showed him the Kal Wis Mani Por talisman had he made a decision only to change it? Change it to accommodate Althea?

"You can't do anything that displeases me."

Jordan tugged Drum's sleeve. He hobbled a few steps beyond Althea's hearing, towing the farrier behind him. "That damned beldame and her tricky cards have baffled Althea. We've got to prove that she's wrong about this."

Drum didn't say a word.

"Well, she *is* wrong. I'm not doing this for Balthan, and I'm not doing this for her—I'm doing it for myself and to prove something to my father."

"I'm here because of her, and only her. Even now, I'll do what pleases her. That talisman of Balthan's is no safe thing. If it's taken him and her in evil, it's taken me as well."

A lock of dirty hair flopped between Jordan's eyes. He paused to hook it behind his ear, yearning for the hot baths of the Hawksnest hypocaust. "We could turn around and go home tomorrow. That would prove she's not at fault for leading." Jordan spoke in jest, but Drum's face soured.

"Nay—that's just what she wants. That, and to abase herself to your lord father and any other who'll listen and punish her."

Jordan scratched his bristly chin. He wasn't used to being filthy day after day. He itched and stung all over. Pushing up his sleeve, he dug his nails into a particularly irritating spot, then looked down to see a pattern of pricks and welts along his forearm. A tiny black dot appeared, and disappeared. Fleas. As if the gypsy wagon hadn't caused him enough trouble, now he had fleas. He'd need a dose of Agatha's naphtha-and-lye soap before he'd be rid of them.

But—did he really want to go home? Was that truly his

own idea? He'd felt the darkning power on the scrying table. Once doubt and magic snarled together, there was no untangling them.

"I'm for going ahead, then," Jordan said flatly, not looking at the farrier. "At least to Britain City. It's what I planned to do when I left home." Not before he'd seen the talisman, of course, but before he knew he'd have company for the length of the journey, and long before he'd met up with the gypsy and her cards. "Maybe there's something there. You know the way home, if that's what you and she want to do."

Drum grunted—the sound conveyed his expectations: He was going to Britain City, too, and that it would be a fool's errand. Then the farrier uttered an opinion. "I don't like anything about this place. I think we should set a watch. Are you game?"

Jordan swallowed his surprise. "I hadn't gotten that far. I'm game," he agreed. "I slept all afternoon and I ache too much right now. I'll take first watch—'til midnight."

"Maybe it's just as well we're both awake—until the gypsies sleep."

They settled on either side of Althea, facing the gypsies. She fell asleep in the midst of another rambling apology. Drum covered her with blankets; Jordan retrieved his sword and whetstone. The blade was crusted and nicked where it had clipped the brigands' armor. Jordan appraised the burrs with his fingertips; he judged he had about three hours' work restoring the edge. It would be exacting work, and mind-numbing as well.

He looked forward to it until he swept the stone along the steel. With difficulty he could balance the sword across one leg, but he couldn't keep it angled properly without getting a twinge in the wounded thigh each time he swept the whetstone toward the tip. Muttering to himself, he returned the sword to its scabbard. He stared at the stars, trying not to think or feel.

"The old woman said you'd be right as rain tomorrow morning. Said that paste she used would draw out the poison and cobble the flesh together again. I'd sooner trust a cautery iron." The farrier stroked his own leg in sympathy. "It was an awful-looking piece of work. She cut out a piece of flesh the size—"

"Spare me the details, Drum," Jordan said, still studying the heavens. "It worked. I was hungry enough to grow myself a new leg. The crone knows her healcraft."

Drum was chastened, but the damage had been done. The gypsy knew her healcraft—what more did she know? What about the curses she hurled so readily? And what about her cards and that cursed scrying table? The questions followed Jordan into the bushes and were waiting for him when he returned. The stars completed the first part of their nightly journey from east to west.

The gypsy women and children disappeared but the men lingered around their fire, passing a straw-wrapped jug and—to judge by their shouts and gestures—embellishing their own parts in the day's misadventures.

For the first time in memory, Jordan didn't care if he received his share of glory—though he wouldn't have minded a swig from the jug to take his mind off darkning magic and the intractable ache in his leg. But he wouldn't join the gypsies, or invite them to join him and Drum, so slaking his thirst was just another frustrating wish until a gypsy started for the bushes.

He understood the wistful look on Jordan's face and tucked the jug under his arm. "Eh—you deserved the first swallow. You should come, join us by the fire, not sit by yourself." His words slurred together. He wiped his mouth on his sleeve. Wine slopped onto the straw wrapping when he thrust the jug at Jordan.

"Leg hurts," the young man explained before taking a pull from the jug. The wine had a kick worthy of Baron Hrothgar's mule and enough acid to pickle anything unfortunate enough to fall in. At Hawksnest Jordan would use wine this sour to clean his mail shirt, but under the stars in the middle of nowhere, it was everything a man in search of oblivion wanted. Jordan took another pull and passed it on to Drum.

"You worried about that—about what the old woman says?" The gypsy dropped into a deep crouch without losing his balance. "There's nothing to worry about. The table— she did not get scarred at all. And the cards? Ha! I tell you—I painted those cards myself not two months ago, and I'll paint 'em again tomorrow. The old woman, she yells like that because she likes to see a man squirm, not because she's got any—what do you call it—*power*."

The wine simmered in Jordan's stomach, driving out the damp and cold of the night air and the ache in his leg. He intercepted the jug on its way back to the gypsy. The wine was starting to taste good. "She's got the power, all right," he averred. "I saw it on that table."

Cradling the jug in his lap, the gypsy waved Jordan's concerns away. "The old woman—she's not the table."

Jordan stared at the jug. "She cursed me for fair. I'll be looking over my shoulder."

"The mother of my wife—if she had *power*, you know what I'd be? I'd be like this." He held up his hand, the fingers nearly touching one another. "I'd be less than that. She got a mouth full of dust—that's all: A mouth full of dust. You don't worry about it. You sleep. You get well. You don't worry." He got to his feet and took the jug back to the fire.

"You believe him?" Drum asked through a jaw-cracking yawn.

The yawn was contagious. Jordan flexed and stretched every muscle that didn't hurt before answering, "I don't believe him or his mother-in-law."

The farrier squinted at the sky, seeking a recognizable pattern of stars. "I'm going to sleep now. You wake me when the Lazy Hunter sets."

Jordan nodded. His thoughts floated on the surface of the wine. Nothing hurt, nothing worried him: not Balthan, not the talisman, not Althea, not his father—nothing at all. He was calm, serene, watching the gypsy men bank their fire. Drum began to snore—he'd fallen asleep before he'd gotten wrapped up in his cloak. He'd be stiff as a board when he got up if he slept all night—even half the night—with nothing to warm him. Jordan decided to have pity on the farrier and tuck him in.

The heir of Ironhawk got to his feet carefully, expecting his leg to be weak, but it was no weaker than the rest of him. Three gulps of gypsy wine and he was lightheaded.

That didn't seem quite right. He'd been drinking wine since he was old enough to see over the edge of the high table. He'd been falling-down drunk only twice in his whole life and both times it had taken a lot more than three swallows. A whole lot more.

He'd been through a lot. There was no telling what happened when the wine hit whatever healcraft was left inside of him. Though something still didn't seem quite right: He'd eaten enough stew for a week, but three swallows of raw gypsy wine gave him the blind staggers?

Jordan took a cautious step toward the snoring farrier. At least his wound didn't hurt; he couldn't feel it at all. It was as if he didn't have feet, or legs. He wasn't dizzy, or tired, but perhaps crawling to Drum would be wiser than walking.

He was on his hands and knees when, with ponderous majesty, the young man recalled that he'd seen the gypsy holding the jug, and he'd seen him wiping his mouth—but he hadn't actually seen him take a drink.

Set a watch, Jordan. Don't trust the gypsies, Jordan. Stupid, Jordan, he chided himself, knowing then what was going to happen next. *Stu . . .*

He was warm; that was the first thing Jordan noticed. His cloak covered him from buskins to brow, the rolled-up hood beneath his head was his pillow. The young man was drifting back to his dreams when he remembered how he'd fallen —literally—to sleep the night before. He sat bolt-upright and reached for the knife in his buskin before his eyes focused.

All in all, Jordan wasn't as bad off as he feared. The muzziness inside his head faded as his vision cleared. Whatever the gypsies put in the wine wasn't meant to linger or cripple. The knife was where it belonged against his calf, and his purse of silver was tied through his belt where it belonged, too. Drum lay under his cloak a half-step away, his shoulders rising and falling exactly as they should.

Althea!

Jordan kicked out of his cloak and spun around. Althea was wrapped in her cloak *and* a blanket. Nervously poised on fingertips and the balls of his feet, Jordan studied the camp beyond her—or, rather, the empty clearing beyond. The wagon, and every other trace of the gypsies, was gone. The loose dirt mounds of three graves and scattered charcoal from the fire pit were all that remained. Hrothgar's mule and pony were hobbled in the grass; their gear was scattered in a half-dozen piles, but that was the way they had left it. The pony raised its head and whickered, disturbing neither Althea nor Drum. Jordan shifted his weight into a one-knee-down squat. He'd held that position a few moments before realizing that his left thigh felt no different from his right.

The bandage came off easily. His trousers were badly torn and crusted with gore, but a reddish splotch, slightly warm and touch-tender like sunburn, was all that remained of yesterday's wound.

"She said it would scar," Jordan whispered, "but it won't. No one will believe I fought seven wolfshead brigands. It's like it never happened." His thoughts and eyes were drawn to the dirt mounds. Were they the graves of men, or merely piles of dirt? Jordan had suspicions, but he wouldn't dig through the graves to prove them.

"They drugged us. There was something in the wine to make certain we slept through their departure. But why? Why? They didn't harm us—not really. They didn't steal anything."

There were no shadows—the sun had not risen above the eastern treetops. Leaving his companions asleep, Jordan explored the abandoned camp by himself. There was little left behind to answer his questions. Wagon tracks were easy to read through the ashes and the soft dirt of the embankment, but they blended quickly into the rutted surface of the road. Jordan studied the gravelly surface. He thought the freshest tracks went south; he couldn't be certain.

A ranger would know, Jordan thought. He'd know which way they went, and when . . . Hawksnest employed rangers when they hunted, but Lord Ironhawk had not compelled Jordan to master their craft. Jordan knew that Lord Shamino could tell what they were wearing and what they ate for breakfast—

Jordan jerked upright. He scanned the forest instead of the road. Lord Shamino—the gypsies weren't awed to have Lord British's Companion among them. Now that his head wasn't muddled with pain, Jordan realized the old crone and the ranger lord must have known each other well.

A slight breeze blew from the northwest, not enough to account for the movement in the scrub beyond their animals. Jordan didn't seriously think that Lord Shamino still followed them, much less that he could spy out the ranger, but that the movement might be dinner—and food was more important than all the gypsies and Companions in Britannia combined.

Jordan descended from the road, drew his knife, and stalked the rustling brush.

"Jor-*dan!*"

Against all logic, Jordan recognized the voice coming through the blackthorn bushes. But what was his younger brother, the Squirt, doing *here*? Jordan had no time to consider all the wild impossibilities. The tangled blackthorn bushes, their branches covered with new spring leaves, whipped and broke as someone—perhaps some*thing*—ran closer.

Jordan reversed his grip on the knife, ready to throw it if he had to, and braced for the worst.

"Jor-*dan!*"

The blackthorns parted.

"Squirt—by the Eight, the Three, and the One-around-all—what are you doing *here*?!"

Darrel ran full-tilt into his big brother. The force knocked Jordan's knife from his hand and left both Hawsons sprawled on the ground. They wrestled briefly. Darrel flailed with all his might, sublimely confident that there was no way he could possibly injure his big brother, while Jordan was obliged to restrain himself.

Jordan finally got the boy pinned down. "Have a care— I lost my knife."

The Hawksnest servants had nicknamed the boy "Squirt" not because of his size but for his uncanny ability to wriggle away from almost anyone and anything. After giving Jordan an unintentional, but solid, kick in the stomach, Squirt pounced on the knife.

"I found it!" he exalted.

"Give it here," Jordan scowled. With one hand catching the knife and the other twisting Darrel's tunic, he separated them. He held the boy at arm's length, toes dangling above the ground. "Where's our father? Where's Lord Iron-hawk?"

The light went out of Darrel's eyes. He struggled to free himself before Jordan threw him into the blackthorns. "At Hawksnest," he swore.

"Don't lie to me, Squirt." A twig snapped nearby. Jordan dropped the boy and spun on his heel. "Father?" No answer. Nothing. He turned back to Darrel. "He's out there, isn't he? Who else is with him? Dragon's blood! I knew he'd follow me."

Darrel hovered just out reach. There weren't many things his big brother openly feared, but their father on a rampage was one of them. The boy savored the look of panic on Jordan's face a moment before he smoothed his tunic and answered the questions. "He's not out there. He's not looking for you."

"He's not?" Jordan's distress collapsed into disappointment.

"Oh—he was in a fury when he found out: breaking things, throwing things the whole day. He swore he'd drop you in the well when he found you. And when he found out that Althea was gone too! His face was *purple,* and our lady mother begged him to calm down."

"And he did?"

"Of course not. You know that big statue in the atrium

by the arbor? He knocked it off its pedestal and smashed it with his sword. Broke his sword, too.''

Jordan hid behind his hands. "But he *didn't* come after us?''

"Companion Lord DuPre told him not to.''

Stunned and nearly speechless, Jordan peeked through his fingers at Darrel's beaming face. " 'Told'?''

"He said that he'd spoken with Companion Shamino and knew you were all headed for Britain City and that nothing—meaning our lord father—should stand in your way. That's how I knew what I had to do to catch up with you. I hid in Creaky Colin's baggage, under his padded chair, because he said he was going straight to Britain City and the palace to complain—''

Jordan raised his hand. "Forget about Colin the unSteady. Tell me everything Companion Lord DuPre said to our lord father.''

"He said—'' the boy puffed out his cheek and tucked one arm behind his back, credibly catching the essence of the paladin Companion in mid-oration. " 'Ironhawk, if you'd Nominated your son, he'd have taken up a proper Virtue Quest. But as you have denied him what he'd earned, he's taken up another that serves Britannia's purpose just as well.' ''

"Lord DuPre said *that*—to our lord father?''

The boy nodded; whooping like a troll, Jordan hoisted his brother over his head. "The bear may growl, but he'll have to Nominate me now!'' Jordan would have hugged his brother, but true to his nickname, Squirt was loose before he could be smothered in maudlin affection.

"You stink!'' he sneered, wrinkling his nose and dodging easily under Jordan's arms. "You're covered with crud. Your face looks like you've got the mange!'' Darrel didn't actually prefer to have his family angry at him but it was the situation with which he was most familiar. "Your mail's gone dung-y with rust—"

Jordan made a halfhearted attempt to catch his brother, then laughed and let him run into the blackthorns. He shouted reassurances to Althea and Drum, who'd been awakened by the ruckus and, understandably, thought the worst. They asked the practical questions, but Jordan's thoughts had gotten as far as Nomination and no further.

He'd ask for Honor first, not Valor as he'd always planned. Honor was a paladin's cardinal virtue . . .

"Jordan Hawson—pull your head down from the clouds," Althea chided. "We're not on your Virtue Quest. What are we going to do with him? What are we going to do with your brother? Your lord father and lady mother must be beside themselves with worry." When Jordan stared dumbly at her, she answered her own question: "Someone's got to take him back to Hawksnest."

The three of them—Jordan, Drum, and Althea—sat around the cold fire. Their gear was packed and loaded on the animals, but they couldn't leave until they decided who was going to Britain City and who was taking the boy back to Hawksnest. There were no volunteers for Squirt and Hawksnest. More than one person at the villa was convinced their lord's second son was a changeling: a gremlin foisted off on them like a cowbird chick in a sparrow's nest. During the few hours since his arrival, the boy spooked the mule —a challenge in itself—and put Drum in a sour mood by losing the plug of the farrier's waterskin.

Chips of wood flew like sparks as Drum whittled a replacement. "Ask him again how he caught up with us. That brat can't hold still for two minutes. No way he hid for eight days in a Peer's baggage. Ask him."

Jordan sighed and looked around. Squirt had made a truce

with the mule and was pawing through the packs tied to its saddle. "Hey, Squirt. Get over here!"

The boy leaped away from the mule, his face radiating guilt and fear. A familiar silk pouch lay on the ground in front of him. Althea ran to see if the talisman was intact; Jordan and Drum ran after Squirt. Drum caught him as he scrambled up the road embankment—which was lucky for the boy. For all his anger, the farrier didn't think he had the right to thrash a lord's son; Jordan had no such hesitations. Drum's thick arms offered Darrel some protection when he faced his brother, and, for once, the boy did not try to escape.

"Don't you *ever* touch anything of Althea's. Ever. Anything—"

"It's not broken," Althea shouted. "No harm done."

Jordan could change the expression of his anger, but not its power. "What were you looking for? What did you hope to find in Althea's things?"

Darrel tested the farrier's hold on him before answering. "Shamino said Althea had whatever it was that was drawing the shadows. I wanted to see it for myself—" He dropped his shoulders and squirted toward the blackthorns. Jordan lunged after him, but the boy stiff-armed his big brother in the gut and vanished into the bushes. "Wait—I've got something to show you," he called out.

Twelve

Darrel Hawson huddled among the bundles atop the mule. He itched in five separate places; a sharp reed from Althea's basket jabbed between his ribs with every plodding step the animal took. The boy endured it all. He hadn't twitched since Jordan set him in the saddle. Except for that one spot between his ribs, Darrel didn't hurt anywhere. He wished he did. A thorough thrashing would have been easier to bear than his brother's grim silence.

The boy honestly thought the bow and arrows he'd retrieved from the bushes would explain everything and that they'd understand why he *had* to see that talisman-thing for himself. When they realized that Lord Shamino trusted him—had given him a friendship token—they'd trust him, too. And perhaps *they* would have, if they were Althea and Drum alone, but *they* included Jordan, who took the bow, all the red-and-blue-fletched arrows, and shook them as if they were a sheaf of serpents . . .

"Where'd you get these, Squirt?" Jordan had demanded. "Lord Shamino wouldn't give them to you—you couldn't draw this bow. Your arms aren't long enough. Your shoulders aren't steady enough. Don't lie to me, Squirt. Did you steal them from one of the Peers? Did you steal them from Lord Colin?"

Adults—and Jordan was acting like an adult—were prickly about honesty. They always expected the truth, though they fibbed whenever it pleased them. The boy told Jordan everything, and his brother's face got gloomier every time he paused to breathe.

Squirt hadn't lied. He had been in the baggage cart for about a furlong: until he sneezed and Lord Colin's steward dragged him out by his ear. Escaping was simple—getting loose always hurt less than staying put—although it helped to have nimble joints and narrow shoulders. The boy hadn't been lost, either, when Lord Shamino found him near the Hawksnest boundary stones. He knew where he was going; he was just having a little trouble choosing the best way. When the Companion appeared, and said he *knew* where Jordan was—Squirt simply invited himself along.

The ranger knew every shortcut in Britannia, and he didn't mind having a boy for company. He showed Squirt how to tie a piece of suede over his thumb to grip the wooden bow and guide the arrow as it slid over his hand—a trick which Darrel would be pleased to teach his brother. And—most remarkable of all—three nights back Lord Shamino summoned a moon gate with a smooth black stone!

"What about shadows?" Jordan had asked when it was clear Squirt had finished talking. "Did Lord Shamino say how or why he was following us, and why he didn't join us?"

"Lord Shamino said there were three shadows, each one worse than the other, and the smell of them—Lord Shamino said *smell*, he truly did, I swear it, Jordan—he said the smell of them was in a hollow glass Althea carried. Lord Shamino said I could be a ranger, if I wanted to—if our lord father would permit it, so I had to see if I could smell through glass, too. But I couldn't.''

Darrel had never seen Jordan look so angry. He'd thought he'd lose all his teeth, his nose, and maybe an eye. Jordan's chin jutted forward like an axe. His shoulders were so tight that his neck disappeared; he looked frighteningly like their father. Then Jordan had sighed and said, "The Squirt's coming with us, and we're all going to Britain City."

They'd been on the road ever since. Around midafternoon, they passed a ramshackle charterhouse. Jordan, Drum, and Althea went inside to eat and purchase provisions, leaving Darrel on top of the mule. When they came out Althea surreptitiously tucked something into the boy's hand—a wad of bread stuffed with cooked onions, parsnips, and force-meat. Darrel wolfed it down gratefully, but what held his attention, and gave him the strength to endure the itches, saddle cramps, and the reed pricking his ribs, was the arm-long bundle—wider at one end than the other, and very stiff—Jordan had purchased in the charterhouse.

It had to be a sword. Darrel hadn't lived at Hawksnest for all his eleven years without learning what a sword looked like, wrapped in canvas or anything else. The bundle was about two-thirds the length of Jordan's bastard-sword which meant Jordan would never use it, and that meant—since it was inconceivable that a son of Erwald Ironhawk would give a sword to a blacksmith, except for reforging—Darrel was finally going to have his very own sword. The prospect almost made up for the way Jordan had appropriated Lord Shamino's bow and arrows.

The road widened just beyond the charterhouse: Two carts

could squeeze past each other and the travellers from Hawksnest no longer had to climb the embankment every time they met or were passed by a galloping court-herald. They came to a crossroad. The stone marker proclaimed the distance in furlongs to the nearby villas and the distance in miles, twelve, to Britain City.

Darrel could read that much for himself; he'd mastered the angular runic alphabet carved into the stone, but the scrawls on the piece of parchment hung from hooks on the stone were just so many worm trails. Althea and Jordan could read script, and write it, too—but the farrier was completely unlettered. Darrel linked his thumbs and forefingers together, imitating the symbol of Infinity—the One-all-around by which Jordan so often swore—and hoped Drum would ask what was on the parchment that left both Althea and Jordan with scowls on their faces.

Granite had more curiosity than the farrier. Darrel had to ask for himself: "What's it say?"

"Twelve miles to Britain City, dunderhead."

Darrel pressed his fingers harder. Sometimes—most of the time—Jordan's insults meant only that Jordan was the elder brother, the heir, and could get away with teasing; but sometimes it meant Jordan was on a short fuse. The boy risked an explosion. "What's it say on the parchment?"

Grimacing, Jordan tore the sheepskin from the hooks and rolled it into a tube. "It says it's treason to ask too many questions, and the punishment for treason is death by quartering. Here, Squirt, read it yourself," he said and bounced the tube against the boy's wrist.

Squirt unmade his Infinity sign. "You know I can't. Our lady mother says the letters won't hold still for me—"

"You won't hold still for them, you mean." Jordan creased the tube and stuffed it deep inside one of their packs. "But that *is* what it says—more or less. The Council of

Mages stands condemned and disbanded by Lord Blackthorn's order, for the good of Britannia. Say otherwise—
where the wrong ears overhear you—and you'll be quartered
for treason.''

"That's not right, is it? Just asking questions . . . talking.
That can't be treason, can it? Lord British said we have the
right to say whatever we want—even to him.''

The brothers' eyes met for the first time since the morning. "Something's happened to Lord British, something
more than getting lost in those caverns. Those shadows Lord
Shamino told you about, they're not ordinary shadows. I
don't know what they are, but, well, maybe they've got
Lord British, and Balthan—and maybe Lord Blackthorn's
part and parcel of them. Didn't Lord Shamino explain it to
you?''

The stoniness hadn't quite left Jordan's face and voice,
but it was no longer aimed at the boy. Darrel relaxed. "I
didn't listen too good. It's all that boring stuff our lord
father likes to talk about after dinner and even our lady
mother falls asleep.'' When Jordan smiled, Darrel's
thoughts and eyes turned immediately to the wrapped sword.
"Are you still angry at me?''

Jordan started to walk away. "No more than usual,
Squirt.'' He heard what he was saying, the way it sounded,
and turned back. "I'm angry because you followed me—
just like Lord Ironhawk's angry at me in the first place. I
wanted to do this by myself. I can take care of myself, but
now I've got to take care of you, and Althea, and Drumon
the farrier. In the last two weeks I've killed trolls and men.
I've been wounded, healed, and drugged by gypsies. Lord
Shamino says he's been following us because what *we're*
trying to do is what *he's* trying to do. But he's talking about
Lord British in the Underground and shadows and evil when

I thought the worst I'd have to do is listen to Balthan brag while he sobered up."

Darrel heard and remembered only three words: "You killed *trolls*?"

"Yes." Jordan shook his head with bemusement. "Three, at least. It was dark, I couldn't see." He was thinking of the blond, blue-eyed one he'd seen very clearly.

"What was it like? Did you cut off their heads? How big were they? Did you keep their ears? Can I see?"

Jordan heard himself in Squirt's bloodthirsty enthusiasm; worse, he was about to quote Erwald Lord Ironhawk for the unavoidable reason that their father, once again, was right: "It wasn't like that, Darrel. I killed them because they would have killed me—and there was one I didn't kill . . ." He ransacked his memory for the words that explained how he felt when he plunged his sword in the troll's chest. "He was going to die, but he wasn't dead. He looked at me—"

"And you thrust your bastard-sword right between his eyes!"

"Aye," Jordan shrugged and nodded, "something like that." He joined Drum beside Althea's pony.

What Lord Erwald called the commonweal of Britannia and discoursed upon while his gut digested his supper was as boring to Jordan as it was to Darrel. A virtuous man a Peer—should not have to worry about laws, writs, decrees, and the myriad details of government. Lord British said so himself when he refused a monarch's sovereign title. What was good enough for Lord British was certainly good enough for Jordan Hawson—

"But, remembering how we were greeted in Paws, I don't think I want to arrive in Britain City an hour before sunset. I'd sooner spend another night outside the walls and have a full day to sound things out before we sign our names to some innkeeper's book.''

Althea wrinkled her nose. Another night on the cold ground held little appeal. "What about a charterhouse? Shouldn't there be one a league from the city?"

Drum offered another suggestion: "The smithguild has freehold outside the eastern gate. My mark and vouchsafe would get us a room there.''

A freehold—Jordan bridled at the mere thought. A freehold was a place outside of any lord's desmene, beyond the limits of a city's charter. Jordan would sleep in a snowbank before he set foot in a freehold. The guilds waxed eloquent about their unwritten guild laws, but thieves, pirates, and even wolfshead brigands claimed to have guilds. The blacksmiths, the vintners, the coopers, and all the rest disavowed their shady imitators; Jordan Hawson was not convinced or fooled. But he had other, more practical reasons to avoid the freehold that would not start a debate between Drum and himself.

"We'd still have to leave our marks and if Balthan's in Britain City, I don't want anyone to know people from Hawksnest villa have come looking for him.''

"Do you think Balthan's run afoul of Lord Blackthorn's . . . warnings?'' Althea asked in a small voice. She could not bring herself to dignify the parchment proclamation with the word of law.

"I'd bet my last piece of silver on it. If everything we've heard is true: Lord Blackthorn wants the power to open all the dungeons himself. He condemned the council when they refused to give in to him. He put Felespar in prison and tortured him. Can't you *hear* Balthan bending every ear he can find—and damning the consequences?''

Crestfallen, Althea admitted that she could. Much of the picture remained cloudy, but those pieces which could be

seen placed her brother at cross purposes with Lord Blackthorn. And all Britannia was learning that was a very dangerous place to be.

Late afternoon found the travellers outside a thatched
cottage with two chimneys and a wreath of out-buildings.

"Goodwife—may we use your well to water our animals
and make ourselves a nightfire along the lane?"

Scruffy chin and stained tunic notwithstanding, Jordan
had the manners of a Peer's son and usually his flattery was
sufficient to get all of them invited inside for supper. He
expected no less close by Lord British's city. The holding
was well-run and prosperous. The goodwife at the window
wore a madder-dyed gown and a bonnet trimmed with a
piece of lace. Another four settings at her supper table would
not strain her resources—even if three of those four were
hungry menfolk.

Instead of greeting them hospitably, the woman beat the
scrap-metal gong hanging beside the window.

"Water your beasts quickly—then begone!" she growled.
"There's no place for strangers here."

Men from the holding gathered in the yard, rakes, shov-
els, and forks at their sides, as if trouble were a frequent
visitor. Jordan consciously kept his hand away from the hilt
of his sword where he wanted very much to put it.

"We're from the south, bound for Britain City—"

"Then go there!" the brawniest of the hold men shouted.
"There's time enough for the likes of you to reach the gates
before they close."

"We ask for nothing an honest man would not freely
give: water and leave to build a nightfire."

"Can't you read the markers—Britain City's four miles
yonder. Hie yourselves there."

A younger man with a walleyed squint and dunnish hair
whacked straight across his brow skulked forward bearing

his rake two-handed across his chest. He wasn't a serious threat to a man with a mail shirt and a sword, but the fact that he was a threat at all came as a cold surprise to Jordan and his companions.

"Let's go," Althea whispered urgently. "We're not welcome here."

That much was obvious—but why? "What plague visits Lord British's charter holding that honest travellers are chased away like vermin?" Jordan demanded as he retreated.

The goodwife exchanged a guilty glance with her husband. "See for yourself in the city," she said. "Where Lord Black—"

"Wife!" The brawny holder smacked his shovel against the ground. "Mind your waspish tongue." Then, turning to face Jordan he growled, "Go to the city."

Althea needed no greater urging. Reining the pony with hard-earned expertise, she clapped her heels against its barrel ribs. They went down the lane at a canter.

"We better go," Drum announced as he ran after her.

Jordan walked backward until he bumped into the mule. Taking its reins near the bridle, he completed their retreat.

"I don't believe you let them get away with that." Darrel sawed uselessly on the reins his brother continued to hold. "We were entitled to water. What right has some churl to tell *us* where we can draw water or build a fire? Or to threaten you with—"

"Be quiet, Squirt. This has nothing to do with Peerage rights. They were afraid of us. Afraid of us, of the city, and above all else—Lord Blackthorn."

"But our rights—they can't deny our rights!"

Jordan understood his brother's indignation. The decision —his own decision—not to impose his will and rights on the holders had burst into his mind with an unprecedented

deep-voiced authority. Instinctively Jordan knew his father would, for once, be proud of him: He was acting as
a responsible lord ought to act. But any sense of pride
Jordan felt toward his sudden maturity was overshadowed
by the distasteful realization that manhood was not a
complete freedom from the externally imposed restraints
of childhood. Manhood was, instead, the unrewarded ac-
ceptance of more restraints than any adolescent could imagine.

Jordan could have explained all this to his younger
brother, but in doing so he would not only sound like a
man, he might very well *become* a full-grown man just like
his father. That was a risk he was not ready to take, so
Jordan clamped his teeth together and pulled the mule into
slow trot that kept Squirt too preoccupied with keeping his
seat amid the bundles to ask any more questions.

The boy remained silent even after they caught up with
Althea's pony and, as a group, resumed walking toward the
city.

"Will you come to the freehold now?" Drum asked
smugly. "We smiths never asked anything from Lord British or his city. What we never took in the first place Lord
Blackthorn can't have taken away now."

Jordan shook his head. None of them understood, and he
was forced to take his father's part. "Any lord can take
anything he wants—if he wants to take it. I—with my sword
and nothing more—could have taken that holding back
there. Every Peer has a cohort. Lord Ironhawk has forty
men-at-arms retained in his desmene, eating at his table,
and living from his purse. That's a small army. How many
men do you think Lord Blackthorn has? How many court-
heralds have we seen pound by us this day alone? Lord
Blackthorn has taken all of Britannia."

"He wouldn't dare," Drum retorted.

"I think he already has," Althea interjected. "That's what Lord Colin was trying to say at the Conclave invocation."

"And saying it poorly, as usual. If the Peerage stood firm—but they won't. They'll whine, wheedle, and worry until it's too bloody damn late." Jordan picked up a stone and threw it toward the now-hidden cottage. Then he pounded the fist of one hand against the palm of the other, emphasizing each word as he repeated, "Too . . . bloody . . . damn . . . late." He heaved another stone, this one aimed at Britain City. "Balthan was right—and no one listened!"

Jordan ran ahead of them, pausing every few strides to pick up another stone and hurl it toward the city. Drum eyed Althea who shrugged and looked up at Darrel on the mule beside her. The boy clicked his tongue to get the mule moving.

"He won't wait for us."

"We should still go to the guild's freehold," Drum advised Althea when they were left behind together. His hand rested on the pony's shoulder, keeping it from following the mule. The "we" he had in mind did not include either Hawson.

"And try to get all three of them out of Lord Blackthorn's jails?"

"You Peerage folk with your virtues and guests—you're all alike," the farrier muttered, but he followed her anyway.

All the rashness and anger left Jordan when he came to the crest of a rolling hill and got his first sight of the city walls. Nothing proclaimed the city within the walls different now from what it had been any other time the young man had visited it. At this distance he could not see if the gates were open or how many men patrolled the narrow barbican. Fingers of dark smoke rose from several quarters, but that was as it should be. Several thousand citizens dwelt in Britain City, where they plied every trade imaginable. In times long past, New Magincia was the greatest city in the land, but since the triumph of the Avatar, Britain City, a half-day's ride from Lord British's castle, was the heart of the realm.

An army would think long and hard before storming its steep granite walls. An eighteen-year-old Peer's son certainly did. He waited at the hillcrest for the others to join him.

"We're not going in. We'll camp over there—in those trees."

Althea looked past the copse to the freshly turned fields and the home of the family that worked them. "What of the holders? We're even closer to the city now."

"We're not going to ask. We'll set a cold camp; no one will know we're there."

There was less to do without a fire, especially for Althea, who usually prepared supper. She took the talisman from her basket and carried it to the edge of the grove. Out of sight of the road, the nearest cottage, and her three companions, she studied the glass in the reddish light of the setting sun. The darkning band divided the globe at the middle. It seemed thicker than it had been the last time she looked, but no darker. Her brother's homunculus floated in the lower portion, looking up at the darkning. Its stubby hand pointed toward the city, but its head pointed north-northeast, beyond it.

Althea shook the smaller vial of volatile oil into her lap. "*Kal Wis Por Mani.*" She rubbed the oil over the globe. The colored ribbons above and below the darkning came alive. The evanescent glow on the surface of the globe was lost in the waning sunlight, but palpable to Althea's fingers. "*Kal Wis Por Mani.*"

The homunculus began to move. It tried to stand, but the darkning moved also, and there was not enough room. The iridescent ribbons in the lower portion dissolved and re-formed, weakly, in the upper portion. There was nothing to obscure Althea's view of the homunculus as its little head disappeared. She swallowed a cry of terror. Her hands trembled, but not so much that she could not see the stubby arm point beyond the city, or the homunculus vanishing slowly into the darkning.

"Balthan—" she whispered.

"Is that truly Balthan—your brother—in that glass?"

Squirt's question destroyed Althea's concentration. The strangled whisper became a full-fledged shriek. Mindlessly, the young woman scrambled to her feet. The globe flew from her hands. She covered her eyes and screamed.

Darrel caught the talisman. It tickled his palms like velvet—but he held it easily. "I caught it, Althea," he told her, though it was unlikely she heard anything but her own screaming, which he ignored. No one trusted Squirt with fragile things. Agatha swore he could shatter a goblet by looking at it—and sometimes the boy feared she was right. But he knew he wasn't going to drop the fascinating talisman. He just *knew*.

It balanced on the fingertips of his right hand. He held it above his head. Sunlight shone clearly through it.

"Hammers and bells!" Drum burst through the trees behind both Althea and Darrel, with Jordan close at his heels. His instinct, as always, drew him to Althea, not the talisman.

Rescuing the glass fell to Jordan, who paused before trying to snatch it out of his notoriously inept brother's hands. While his mind sought the best tactical solution, his eyes focused on the shimmering globe. The problem was suddenly different.

"Squirt," he said slowly, then corrected himself, "Darrel . . . Darrel, what are you doing?" Althea had stopped screaming; she meant to rescue the talisman herself. Jordan shot his arm across her waist, stopping her before she reached the boy. "Look at it. *Look!*"

Althea smothered another cry behind her hands. Her strength left her; Jordan thought she was going to faint and held her tightly in front of him.

"It's clear," she whispered. "The darkning's gone . . ."

The oil within the talisman globe was the same color as the setting sun behind it. The darkning streak and the shifting ribbons were gone. Jordan could not see if the homunculus had vanished as well.

"Darrel?"

Neither the boy nor the talisman moved. Jordan released Althea and stood in front of his brother. Squirt's face was bathed in ruddy light. His eyes were wide; his pupils dangerously large for someone looking into the sun, even the setting sun. Jordan moved the shadow of his hand across the boy's face. He didn't blink.

"Darrel—Darrel, can you hear me?"

The boy didn't answer but Althea did.

"Jordie, can you see Balthan—the homunculus? Is it still in there?"

Hang Balthan and his talisman, Jordan thought, if they left his brother blind and dumb. All the same, taking the globe from the boy's hands might be the best way to break whatever enchantment had come over him. The glass was slick with oil, as slippery as a bucket of eels. Jordan wanted to use both hands to hold it, but Darrel went limp the instant it was lifted off his fingertips. The older brother hugged the younger and snared the globe between them.

Squirt's eyes had closed. His breathing was shallow, but not dangerously slow. Jordan shifted the boy's weight into his left arm and reached for the talisman pressed against his breastbone.

"Let me see it!" Althea took it from Jordan's hand.

"Be careful," he chided.

"He's there—Balthan's there—right in the center. He's safe. He's—" her voice dropped ominously "—it's coming back. The darkning's coming back."

Thirteen

Thick clouds rose from the water of Britanny Bay before the sunset glow faded. The stars and moons were hidden, and in the fireless camp where the travellers from Hawksnest ate a cold supper, it was impossible to see hands, food, or the ground beneath their feet.

Darrel lay in his cloak. He hadn't moved of his own will since Jordan lifted the talisman from his fingertips. By all they knew of illness and healcraft, the boy was unharmed from his brush with Balthan's magic. His flesh was neither too warm nor cold. His breathing remained steady, neither loud nor labored. In the soft light of Althea's handfire, Jordan opened the boy's eyes gently with his thumbs. Both pupils contracted swiftly and equally.

"There's nothing the matter with him," Althea concluded. "He's asleep."

"Then why doesn't he move? Why doesn't he wake up when I open his eyes?"

"I don't know!" Althea's tongue was as sharp as it had been since their journey began at Hawksnest. She had no concern to spare for a healthy boy. When the darkning reappeared in the talisman, it was blacker than ever before. As for Balthan's homunculus, it remained within the darkning and whether it pointed north-northeast or north to the city was anyone's guess.

If Jordan, to whom she had given her vassal's oath, had asked, Althea would have used the remaining volatile oil. She would have broken the glass itself to free the homunculus—if Jordan had been the least bit curious or anxious for *her* brother. Her mood was as dark as the sky . . . or the streak within the talisman.

"I'll take the first watch. I'll sit outside the trees. If there's light on the road or in the holding I'll see it and call," Drum offered. His generosity was tempered by a strong desire to be somewhere, anywhere, else.

"I can watch from here," Jordan countered from the boy's side. "There's no need for either of you to watch. I'm not planning to sleep until the Squirt wakes up."

Shrugging silently, Drum returned to his usual place between Althea and Jordan. His cloak snapped when he shook it out; his basket creaked when he settled his shoulders against it. "Wake me—if you change your mind."

Jordan wouldn't change his mind until the boy was lively again. He heard Drum yawn, stretch, and sink quickly into the rhythms of sleep. He waited for the telltale sounds of Althea making her nest against the pony's saddle.

"Go to sleep," he advised when the sounds were not forthcoming.

"Do you think we'll find Balthan tomorrow in the city?"

"Find him—probably. Rescue him—your guess is as good as mine. We'll learn soon enough. Go to sleep."

Althea rearranged her cloak into a blanket cocoon. "Are you sorry you came?" When Jordan did not answer straightaway, she guessed she knew the answer and drew the cloak around her like a turtle retreating into its shell.

"No—" Jordan said finally. "It's made a man of me as nothing else could. More than a Virtue Quest with my father's name and wealth beside me and twenty or more in the cohort at my back. I've become a lord, an oath-holder, with vassals to defend."

"He's going to be all right. I'm sure of it."

Jordan didn't know which brother she meant and at that moment didn't much care. "Aye—go to sleep." Squirt's head rested in his lap; Jordan could feel his brother's breath on his forearm. If he should doze off, the boy's first move would waken him.

The hours passed beneath him, like waves beneath an anchored boat. Drum snored when he rolled onto his back. Althea dreamed restlessly. She cried out once. Jordan was just about to leave Squirt when Althea's nightmare ended, and, with a contented sigh, she escaped whatever had frightened her.

Another motionless hour slipped into eternity. Jordan scarcely knew if his eyes were open when he saw Lord Shamino stride into the camp. The ranger's features limed with silver. He reached into Althea's basket; he removed the talisman. His teeth shone when he held the globe up to study it. Long, pointed teeth—like a wolf or a bear. Jordan raised his arm; his eyes were open. Shamino looked at him and frowned.

A frogish syllable fell off Jordan's tongue. The Companion vanished utterly before he uttered another. Lord Shamino was the object of many legends and mysteries, but he wasn't a ghost. Nor had there been a ghost beside Althea's basket—merely Jordan's unrelieved worries.

An owl came hooting to its roost; then, it, too, was silent. Another figure appeared by the basket—silvery as Lord Shamino had been except for his crown, which was gold. He looked for the talisman, but could not find it.

"My lord?" Jordan's voice was too faint to reach his own ears, much less the man at the basket. He cleared his throat and tried again. "My Lord British?"

The crowned head turned, but the face was not the familiar one impressed on Britannia's coins. This strange lord had a long aquiline nose and eyes as sharp as any knife.

"Jordan?"

The voice belonged to Althea and the apparition vanished.

"Jordan—is something wrong?"

No longer drifting above his dreams, Jordan crashed through them. His limbs were stiff with neglect and cold. He could not feel Squirt's breath. Panic surged through the older brother. When the paralysis had boiled away, Jordan could feel his brother's chest rise and the faint breeze across his arm when it fell.

"No—nothing."

"You said something. Do you remember? Were you dreaming?"

"I must have been." Peers on their Quest occasionally received guidance from an apparition. Lord Erwald said he knew it was time to end his Quest when the Avatar came to him in a dream, warning him that Spirituality lay beyond his grasp. But the Avatar never wore a crown.

"How is Darrel?"

Jordan smoothed the boy's unmussed hair. "The same. Sleeping, I guess. I hope."

"I dreamt about Balthan."

"And how was *he*?"

"Sleeping, too. I—I couldn't wake him. When I tried to touch him, my hands disappeared."

A shiver raced up Jordan's spine. The boy moved beneath his arms. "Squirt. Squirt—wake up!"

The boy did not, but he moved of his own will, turning on his side and tucking a hand between his cheek and the torn, stiff cloth of Jordan's trousers.

"He moved! All by himself!" Jordan sat up straight. Squirt resisted the sudden movement, digging his bitten, ragged fingernails into the still-tender flesh of his brother's left thigh. Jordan winced, then something brushed against his hair, and, without thinking, he shoved his brother aside to reach for his sword.

"Did I scare you?" Althea asked, all innocence and concern. "I just thought—well, I'm awake now, and if Darrel's all right—maybe you'd want to get some sleep?"

"Aye," Jordan said, not daring to say more. His heart hammered and the need to attack the nearest moving object was still strong within him.

On hands and knees, Jordan felt his way to Althea's cloak. It was too short, but it smelled of her. Jordan's dreams kept him warm.

"Darrel! What's—? *Squirt!*"

All-too-familiar shouts yanked Jordan out of his sleep. Instead of Althea smiling lustily in his arms, there was Althea with her arms full of his brother and a disgusted grimace on her face. The idyll hadn't quite escaped; if he closed his eyes quickly, without moving another muscle, he might be able to catch up with it—

"Look what you've done!"

Jordan had to look. The dream Althea disappeared into fond memory. The front of the real Althea's tunic was streaked with broken eggs. Jordan struck out with his leg as his brother squirted by. The boy went sprawling; Jordan caught and held onto a flailing foot.

"What did you do?" he demanded, morning grogginess making him sound angrier than he was—if that were possible.

The boy spun, his shoe slipped and he was almost free before Jordan clamped down. Squirt lay on his back, acutely aware that the least twitch of protest would leave him with a sprained ankle.

"I got you breakfast." The boy's voice was thick with tears.

"Cat's-in-the-coop," Jordan exclaimed before realizing how appropriate the comment was. Letting go of Squirt's shoe, he got to his feet. "Did anyone see you?"

"No," Darrel insisted, wiping his nose on an already filthy sleeve.

Drum contradicted him. "Aye—there's a long-strider coming through the fields. His hair is long and grey. His beard as well. He wears a long robe and carries a crook."

Jordan caught his brother's arm and hauled him, sobbing, to his feet. "Hythloth take you and keep you—don't you remember *why* we didn't approach the hold for hospitality?"

The boy twisted and tugged; his brother's grip remained an iron manacle over his wrist. Jordan knew all his tricks.

"I didn't mean it!" he insisted.

"You didn't mean to get caught, that's all." Jordan shook the boy until his teeth rattled, then turned to Drum. "How many—just one, just a staff?"

"Aye. Lean and spare. Looks like he knows what he's about."

"And we can't give the eggs back," Althea reminded them all as she shook gooey mess from her fingers. "Oh, Darrel, I turned my back on you for one moment and you were gone. You promised . . . you swore—"

"It's not my fault—"

"Then who's fault is it?"

Jordan began to shake Squirt again, but this time the boy was ready and used the motion to free himself. He ran out the opposite side of the grove. Jordan was ready to follow until Drum stopped him.

"There's no time for that now. He'll come back like a bad meal. Worry about the long-strider."

Taking a swipe at his hair and the seams of his tunic, Jordan was as ready as he could be when a man his own height and his father's age strode into their camp.

"What leaves travellers on the hill over a cold night and brings visitors to the chicken coop at sunrise?"

When Jordan did not immediately answer, Althea started to explain for him. He silenced her with a curt gesture the holder could not see. There was something odd about the man—he didn't seem particularly angry, for one thing. The Peer's son wanted a few moments to think. The holder's clothes were plain, but not poor—if he was the holder. He wore no jewelry, not even the signet of his holder's oath. Or did he? Jordan spotted the wink of precious metal beneath the rough collar.

"We are on a Quest, my lord."

The man stiffened. Jordan did the same, fearing that he'd guessed wrong. Then the holder smiled and extended his right hand.

"No lord here." He clapped his left hand over Jordan's right hand and seemed a bit surprised when the young man did not complete the four-hand greeting one Peer gave to another. "I was Menagel when I was born and will be so when I die. You've sharp eyes." Menagel hooked a finger under the silver chain and lifted out his Virtue Quest medallion.

There were tiny pits along the circumference and nowhere else. Somewhere Menagel had thirty-three small, perfect diamonds—unless he had given them away. Peers who received Humility's enlightenment often did that. Jordan, by contrast, was unabashedly proud to have guessed the holder's virtue.

"Thank you, my lord."

Menagel smiled wisely as he shook his head and released Jordan's hand. "Not 'lord,' remember? But tell me: Why did you shun my door? Have you lost your way to Compassion's shrine? Did you leave the road so late you feared to wake an old man?"

Jordan stared at his feet. He rubbed the toe of one buskin against the heel of the other before answering. "We're—" he coughed and cleared his throat—"we're not on a Quest. And, truth to tell, we've not found much hospitality on the road to Britain City. We saw nothing from the road to think your door would be open where others had not been."

Menagel stroked his flowing beard. "It is open to all—but, though it grieves me, I understand why you would shun it. Now I invite you to Serenity for a meal. All of you, even that rascal who got among the chickens. Your brother, by the looks of you both."

"Darrel—we call him Squirt. You know why."

"He is welcome at Serenity, whatever you call him."

Serenity's roofbeams were high. Its walls were whitewashed within and without. A modest woman—Menagel's wife or daughter, she didn't say which—worked at an open hearth framed with glazed tiles, each of which shone like glass. The pots and spoons were clean at Hawksnest, but at Serenity even the pothooks were polished until they glittered in the morning light. Earthware bricks were laid in geometric patterns across the floor, with drain channels grouted between them. The floors at Hawksnest were invariably planking or rough stone covered with straw that was shovelled into the midden when it became too rank.

Althea got two steps into the pristine kitchen and retreated to the garth where she unlaced her buskins. She left them on the clean-swept threshold stone. Jordan followed her lead, wishing that he had presentable clothes and a suitable house-gift as well. Drum understood what was required once Althea tugged on his sleeve and tilted her head at the four buskins lined up outside the door, but Squirt had to be carried from the kitchen by his brother.

"He's just another peasant," Darrel said, refusing to undo the buckles of his ankle-high shoes.

"He's a *Peer*."

"His clothes are undyed and homespun."

"His Quest medallion's marked for Humility. And you're not tracking road dirt on his floors. Get your shoes off—*now!*"

"He *looks* like a peasant. Why doesn't he dress like us if he's a Peer?"

"Because he's got humility the way you're going to have a tanned backside . . ."

Squirt shed his shoes and scampered into the kitchen, aided by the breeze from his brother's hand.

Lord Ironhawk insisted his sons be taught that Humility was a virtue as valued as any of the rest, but the tutors he hired and the richly illuminated manuscripts in his library conveyed a different message: Humility led to humbleness, and humbleness to meekness, from which it was only a small step to submissiveness, a very dangerous attitude for those who also valued Honor and Valor.

Jordan could humble himself easily before the Companions, and before his father—especially when Lord Ironhawk was florid with rage—but otherwise he regarded Humility as something of an imperfection in the Avatar's moral philosophy. How, after all, could a man adequately display the courageous virtues from his knees?

Menagel showed him. Life on Serenity holding was sim-

ple without being impoverished. The food was as good as
any served at his father's table for all that it was served on
plain wooden plates and—for this breakfast at least—was
both meatless and eggless. Countless questions about virtue
and enlightenment swirled in Jordan's mind—none of which
could be politely asked until they'd answered all the questions their host put to them. When Althea, Drum, and Jordan
were finished with a truthful, but abbreviated, account of
their journey, the boy plunged into the lull.

"Why do you live like this?" Darrel demanded. "Why
don't you have retainers to serve your food? Is it because
you're *humble*?"

Jordan groaned and Althea rolled her eyes heavenward,
but Menagel was unperturbed. "Exactly so," he explained.
"The essence of humility lies in never confusing your wants
with your needs. Once I understood that, my Quest was
over and I was content."

The boy squirmed on the bench, studying the kitchen and
what else could be seen of the modest house. "I'd need a
wall for my weapons," he decided, thinking of Erwald's
imposing armory. "But I'd keep the rest just as it is—"

"Squirt!" Jordan lashed out beneath the table.

The boy rubbed his leg. "He doesn't have to get all
dressed up to eat his supper."

Menagel tousled the boy's hair, agreeing that quilted sur-
cotes with stiff, high collars formed no part of Serenity's
life. Which was why, though he was invited to the twice-
a-year Conclaves, he never attended. "Peers like your father
admire my virtue best from a distance. Up close I make
them very uncomfortable." He winked at Darrel, who
grinned and forgot his bruised shin.

"But I am not ignorant of the world." Menagel turned
from the boy to his brother. "It is not a good time for the

sons of Lord Ironhawk to be loose in Britain City. It is not, I fear, a good time for any citizen of Britannia, anywhere.''

Menagel of Serenity hold told them what he knew of the great city he could see clearly from his front door. ''There is a miasma over the city; some days I can see it like the harbor fog, other days are clear. It is no natural fog—''

''A shadow?'' Althea asked, thinking of Balthan's talisman.

Shadow or miasma, what mattered was that each time it oozed out of the harbor, Britain City became, and remained, a less pleasant, less virtuous place.

''I've heard it said Lord Blackthorn walks with heavy feet,'' Jordan ventured, repeating once again the words he'd heard from Iolo Arbelest.

''So does any man who bears a great burden,'' Menagel replied. He was humble; he did not judge or mete out justice. ''I am not privy to Lord Blackthorn's thoughts, but I am certain he is as much a victim of the miasma as any man.''

Generosity came naturally to Menagel of Serenity. He could see a victim in a man who saw enemies and traitors everywhere, and who imposed his own rigid interpretation of the Avatar's virtues on the citizens of Britannia.

''He is not a victim of anything,'' Jordan asserted. ''He's become an oppressor, pure and simple. He must be removed before things get worse.''

Jordan did not want to imagine what could be worse than what he had learned sitting in the bright, congenial kitchen. Since disbanding the Great Council, Lord Blackthorn had placed all the cities of Britannia under his personal desmene's justice.

''Why would the citizens tolerate it? Why did they not appeal quickly to the guilds and the peers?'' Althea mused.

''The miasma,'' Menagel repeated. ''We have not felt it

outside the walls and I pray—yes, *pray*, though I know not to whom—that we never shall. I was there one day when it came off the harbor. I felt a cold hand around my heart, clouding my eyes. I was walking down a quiet street, there was a little girl playing with a kitten; she picked it up and began smashing it against the wall. I told her to stop; she looked at me, but went ahead, though the kitten—poor thing—was already dead.

"A rage took me. I saw my hand moving toward her, taking her by the neck as she held the kitten. I lifted her off the ground; I meant to kill her, Jordan—I, who eat no butchered meat, *I* meant to kill her."

Althea swallowed hard and found her voice. "But you didn't?"

Menagel shook his head. "I did not. The hand of destiny intervened; the girl's mother dropped a honey jar on my head. When I awoke, I was alone in an alley. The air was clear again, but I could not—cannot ever—forget what I would have done." He concealed his grief-stricken face behind his hands. "Don't go into the city," he begged them. "The laws are not enough. The Inquisitors are not enough. Lord British was wrong, I fear. The Avatar was wrong, also. Evil was never banished—it has hidden in the hearts of each of us, and the miasma awakens it. Lord Blackthorn's laws and his Inquisitors stand between Britannia and the abyss."

Squirt returned his brother's earlier favor and kicked Jordan in the shin. *What laws?* he mouthed. Althea and even Drum added their own curiosity with raised eyebrows their host could not see.

Oppressors created laws and laws created oppressors, Jordan wanted to tell them, the two went hand-in-hand. No miasma, no magic, and no evil were necessary. Why else had Lord British always refused to issue laws just as he refused the title and dignities of a king? But, since Jordan himself did not wish to seem like an oppressor, he bowed to their will. "Menagel—what laws?" Then he added, to satisfy his own curiosity, "What Inquisitors?"

There were only eight laws, one for each of the Avatar's virtues, reducing them to rigid precepts. As with any such reduction, Lord Blackthorn's code clearly stated the consequences of failure but left the definition of that failure open for interpretation. The black-robed Inquisitors made that interpretation and their verdict could not be appealed.

"Don't go into the city," Menagel pleaded. "Go back to your homes. Warn your father. Warn the others. Some are more susceptible to the miasma than others, but none are safe. By the Eight, the Three, and the One, I have seen it for myself—*in* myself."

They stayed in the kitchen of Serenity hold through the morning. Jordan asked questions about Lord Blackthorn, the eight laws, and, especially, the Inquisitors. Menagel answered each the same way: Virtue was moribund in Britain City. The miasma infected its citizens. Humbly, Menagel acknowledged that he, himself, was infected.

"Don't go into the city. There is nothing there that can help you. If the one you seek has been in the hands of the Inquisition all this time—then he has become one of them."

With her mind's eye, Althea watched as the homunculus rose into the darkning. "Magicians follow their own path through the eight circles of magic," she muttered. "They aspire to knowledge and mastery of the eight reagent elements. Balthan turned his back to the straight paths of virtue while he was still a child." She folded her hands on the table to hide her trembling fingers. "He would become an excellent Inquisitor," she concluded in a sad, resigned tone.

Menagel wrapped his hands over hers. "Pray for him, then, but do not go near him."

Jordan paced the length of the room. The white walls, scrubbed floor, and shiny hearth had lost their attraction. "We do not pray, beg, plead, or beseech," he asserted. "We do not *submit* to fate. I will not humble myself. If I must have a flaw, I'm glad my flaw is pride. I'm leaving now. Which of you is coming with me?"

Squirt was at his brother's side before the speech was finished. Althea left her hands beneath Menagel's, and Drum, for once, was visibly torn. He reached for Althea; his hand fell short. He opened his mouth, and said nothing. Jordan sat on the threshold stone, lacing his buskins with grim determination.

"The risks are too great, Jordie. I can't let you go," Althea called after him.

Jordan stomped his feet as he stood. The earthenware tiles echoed the sound. "You can't stop me, either."

"Not for my brother. Not for Balthan."

"No, not for Balthan—for *me*. I wouldn't turn back if a dragon blocked the path to a shrine—and I'm certainly not going to turn back for a *cloud*." Jordan returned to the table. He took a broken loaf of bread and gestured with it at Althea. "I never thought I'd hear myself say this, but you're wrong about your brother. He's an arrogant bastard, not an Inquisitor." Then, tucking the loaf under his arm, he put Serenity behind him.

"Althea?" Drum found his voice and the strength to touch the woman he adored. "Althea—let's go."

"Don't go," Menagel pleaded. "If the miasma touches you, it will corrupt you. I *know*."

"Aye," the farrier agreed. "He knows." Gently, Drum freed Althea's hands. "And he's too humble to fight back. Come on."

* * *

The sky over Britain City was a cloudless blue when Jordan led his three companions into the angled barbican. Lord Blackthorn's so-called Code of Virtue was posted prominently on either side of the gate, along with a list of proscribed citizens who'd incurred the Inquisition's wrath. Balthan Wanderson's name was not among them.

The new law of Compassion dictated that every citizen should surrender one-half his income to charitable causes. Jordan argued that the silver he carried was not income from rents, taxes, dues, or customs; it was a loan and therefore exempt from the law. He was prepared to challenge the law itself, but that proved unnecessary. The guards succumbed to old-fashioned bribery, passing the foursome through the gate with what had become the customary warning:

"Keep clear of trouble and the Inquisition will keep clear of you."

It was advice the citizens of Britain City seemed to have taken to heart. The streets were uncommonly quiet. Merchants waited silently for customers who either paid the asking price or departed without bargaining. Neighbors recognized each other with barely perceptible smiles and even the children played singly or in small groups close by the family stoop.

"It seems so peaceful," Althea observed, "so extraordinarily peaceful and perfect."

"Like the eye of a storm," Jordan added in a hoarse whisper.

Fourteen

*D*usk came quietly to Britain City. The tower bells rang the evening peal to empty streets. Though the night remained warm and fair despite clouds above the horizon, no lovers promenaded through the plaza; no bodyguarded merchants scurried to their moneychangers with the day's receipts; no unhappy souls staggered toward the flickering lamps of neighborhood taverns. The night-watch patrolled the walls in tight quartets, their festooned pikes resting uneasily against their shoulders, but, long before midnight, even they took shelter in the corner block-houses.

Jordan used a silver piece to rent a room at an establishment called the Hunter's Horn. It was a reputable place although the ceilings were still too low for him or Drum, and the barren rope-mattress bed dominated the room. He availed himself of a bath in the inn's kitchen and offered to provide the pence for anyone else who wanted one. Drum and Squirt shook their heads to say no; Althea longed to scrub herself from toe to scalp but not—thank you very much, just the same—in the middle of a tavern kitchen.

When Jordan returned, looking relaxed, refreshed, and radish-red, Althea pulled the blanket over her head and softly cried herself to sleep.

The change-ringers played mumble-the-peg, as was their nightly custom, below the rope room of the tower. They kept one eye on the hour-candle in its glass chimney. When the fifth knob was a puddle around the wick, the loser climbed the steep, narrow steps to the rope room and clanged the great bass bell once for midnight.

In all of Britain City, the change-ringer was the only one to see the billowing cloud above the harbor bear down on the city like a mailed fist.

"Black fog's rising," he said to the other ringers on rejoining them.

Nothing more had to be said. The man who owned the knife reclaimed it and lashed it carefully into its sheath.

The four travellers from Hawksnest slept soundly, but restlessly. The blanket migrated from shoulders to feet, from one side of the bed to the other as they contended for it in their dreams. The sun had not risen when Drum, eyes closed and snoring, shoved Jordan over the edge. Normally a cheerful riser, Jordan got up from the floor with his teeth showing. The farrier lay on his back, a child's grin in the middle of his dark, wiry beard. Jordan lowered his fists.

Their room had a window, which cost an extra pence. The shutters were closed when they first entered the room, and they'd left them that way to keep out the damp sea air while they slept. Jordan unwound the thong. A little sea air couldn't possibly hurt his unbathed companions who were surely responsible for the tight feeling around his eyes and down into his neck and shoulders.

He didn't expect a panorama of the city and the harbor for a single copper coin, but all he could see was fog that reeked of everything that had ever lived or died on the tidal flats. It made Jordan's eyes water and, a half-moment later, it dislodged his companions from their slumber.

"Hammers and bells!" Drum was the first on his feet. He wobbled noticeably and warded his eyes with his forearm when he looked toward the window. "Close it up, for love or pity's sake." He massaged the ridge of bone above his eyes and an arc that went behind his ear and down his neck.

Jordan winced in sympathy when the farrier reached the knotted sinews in the crook of his neck. His were throbbing too. He closed the shutters, for all the good it did. Althea was awake, and unwilling to sit, much less stand.

"My whole head hurts," she complained. "My eyes hurt. My *hair* hurts."

Drum and Jordan exchanged identical glances—*she* didn't have to contend with an achy beard.

"I must have drunk too much wine with dinner."

Althea continued to moan, but unless the wine was bad or drugged, it was not the source of their agony. Then the boy was awake. He actually sprang out of the bed; Althea clung to the rope-mattress like a storm-tossed bee.

"Ow—don't do that!"

Darrel made an eyeblink study of the almost-adults with their bleary eyes and pained expressions. "What's the matter with you?" he demanded. Jordan swore at him and told him in blunt terms to be quiet. The boy retreated to the wash basin in the corner to reassess the situation. He felt fine; they clearly did not, and that, Squirt knew, boded ill for him. He put on his sincerest smile. "May I please go down for breakfast? Please?"

Jordan massaged his whole face before replying, "That sounds like a good idea. Maybe what we need is food."

The mere thought of food, Althea proclaimed from beneath the blanket which she no longer had to share, made her nauseous. If they would close the door quietly as they left, she would go back to sleep. They obliged. The click of the latch was no louder than the creak of the ropes when she turned over. There were no other sounds piercing the walls or floor. The only distraction came from within her skull; but it trampled any hope the young woman nurtured of sleeping through her misery.

Leaving her buskins by the door, Althea padded barefoot into the hallway. Her hair fell in tangled coils around her face and in front of her eyes. Sleeve laces dangled from her elbows. Her belt was twisted with the knot pressed into the small of her back; one end was long enough to trip her as she walked. Althea of Hawksnest would never appear in such disarray, but Althea of Hawksnest was not herself. She gripped the banister with both hands.

Strangers filled the common room—all quiet, all staring. Althea stared back, wondering where Drum and the others had gotten to, then the kitchen erupted.

"I don't want to hear about it! Cold meat and turnips is not—I repeat, *not* —the breakfast I paid for!"

Jordan's voice was loud enough to wake the dead. Althea winced and made her way to the kitchen. Four drudges cowered together while Jordan threatened them.

"The hearth's cold," Drum whispered to Althea when he noticed her. "And the innkeeper's locked up all the knives."

"I'm hungry. My brother's hungry. My friends—"

The double door to the courtyard burst open. "—have headaches as have we all," finished the innkeeper's wife, who was also the cook, as she slammed a basket on the carving board before confronting Jordan. "The air's bad," she explained both softly and emphatically. "And listening to you rant isn't helping anyone, including you. You were told at the gate to stay out of trouble—now is the time to do just that. Fill your plate with what's there. Starve for all we care—but do it quietly or you'll find yourself in a place you'd rather not be."

"I'll not be threatened by the likes of you."

Jordan's right hand dropped to his left hip. Everyone in the kitchen drew a frightened breath, but Jordan's sword was in the room where he'd left it. The cook filled Jordan's empty hands with small round loaves of day-old bread.

"I will try to remember that you're new to Britain City and don't know to keep to yourself when the fog clings like this. But one more peep and I'll summon the guard *and* the Inquisition—if they haven't heard you already."

Squirt slipped away from Althea, who never pinched him hard enough to hold him. Diving under the table, he crept to Jordan's side. In the normal order of life, there was nothing Squirt enjoyed more than watching his brother fight. If a thing could be swung, thrust, or thrown, Jordan could wield it as a weapon. But there was nothing normal in this kitchen—in this whole city.

When Jordan's fingers began to twitch, Squirt grabbed his brother's right forearm. Bread went flying. Jordan cuffed his brother's ear and shook his arm mightily, but the boy held on. Murderous rage contorted Jordan's face when Squirt got a quick glimpse of it.

"It's the air, Jordie," the boy gasped. "The *air!*"

It wasn't the air. *It* was akin to Squirt's secret demon, that tightly coiled monster lurking behind his conscious self, always ready to spring free and reduce his thoughts to chaos. When the demon unwound, and his thoughts raced, everything in the world was transformed into threats. The boy had to defend himself from the danger he felt with the demon's sharp senses. He had to kick and scream until he was exhausted. He *had* to—or the demon would devour him.

Jordan didn't have a secret demon in his head. Jordan's demon was everywhere and shared by everyone in Britain City, except by Squirt himself whose mind already had a demon in residence. The boy couldn't tell if Jordan resisted the demon, or if he'd surrendered to it. In practical terms, that didn't matter very much. If Jordan Hawson was going to fight until he was exhausted, everyone in the kitchen might die.

Unless Squirt could scare the demon out of Jordan the way their lord father could scare it out of Squirt. The boy was seriously handicapped; he was smaller and weaker than his brother. Intimidation was out of the question, so he tried the opposite tack: When Jordan bashed him into the table, Squirt pretended—quite convincingly—that the collision had killed him.

Jordan froze in mid-motion, staring at the overturned table and his brother sprawled between the legs. He might well have been pole-axed. His eyes were dazed; his mouth hung open. His legs held him up by habit, not will. Squirt knew the feeling. Lord Erwald or some other adult would slap the sense back into him after his enemy left him, but slapping Jordan—even a dumb-struck Jordan—called for more bravery than the boy possessed.

The kitchen was stone-quiet until Jordan shuddered.

"I had to do it. I *had* to," Squirt explained hastily, ready to run if he needed to.

Jordan dragged his hands through his hair. "My headache's gone," he mumbled in amazement.

"Mine too," Althea agreed, and after her, the inn's cook and Drum.

The drudges said nothing, but, like Jordan, they touched their scalps and their sour expressions melted into giddy smiles. Squirt smiled broadly himself. He stood up and dusted himself off.

"You knew . . ." Jordan mused. "You knew."

Jordan could no more explain what had happened than Squirt could. There was magic involved, a malevolent magic that hurt his head, and drove him mad. Jordan had no aptitude for magic. He could read the magicians' alphabet, recite their runes, mix reagents until the moons fell into the sea and nothing would happen.

Everyone at Hawksnest simply assumed Darrel was similarly head-blind. There was no alternative: Squirt defeated every attempt to teach him to read cursive script. Who had the time, or energy, to try him with runes?

"Come here," Jordan told the boy, who immediately ducked between the table legs. The older brother tried to catch him, but his timing was off. The boy was uncanny. If there was one chance in a hundred to escape, Squirt seized chance as certainty and was gone.

Uncanny.

Balthan was uncanny, too, doing things with linear magic no one else ever dreamed of. But Balthan never let anyone forget his ambition to become an eighth circle mage . . .

Jordan shook the thought of Squirt in a magician's long, embroidered robes out of his head, and realized that the headache had returned. The throbbing was faint and muffled. A month ago, even a day ago, the young man would have ignored it, but he was a warrior and if a magician's motto was *know thyself*, a warrior's was *know thine enemy*. Jordan Hawson's newest enemy had returned. He studied the faces around him. Smiles were fading, heads tilting, shoulders rising. None of them seemed aware that their pain had returned, and without awareness they could not fight.

"Relax," he told everyone, shrugging the tension out of his neck and shoulders. His enemy retreated, but no one imitated him. Jordan knew instinctively that this was no time to demand obedience.

Jordan fought a losing battle. Through exercise and concentration, he was able to keep the unseen enemy from reducing him to a mindless beast again, but the enemy was in the air and so long as he breathed, it assaulted him. The cold meat and turnips rumbled through his gut like stones in a rattle. He sat between Althea and Drum in the public room of the inn pondering the question: Did he feel well enough to vomit?

A bit before noon there was a ruckus in the street and, after thinking of his absent brother, Jordan staggered to the window. A trio of mail-shirted guards had cornered someone and were pummeling the poor wretch with sticks. Nearby —not taking part in the beating, but not stopping it either —was a nondescript woman in a black robe. An Inquisitor, Jordan decided.

The guards dragged their quarry before her. The wretch's face was bloodied beyond recognition, but his hair was dark brown and he was too tall by half. Jordan lost interest and returned to the bench being very careful not to tread on anyone's toes.

"What was it?" Althea whispered.

"Nothing."

She slumped against him. Her jaw pressed a nerve each time she swallowed. Strands of her hair tickled his nose. What could have been pleasant was instead torture. Jordan's arm was moving before he recognized the mark of his enemy. He could keep himself from striking her, but he couldn't make himself enjoy having her snuggled against him.

"Thea—you'll have to move." His voice was as gentle as he could make it.

Althea straightened. "You don't have to get nasty about it," she snarled.

"I'm—" Jordan began in the same tone, then pressed his fingertips in circles around his aching eyes "—I'm sorry."

She called Jordan a name he wouldn't have hung on his worst enemy, and, once again, the omnipresent enemy sought control. Jordan's beleaguered conscience reminded the rest of him that Althea hadn't said anything: Her pain was talking, and she was not hardened against it as he was.

"I'm sorry. Lean if you want."

By then, of course, Althea wanted nothing to do with him. She sat erect on the bench with her back pressed flat against the wall, exchanging one pain for another.

There was an outbreak of nearly civil conversation when the noon peal was abbreviated to a single chime. Be grateful for the little things, several people said together. My mother-in-law doesn't arrive until tomorrow, added a weary little man by the cold hearth.

"Did you hear that?" Jordan whispered to his companions who did not respond. "That means it's not going to last forever. By tomorrow it will be over—"

"Oh—be quiet, Jordie. How do you know what anything means?"

Jordan sighed. He didn't know anything, perhaps, but he needed to believe something.

"I hope you're right," Drum agreed belatedly. "I can last a day and a night, if I have to, but much longer than that, and I'm going to have to get out of here."

"Aye—no matter what, we leave tomorrow." But not today. Jordan's eyes and thoughts came slowly into focus: a roomful of strangers sitting silently in a darkened room.

Not one of them, including himself, had ventured onto the street. He'd seen guards patrolling through the dense fog; he'd seen them, the Inquisitor, and their victim; but no one else. The cook had been in the courtyard, not the street.

The enemy had a larger purpose, Jordan reasoned. It used pain to keep people pinned down in one spot. Maybe he should try going to the door to learn if the pain was worse there? It was certainly worse when Jordan stood up, but only for a heartbeat or two, then the throbs subsided to their former level. After that, it didn't matter whether Jordan walked to the stairwell, the kitchen, or the front door—so he opened it and stood on the threshold. As far as the young man could see—which, in the fog, was not far—the street was deserted. Doors were shut tight, and the windows remained shuttered from the previous night.

"Shut the damned door!" a none-too-friendly voice barked from the room behind Jordan.

"You're letting in the damned air!" came a different voice, no friendlier.

Jordan had more trouble controlling the urge to lash out when the likely victims were strangers. Leaving the door wide open, he strode to the middle of the street and took a deep breath of the damned air. The streets were not completely quiet. There were shouts—screams—coming from the center of the city. Since his headache had gotten no worse, Jordan considered taking a walk in that direction. He'd gotten a few steps when he heard other sounds: horseshoes clattering against cobblestones. Fog played tricks with sound; Jordan cocked his head to unscramble them.

He'd figured that they weren't far when Squirt jumped from the eaves to land beside him.

"Get inside—*quick*—before they get here."

"Who? Why?"

Jordan resisted the frantic tugging on his sleeve until a

moving wall of horseflesh separated from the fog, but by then it was too late. The guards saw Jordan and Squirt, and the door they pulled shut behind them. They dismounted, and now pounded on the door in Lord Blackthorn's name.

The faces in the public room were painfully easy to read. The only person able or willing to stand beside Jordan was his hapless brother. Whatever trouble Jordan reaped by standing in the fog-shrouded street, he was going to confront it alone.

Five men crowded through the door. They wore knee-length hauberks that were slit up the middle. Their helmets were trimmed with chain mail and fitted with heavy nose guards. Two had beards, one carried a parrying dagger in addition to his longsword. He was the one who stood nose-to-nose with Jordan.

"What's your name, *boy*? Why were you sneaking around in the street, *boy*? What did you think you'd see, *boy*?"

The guard shouted as if he knew he was the only one in the world without a headache. He blasted Jordan with breath as rank as any dragon's.

Jordan bent, but he didn't retreat. "Jordan Hawson, heir of Hawksnest, off the Old Paladin's Road. Who—"

"I'll do the asking, *boy*!" Dragon-mouth planted a gauntleted hand on Jordan's chest and shoved him against the wall. "What were you looking for out there, *boy*?"

Nothing—not the world's worst breath or headache—could make Jordan suicidal, which is what he'd be if he kicked Dragon-mouth in his unprotected groin. He was unarmed and unarmored. The other four guards had the look of bullies who wouldn't hesitate to skewer a defenseless man. Jordan perceived that his best chance—his only chance—lay in grovelling like the laziest churl under the sun, but something was lost between perception and action.

His knees remained unbent, his eyes continued to radiate disbelief and defiance.

"One last chance, *boy*, or you'll do your talking to an Inquisitor—"

"He was l-l-looking for m-m-me." Squirt skidded between them, adding an array of tics to his stuttering enunciation. A palsied youth lived at Hawksnest and, with the cruelty common to children, Squirt led the way in teasing him. The precision of his mimicry did not excuse those taunts and slurs, but it saved Jordan. The boy jerked his arms and legs like a demented puppet. He crossed his eyes and spat his words. A gob of spittle landed on Dragon-mouth's cheek. Jordan feared for the worst, but Squirt's contortions were too sincere to invite retaliation.

The boy moistened his lips. "*Got* th-the shakes!" he exclaimed, launching another gob. Dragon-mouth retreated. "*Go* t-t-to healer. At h-home. *No* g-g-good! *K-k-come* h-h—"

Jordan dropped his arms protectively over Squirt's shoulders. He was ready to resume his role as older brother. "The boy's not right. They say the greatest healer of Britannia is Milan of Britain City. We thought—we hoped she could help him. Nobody at home can—" Squirt barked like a dog and drooled on his brother's hand. Jordan casually wiped it dry on the boy's shirt. "He's getting worse," he confided. "I don't know what we'll do if Milan can't help him."

Dragon-mouth locked his fingers in the Infinity ward-sign. "She can't help him today," he said, looking at Jordan, not Squirt. "Everybody stays indoors when the fog rolls in—it's posted at the barbican gate. You should've read the notices."

"I can see that now, sir. It won't happen again. I'll take

my brother to the healer's once the fog lifts and then, Destiny willing, we'll go home." Jordan's humility was less convincing than Squirt's palsy, but sufficient to impress Dragon-mouth.

"I'll let this pass if you give me your oath you'll keep—" the burly guard glanced down at Squirt who was drooling again, and looked away quickly "—keep *him* out of sight."

Dragon-mouth walked away. His cohort preceded him toward the door. Jordan was giving Squirt a congratulatory pat on the head when the guard turned around again.

"Just the two of you?" he asked. "When did you arrive in Britain City?"

"Yesterday. Sir."

"Through the barbican, or one of the other gates?"

Jordan swallowed hard. Beyond a doubt, the question had a right and a wrong answer, but he couldn't guess which might be which. He took refuge in the truth. "Through the barbican, sir. There were four of us."

"Where're the other two? Either of them magicians?" Dragon-mouth watched Jordan shake his head, then he picked another guest of the inn to intimidate. "Any magicians here? By the order of the regent, Lord Blackthorn, all magicians are to present themselves to the Inquisition for examination. Any magician failing to do this will be punished by dismemberment and death."

"Same if he does."

All eyes sought the source of the seditious whisper, but the rebel was indistinguishable among the pain-wearied guests.

"Reveal yourself!" Dragon-mouth commanded. "Pain of death—the traitor will reveal himself." The room remained silent. "Someone stands next to him—reveal him, or share his punishment!"

Two guests, standing far apart from each other, pointed fingers at the men standing closest to them. Dragon-mouth shoved his helmet up and pinched the bridge of his nose— the first indication Jordan had that the guards were not completely immune to headaches. "Search them all," he muttered to the four men in his cohort.

Pouches and purses were probed and returned to their owners lighter than they started. Jordan thought of the silver hanging from his belt and positioned Squirt to hide it, but neither he nor the boy was searched. The guard claimed four of Drum's pence were counterfeit, and added them to his own bulging pouch. The farrier's nostrils flared and his cheeks turned a dangerous red shade, but he kept his peace. The guard moved on to Althea.

Jordan couldn't imagine how the guards or anyone else expected to find a magician. Unlike guildsmen, magicians bore no achievement scars. Their style of dress was distinct; still, if a magician exchanged his long, embroidered robes for plainer stuff and denied any knowledge of magic, no one would be the wiser. But the guard took extra time with Althea. He examined her hands. He turned her head from right to left as if she were a beast for sale at the fair and he the prospective buyer. Althea was ash-white with terror. The color drained from Drum's face as well, but not from terror.

"What do you know of magic and magicians, dear lady?"

Althea gasped, but did not answer.

Dragon-mouth pushed Jordan and the boy aside in his eagerness to pursue the examination. "Maybe she knows a few spells herself."

He pushed the flaring sleeve of her woolen gown past her elbow then did the same with the tighter sleeve of the linen shift she wore beneath it. Pain darkened and dulled her eyes; the sun had raised a crop of freckles on her cheeks. Even so, any man could see that Althea was a beautiful, vulnerable, young woman.

"I have house-magic, the linear spells, and not all of them," Althea confessed softly.

" 'Linear spells.' " Dragon-mouth parodied Althea's tremulous voice, " 'and not all of them.' Well, now, dear lady —how would you know which ones you *didn't* have without someone to tell you. A lover. A magician lover . . . ?" He stroked Althea's hair and held her head at a dramatic angle. "A lover who told you his *secrets*? A lover you might be foolish enough to try to protect?"

The boy kicked Jordan deliberately among his other, aimless, twitches. "Do something!" he hissed.

Jordan began lamely: "The lady is with me."

Dragon-mouth appraised Ironhawk's heir with the same look he'd use for a dwarf mounted on a Valorian stallion. Jordan understood he'd have to do better if he hoped to improve the situation.

"She is an orphan, the ward of Erwald Lord Ironhawk. She tends the boy—" Squirt gave a timely sputter and twitch. "Lord Ironhawk has seen her taught such spells as she needs to be useful. He would have taught her more, but she is stupid. He has *plans* for her once the boy is healed."

It was just as well that Dragon-mouth released Althea's chin without looking at her again. If he'd seen the outrage replacing fear in her eyes, he'd never have believed Jordan's bold lies.

"So you're Lord Ironhawk's whelp, eh?" Dragon-mouth gave Jordan another, slightly less critical, top-to-toe stare. If he'd heard Jordan's previous assertions, he did not remember them. "Which side of the bed did you fall out of?"

"I am the rightful heir." This time there was no uncertainty in Jordan's voice.

"You might be at that." Dragon-mouth snapped his fingers and pointed to the door. His cohort reassembled and awaited him there. "Keep your nose clean, Hawk's son. A hero's name won't take you very far these days." He looked around the public room one last time. "There's a traitor here; mind you all, we mark it and we'll keep a close watch on this place until we find him. Stay put until the fog lifts. Live by the Code and you'll not suffer; break it and you'll find no mercy."

Althea fled the room as soon as the five men were gone. Drum followed her, then Jordan, and finally Squirt. The boy paused by the closed door of their room. Althea was sobbing, Jordan and Drum snarling at each other. He could go in, and maybe they'd all snarl at him instead of each other, but he'd done them enough favors for one day and didn't owe them any more. Tiptoeing past the door, Squirt scampered up a ladder, through a trapdoor, and emerged onto the fogclad roof of the inn.

Fifteen

*E*rwald Lord Ironhawk believed his sons should know
       something about city life in addition to the self-
       contained life of the Hawksnest estate. He began
taking his son with him on his seasonal treks to his native
city of Trinsic when Jordan was five, and he intended to
continue the tradition when his younger son reached the
same age. If anything, it was more important that Darrel
be familiar with a merchant's life because the boy would
not inherit the estate. Erwald wouldn't leave his younger
boy landless—he'd find a suitable cadet property somewhere when the time came—but Darrel was a second son,
a spare son in case anything happened to Jordan before
another generation was firmly established.

When Darrel was four, Erwald arranged to foster him
with his Trinsic relations. The following year the whole
family travelled down the Paladin's Road to see the boy
established in his new life. Not all the disasters of that

journey were Darrel's fault: He wasn't responsible for the flood that washed away the bridges, or the algae blight that turned Trinsic harbor into a sewer. The rain barrel that fell through the roof of the family mansion—that could have been a complete accident, too. Everything else could be traced directly back to the boy—or one of the household children he corrupted with his wild mischief.

Needless to say, the fosterage was cancelled and on those rare occasions since when Lord Erwald took his youngest son with him to Trinsic, he brought along extra men whose sole duty was keeping the boy in his proper place.

Britain City was much larger than Trinsic, and, with all its citizens cowering indoors waiting out the fog, virtually deserted. Squirt, standing with one foot on either side of the crown-tiles and his scrawny arms folded over his chest, couldn't decide whether to explore the quarters between himself and the bell-tower plaza or head the other way, toward the wall. He'd already explored the inn and its quarter thoroughly.

The adults, with their headaches, might be content with cold meat and mashed turnips but Squirt yearned for a more palatable meal. The boy filled his lungs with the thick air, sorting through the tastes and smells until he found one that appealed to him—frumenty custard—and set his course accordingly.

There was no need to descend to the cobbled streets where a wandering patrol might surprise him—not when every building leaned over the streets and the gap between quarters could be easily spanned by a surefooted, fearless boy. Here and there Squirt spied a dormer window that cried for closer examination. A toymaker's attic storeroom made the boy's heart ache, with its brightly painted puppets, hobby-horses, and shelf-upon-shelf of enamelled cohorts just waiting for a Peer's son to bring them to life. That is, Darrel understood that Peers were the only citizens rich enough to buy those dazzling statuettes for their children; not that he, personally, was allowed such luxuries.

His lord father's idea of a birthday present was a hand-lettered book about virtue—which Squirt wasn't allowed to touch anyway because his hands were always dirty.

The storeroom was deserted; the window was unlocked; and there were so many knights and paladins. No one would know. Squirt opened the window just a bit, then eased it down again. The Eye of Destiny would know. It saw everything—even through the fog. The boy didn't worry about the Eye when he stole food—he ate the food right away so the Eye would forget—but an enameled paladin; the Eye would see *that* no matter where he put it. Althea would buy it for him, if she had any money. Jordan might; he had that fistful of silver, and beneath the layers of bluster and bullying, Jordan was as mushy as ripe cheese. Getting through those layers, though, could take a long time.

Wearing a long, sad face, Squirt tore himself away from the window. He clambered up a narrow chimney and sifted the air for the scent of frumenty. The alluring aroma had vanished and, belatedly, Squirt realized that there was no scent at all to lead him back to the inn whose name had also vanished from his mind. The fog was as heavy as, or heavier than, it had been when he set out. No matter which way he turned, the rooftops looked alike and unfamiliar.

The Eye must have seen him at the toymaker's unbarred window and seen the unvirtuous yearning in his heart.

"I'm sorry," he apologized aloud. "I wouldn't have taken it. I *try* to be virtuous. You know I *try*. Please— which way is back along the way I came?"

The Eye wasn't listening. Nothing changed—except that Squirt couldn't refind the toymaker's, either. If the Eye wouldn't reward him for *not* stealing, he had decided he might just as well go back and take one of the paladins.

Squirt wasn't scared—not yet—though his throat was getting uncomfortably tight and the steep, slate rooftops weren't fun to climb anymore.

"I'll stay right here," the boy told himself after he'd nearly lost his footing. "Jordie will come looking for me. Jordie will find me . . ."

His brother would look, but *find*—when Jordan didn't know Britain City any better than Squirt, himself, knew it? And here he was tucked behind the chimney of a roof that sagged ominously under his own, much smaller, weight. If Darrel wanted to be found, he'd have to be someplace where he could be found, so he abandoned his perch and ventured onto the slate again, searching for a spot where the roof descended to the lintel of a front door.

Finding such a place was harder than Squirt expected. He'd wandered into a neighborhood where the houses rose straight from the streets with tall facades designed to discourage thieves. No matter how many times the boy approached the gutter, the drop to the cobblestones was easily three times a man's height—four times his own. Even if he hung from the edge by his fingers before dropping, there was no way he'd land without hurting himself.

"Please let me land safe," Squirt begged the all-seeing Eye of Destiny. "Don't let me break my legs. Don't leave me crippled. Kill me first, but *please* let me land safe. I'll be good. I swear it."

There were too many things to worry about, too much fear, too much doubt. The boy's secret demon loomed over him, rattling his thoughts, destroying his concentration.

Squirt's hands were slick when he lowered one leg over the gutter. He caught himself before he plunged back-first to the street, but he couldn't find the strength to pull himself to safety. He closed his eyes and tried to calm himself the way Jordan and the other men did before they cleared their swords—but they didn't have to fight demons that lived inside their heads.

Squirt's eyes popped open. His head dropped back and he screamed from the depths of his spirit and heaved his hips toward the sky.

"Up there—clinging to the gutter!"

"He's going to fall!"

Voices—the deep voices of full-grown men. Strong arms to catch him when he fell. Squirt almost let go before he looked down at his rescuers. They had strong arms—and helmets, mail shirts, and swords. Not the same guards who had hassled everyone at the inn, but Lord Blackthorn's guards just the same. Squirt was ready to surrender to them anyway, until he glimpsed the lean, black-robed figure behind them. One look at that cadaverous face, those hollow eye sockets, was enough.

The screaming inside Squirt's head stopped. His thoughts cleared and he was back on the roof in a single moment. He scrambled for the crown-tiles as if he'd been born and raised on a steep, slate roof. The guards hammered on the front door of the house, but Squirt was running along the crown-tiles of the next house by the time the retainers got the door open.

Squirt had jumped onto these tricky roofs from someplace else, but when he'd travelled the length of three houses without finding a street or alley he could leap across, the boy began to panic again. Shielding himself behind an empty dovecote, he looked back the way he came. There were city guards on the rooftops. They were heavier and their thick-soled boots weren't meant for walking on slippery or angled surfaces, but they'd reach him eventually.

"Think, Squirt," the boy ordered himself. "You can't jump to another quarter. You can't jump down to the cobblestones. You can't fly . . . You know what you *can't* do. What *can* you do? Think. Think. *Think!*"

He bounced his head against the peeling paint of the dovecote. The shutters rattled on their hinges. The wood was rotten from neglect; the next storm might blow the whole dovecote from the roof. Whoever lived in the house probably hadn't kept birds for years.

"Forget about that! Think about getting out of here before they get you!"

The shutter swung open. It wasn't locked, only weather-stuck. Fool household probably had locks on all its doors and windows and left the roof open to any thief.

"Forget it! Thieves couldn't get up here anyway, stupid. That's your whole problem, Squirt—you're up where thieves couldn't get—"

Grinning broadly, the boy heard his own words and, squeezed into the cote, pulling the shutter tight behind him. The little turret was dusty as only a dovecote could be. Squirt sneezed. The sound seemed louder than thunder. He clamped his fingers over his nose before he sneezed again. His ears popped and, for a moment, he couldn't hear anything. When his ears cleared he heard the worst sound imaginable: leather scraping on slate. Peeking through the slats Squirt watched an angry man climb onto *his* roof. He didn't dare make a sound, so he mouthed a plea to his imaginary guardian:

Eye of Destiny watch over me. Eye of Destiny watch over me, please . . .

He fastened both hands over his nose and forbade himself to breathe, but that didn't work. The guard was moving slowly, latching onto anything he could reach to keep his balance. He was certain to grab onto the dovecote. Squirt breathed through his mouth and used his hands to feel through the layer of debris on the floor of his hiding place.

There had to be a trapdoor.

Eye of Destiny—let it not be nailed shut . . .

A board shifted beneath Squirt's fingers. When it was loose there was just enough room for him to wriggle through, and into a square, cobweb-filled shaft whose purpose and depth the boy could not guess. His feet found, and promptly broke, a wooden rung jutting the length of one side.

No wonder they stopped keeping birds, if this is what they had to go through . . .

The shaft was small enough that Squirt could brace his back against one wall and hold himself in place with his feet on the opposite wall. That freed his hands to peel the cobwebs from his face and replace the loose board across the opening. He could only hope the guard wouldn't notice how the dust had been disturbed.

Shinnying down the shaft wasn't difficult. The cobwebs were the only obstacle. They felt like dead man's flesh. He couldn't keep from batting at them when they tickled his face, and he didn't want to encounter the family of spiders that spun them. But all in all, getting down the shaft was simply a matter of sliding and bracing—except that the shaft seemed to go on forever. The texture of the walls changed from wood to masonry and back again. Squirt was sure he was below the level of the street; he feared he was headed for the Underworld. No light had appeared above him.

Ten more, then I'll head back up—

And then what? Even if the guards were gone, he was still trapped on the steep roofs of this quarter. The boy's only choice was to continue downward. And he did, until he struck hard, seamless stone at the bottom of the shaft. Squirt pressed against the walls with all his might; they didn't budge. He jumped on the stone floor until he thought about what would happen if it gave way beneath his feet, then he panicked completely. There had to be a way out. No one would put a dovecote on top of an oubliette—and it wasn't really an oubliette. The wooden rungs running from the top almost to the bottom of one wall were rotten now, true, but they were spaced like the rungs of a ladder. Somebody was meant to stand where the boy stood, lift his foot to the first rung, and climb up to the roof.

The door, then, had to be behind him. Squirt pushed. The sturdy planking didn't give at all. Maybe he wasn't strong enough. Maybe the boards had been bricked over on the other side. Maybe it opened toward the inside? The boy felt along the cracks for hinges; there weren't any.

I'm going to die down here. I'll starve. I'll die of thirst. I'll suffocate.

The boy could feel it already: stomach shrivelled to the size of a chestnut, throat parched and cracked like a dry creek. And then the spiders would come for him with poison fangs and prickly feet. Squirt slid slowly and dramatically to the stone floor—he had to curl up in order to fit—and when his cheek was against the stone he felt the faint stirring of a draft between the floor and the wall.

There had to be a door. It didn't swing in and it didn't swing out. It didn't rise like a portcullis, and it couldn't sink into the stone floor. Squirt spat on his palms and tried pushing it sideways. It moved quietly. It didn't begin to open until he'd pushed it a bit further; after that the boy forgot he'd been scared.

A heavy wool-backed tapestry covered the doorway. Beyond the tapestry was a room—Squirt could be sure of that because he heard a man humming. The boy resolved to wait until the room was quiet before venturing away from the door as the tapestry was certain to ripple no matter how carefully or slowly he moved behind it. That resolution lasted through four repetitions of the same snippet of melody, then Squirt was on the move.

He sidled along the wall, thanking the Eye of Destiny after each step that the humming never stopped. His outstretched fingers felt the silky fringe at the edge of the tapestry and then he was in the room, in the light.

Squirt had been in the dark long enough that candlelight would have blinded him momentarily—and the room was considerably brighter than that. The boy couldn't see anything, and he couldn't hear anything—because the humming had stopped. He ground his knuckles into his eyes and blinked furiously. Squirt turned to the right: shelves, lots of them, filled with books, scrolls, and odd-shaped bottles. Tapestries on the floor, on the walls, too—very bright and covered with magical beasts. Squirt turned left and his blood ran cold.

A magician. Squirt knew he stood before a magician because only a magician would be wearing such a long robe. What the boy didn't know was what kind of magician—as in human or not human. The creature in the bloodred robe was shaped like a man and bearded like a man. But his eyes were very blue, very round, and very large. They were so large and so round that they seemed—impossibly—to protrude beyond his face.

Squirt was fascinated by demons. He'd seen pictures of them in his father's illuminated books: huge demons with leathery wings and fangs that hung below their chins; tiny demons with stubby tails and pointed ears; feathered demons; and demons with extra arms and legs. But when the magician's huge eyes vanished and reappeared—they didn't actually open and close, there were no eyelids that the boy could see—and the black pupils expanded until the blue was almost gone, Squirt knew with his dying breaths that he'd taken himself to the lord of all demonkind.

"Where did *you* come from?"

The demon spoke with a man's voice. Squirt wasn't fooled. Fire was going to spill from those eyes any moment now. Fire, or poison, or some other deadly horror. But, since it hadn't yet, and until it did, he was Darrel Hawson, Ironhawk's son, of Hawksnest, and he knew how to die.

"*IRONHAWK!*"

Darrel Hawson used his head as a battering ram. He ran straight into the demon, knocking them both to the carpeted floor. When that didn't get him killed, the boy picked himself up and made a run at a bottle-covered table. There was an explosion when the bottles hit the floor, but Darrel was still on his feet. He headed for the cluttered shelves.

"Stop!"

Books, scrolls, and a few more bottles flew across the room. One shelf was clear; the boy moved on to the next.

"*Stop!*"

"*Ironhawk!*" And another shelf was empty.

"*An Xen Ex!*"

The spell appeared between the demon-mage's arms. It gathered strength for the space of a single heartbeat, then arched upward before bathing the boy in cool, pale blue light.

Everything came to a halt within and around Darrel Hawson. Dying wasn't such a terrible thing. He didn't hurt anyplace—in fact, he felt *good*. The yammering inside his head—that clutter of thoughts, feelings, sights, and sounds that marked his secret demon's territory—was absolutely quiet. The boy could think one thought at a time without having to say it aloud. He could see just one thing or hear it, without all the others clamoring for his attention.

No—dying was not such a terrible thing. Darrel wanted to thank the demon-mage—if he could.

Moving his feet was difficult, but not impossible. He raised his head. The demon looked completely manlike now, with ordinary eyes set in an ordinary face.

"Well—out with it—tell me the truth, you little gremlin. Who made you do this? Who sent you? Come on—tell me."

Darrel shook his head. He wanted to answer the questions, but he didn't understand them. He wasn't a gremlin. Nobody made him. Nobody sent him.

"What—did they take your voice . . . your memory?" The demon-mage shook his fist at the ceiling. "Anabarces's ghost—they have taken the voice and mind from a child! Blackthorn—wherever you are—you shall never succeed. Never!" He crunched across the shards of countless bottles and thrust his arms into the blue glamour. He held Darrel's face between his hands.

"You're no gremlin—you're not even charmed, except by me. But *how*?" He withdrew his arms and played with his beard a moment before fumbling with a ribbon he wore tied around his neck. "Let me get a good look at you." He propped wire frames on the bridge of his nose and peered at the boy through thick, hand-ground lenses. "Tell me your name."

"Darrel Hawson of Hawksnest, son of Erwald Ironhawk. But everybody calls me Squirt."

"And Darrel Hawson—since you're not a gremlin and not possessed by a demon—what did you hope to gain by invading my privacy and destroying my life's work?"

"Nothing."

"Nothing? Nothing? You did a very thorough job of it, Darrel Hawson, you must have had some reason."

The *An Xen Ex* charm had been hastily constructed. The

boy remained under its compulsion but turned his head away before he answered.

"You're the lord of demons. I couldn't let you kill me without a fight."

A woeful smile appeared on the magician's lips. He removed his pinch-nose spectacles and studied them. "Lord of demons, is it? And why did you visit the lord of demons?"

"I didn't mean to. Everybody at the inn—my brother, Althea, even Drum the farrier—was grouchy because of the air. I didn't want to get yelled at more, and I was hungry, so I went out on the roofs. And then I got lost—"

"There are no inns in this quarter or its neighbors. What inn?" The An Xen Ex charm could force the boy to wrack his memory for the name of the inn, but it couldn't guarantee he'd find it. "Very well—stop trying to remember it," the erstwhile lord of demons commanded when Squirt's face began to turn red. "Why are you and your brother in Britain City? Are you all farriers?"

"No—I'm the son of Erwald Ironhawk and my brother's his heir. We're Peers' sons; *not* farriers. Drum's only with us because of Althea . . ." Squirt raced through the entire quest as he understood it—which was not very well.

The magician polished his spectacles before peering through them again. He caught no more than half the words the boy said, and recognized none of the names until "Balthan" popped out between a stubborn mule and a magic talisman. Balthan was not a common name—he was acquainted with a Balthan who was as stubborn as a mule and knew something about magic—but the boy did not mention the name again.

"The city guards were after me so when I found the old dovecote, I got inside it, but that wasn't going to be safe enough, and then I found the shaft. I thought the Eye of Destiny must have forgiven me and decided to protect me again. But the shaft didn't stop until I got here. So I was wrong again—the Eye hasn't forgiven me: I'm in the Underworld, aren't I?''

"No, Darrel," the magician sighed. "You're merely in Annon's supposedly secret basement. You say there's a door behind my tapestry," he said as he flung the cloth back along its hanging pole. His spectacles fell from his nose. "Mother of the universe—a full-blown bolthole." Placing his spectacles in their accustomed place, the magician stepped into the shaft. "Anabarces—it goes clear up to the roof!" He reappeared with cobwebs clinging to his fine velvet robes. "I should thank my lucky stars it was you and not someone else. A proper warding—that's what it needs. *Vas Tym Sanct Grav . . .*"

The mage fell silent, surveying the wreckage of his study. The reagents for the warding spell, and every other major spell, were hopelessly mixed on the carpet.

"Are you truly Annon the Great?" the boy asked.

"I was." He knelt down. "Mandrake root. Come, Darrel, help me find mandrake root before the whole arcane world knows you've found me."

Darrel learned quickly. After a few false starts, his sharp eyes and fingers proved adept at extracting mandrake from the carnage, but the effects of the An Xen Ex charm began to fade. The wrinkled nubs of mandrake were among the least fascinating objects on the carpet and easy to ignore.

"Mandrake, Darrel," Annon chided from the worktable where he worked desperately with his mortar and pestle. "Those are scarabs—you may have them, if you want— but look for mandrake."

And for a few moments, the boy would—until some other bright-colored or oddly shaped treasure caught his eye.

"Mandrake! Mandrake—Squirt!"

A vial of sapphire glass fell from the boy's fingers. He

redoubled his efforts, but his eyes were no longer sharp and his fingers shook when he picked up what little mandrake he could see. He hadn't meant to get distracted—it just happened. The secret demon would spin his thoughts and he'd follow them. The calm of the An Xen Ex charm was a memory belonging to some other boy, not him. He handed Annon what he'd collected and would not look up from his feet when the mage spoke to him.

So Annon left his stool and spellcrafting. His knees creaked when he crouched down and a timid smile appeared on the boy's face.

"You were born with wild and wandering thoughts, Darrel, but you *can* control them."

"That's easy for *you* to say—you're Annon the Great. You know every spell in the whole world. You can make anything happen. I can't. I can't do anything without getting lost halfway through."

"You must try harder."

"I can't try *harder*. I try so hard my eyes and ears hurt. It doesn't do any good. The harder I try, the harder it gets. Cast that spell on me again—I did what I was told when you made me."

"Cast it yourself."

Squirt thrust his lower lip forward. Annon the Great, with his funny-strange eyes, was no different from his lord father or any other adult. "I'm not a magician," he said bitterly. "I can't even *read*."

Annon smoothed the frown lines from the boy's forehead with his thumbs. "You don't need to be a magician to cast a spell *inside*, in your own world. At this moment you believe you can't do anything right—that's one spell. If you believe something different—if you believe you can control your wayward thoughts—that's a different spell, the counterspell.

"Whatever you believe about yourself *will* happen. And when you are your own master—"

Wood clattered against the stone floor of the bolthole shaft; Annon's minor prophecy went unspoken.

"Quickly, Darrel—there's no time for warding. I cannot take you with me. There's a stairway behind the dragon tapestry. Get to the street and go home quickly. No one will follow you—not when they think they can follow me." Annon twirled his fingers through the cobwebs clinging to his robe and then dipped them in a powdery red stain on his worktable. "*Des Por*," he murmured. The spectacles fell from his nose. "*Des Por Vas*."

"Take me with you," Squirt pleaded. Another piece of wood struck the floor. The boy recognized the faded paint of the dovecote shutters. "Please—I won't be any trouble."

"No!" Annon sounded and looked more like a powerful mage. "Go home! It's too dangerous. You can't be found with a magician. Go home, now!"

"I can't go home! I don't live here—don't you remember—I can't remember the name of the inn where we're staying. You've got to take me with you. Take me to Felespar. He could tell me where Balthan is and then I'll go find Balthan, because if I'm with Balthan they'll find me when they find him."

A coil of rope landed at the bottom of the shaft. Wisps of foul-smelling smoke rose from Annon's fingers when he rubbed them together. There was no time left, so Annon made time with the blood-moss powder and mandrake pellets.

"*Rel Tym!*"

The first spell Annon cast quieted the noise within the boy's mind. The second spell made the room unnaturally quiet instead. Squirt looked at the open door of the bolthole:

He'd never seen a rope, or anything else, move so slowly. It made no noise when it struck the wall.

"What did you do?" he demanded.

Annon caught Squirt before he could explore the rope in the bolthole. "There's still no time to waste. Tell me— exactly what do you know about Felespar of Yew?"

The boy shrugged. Any other time that movement would have freed him, but within the sphere of Annon's spellcraft, his agility was negated. "I don't know anything except that he's in trouble, and so is Balthan. We're really looking for Balthan because he's Althea's—"

"Balthan Wanderson—Felespar's amanuensis? What about this Balthan? Why do you seek him?"

Adults—always interrupting to ask a question when, if they'd stay quiet, they'd already have the answer: "We're looking for Balthan because he's Althea's brother. And she thinks something happened to him when Felespar got into trouble because the talisman she's got has been all strange since then."

"Your friend's brother, my friend's amanuensis, was not captured that night in Yew. He was seen once, hiring an oar-boat in the village of Merdaunt, presumably bound for Cove, possibly with a heavy conscience. There are those among us who say he could not have escaped without help. I believe Felespar helped your friend, but the longer Balthan shuns us, the harder it becomes to defend him. Tell him for me—if you find him in Cove—that his actions speak of cowardice and falsehood. Tell him to seek Annon of Britannia before his friends become his enemies!

"Now—go! Before the spell breaks."

Annon wrapped his fingers in spider-silk again, then touched them to the last of the red powder on the table.

"*Des Por* Vas!"

Incredibly, the magician began to sink through the floor.

"I can't go—I'm lost. I can't remember where I started or how to get back there. I don't remember the name—"

Annon was half-gone. "You can remember, Darrel. Cast your own spell. Cast it inside—on your—"

He was gone. There was a bright, clean circle on the tapestry carpet but the magician was gone. Squirt recited the syllables of the spell Annon had used to calm him; nothing happened.

"I can't do it!" he wailed. "I can't. I can't. I can't!" Squirt willed for the magician to return; that didn't work either and the rope had begun to writhe like a snake—a noisy snake. The boy could hear boots striking the walls of the shaft, and men's voices. He pleaded with the Eye of Destiny and then, for no good reason at all, thought of Lord Shamino who could shoot his arrows blindfolded.

An arrow appeared in the boy's mind. Not one of Lord Shamino's red-and-blue-fletched arrows, but a strange arrow fashioned from a hollow brass pipe. Instead of having a sharp point, the pipe came to a flaring end, like a horn. A horn! The brass arrow sped past. It had writing along the shaft. Squirt could not read it, but he knew it said: "The Hunter's Horn." He followed it safely through the corridors of the house and the fog-shrouded streets of Britain City.

Sixteen

The sanctuary of Cove lay on the shores of a lake
north-northeast of both Hawksnest and Britain City
—as Jordan observed repeatedly in the hours after
Squirt's return to the Hunter's Horn. The lake, known ap-
propriately as Lock Lake, was in the center of impassable
mountains. Lock Lake's sole outlet was a swift-flowing
mountain river which would be judged unnavigable were it
not for Cove itself and the nearby shrine of Compassion.

"We'll need a boat," Jordan would mutter, then he'd
look at the dwindling silver in his purse and pace the length
of the room again.

If the young man were on his Virtue Quest, armed with
Compassion's mantra and Lord Ironhawk's blessing, getting
to Cove would be no problem. He'd simply go down to the
harbor, hire a seaworthy craft to sail him and his cohort to
the village of Merdaunt at the mouth of the mountain river.

At Merdaunt he'd hire several flatbottom oar-boats and thick-sinewed men to row them against the current the length of the river to Lock Lake.

The coins left in his purse wouldn't buy a sea passage for one to the mouth of the river.

"Can't we go as we've gone—at least until we reach the river village?" Althea said reasonably. "We'd only need one skiff—we could make the same sort of trade you make with Baron Hrothgar except this time we'll swap the mule and pony for the boat until we return it."

Jordan tried to explain that there was no road beyond Britain City, merely uninhabited wilderness where nothing kept the night creatures at bay. He'd never been in a swamp himself, but that didn't hinder the young man as he described the manifold horrors they'd find amid the bogs and mires.

"We've gone as far as we can. If Balthan's in Cove he's safe enough," Jordan concluded. "I think it's time we went back to Hawksnest. It's time for me to face my lord father *and* tell him what I've learned of the world."

Althea agreed, then she turned her emerald green eyes on Drum. "Will you come with me to Cove, or will you return to Hawksnest with Jordan and the boy?"

They all left Britain City together, as they'd arrived, except that Jordan's purse was nearly empty and Drum was in debt to his guild. Althea rode the pony. The mule carried the poles and canvas for a small tent as well as ten days' food for each of them; there was no room on its back for Squirt—which pleased the boy. He couldn't swagger atop a jumble of food sacks as he could when he walked with his new sword thumping against his hip.

"I did it, didn't I?" The boy struggled to match both the length of his brother's strides and their rhythm. "I wager you didn't think *I'd* be the one to find out where Balthan was—but I did. I found Annon the Great of Britain City. He told me what happened to Balthan, and he told me how to cast a spell inside myself—''

''Aye,'' Jordan agreed—not for the first time. ''I'd be as poor as a tinker's widow wagering against you, Darrel.'' Then he poured a little more effort into each step and left the boy behind.

Squirt didn't mind. Jordan was surly with everyone now that they were getting close to the fen country. He kept them all looking over their shoulders, scanning the horizon for anything that might spell trouble. Each morning, while Althea fixed breakfast, Jordan practiced his swordwork against imaginary, fast-moving enemies, then he drilled Squirt with his sword, Drum with his axe, and even Althea with her knife.

''I'm going to beat him bloody,'' Drum confided to Squirt as Jordan leered at Althea, defying her to attack his out-thrust leg and then sweeping her off her feet when she slashed at his arm instead.

''You'd have to catch him first.''

Althea charged her tormentor from a crouch. Jordan was ready. He praised her for keeping her body behind her attack as he easily wrestled her aside. ''Go for the hand,'' he advised. ''Try to push the blade clear through the palm. You're not strong enough to kill an armored man—you want to make him hurt too much to follow you.''

''I'll catch him. There's no reason to teach her these things. A lady like Althea shouldn't roll on the ground with her skirts hiked up like a whore's,'' Drum muttered. ''One of these damn mornings, I'll catch him good.''

That morning might never come. Though Jordan was a surprisingly patient teacher, there was a limit to what he could teach to Drum and Althea who measured their expertise in hours of practice, not years.

The heir of Hawksnest kept his little cohort on the lookout for a fight he hoped they would not have. Though they saw the tracks of wild and magical beasts several times, the closest they came to danger was a giant snake sunning itself on the natural dike ahead of them. It was sluggish and swollen with a recent meal. It caught sight of Jordan banging his bastard-sword against the shorter one he'd momentarily reclaimed from Squirt and hit the shallow water with a splash.

"We could've taken it," Squirt insisted, feinting at the empty dike. "You and me together. I'd do everything you'd tell me to do."

"Then put your sword away. Everything in the swamp's poisonous—no trouble if you've hired a magician for your cohort, but sure death if you haven't."

The boy rammed his sword into its scabbard.

They were twelve days beyond Britain City when they spied the stilt houses of Merdaunt rising out of the estuary like huge herons browsing through the brackish water. In the bay, beyond the village, a two-masted sloop was lowering its sails. A Peer's ship, Jordan proclaimed, and the answer to all their problems. Rather than emptying their purses by hiring a skiff to ferry them upriver to Cove, they would offer their services to the cohort instead.

Or, at least he and Drum would. The lord and his lady, who were Questing together, were pleased to hire the heir of Ironhawk and his sturdy companion. Althea and Squirt travelled with the baggage while Jordan and Drum joined the men of Merdaunt as rowers.

Three backbreaking days later, as soon as they reached Cove, the men of Merdaunt went into the forest to cut down the trees they needed for the never-ending repair of their stilt homes. The peerage lord and lady gathered the men of their cohort for the short overland trek to the standing stones of the shrine of Compassion. Jordan stood by himself on the gravel beach and watched them depart.

Althea approached him quietly. "You could have gone with them. Drum and I can find Balthan in Cove; we'd take care of Darrel, too. I spoke with Lady Alinore—she thought what you were doing bespoke true compassion *and* humility. She was sure you'd receive enlightenment. You'd be a Peer in your own right."

"It wouldn't be my own right, Althea. They'd chant the mantra; I'd never learn it."

"Is that so important?"

"You know it is."

There was an edge to Jordan's tongue that made Althea retreat. "I don't know what you mean."

"You don't? Why didn't you go with them—do you mean to say Lady Alinore didn't invite you? They are going to the shrine of Compassion, after all—they asked every man of Merdaunt. It would hardly be compassionate to leave you out."

"I have to rescue my brother."

Tendons snapped as Jordan flexed his aching shoulders. "Then let's rescue him and get it over with."

"You sound very bitter. Are you *that* sorry you came?"

Jordan got another crackling outburst from his joints before straightening his stained tunic. "No—just weary." He started up the path ahead of Althea, then stopped short and faced her again. "Questing is nothing like I thought it would be. I always knew exactly what I wanted—what I wanted to do with my life: I'd do what was expected of me, make my father proud of me, quest all around Britannia seeking virtue. I'd become a Peer like Lord Ironhawk, or Lady Alinore and Lord Herdic—except I find I don't like killing, I'm not sure of virtue, and I don't like Peers."

"At least you'll have something to talk to Balthan about on the way home. He feels the same way."

Althea didn't mean to be funny, but Jordan laughed. "I can just see him, that owl-y face he puts on when he's afraid he missed something important—you know the one." Jordan raised his eyebrows and pursed his lips as if he were stifling a yawn.

"He only does that with you," she amended, stifling a real laugh. "I don't think he knows what to make of you. Balthan doesn't like surprises, and you surprise him."

"Aye—he thinks I'm dumb as a stone, when, truly, I'm at least as smart as a tree."

"A chestnut or apple tree, perhaps," Althea sidestepped out of his reach—as she'd learned to in their morning practices— "But nowhere near as smart as a big old oak tree."

Jordan caught Althea's wrist and twisted it slightly; she replied with another move he'd taught her. The young man was in the midst of a game he'd played all his life. Without thinking, he countered with a move he'd never shown her. Suddenly they were pressed against each other and the rules changed completely. Jordan lost interest in Althea's wrist when the rest of her was in reach. His fingers relaxed and she spun away from him the moment she was free. He was left with empty arms and a brilliantly red face.

Althea lifted her skirt with both hands. "Forgive me," she gasped. "I forgot you're a man," then she ran for the village of Cove.

Jordan was a good-looking youth with excellent prospects. He'd learned more than weaponcraft from the men his father hired to tutor him. He had his share of opportunities both on the estate and, especially, when the family made its regular treks to Trinsic. He could have chased her, caught her, and made certain she never again forgot what he was. But the thought that merged Althea with the blowzy wenches of the Trinsic stews also turned Jordan's feet to lead.

Jordan didn't start moving until Althea vanished behind the whitewashed walls of the apothecary, and even then he walked slowly, rehearsing what he'd say when they were alone together again. If they dared to be alone together again. If he could even trust himself to look into her eyes again, which, giving the matter careful consideration, Jordan concluded he could not. He'd look at his feet whenever he had to speak to Althea—that way, he reasoned, neither of them would have anything to forgive or regret.

He needn't have worried. Althea had never been more demure. She was ensconced on a stone bench outside the apothecary with Squirt and Drum beside her like mismatched guardians. Her brother's talisman pouch rested openly in her lap. She never lifted her eyes from it and used it as a mirror to watch Jordan approach. He couldn't see the tip of her nose, much less those dangerous green eyes.

"There's a mage in the sanatorium," Squirt announced. "I spied him out through the window. He was turned to the wall. His hair was dark, but I couldn't get a look at his face before . . ."

"Before what?" Jordan asked wearily.

"The nurses caught him on the roof," Drum replied in the same tone.

"I said I wanted to see his face, or if they'd tell me his name, that would do just as well. But they threw me out instead!"

"That's not the worst of it." Althea picked up the thread of the tale. "While we—while I—while you and I were talking on the shore, Drum asked the same questions. The nurses said he never gave them his name and had neither spoken nor eaten since he arrived almost two months ago.

They said they feared for his soul as well as his life because he raves so whenever a stranger comes near him.''

"You're his sister." Jordan readily joined the consensus that the afflicted mage was indeed the long-sought Balthan. "You're not a stranger. They ought to let you see him."

"They said there was no resemblance," Drum spoke when Althea would not.

"There never was. There's none between the Squirt and me," Jordan said, which was wishful thinking rather than the truth, though there was, in fact, very little family resemblance between Althea and her brother.

"I thought if I invoked the homunculus one last time. I have just enough oil left, I think—"

Jordan agreed. "That ought to convince them."

Althea raised her head. Their eyes met and they hastily looked in opposite directions.

"I was afraid—it's so peaceful here. Not like Paws or Britain City or anywhere else we've been. Maybe Cove hasn't been affected by Lord Blackthorn yet. Maybe if I use the talisman, I'll bring ill fortune to this village."

Drum and the boy shared Althea's concern. Squirt added, "Once it's dark we can climb up on the roof and get him out ourselves."

"No." Jordan shook his head vigorously. "The privilege of the sanatorium is the same as any other place of sanctuary. We'll be dishonored if we break it—even if we have good reasons. Besides, if Balthan's been here raving for two months without drawing Blackthorn or his goons, then rubbing the talisman once or twice isn't apt to cause trouble."

Althea looked at him again. This time they did not shy away from each other. "Do you truly think so, Jordie?"

"I do."

Calmly, Althea unknotted the silk cords. She retrieved

the little vial of oil first and gave it to Drum, then she lifted the talisman out of the pouch. They all gasped at its dusky grey color. Only the opposite poles of the sphere retained their shifting amber beauty. The homunculus was in the upper portion. It floated above the stagnant oil, and seemed in no danger of sinking, but its movements were severely restricted.

"It points at the sun," Althea commented. "I've seen pictures that show the spirits of the dead swimming to the sun to be cleansed—"

"Put the oil on it," Jordan advised, "then give it to my brother to hold."

"The shadows come back stronger after he touches it." Althea clutched the talisman beneath her breast, refusing to surrender it.

Jordan examined the shining roof of the Temple of the Avatar. "You said this is the last of the oil, right? So what difference does it make how dark it gets after this time so long as we can show the nursing-sisters that we have a reason to see their patient?"

Althea glanced over her shoulder. She saw nothing unusual about the roof of the temple but was willing to let the boy touch the talisman while she remained responsible for holding it. Squirt knelt in the gravel at Althea's feet, his hands palm-up in her lap beneath the globe. Jordan continued to study the roof of the temple while Althea shook the last of the volatile oil onto the glass and began the invocation.

"It's clearing!" Squirt exclaimed.

"Be careful!"

The talisman darkened when Althea abandoned the invocation to chide Squirt for carelessness. The young woman gasped and Jordan abandoned his examination of the temple's architecture to clamp both hands over the boy's thin shoulders.

"We trust you," Jordan assured his brother, though his hands contradicted his words. "Hold steady while Thea wakes it up. You can do it."

The boy straightened under the pressure of Jordan's hands. "I can do it," he repeated, following the prescription Annon of Britain City had given him. "I can *do* it. I *can* do it."

Golds and yellows blossomed in the polar reaches of the talisman. They dove into the turgid grey band. The colors faded, but with each successive bloom the turgid band narrowed and yielded more easily. The homunculus stood upright but did not move freely until Althea concluded the invocation and the talisman seethed with brilliant colors.

"It's hard to see," Althea complained, peering at it from the top. "There's so much color—more than there's ever been, even when he first made it. I can't see its little arm."

"I can," Squirt announced from his vantage point. "But—it's *not* pointing at the sanatorium. It points to the temple."

Jordan's hands relaxed against the boy's shoulders. He looked again at the Temple of the Avatar, imagining the Flame of Virtue burning brightly within it. By the Avatar's decree, his temple was open to everyone. It was the place where doubts were purged, where a troubled conscience might be cleansed, where a citizen might improve his perception of virtue. In practice, however, those who came to the temple were usually Peers whose quests were in the throes of unenlightenment.

Magicians almost never came to the temple; they seldom sought enlightenment within the stone-ringed shrines. Extracting the virtue they needed from their studies of the eight reagent elements of magic, they acknowledged the morality of Enlightenment and publicly organized their discipline into eight spellcraft circles corresponding to the eight virtues. But it was no secret that their true way was a meandering spiral with no unitary purpose or goal. The Peerage considered magicians a necessary inconvenience, while magicians did not need the Peerage or anyone else at all.

"It's hard to imagine Balthan taking refuge *there*," Drum acknowledged.

"Remember Britain City," Jordan advised. "Just because the temple's in front of us doesn't mean Balthan's inside. Come on, Squirt, let's take a little walk."

Before Althea could object, Squirt took the talisman from her lap and followed his brother to the temple. The stubby arm of the homunculus pointed due north until the brothers turned east, where it began to swing slowly toward the west. It did not point west until they neared the rear wall, then it began to swing south. Squirt stopped midway along the rear wall with the homunculus pointing due south and wisps of darkning clotting the oil.

"Nobody *lives* at the Temple of the Avatar, do they?" the boy asked his brother, who was supposed to know everything.

"Not that I've heard of, or read in any of our lord father's books. The *Notebooks of the Grimaldi* say the Avatar's sisters guard the Flame until he returns. But they were written over a hundred years ago and also claim that the shrine of Spirituality sits atop a mountain in the Underworld."

Althea caught up with them. She cried out when she saw the darkning had reappeared. Moments after she took the talisman from the boy's hand it was completely dark.

"Why does it do that?" Squirt asked. All three of his

older companions looked at him in ways that made him regret asking. "Should we go inside?" he asked, hoping to divert their attention.

"There's nowhere else," Althea said when neither Jordan nor Drum would decide.

The Avatar's temple was not large: some twenty paces long, half that in width on the outside and only slightly smaller within. The roofbeams were exposed and unless there were a crypt beneath the floor, there was no place to hide, or live. Two women meditated beside the eternal Flame; neither of them looked older than Althea.

They tried not to disturb the acolytes as they searched the temple with the inert talisman, hoping that Balthan's presence would bring it back to life. Althea and Drum left their baskets against a marble column, but none of the men would be parted from his weapon, and their hard-soled shoes tapped against the polished stone floor despite their best efforts to move silently.

The darker-haired woman was roused from her meditation. "I am called Ava—"

The four visitors were startled. Althea clutched the talisman in both hands.

"I did not mean to disturb you," the sloe-eyed girl said. Her voice was sonorous and slow, as were her movements, yet she did not seem to be ill or in a trance. She stared at Jordan because his sword, the bow, and mail shirt made him the obvious leader. "Have you come in search of understanding? You may step into the Flame whenever you're ready—but if it is your first time, we suggest you leave your weapons, your mail, and any other metal behind."

Jordan stiffened. The Flame of Virtue blazed to a man's height above the wide, empty brazier. It roared; it made the air around it shimmer. Looking at it, the young man did not believe he could enter it without being harmed. "My lady Ava, many thanks for your advice, but I had not planned to—to avail myself of the Flame. We are looking for a man about my age, a magician. A talisman he left us has guided us this far.''

Ava faced the flame and her companion. The other girl's eyes opened; she shuddered, then rose effortlessly to her feet and joined them.

"Leona, they seek a man, a magician their own age," Ava said. "They say they have followed a *talisman*." There was no mistaking the emphasis the darkhaired girl placed on the final word.

There was some resemblance between the girls, though Leona's hair was several shades lighter and her eyes were hazel rather than brown.

"I don't recall anything about a talisman." They both spoke slowly, with deep-pitched yet musical voices.

"He is my brother—Balthan, he calls himself Wanderson."

Ava and Leona looked into each other's eyes, and though both nature and magic proclaimed it impossible, the four visitors were each certain that the girls conversed with thought alone.

"You say you are this mage's sister," Ava said. "May we see the talisman you followed?"

"You know him! You know Balthan—is he here? Is he well? You can't imagine how worried I've been about him. We've come all the way—"

"May we see the talisman?" Leona repeated her companion's request.

The acolyte's expression had not changed, nor her tone, yet Althea was humiliated. She nearly dropped the talisman while placing it in Ava's outstretched hand.

"He did not mention this, sister." Leona examined the sphere which remained dark in her hands—to Althea's relief. "Perhaps he did not believe anyone could learn anything from it."

Althea opened her mouth and shut it again. Let them think what they wish; she'd learned her lesson.

"Your brother is no longer here. He entered the Flame to place a message for one who would come after him. He did not come out of the Flame," Leona told Althea.

"That's impossible," Jordan exclaimed.

"Impossible or not, he did not come out," Ava said. "He would not tell us anything more—for fear that if we knew more, we would, ourselves, be endangered." She looked at her sister who nodded slightly. "He was a very anxious young man. I do not think he had slept for many, many nights. We advised him against entering the Flame. It was nothing he said, of course, but I don't think he expected anyone he *knew* to seek him. He expected his enemies, certainly—and they came, several times. But he did not seem to have family or friends—"

"It was Balthan, all right," Jordan interjected.

Althea scowled at him. "We are his friends and family. Is he *still* in the Flame?"

"He is no longer here." Ava repeated Leona's earlier assertion. It could have been the simple truth, but there was something in the smooth, deep voice that made Ava's words sound like an evasion.

Drum cleared his throat, attracting more attention than he wanted and nearly abandoning his question: "What enemies? Who else came looking for him? Magicians? Inquisitors?"

The sisters exchanged knowing glances again. When Ava spoke she had lost much of her composure. "Inquisitors. My lady," she faced Althea squarely, "your brother feared his enemies could separate knowledge from the spirit and was careful that we know *nothing* that could hurt us. Foolishly we chided him for this caution—but we have met the Inquisitors, and are grateful for his foresight. I cannot but think you would be wiser not to seek your brother or his message. Together we could barely stand against Balthan's enemies—you would not fare even so well. Leave your brother's destiny to others."

Althea was stunned by the girl's bluntness, but Jordan was galvanized. He seized Ava's arm and held it in a nerve-pinching grip Squirt recognized very well.

"Balthan Wanderson has enemies, and he has us. We'll take our chances with his enemies. You have to take yours with us. Now—where is Balthan or his damned message?"

The air around Leona crackled until Ava glanced back over her shoulder. "The message lies beyond the Flame. Where Balthan lies, I do not know."

Jordan released her.

"Be wary, Peer," Leona said ominously. "The Flame will burn those who misuse it."

"I'm not a Peer," Jordan snapped. He stalked toward the brazier, his footfalls echoing through the austere chamber.

"Jordie—remember your weapons and your shirt!" Althea called after him.

But Jordan never hesitated. He strode into the Flame and vanished.

Seventeen

*S*tepping into the Flame of Virtue was not unlike plunging into a bath on a winter morning when ice capped the water, an experience Jordan had survived hundreds, if not thousands, of times. However, the sensation of being reduced to dust motes and whisked away on the wind was incomparable, and when the young man found himself reassembled on a misty, narrow marble stairway, he collapsed, whimpering like a terrified gremlin.

"Greetings. *Vas Wis?*"

Certain he had passed from the realm of the living to the Underworld or worse, Jordan slowly opened his eyes and raised his head.

"Balthan?"

Balthan leaned casually against the wall some ten steps above Jordan. His hair was many shades darker than Althea's and his eyes were a glinting brown. His face seemed sharper than his sister's until he smiled and their common parentage was revealed.

"I have waited for you. *Sanct Uus. Vannen mire.*"

Balthan used words from a language like no other in Britannia, though Jordan thought he recognized spell-words amid the gibberish. Mages, Jordan realized, must have their own cant. Why not? Thieves, gypsies, and pirates did—and magicians were no less secretive about *their* knowledge.

Jordan found his dignity and rose to his feet. "Balthan?"

"*Vannen mire.*" He gestured at the ascending stairs.

Jordan understood that he was supposed to follow. "I'd rather not."

The magician slouched against the wall. Jordan tried not to stare until he realized that "Balthan" didn't blink and wasn't breathing. For that matter, he wasn't dressed in the drab blue gown of a low-circle mage. The apparition wore a pair of snug suede boots with deep cuffs that Jordan wouldn't mind owning himself. The collar of his black damask tunic tapered to long points that were a bit too delicate for a swordsman's taste, though the wide silver-buckle belt was nice.

Jordan's envy died quickly when Althea, then Drum, and finally Squirt tumbled onto the stairway around him.

Althea recovered from her disorientation as soon as she saw her brother. "Balthan!"

"Greetings. *Vas Wis?*" the apparition repeated its salutation.

"It's not him," Jordan said, catching Althea before she fainted.

"What is he—*it* saying?" Drum put his arms protectively around Althea as he asked. "Sounds like nonsense to me."

"Me, too," Jordan agreed, refusing to let go. "Either it's some sort of cant that magicians use or Balthan lost his mind completely once he got this far."

The boy squeezed around the larger people. He ran to give Balthan his customary body-check greeting.

"He's not *here*!" Squirt complained, slashing his arms through Balthan's image until Jordan looked away.

"*Vannen mire*," the psuedoBalthan concluded, unaffected by the head jutting out of its chest.

"Should we follow it?" Drum asked.

"We can either follow it *up* the stairs, or go down by ourselves."

"What's up there?"

"I don't know, Drum—I've never been here before."

The farrier grunted something that might have been an apology, or an insult. Jordan didn't wait to find out. The heir of Hawksnest charged up the marble stairs. The others came behind him.

"Do you think we're dead, Jordie?" the boy asked when they were all panting from exertion. "And our destiny is to climb these stairs *forever*? Do you think we should go downstairs, instead? Would you recognize—"

"Shut up, Squirt."

The foursome had climbed as high as the roof of the Temple of the Avatar many times over without coming to the top of the foggy stairway. Whenever they paused, Balthan's apparition repeated its cant-laced salutation.

"We're missing something." Althea paused to catch her breath. "There's something we should say to complete the spell."

While she and Jordan shouted every syllable of magic they could remember from their lessons, Drum scuffed the light-colored walls with a frustrated kick. "If we're climbing round in circles, I'll see it."

"*Vannen mire*," the apparition concluded its salutation again.

Jordan took a deep breath and ascended the stairs two at a time. "Enough!" he shouted, getting ahead of the apparition.

"Greeting. *Vas Wis?*"

"No *Vas Wis!*" Jordan replied, imitating the accent as best he could. "No *Sanct Uus*. No *vannen mire.*"

"Here, Jordie." Althea sat on the steps fumbling for the talisman pouch. "Show it this—"

"Bring it up here, Squirt—I've got this thing cornered now and I don't want it to get away."

The boy obeyed. "She says: '*Kal Wis Por Mani,*' " he whispered, offering the globe to his brother. "I wiped it off on my tunic. It's not slippery anymore."

Jordan held the defunct talisman in front of the unblinking eyes. He raised it and lowered it; he moved it from side to side and even whispered the syllables of invocation. "Is there any oil left?" he called back to Althea when the apparition restarted its salutation.

"Not a drop."

Squirt tugged on his brother's sleeve. "Balthan always gets upset if you walk *away* when he's talking."

"Destiny's hind foot, Squirt, all we need is an angry ghost."

"At least it would be paying attention to us," the boy said with the voice of experience. "Right now it doesn't know we're here."

Jordan waggled the globe one last time. He didn't have a better idea. "Start going *down*stairs. You, too, Squirt. If Balthan's up to his tricks again, I don't want you getting hurt anymore than Thea or Drum."

"Everybody needs you more than they need me. I should—"

"*Down! Now!* Or I'll bounce you down like a ball."

Squirt scurried. Jordan gave them a four-step lead before descending the stairs himself. An eerie wind blew past his left ear.

"Please don't forget me. Please don't leave me beneath the ground."

The apparition's damask-cuffed wrist emerged from Jordan's mail shirt. It reached toward Althea who shivered at the implications.

"That night after Lord Blackthorn came from my mentor —when I had fallen asleep in the forest and the shadows surrounded me—you appeared to me. You drove the shadows back and told me to come here, to your temple in Cove. When I entered the Flame you showed me how to use the scrolls I was carrying to leave this message for the future. I beg you—O Once and Future Hero of Britannia—do not leave me behind."

Balthan's image covered its eyes and turned away. Althea tried to comfort him as she'd tried many times in the early years when Simon the Wanderer dragged his broken family from one seedy inn to the next. "It's not your fault," she whispered.

"It's not him, Thea." Jordan lifted her hand and held it tightly. "He's not here. He can't hear you—but at least this thing he's left is talking some sort of sense."

Balthan would not have listened to Althea had he been there in the stairwell with them. In his world there was no difference between shame and guilt; if he felt one, he felt the other. And after Lord Blackthorn's men came looking for Felespar and the word of power, Balthan had reason to feel both emotions.

The young mage had been finishing up the day's work in the closet behind Felespar's magic-chamber when the armed and armored men appeared. Voices were raised. The amanuensis knelt by the keyhole, filled at first with curiosity.

But curiosity changed swiftly to dread as Felespar was bound by the guards and threatened with a dagger pressed hard against the corner of his eye. The scrolls which Balthan had been illuminating were scrolls of Eighth Circle magic—spells that could freeze time or slay a man wherever he stood, among other wondrous things—but before Balthan could retrieve or use them, Lord Blackthorn himself passed in front of the keyhole; the amanuensis's blood turned to water.

Britannia's regent was not alone. A dark presence surrounded him. Balthan recognized the shadow. For much of the past year Balthan had been plagued with nightmares in which faceless shadows enticed him to steal Felespar's Word and tempted him with visions of the rewards that would fall to him once the Word was uttered and the dungeon unsealed. Balthan had resisted the temptations, though not without great difficulty. The nightmares gradually ceased, and Balthan judged himself a better man for overcoming them, still, his first reaction, when he saw that Blackthorn did the shadows' bidding, was searing jealousy: the regent would reap the rewards that should have been his alone. Then Balthan saw Lord Blackthorn's white-rimmed eyes and he saw the shadows for what they truly were: relentless soul-consuming evil—and he knew how close he'd come to eternal doom.

A vision of the Avatar had rescued Balthan from the depths of a nightmare later that same night. Balthan learned his lesson. Sustained by magic and a mixture of ginseng and garlic, he journeyed across Britannia to Cove without allowing his body or mind to drift into sleep. He bared himself in the Flame of Virtue where a second vision showed him how to construct the stairwell.

"Now I wait for you beyond. Please come for me," the apparition pleaded. "Please let me join you. Let me redeem myself fighting at your side against the evil which has entered our world—if not for myself, then for my mentor, Felespar. I beg you.'' Balthan's image fell to one knee and extended its arm, then it began to flicker.

"He wasn't expecting us to come here after him, that's for certain,'' Jordan said after the apparition's features had begun to fade and it seemed very unlikely that it would speak again.

"Maybe he hoped Felespar would look for him, or one of the other Council Mages,'' Althea countered hopefully.

Jordan shook his head. "Not the way I heard him. He didn't think Felespar survived the night. No, I think that in his usual arrogant way, Balthan just assumed he was so important that the Avatar would come to him in his dreams and then come in person from his other world to rescue him. It would take more than the Flame of Virtue to give your brother Humility, Thea.''

Before Althea could defend her brother from Jordan's charges, Drum directed their attention to a more immediate problem.

"The light's fading—not just Balthan's ghost. Everything's fading. How do we get out of here?''

Jordan took a moment to assure himself that the farrier's words were true. The sourceless light was dimming, although the stairwell had, so far, retained its solidity. "Thump the wall up and down from here,'' he suggested. "We must be behind the Flame, somewhere in the wall of the temple.''

He took his own advice until the light was nearly gone and Althea wrapped her arms around him.

"Don't go off in the dark. We've got to stay close together.''

"We can't get too far apart,'' Jordan rebutted.

Balthan's image was gone. Enough light remained in the stairway to see shapes but not color.

"We're trapped!" Althea cried. She stumbled up a few steps before Jordan caught her. "There's no way out. We're trapped!"

Althea's panic was contagious. The stairway was dark before Drum suggested that she make a small handfire. Squirt was missing.

"Down here," the boy replied after they'd all shouted his name. "It's light down here. I think there's a way out."

Squirt sat on the bottom step waiting for his brother and the others. He could not see his hand in front of his face, but he could see the ground beneath his feet through a layer of shimmering blue light—a long way beneath his feet. The stairway came to a rain-spout's end over a piece of ground that wasn't any part of the Temple of the Avatar and probably wasn't even in Cove.

"Hammers and bells!" Drum exclaimed when he saw the straight drop to the moss-covered ground. He braced his hands on opposite walls of the stairway. "Where are we?"

"I was afraid to stick my head out," Squirt admitted. "I imagined my head sticking down out of *nowhere* and I couldn't do it. Maybe we're behind the temple someplace."

Jordan added his own oaths and exclamations, but Althea knew the light for what it was.

"A moon gate."

The heir of Hawksnest was skeptical. "A moon gate that works in the daylight and opens *down*?"

"Balthan said he was carrying scrolls and that the Avatar showed him how to use them together. He was Felespar's amanuensis—he told me once that the spell he illuminated most often was one that opened a moon gate at any time and from any place."

"Probably cost a small fortune in gold. Who'd use it?" Jordan wondered.

Drum knew. "Peers on Virtue Quests—who else? The question is: Are *we* going to use this one? Looks like Balthan smeared the ink, if you ask me."

Jordan produced a copper pence and threw it into the blue light. The coin landed on the ground where they could see it, but the blue light began to ripple like water in a stiff breeze.

"There's no use waiting," Jordan muttered. "Balthan made his little speech facing this way, so this is the way he expected the Avatar to leave."

Before the others objected, Jordan plunged through the light. He broke his fall by rolling as he struck the ground. After brushing himself off, Jordan took a quick survey of his surroundings, then found the copper coin and looked up.

"We're deep in a forest. I can't see any mountains. I can't see you—say something!"

The trio in the stairway didn't need any encouragement to shout. They didn't stop shouting until they realized he couldn't hear them, and, though they could see his lips moving, they couldn't hear him. When Jordan tossed the copper pence over his head, Squirt leaned out to catch it, roiling the light further as he did.

"I didn't miss," the boy insisted, "it wasn't there!"

"We can see him," Althea concluded, "but he's not anywhere near us. What can we do?"

Squirt had his own answer to that. He hooked one hand into the laces of Drum's buskin, then did exactly what he'd been afraid to do: He thrust his head and shoulders into the light.

"Jordie! Jordie! Over here!"

A frigid wind ripped the words away from the boy and carried them to his brother who turned to see Darrel swing across the glade, disappear momentarily into a tree trunk, then reemerge like the clapper of an enormous bell.

"Catch my hand!"

Weighed down by his heavy sword and the mail shirt— neither of which he was about to remove—Jordan's leaps fell short by the length of Squirt's arm. The boy stretched as far as he could without falling, then Drum pulled him back into the stairwell.

"Hold my ankles," Squirt pleaded. "He can reach me if you dangle me out by my ankles."

Afterward, Drum wondered aloud why he did as the boy asked when he'd never been tempted to listen to him before. Althea chastised herself for not thinking of her belt which was as strong as any lightweight rope and twice as long as the boy was tall. Jordan reminded them that if he hadn't grabbed the boy's arms nothing could have happened.

Darrel kept his mouth shut. He had been frightened. The wind whipping past him was winter-cold and stinging. It was strong enough to rip the seams of his tunic and no one wanted to guess where he'd have landed if Drum had lost his grip. But bad as it was, he hadn't been as frightened as he'd been in Annon's chamber when he thought the magician was a demon.

He hurt. He'd been stretched between Drum and Jordan for an eternity until they all fell to the moss. That was one of the reasons he hadn't said anything. His joints burned and he was probably an inch or more taller than he'd been in the morning. It was a different sort of pain, and he'd be glad when it was gone, but as pain went it was nothing compared to Lord Erwald Ironhawk's leather belt when he doubled and redoubled it before applying it emphatically to his younger son's backside.

"We're all together," he announced when they seemed to have run out of new ways to criticize themselves. "And we're in the right place."

Jordan looked up from sharpening his boot-knife. "Be quiet, Squirt."

"No, he's right," Althea defended the boy. "We are in the right place. Balthan cut his mark into this piece of wood. He made a map."

Althea stared at the carved and painted wooden shingle they found propped against a tree trunk. Balthan's mark was legible in each of the corners. She went over to it, gave it a quarter-turn, then retreated to study it again.

"Aye—" Jordan agreed when he saw her brow knotted with frown wrinkles. "Balthan's left a map the same way he left a message—and it's as certain as sunrise that neither were meant for us. We'll never find him with that to guide us."

The farrier snatched the shingle and threw it aside. "Hammers and bells—stop worrying about Balthan! He's the least of our problems. Where *are* we?"

No one answered. No one could answer.

Jordan climbed a tree and reported that they weren't anywhere near Cove or Lock Lake. There were rocky hills to the west of them, but no sign of a cave or dungeon. There were no roads that he could make out. There was no sign that the forest was inhabited—no plumes of smoke, none of the sharp-edged clearings that marked an assart, and no sign at all of a city or village. They could easily think they were the first people to set foot in this part of Britannia— assuming they remained in Britannia—except for the decorated shingle someone, possibly Balthan, left behind.

"What are we going to do about food?" the farrier continued his litany of complaints. "Or shelter. The blackthorns here haven't put their leaves out yet. We must be leagues north of where we started. There's going to be a frost to-night, I'll wager. And our extra blanket is sitting in a basket beside a marble pillar in the temple doing us no good what-soever.''

Jordan tested the edge of his knife with a callused thumb. ''Are you sure you haven't forgotten anything, Drumon? I figure we've got two days walking to get to anywhere. What about the mule and pony—they're still at Merdaunt.''

''Balthan will know the way back, once we find him,'' Althea said with more confidence than Jordan felt the sit-uation justified.

''You don't honestly think that moonlight is going to decipher that shingle, do you?''

Althea retrieved the piece of wood. She brushed dirt from one corner and set it back where it had been, against the tree. ''I just have to remember how he thinks, then I'll know why he made the marks the way he did, and I'll know how to find him.''

Jordan's reply of disbelief mixed with sarcasm was lost to a single shrill cry. It brought the young man to his feet, reaching for the unstrung bow even though the sound came from far away. Squirt drew his scaled-down sword.

''It sounded like a hawk,'' Squirt said, staring at the sky with his brother. ''Didn't it?''

Jordan shook his head but continued to scan the sky above them. He didn't doubt that the sound came from the throat of something that flew, but no hawk he knew cried so loud. And Lord Ironhawk of Hawksnest kept breeding-pairs of every type of hawk and falcon that could be trained to the lure.

''An eagle?'' he whispered to himself, then shook his head again. There might well be eagles in this wilderness, but his imagination insisted that not even an eagle with a wingspan as wide as a man's outstretched arms could have made the cry they'd heard. The part of him that continued to believe he lived at Hawksnest, surrounded by thick walls and retainers, wanted to hear the cry again, to see the creature that made it. The other part, the wiser part, was grateful for silence.

He finished stringing the bow and adjusted the quiver across his back. "Stay under the trees while I'm gone," he told the others curtly.

"Where're you going?" the boy demanded. "Can I come?"

"Hunting down by the stream—and you can't come because you make too much noise."

Althea looked worried. "You aren't hunting for that *thing*, whatever it was?" she asked.

Jordan swallowed a cutting reply. Lady Barbara relished hunting, whether it was riding after stag with the hounds or casting her sparrowhawk after woodcock and partridge; but as far as Althea was concerned, hunting was a form of magic she did not wish to learn. "No, nothing like that," he said finally.

"What was it, then?" Drum asked. He'd reached his own conclusions and was examining the bits of his axe.

"I'm not certain."

"What do you think it was?" Squirt pressed.

"You don't want to know."

The boy's imagination soared: "A *dragon*!"

"Do you think Balthan's sought the protection of a dragon?" Althea added almost as breathlessly.

Jordan shook his head in bewilderment. "Not dragons," he began. "Dragons don't scream, they roar—like cannon—and only when they're shooting fireballs. I was thinking, maybe a harpy—except they're not supposed to live as far north as we seem to be, and they usually fly in small flocks."

"Harpies." Drum put his axe behind him again. His first thought had also been of dragons. "Harpies—that doesn't sound so bad."

Walking slowly and trying to convince himself that the cry had come from an eagle, Jordan made his way to the stream he'd spotted from the tree he'd climbed earlier. If he had his way, come sunrise they'd follow the water downstream as far as they could. After a night which would probably be every bit as cold as Drum feared it would be, Jordan expected Althea would admit her brother's map wasn't going to yield its secrets. In the meantime, he hid himself in a tree overlooking a deep pool and waited with his arrow nocked to see what was thirsty.

A wood-pig and her kits were the first to appear and, out of deference to Althea, Jordan let her drink in peace. The next animal was a yearling deer. Jordan drew the arrow, held his breath, and waited for supper to raise its head— which it did just as the shrill cry was repeated. Jordan shot before he looked at the sky. Three huge birds circled downstream of his own lair. Their wings were powerful, but they'd never get their massive heads, necks, and talons off the ground without arcane assistance. They were harpies and, though they weren't dragons, they were a more formidable opponent than he ever imagined facing alone.

The shrill cry was repeated. One by one, the birds plummeted into the trees. The heir of Hawksnest wasn't the only one hunting the stream banks in the late afternoon. Jordan jumped to the ground and cut the undamaged arrow out of the dead deer's neck. After unstringing the bow and attaching it to his quiver, he draped the carcass over his shoulders and hurried back to the glade where he'd left the others.

Squirt was the first to see him and the loudest with the

predictable greeting, "Did you hear it? Twice and closer this time. Are you *sure* they're not dragons?"

The boy unsheathed his sword, which further soured Jordan's mood. "By the Eight, the Three, and the One, Squirt, put that *away!*" He let the deer fall from his shoulders and reached for his brother, who, as usual, eluded him. "Now! Or I'll take it away from you, I swear I will."

Althea and Drum didn't say anything. Their questions showed on their faces and they were no different than the boy's.

"I'm pretty sure they're harpies, but I'm absolutely certain they aren't dragons."

"Damn!" Squirt swore as he slammed the sword into its scabbard.

"You can't fight dragons with swords, dunderhead." Jordan clouted Squirt to the ground with the back of his hand—teaching the boy a lesson was not nearly as difficult as catching him. "I don't know if we could fight harpies with swords."

Squirt's eyes swam with tears and he refused to grasp Jordan's outstretched, forgiving hand.

"Why not?" Drum demanded.

"They're left over from ancient times when sorcerers bred magic into their slaves and pets. They don't live the way natural things do—the way we do—and they don't always die. If I had a magic sword, but I don't. There's a little linear spellcraft in this—" Jordan touched the bastard-blade at his side "—to help against rust but nothing to make it lethal. And that—" he confronted his brother who decided he still wasn't ready to stand up again "—that sticker will rust like a pig-iron if you don't take care of it. Brandish a rusty sword at me, will you?"

The boy rolled on top of the scabbard. "I'm sorry, Jordan. I forgot. I won't—ever again."

Althea distracted Jordan with another question: "I thought you said harpies didn't live this far north?"

"They're supposed to have a rookery on the cliffs above the dungeon of Hythloth. But they're magical birds—they can probably live anywhere they want. Nothing's going to chase them away."

"Could something have lured them away from Hythloth?" Althea asked.

Jordan noticed she was hugging Balthan's map against her heart. "Why don't you tell me."

"Balthan's in a cave near the Dungeon of Wrong—the dungeon Felespar had . . . has the Word for."

The preciseness of Althea's answer stunned Jordan. He stood with his mouth open while Althea showed him how the shingle could be opened like a student's diptych to reveal a carefully drawn, easily interpreted map on the wax inside.

"Simon would split shingles like this and wax them when he taught us our letters. We couldn't ever afford vellum and ink."

Their glade was clearly marked; the stream where Jordan hunted; the downstream path they should follow to the cave; the distinctive skull sigil of the dungeon nearby.

"I'm sorry," Jordan whispered. "I'm sorry I didn't believe you. But, that's *where* the harpies are right now. They could have come from the dungeon—if Balthan was correct and Blackthorn's gotten Wrong's Word from Felespar."

"We—you'll have to fight them, then."

Jordan shook his head. "I *can't* fight three of them, Althea. Let me have tonight to think about it. Maybe there's a way to separate them. Or draw them off."

"You could try to drug them like the gypsies drugged us," Drum suggested.

"It's a good idea, Drumon." When Jordan's first impulse was to tell someone to shut up or clout them on the head, and that someone wasn't Squirt, his second impulse was often superciliously polite. "But we don't have any drugs." He touched Althea's hand lightly. "Let me think about it tonight. I'll think of something before the morning comes. You have my oath on it."

Eighteen

With a broken twig for a stylus, Jordan noted everything he knew about harpies in the margins of Balthan's wax map: They were magical. They were less magical than dragons which had magic woven into their bodies and used spellcraft as a weapon. They were more magical than Althea's linear spellcraft or his rust-resistant sword.

And there were three of them.

Deep in his own thoughts, Jordan ignored the activity around him: Drum making a fire; Darrel dressing and flaying the yearling deer; Althea making a spit out of blackthorn withies. But the smell of venison sizzling as it roasted shattered his concentration. It reminded the young man of his empty stomach, nothing more.

Jordan smoothed the wax with the side of his hand. He had given an oath; he meant to keep it, but the problem had no satisfying solution. There was no way to conquer the harpies beside Balthan's cave, even if he was willing to sacrifice his life. He was almost relieved, then, when the quiet sunset was torn with the shrill cries booming through the calm evening air.

Ironhawk's heir jumped to his feet. The diptych fell to the ground beside him. "They've left their roost," he announced. He had the silk-and-sinew bow string caught at one end of the bow and was bending the wood to attach the string to the other. "Squirt—help Althea into one of these trees—and *stay* with her."

"What about me?" Drum asked.

"If they're anything like hawks, they attack mostly with their talons. Their first attack will be a stoop: They'll come in like a stone, spread their wings to slow themselves, then swing their talons forward. If you can survive *that*, they'll lose their advantage. Try to stay back and go after their wings. With those talons, they won't be able to walk on the ground like ducks or chickens. Break their wings, and they'll be almost helpless."

"You're going to try to put an arrow in them while they're diving?"

"That's the idea—but don't count on it. I'll be lucky if I get three shots; I'll be even luckier if I hit anything. It'll be like hitting a cannonball in flight."

"Good luck, then."

Jordan selected the best four arrows from the quiver and arranged them carefully on the ground beside him. He flashed a confident grin toward the tree where Althea and his brother had concealed themselves.

"They're probably not interested in us," Jordan reassured them with a bald lie. The noblest falcons ate carrion whenever it was available. The harpies were drawn to the scent of their fire. Roasting venison had become the best chance the young man would get to keep his oath and survive.

Drum spotted the birds first, pointing to the silhouettes spiraling against the gaudy sunset. "You're right. They don't seem to have noticed us at all."

Jordan frowned. "They've seen us. They're riding the air up high enough for a dive. See—they aren't beating their wings—"

"They are now."

One bird left the spiral and vanished in the glare. Jordan cursed—the harpies were intelligent enough to hide in the sun. "Get ready. They'll probably come from right about *there*—" He indicated a portion of the sky between the zenith and the setting sun. "You can let your eyes drift just a bit, not too much. I wouldn't turn my head."

Jordan took his own advice. He retrieved his arrows without looking at them, and put three of them between his teeth. After several deep breaths, he nocked the fourth against the flat silk portion of the string. "They're coming down." The words were barely intelligible.

"Luck to you, Jordan Hawson."

"And you."

The second bird was visible beyond the first before Jordan loosed the arrow. He couldn't wait to see if it caught or went wide. Holding his breath, Jordan drew and shot the second arrow before the first bird spread its wings and lashed out with talons as sharp as the farrier's axe. Jordan's concentration broke. He looked to his right to see if the farrier survived the stoop. He couldn't find the birds when he looked up again. Panicking, Jordan sought a target wildly and unsuccessfully. He was about to throw the bow aside when he saw a black silhouette coming from the same quarter as the tree where Darrel and Althea were hiding.

Jordan got the arrow off just before he felt the air move behind him. Ridding himself of the now-useless bow and arrows, he cleared the sword and made an upward cut in a continuous motion. The bird screamed, but neither Jordan nor it struck the other. The harpy's head was the size of a horse's, and naked as a vulture's. Its neck was scaled and crested: a clear sign of its magical ancestry. Its pale iridescent plumage had a certain beauty, but Jordan thought the arrow sticking out of its breast was infinitely more attractive.

"They bleed; they die."

The harpy kept its wings spread for balance when it lashed out with its talons or snapped its hooked beak. Jordan put both hands on the hilt and wove the bastard-sword through the tight curves of an upright infinity-loop. He had the strength to deflect the bird's attacks, but the talons were as hard as steel; his weapon could not damage them. Jordan struck the creature's beak, chipping the cartilage. The harpy responded with a shriek that forced Jordan backward. With his ears ringing, the young man yelled his war cry and with a flurry of cuts and slashes beat the magical bird back.

Jordan was trapped in a stalemate until the arrow-wound weakened the harpy enough to make it careless. He did not dare look beyond it to see how Drum fared; although the fact that he faced only one of the magic creatures, not two or three, could be an omen that the farrier survived. The harpy's hard red eyes followed Jordan's every move; it had the intelligence to exploit his patterns to its advantage. After a few close calls, Jordan was careful to keep his moves unpredictable. His wrists felt like frayed rope.

Finally, the harpy made its mistake. Listing to its weakened side, the wing struck the ground. Primary feathers snapped, but before the bird reacted to the damage, Jordan lunged forward, driving the bastard-sword into the harpy's heart.

"IRONHAWK!"

The harpy died with its crest raised and beak open for a final strike. It slid off the sword as it fell to the ground.

"IRONHAWK!"

Jordan allowed his perceptions to widen; he looked for the other harpies. Drum held his own against one of them. The farrier had gotten lucky; Jordan's arrows had put out one of the harpy's eyes. The third bird spread its wings on the opposite side of the glade. Darrel was astride its back flailing with his sword. The harpy's crest was a bloody ruin, and Jordan allowed himself a smile—until he saw Althea playing tempt-the-target in front of the creature.

The farrier would have to take care of himself a few moments longer.

Circling wide, Jordan approached the third harpy. The arrival of assistance was a dangerous moment for any warrior, but it could be a fatal distraction for an inexperienced one. The harpy saw Jordan before Althea knew he was there. While it shifted its attention to the greater threat of Jordan's bastard-sword, Darrel drove his sword up the bird's neck into its skull.

Drum's harpy went down quickly, after Jordan came on its blind side and slashed through the wrist-joint of its wing.

Squirt hollered the family war cry. He ran at Jordan who dropped his sword and caught him before they collided.

"He crashed into the tree after us—*splat*!—I jumped on top of him and rode him to the ground. He tried to bite, but I wouldn't let him. I had my sword and kept hitting his nose every time he tried. And when he went after Althea I'd cut at his neck. I'd've had him—even if you hadn't been there—"

Jordan was proud of his brother, and angry with him at the same time. "Didn't I tell you to stay with Althea?"

"I did—she fell out of the tree, so I had to jump on his back and make sure he didn't hurt her."

Althea assured Jordan, and Drum, that Squirt's story was truthful. She admitted she'd been stunned and bruised by the fall, but was adamant that the harpy never touched her. When she saw the boy clinging to the harpy she'd done her best to keep *him* from getting hurt.

Jordan was full of the reasons she should never have tried to bait a harpy, or anything else, but Althea stopped him before he'd uttered any of them.

"Your hand's bleeding."

A cut ran the width of Jordan's left hand along the knuckles. Looking at it, he remembered his harpy going for the swordhilt rather than the blade. He thought he'd pulled back cleanly, if a bit desperately, winning the exchange when he'd chipped the bird's beak. He assessed the damage by splaying his fingers then making a fist. Blood flowed thickly, but everything moved as it ought: The wound was superficial. It had probably bled itself clean by the time Althea noticed it, but Jordan couldn't take the chance. With no healcraft available, an injured warrior applied cruder methods. He sucked a mouthful of his own blood and spat it loudly to the ground.

Althea squealed with disgust and the boy laughed. Drum made a queer little noise and sank to his knees. Squirt doubled his laughter until they realized the farrier was injured. Drum's arm was open along from wrist to elbow; the sight of his living bone had unnerved him. He tried to stand up, and would have kept trying, if Jordan hadn't restrained him.

"I never felt it," the big man whispered as Jordan helped him lie down with the injured arm resting above his heart.

"That's always the way," Jordan agreed.

"You'll . . . do something before you cut it off?"

"Aye—I'll sew it up."

The farrier's eyes widened with terror, and Althea upbraided him acidly for joking at the worst possible moment, but Jordan knew what he had to do.

Stars shone in the clearing skies before Jordan had the gash cleaned as best he could without boiled water. He sewed it shut with a length of gut and sinew cut from the deer and seared in the fire Althea rekindled. They made a sling out of Darrel's belt. Drum felt well enough to eat dinner with the rest of them.

"You're not keeping watch tonight," Jordan said firmly. "These harpies will have kept out any other predator and scavengers. Squirt and I can handle the watch."

The boy beamed and announced he'd take the first watch. Jordan had no objection. He was ready to curl up in his cloak. There was reason to hope they'd been through the worst, and that following Balthan's map in the morning would present no new challenges, but he learned better than to count on hope or reason. He was loosening the laces of his buskins when Althea sat beside him on his cloak. Their encounter on the lakefront at Cove had happened earlier this same day—to Jordan it belonged in another lifetime.

"I didn't know you knew so many different things." She reached for his hand. "Not just swordwork and fighting. I wish I could do half the things you do."

Jordan put his injured right hand over hers. "You could sew this up. You've got to be better with a needle than I am."

Althea shivered. "I can't even think about it. Doesn't drawing the *gut* through hurt?"

"It hurts either way—but it heals better if it's cleaned and sewn. I always thought there was linear healcraft— helping hands, or something like that?"

"Soothing hands. I said I didn't have all the linear

spells. I get stiff inside when I think of healcraft. Soothing hands doesn't work for me. I've made things get worse when I've tried, so I never do. Almost never. Except on myself.''

"Well—we'll find Balthan tomorrow; he can take care of anything I missed. There's probably nothing to worry about. It was a clean cut, and, before Destiny, Drum's as tough as an ox.''

"Most injuries heal themselves,'' Althea mused, "if they're left alone. That's true, isn't it? It's true in the kitchen—we don't go running to Lord Ironhawk's apothecary every time there's a cut or scrape. We get pecked by the hens every morning gathering eggs. Nothing comes of it.''

Jordan yawned. "Aye—there's nothing to worry about at home. And that's where we'll be headed, one way or another, by tomorrow night. Go to sleep, Thea.''

She left quietly, and Jordan had the notion that she was worried. Probably about her brother. Again. He didn't let it keep him awake.

"I only just closed my eyes,'' he protested when Darrel nudged his shoulder.

The stars didn't lie, the boy insisted, and Jordan surrendered his place by the fire. He tried to guess the location of the glade by the angle and movement of the stars. He found the three guide stars and from them he located true north in the sky, which seemed further above the horizon than it had been—as it would be if Balthan's arcane stairway dumped them in the northern forests. But he'd known that much from the blackthorn bushes.

For the remainder of his watch, Jordan crafted his version of the battle with the harpies and imagined reciting it to Lord Ironhawk. The sky was brightening before he realized he was no longer afraid of his father.

Drum beat the sun up. His arm had swollen some during the night; it hurt more than he wanted to admit. But the flesh near Jordan's uneven stitches was a healthy color and not unduly warm to the touch.

"Maybe I should burn it anyway?" the farrier suggested as Jordan reknotted the bandage.

"Destiny's hind foot, Drum, is that all you can think of—hot iron? It's going to be fine. We'll cut the gut out in a few days. By then we'll have Balthan with us."

The boy was the next to awaken. Killing the harpy hadn't completely transformed him, but taken with everything else that had happened, Jordan had begun to think of him as Darrel rather than the Squirt. Darrel studied the diptych map intently and did not break it or smear the wax image.

"When do we go?" he asked.

"As soon as Althea wakes up."

But Althea gave every indication of sleeping until noon. Drum was the one who decided to awaken her.

"She's burning up with fever," the farrier said from his knees beside her cloak.

The young woman did not stir when they called her name. There were countless ways to get a fever in the wilderness. Exhaustion alone could weaken a man, or a woman, into illness.

"Maybe we should wrap her in all the cloaks and see if she'll sweat it out. Or maybe we should cool her off with cold water from the stream. What do you think, Drum?"

Drum, as always, had nothing to say. Jordan wrapped the unresponsive woman in her cloak and his, but when another hour had passed and Althea still hadn't opened her eyes, he went to the stream and came back wringing his shirt. He bathed her face and hands. He loosened the laces of her sleeves and cooled her arms. Under the farrier's disapproving scrutiny, he unwound the cloak layers from her legs.

"I'm going to take off her buskins and wash her feet. If that won't wake—"

There was blood on his hands. There was a hole in her skirt none of them had noticed the previous evening. Fighting back tears, Jordan lifted her skirt. She hadn't fallen from the tree, she'd been dragged. Straight bruises revealed where the harpy had clamped its beak over her thigh. A weeping puncture showed where the hooked tip pierced her flesh. Angry red streaks radiated from the hole.

"She tried to heal herself," Jordan whispered.

The sensation of air, rather than linen, against her leg roused Althea from her stupor. She tried to push her skirt back where it belonged. When she met resistance, she opened her eyes.

"I'll be all right. It's just a scratch. It will take care of itself," she insisted, still trying to yank the cloth out of Jordan's hand. "I'm tired, that's all. Let me sleep."

"You're not tired—you're sick. You knew you were hurt and you didn't tell us. You used that spell, didn't you— and you made it worse. Now there's nothing we can do." Jordan was distraught with anger and helplessness.

Althea got the cloth out of his hand and made it cover her legs. "I wasn't going to let you cut me, or burn me, or sew me up with gut-string. Or suck the blood out of me! I've been pecked by birds before."

Jordan rocked back on his heels, openmouthed and clutching air in his fist. "Chickens, Thea," he stammered. "Chickens—not harpies."

"Then find my brother."

Drum put his good hand on Jordan's shoulder. "That's what we must do."

Numb all over, Jordan wrapped Althea in the cloaks and

got to his feet. An insect buzzed around his head. He swatted it. "We can't leave her here." He gestured at the harpy carcasses.

"I'll stay here until you get back with Balthan," Darrel volunteered, his hand resting manlike on his sword.

"I don't like splitting up like this. It looks like it's only a couple of furlongs to that cave, but we don't know, and we don't know what we'll find when we get there. There's a dungeon around here, and it might be open. I'd rather stay together, even if we have to carry her."

Jordan stood his ground, but both Drum and Darrel stood against him. If the cave wasn't where they thought it was, or if Balthan could not be easily rescued, they could change the plan. Otherwise, they were wasting time.

Balthan's map led the two men out of the trees, face-to-face with a dungeon entrance in a weathered knob of rock. The plug of black rock with its glossy obsidian runes repelled them when they approached. It had not been tampered with by Balthan or anyone else. The harpies roosted near the dungeon of Wrong, but they had not escaped from it.

"A benison," Jordan observed. "Felespar must be one strong-willed old magician."

"Or he died before they could get the Word out of him."

Jordan paused partway up the steep path beyond the sealed dungeon. "Wouldn't it be easier to be hopeful once in a while?"

"Hope is for women, children, and fools, not men."

Ironhawk's heir continued through the rocks in silence. Their path followed a seam of light-colored, porous rock to another tree-ringed clearing where the harpies made their foul-smelling roosts. Fewmets and rotting meat littered the ground beneath the nearest trees. Sharp-edged stones were heaped against the darker rock where Balthan's map showed his cave.

"Well, what do you think?" Jordan asked through the sleeve-cuff he pressed over his face.

"I'd rather clear the cave than root through this." Drum indicated the reeking mess around them.

"You don't think we'll find him in there, do you?"

Drum nodded. He couldn't lift anything heavy, so Jordan did most of the work. The scab on his hand cracked and oozed. He tore the hem from his shirt and bound it over his palm and fingers until they were splinted into a mitten shape. The sun was slipping past its noon zenith before he cleared an opening broad enough for either of them to squeeze through.

"Let's see what's in there before we clear the rest," Jordan suggested, wiping his brow with his bandaged hand.

He went to the rock where he'd left his mail shirt and sword. With a little help from the farrier the mail settled on his shoulders. Jordan took the sword from its scabbard. He probed the opening with it, then led the way into darkness.

Beyond the rubble, the cave was high enough for both to stand erect. "We should have torches and rope," Drum commented.

"Aye, we should, but we don't. Do you want to go outside to cut branches from the trees where the harpies roosted?"

"Maybe we won't need to. See if you can find him."

Jordan's grimace was lost in the dim light. Using the sword as a blind man's stick, he explored the chamber. "Empty," he muttered after several minutes, "except for a hole in the back and to the right."

"I suppose you think a skinny magician filled that entrance up and then crawled through a little hole in the back?"

"I don't think the harpies would guard an empty tomb. The hole's big enough to crawl through."

Barely. They wriggled along on their bellies, Drum protecting his arm and Jordan shoving the long bastard-sword ahead of him until they came to a sharp bend.

"We can't go any further. We've got to turn around," Jordan called when no amount of pushing or twisting would get the steel through.

"How?"

"Well, back up, then."

"Can't you leave the sword here? When I get out of here, I won't come back in, Jordan, I swear it. It's too dark, too tight—like the bowels of the world."

"Thanks, Drum, I hadn't thought of it in quite that way. Let's keep going."

Warning the farrier to be careful of the sword's edge, Jordan wriggled over it. The bend became a downward spiral. Panic snagged Jordan as easily and often as the rough stones of the passageway snagged his mail shirt. He willed himself to breathe evenly and kept the terror at bay until the passageway funneled out.

"We're coming to something!"

Drum didn't respond. Jordan thought he was alone but the farrier eventually emerged beside him in a second, smaller chamber.

"Over there." Jordan took the farrier's arm and pointed it toward a faintly luminous patch in the distance.

Drum took one hunched-over stride before the other young man could restrain him.

"Destiny's sake! We're not standing in my lord father's dining hall! Slide your feet, man—don't charge like a rutting bull."

The farrier paralyzed himself with images of what might have been. Jordan eased past him and made his way to the light, crawling on his hands and knees, testing the rock thoroughly before trusting it with his weight.

"Put your shoulder on the right wall and follow it

around," he told Drum. "I think Balthan's in the chamber below us."

They knelt on either side of a narrow chimney that dropped cleanly into shimmering silver-blue light. They could see the floor of the next chamber through the light. Jordan guessed it was a twenty-foot drop.

"Balthan likes to dump people into things," Drum observed. "How're we going to get down there *and* get back up?"

"Could you hold a rope while I climbed up it?"

"We don't *have* a rope."

"Belts, dunder-Drum. We'll knot our belts together."

Muttering that his name was Drumon, or Drum, the farrier unwound his belt while Jordan did the same. Drum's belt was a utilitarian piece of leather long enough to go around his waist once with a tab that could be tucked out of harm's way at his side, but Jordan's was extravagantly long, circling his waist twice before drooping to the heavy buckle on his right hip. It was, however, typical of belts worn by fighting men who might have to replace a saddle-cinch, bridle-reins or a rope with it.

"We hardly needed mine—" Drum said as Jordan fed the knotted leather down the chimney.

His complaint was truncated by a brilliant flash and acrid tang of singed leather. Jordan hauled the belts back up. He bent the leather to assure himself the damage wasn't serious.

"Remind me never to go questing after a magician again," Jordan said lightly, trying to squelch the tremors in his stomach. "Got to find out what's down there. Balthan's ghost did say he wanted to be rescued—right?"

The farrier had no comment. Jordan lowered the belts again. There was another flash, then calm silence. He helped Drum wrap the end of the belts around his uninjured forearm, then lowered himself down the chimney.

"I'm going to deadfall the rest of the way," Jordan called when his feet were inches above the bottom of the chimney.

With his eyes closed and his arms against his face from the instant he let go of the leather, Jordan protected himself as he dropped to the floor. His hair lifted from his neck; the air of the chamber smelled like lightning, but Jordan survived unharmed.

"I'm going to open my eyes, Drum. Drum—can you hear me? Destiny's hind foot—not *that* again."

"No," Drum replied, "I can hear you—you've opened your eyes. What can you see?"

At that moment Jordan saw the unworked rock wall of the chamber bathed in flickering blue light from a source behind him. Cautiously, the young man turned in place. The metal studs of his dangling belt struck his cheek; they were cool.

"Destiny have mercy on us all—"

Jordan's voice did not carry up the chimney. "What—? What did you say?"

"He's here all right. He's looking at me, but I don't think he sees me."

The magician's chamber was about twelve feet square and very cold. Gooseflesh rose on Jordan's skin; he began to shiver. Balthan sat cross-legged on a bed of crude planks. A richly embossed book with a gilt binding lay beside him, as did a coarse-woven sack. Jordan forced himself to notice these details, but his eyes were drawn to the magician himself. Both his arm were stretched above his head, his eyes were closed and his teeth were bared in a grimace worthy of a cornered troll.

"What do you mean? Is he alive—is he safe? Can you talk to him?"

"Balthan?" Jordan cleared his throat. "Balthan?"

"Well—is he alive?"

"He's stopped time."

This was a slight exaggeration: No mage could halt time completely, but Balthan Wanderson—supposedly a mage of the Second Circle—had come close. He'd gotten what appeared to be a week's worth of food into the underground chamber—Jordan didn't want to guess *how*—and in the course of a month or more, didn't appear to have touched any.

"Is that a problem?" Drum shouted down the chimney.

"I don't know. I'm guessing the light comes from the boundary between the spell and the rest of the chamber, but I don't know what will happen when I cross it."

"You're going to cross it? Do you think that's—"

"I'll prod it first with my knife," Jordan assured the farrier. He drew the boot-knife from the top of his buskin and held it before him.

"Why don't you throw it?"

"When I get clos—" Jordan was in midstride when light blasted through the chamber. Stunned, Jordan dropped to the floor. "I can't see!" he shouted. "I'm blind!"

Nineteen

No amount of weapon practice with a piece of cloth tied over his eyes prepared Jordan for the reality of blindness. The young man's mind believed his eyes had been gouged out—though there was no physical pain and his quivering fingers assured him that his face was not streaked with gore. His eyes opened and closed as he willed, but, open or shut, what he *saw* did not change: bursting brilliance in the sickly colors of a nightmare.

"I can't see!"

Anguish brought tears, warm, salty tears, from Jordan's eyes, but he remained blind—if the crazed light exploding in his skull could be called blindness.

"Talk to me, Drum! Can you hear me? Where are you?"

"Jordan! What happened? I saw another flash—it seemed brighter . . . longer. It blinded my eyes, too. But I can see now. Come back to the chimney, let me see you."

"Where—I don't know where!"

"I'll come down, then. Hold on."

"No!" A certainty erupted in Jordan's panic-tossed thoughts. "Talk to me. Keep talking. Make the belts move. Make them hit the wall. I'll find the sound."

Drum did as he was asked. The swinging leather brushed Jordan's outstretched fingers.

"How do I look?" He pointed his face toward the ceiling.

"You look—no different, Jordan."

"My eyes!"

"No different. Maybe it's the light. Do you want to go after Balthan anyway?"

"I'm blind—dunderhead!"

Drum believed Jordan: the heir of Hawksnest was too proud to panic in jest or deceit. "But what about Bal—"

"Balthan can burn in the hot fires of Hythloth! I'd rather be dead than blind."

Drum braced himself beside the chimney while Jordan pulled himself up arm over arm.

"You lead," Jordan said hoarsely while Drum unwound the belt from his forearm.

"Why? It's pitch-black in that wormhole. I'd be as blind as you—"

"No. I'm blind—but it's not midnight-blind. You lead."

Their journey to the surface took less time than the descent, but for Jordan Hawson, the minutes he spent in the narrow passageway while light burst inside his head were the longest of his life. When Jordan heard the bastard-sword scraping ahead of them, his thoughts turned to falling on it once he could stand up erect.

The light—how, Jordan moaned silently, would he ever know when he was back in the light?

They reached the main chamber. Drum hurried toward the exit hole.

"Say something, Drumon." Jordan's voice was weak. "Talk. Let me follow the sound of your voice."

"Hammers and bells, I'm sorry. Give me your hand."

"No!"

Jordan tripped and fell while eluding Drum's patronizing hand. The bandage on his hand was wet. The blood came from the gash on his hand, not his chin. Jordan's reflexes hadn't deserted him, he'd protected his face when he felt himself falling, but he'd lost the will to move on his own.

"Come on—give me your hand."

This time Jordan held his arm out until the farrier found it, then he followed like a little boy. He knew when they left the cave and sunlight fell on his face: The seething colors merged into a single, white-hot blaze. Closing his eyes did not help, but binding the thick, and sticky, cloth he'd wrapped over his hand around his head did. Jordan pulled the knot tight; he was finally midnight-blind.

Heedless of the stench around them, Jordan found a flat rock and sat down.

"We've got to go back. We've got to tell Althea and the boy what we've found," Drum urged. "Here—take your sword." Drum leaned it and the scabbard against Jordan's shoulder. They clattered to the ground; Jordan made no effort to retrieve them. "Maybe it's no more than sun-blindness. Your face is a bit red."

Jordan didn't respond.

"Damn you, Jordan Hawson, I'm not going to pick your sword out of the dirt and tie it around you!"

In grim silence, Jordan found his possessions in the rubble at his feet. On the second attempt he fed the sword into its scabbard. He rose unsteadily to his feet and buckled it below his left hip.

"Let's go," the farrier said, taking Jordan's hand.

* * *

Althea was dozing when the men entered the glade. She didn't know there was a problem until Darrel wailed. When she saw that there were only two of them, and that Jordan's eyes were covered with a bloody bandage, she forgot her fever and injury.

"What happened? Where's my brother?" She took Jordan's hand from Drum and held it tightly. "Tell me."

Jordan wrenched his hand loose. "Your damned brother laid a trap that blinded me."

"But you found him? You saw him?"

Angered, disgusted, and filled with an anguish words could not describe, Jordan turned away from the sound of her voice. He took two strides before tumbling over a harpy carcass. He pounded it mightily with his fists, but did not try to stand.

Althea looked at Drum who shook his head. "There was a tremendous flash. So bright it hurt my eyes, and I wasn't in the chamber. He says all he can see are swirling colors —except when the sun hit his eyes, then he screamed about a white-hot poker."

"The blood—"

"From his hand."

Althea comforted Jordan with soft words and caresses, as if he were a frightened child. She helped him to his feet and guided him to the pile of cloaks where she rested. By then her fever reasserted herself and she leaned against him as much as he leaned against her.

"We both need Balthan now. If only there was a way to let him know—"

Jordan found her face with his fingers and made her look at him. "Don't you understand? *He* did this. Your damned brother's frozen himself behind a wall of light. He's waiting for the damned Avatar—not his little sister, not some dumb

Peer's son on a whim-quest. Lord British himself couldn't get through that *thing* he's set around himself."

Althea pushed Jordan's hand away. "Are you sure he's not a prisoner?"

Sighing, Jordan conceded, "There might be something wrong. He looked like he's screaming—like he'd go on screaming forever. And that's fine with me."

Althea sniffled. "I'm sorry. I'm sorry for what he's done to you, and I'm sorry for him. Balthan wouldn't mean to . . ." She dried her eyes. "Is there anything I can do—anything at all?"

"Aye—brew me up some poison from the bowels of those stinking birds. Let me get this over quickly."

Althea was speechless, but not Darrel. The boy knelt at Jordan's feet. "Don't *talk* like that. You'll get better. Don't lose hope. Tell yourself over and over again that you're going to be able to see again. Make your eyes heal! You can do it—if anybody can cast a spell on himself and make it work, you can, Jordie."

Squirt was ready to dodge one of Jordan's powerful backhand slaps; he had no defense ready when Jordan wrapped him in a bear hug instead. Jordan hadn't taken off his mail shirt. Any joy the boy got from the affection was tarnished by the discomfort of it. He endured as long as he could, then he wriggled free.

The sight of Jordan's arms weaving aimlessly in search of him sent Darrel running from the glade. Althea hobbled after him.

"Althea, you shouldn't—" Drum said hesitantly.

She fixed the farrier with a stare that reminded him why he never told other people—especially her—what to do.

"Althea shouldn't what?" Jordan asked, turning his bandaged face toward Drum.

Drum considered telling him. Althea might listen to

Jordan; she'd given him an oath of obedience and sometimes she allowed it to bind her. But if she listened? If he
ordered her back and she came, then what? The four of
them could stare at each other. The three of them. Drum
said nothing.

Jordan thought he was alone. He called them all by name.
Althea and the boy couldn't hear him. The farrier simply
didn't answer. Jordan stopped calling. He tightened the
bandage over his eyes; then, on hands and knees, he followed a moss-covered root to its tree and settled against the
trunk like a stone.

Resentment boiled through Drum's thoughts. He wanted
to rail at Jordan for failing them when they needed him
most. Althea was the driving force behind this misguided
quest—that was part of the problem: She was always behind, *pushing*—never leading. Jordan was their leader, and
now—just because he couldn't see . . .

The farrier got a taste of the bile brewing in his throat
and walked away before he spat it out. Getting mad at Jordan
Hawson wasn't going to help. Drum longed for his forge
in the Hawksnest foregate. When there was a problem he
had to solve, he liked to heat an iron ingot until it was
cherry-red, then hammer it flat, fold it, heat it, and hammer
it again until the answer came to him. He had no hammer,
no anvil, just an axe and a forest full of trees.

Drum was no woodsman. His axe was better suited to
splitting logs for the forge fire than felling trees, and his
right arm was useless. But labor loosened his thoughts and
freed him from his anger. As woodchips scattered wildly
around him, notions wove and rewove in his mind. When
the tree was weak enough to topple, Drum was ready.

Everything came back to Balthan Wanderson: He could
heal Althea. He could undo whatever damage his magic

had done to Jordan's eyes. He could get them home. There was one problem: Balthan; and there was one solution: Balthan.

Jordan was as Drum left him: leaning against a tree, his hands limp in his lap. Althea was nearby, wrapped in the cloaks, looking pale and feverish as she slept. Squirt had raided the harpies for feathers and was trying to fly.

"Jordan?"

With the bandage around his head it was impossible to know if the Peer's son was awake or asleep. Drum nudged him with his foot.

"Go away."

"I've got to talk to you. We've got to get Balthan out of that cave."

"Not me, Drum. I'm no good to myself, or you, or anyone. I'm not fit for living. I might just as well die right here. If you want to get Balthan out of that cave, you're going to have to do it all by yourself."

Drum settled against the tree beside Jordan. "I wasn't thinking of doing it myself. I was thinking of your brother, the Squirt. Do you believe in Destiny?"

"No. Not anymore. Look at me, Drum. Look at what Destiny's done to me. Destiny's a joke—but no one laughs."

"Lord Shamino found the boy near Hawksnest, but brings him all the way to us outside of Britain instead of taking him home. While everyone else is crippled with a headache; the boy goes out and finds Annon the Magician who tells him where to find Balthan. He finds the end of the stairway, and because of him we're all here. Whenever Squirt touched Althea's talisman, it got clearer. He's the key. He's the one who can get Balthan out for us . . ."

Drum waited; Jordan said nothing. But the farrier could

be as stolid and stubborn advocating an idea as he was resisting one. While Althea slept and the boy leaped from the pile of carcasses, Drum eroded Jordan's indifference.

"It's Destiny, Jordan—don't you see—understand it? Magic doesn't effect your brother the way it effects the rest of us. He has a talent for finding a way out, no matter how it's hidden. You've said it yourself: You can't hold onto Squirt unless you're willing to hurt him. He'll go right through that light."

"There's a better way." Jordan leaned away from the tree. "There's no way to know what would happen to Darrel—or Balthan, for that matter—if he went through that spell-light. And no need to find out. He can make a grapple-line and pull Balthan out."

"How—with what? I was figuring to take your belt with me again."

Darrel launched himself with a shriek from the head of the uppermost carcass. Both men looked toward the sound. Jordan stiffened when he realized what he had done; his fragile enthusiasm for the farrier's plan faded.

Drum got another idea. "We could gut those birds—that'd give us the length."

The vision of Jordan's mind's eyes was still sharp and its image of fastidious Balthan finding himself trussed in bird intestines overcame his anguish. "I was thinking of tying a rock to one end of Althea's belt. It should be long enough to go though the spell, wrap around Balthan, and come back out again."

"If I'm right that Squirt won't get flashed the way you were."

Jordan's smile faded. "If you're right."

"We should ask the boy which he wants to use: guts or Althea's belt."

"If he wants to do it at all. He'll be heir now; it's got to be his choice."

Darrel needed no time to make up his mind. Drum was still explaining why he, himself, couldn't be the one to climb down the cave chimney, when the boy figured out that *he* would be the hero. But Jordan's calm assertion that he was no longer the heir of Hawksnest left Squirt loose-limbed and gaping.

" 'Of sound mind *and* body,' Squirt. I can't be confirmed to the holding."

The feathers dropped from the boy's hand. "Lord Ironhawk would never make *me* his heir. He really would send for Milan the healer. He'd do anything to get your eyes back. You're the heir, Jordie—not me, I'm just Squirt. I don't want to be the heir. You'll see again. You've got to see again."

Jordan shrugged and grimaced. "I can't see now, and right now *you're* Ironhawk's heir. You've got to think about all of Hawks—"

"I won't be the heir when you can see again, right?" When Jordan nodded, Darrel turned to Drum. "Let's go. There's no time to waste. Should I take my sword?"

"You won't need it, but take it if you want," Jordan said, sounding almost like his old self, until he reached for Squirt and didn't come close to catching him.

Darrel stared at Jordan's hand. The boy's conscience said he should give his hand to his brother, since Jordan couldn't take his, but that was akin to admitting that Jordan wasn't going to get better, and that was more than he could do. He ran toward the stream and Balthan's cave instead. Jordan let his arm fall.

"I better go after him," Drum said. "You'll be . . . You can take care of yourself?"

"I'll find out."

The farrier started to walk away.

"Drum! Don't forget Althea's belt—you don't have time for guts!"

Guiltily grateful that Jordan could not see his flaming cheeks, Drum knelt beside Althea. She woke up babbling about nutmeg for a New Year's pudding. He took her belt and told her to go back to sleep.

"She's worse off than you."

The farrier stood beside Jordan as he spoke. Jordan did not turn his head.

"You've got to take care of her. She doesn't know where she is. If she starts moving—if she tries to get up—you've got to stop her, somehow."

"I'll sit on her. You've got to catch my brother."

By the time Drum finally caught up with him Squirt was inside the cave and eager to crawl through the narrow passage to the second chamber.

"Are you scared?" the boy asked without a trace of tact. "Do you go through first because you're older and bigger, or do I because I'm a Peer's son and the heir of Hawksnest until Balthan heals my brother?"

In the heartbeat before he opened his mouth to admit that he didn't want to reenter that wormhole at all, Drum gained a lifetime of insight into men like Jordan and his father who valued Valor and Honor above Honesty. "I go first. I'm bigger, I'm older, and I've done it before."

The farrier repeated those words to himself as he shouldered himself through the tight curves. He stood where Jordan had, in the second chamber looking at the flickering light on the floor on the other side, and caught the boy charging straight across just like Jordan had caught him.

"We're not standing in your father's dining hall. Test every step before you make it! We didn't mark out this chamber. Stay to the right. Keep your hand on the wall."

"You sound just like my brother."

"He was right," Drum said, forgetting what he'd discovered about the limits of Honesty. The boy didn't move. "Get behind me and *stay* there!"

Darrel tucked his hand through Drum's belt and stretched his legs to step exactly where the big man did. He gasped when the dangling end of Jordan's belt touched off a flash of light.

"*Wo-ho!* Is that the light that *blinded* Jordan?"

"Like enough. Keep your eyes closed and your back against this side as you leave the chimney."

"In case you're not right about me sneaking through?"

"Aye." Drum hung Althea's weighted belt over the boy's neck. "Don't do anything without telling me what you're going to do. You're certain you're ready?"

Darrel answered by dropping his legs down the chimney. He descended the belt-rope faster than Drum would have preferred, and didn't hesitate at all when his toes reached the chimney bottom.

"Ironhawk!" The boy hit the floor without tripping the brilliant defenses of Balthan's chamber. "Damn!"

"What's wrong! What happened?" Drum called anxiously from the top of the cave chimney.

Darrel looked up. "I bit my lip." There was a dark smudge on his lower lip. "It's higher than I thought it was."

"Will you be able to reach the belt-end to climb out?"

The boy nodded slowly. "Aye." He looked away from the ceiling hole before adding, "If I had wings."

The chamber was cold—as his brother said it would be. Balthan looked like he should be screaming, but he wasn't moving—not even as much as the rope had moved in the bolthole after Annon cast his Rel Tym spell.

"It's just the opposite of what Annon did. We were inside the spell and the outside was slow. Balthan's slow inside so we must—"

"Don't worry about that. Can you do it? Remember—keep your back to Balthan and your eyes closed when you move forward."

Darrel mocked the farrier's anxious warning until he took his second backstep and triggered the flash of light. He wasn't blinded; he'd had his eyes closed and his back to the shimmering drapery—but he'd been so certain that he'd stride through all the magician's defenses unscathed and unnoticed. Being wrong shook the boy's confidence more than the flash of light had.

"I'm taking my third step, now."

"Be careful—if you've tripped it once, you'll probably trip it every time now."

Sucking on his swollen lip, Darrel slid his heel back. The hot light flashed immediately. Darrel felt each hair on his head stand straight up. The cold air reeked of lightning and singed hair.

"I'm scared, Drum. I can't do it! I just took a little tiny step and my hair got burnt. I'm coming back!"

"No! Take a deep breath, and take a *bigger* step. You've got to get close enough to swing the belt, Squirt. For Althea, and your brother."

"I can't."

Drum wiped the sweat from his face. They'd come so close only to fail because a boy was afraid.

"Darrel—*Do it!*"

"I can't."

"I'm pulling up the belts . . ."

"No!"

There were two flashes, one as the end of Jordan's belt left the chamber, and the other as the boy took the largest stride his legs allowed. Darrel's flesh tingled and his scalp felt like ants were nesting on it—but the farrier was right: A big step was no worse than a little one, and one more big step would have him close enough to throw the weighted belt.

"Eye of Destiny—can you see me all the way down here? Make it not my time to die—please?"

He took the last step.

"Squirt! What was that—are you all right?"

Darrel opened his mouth twice before he found his voice. "I'm where I'm supposed to be: The blue light is behind me. I'm—I'm going to turn . . . around!"

"Close your eyes!" Drum called after the fact.

The drapery was formed of glittering specks. The blue ones were ice-cold and the white ones massing together not an arm's length from Darrel's nose were the source of the searing hot light. The boy had rubbed a cat's fur the wrong way; he had a pretty good idea what was going to happen when he sent the weighted end of Althea's belt whipping around the frozen magician.

"O All-Seeing Eye of Destiny—remember: I'm doing this for my brother and for Althea. I don't want to be a hero. I don't want to be my lord father's heir. My heart is *pure* as the fresh-fallen snow."

The Eye hadn't failed him, but the Eye was All-Seeing, not All-Powerful. Darrel turned again. "I've got my back to it. I'm going to throw the belt in now," he shouted to Drum and the Eye.

"Squirt—if you can't watch what you're doing, you might miss. We may only have one try. Squirt—listen to me! Turn around. Keep your eyes open until you've thrown it, then close them."

"My name is *Darrel*, farrier."

Darrel draped the weighted belt over his fingers, letting the feel of it penetrate to his muscles and memory. It was a little like a whip, a little like a sling, and a lot like nothing the boy had ever held before. Jordan said the weighted belt would work. Jordan was a master in the art of fighting: He understood how anything could become a weapon—but did that mean Jordan was right about rescuing Balthan with a rock tied to a strip of embroidered cloth?

The boy let a bit more of Althea's belt slip through his fingers. The rock swayed in front of his knees. He could have spun it in front of him like the vanes of a windmill. But spinning a rock in front of him wasn't at all the same as whirling it through the spellcurtain and around Balthan. Squirt's old enemy, his secret demon, reappeared to addle his thoughts.

"Jordie! You should've showed me how!"

"What? Squir—Darrel, what did you say?"

"I don't know what to do!"

"Throw it."

"When did you ever throw a stone and have it come back to you, farrier? I can't just *throw* it. I've got to make it go fast, and I've got to make it go around, and there's not enough room! He should've showed me!"

"Jordan didn't *show* you because he's blind!" Drum threw the rope made from his and Jordan's belt down the chimney. "All right—give it up."

The studded leather struck one part of the opening after another before slowly spiraling to the center where it hung straight and motionless. By then Darrel understood how he could start with a rock whirling around in front of him and transform it into one that spun away from him and around Balthan.

There was thunder along with the lightning when the rock

pierced the spell curtain. It lifted Darrel up and threw him into the far wall.

"What happened? The light's gone. All gone. Darrel. Darrel! *Squirt!*" Drum shouted from above.

"Who's there? What is happening? Damn—I must still be asleep. I must be dreaming again. *In Lor!*" another voice replied from the far side of the lower room.

An amber glow, not unlike Althea's handfire, bloomed at the carved end of a magician's staff.

"Squirt? Squirt Hawson? Darrel Hawson?" Balthan's head appeared in the light.

The boy crawled forward. "We came to rescue you."

"*You* came to rescue me?"

The staff fell from Balthan's fingers, extinguishing the lesser light spell. The magician made noises that could have been laughs, or sobs, or agonized moans—in the darkness neither Drum at the top of the chimney nor Darrel at the bottom could say for sure. Then everything was quiet again.

"Balthan—are you still there, Balthan? Could you make your light again, please?" The boy was afraid to move.

"How did you find me?" the magician asked after making light bloom at the end of his staff again. "How—*why* did you find me? Don't you know what's happened?" A stray thought turned the tide in Balthan's mind: "Lord British is back! Blackthorn and the shadows of evil have been vanquished—"

The boy shook his head. "We found you because Althea had a talisman that led us to Cove."

"Althea—Althea my sister? Is she with you? That talisman I made for her—sweet heaven, I forgot. That's how you found me?"

Darrel nodded. Balthan's knees hit the stone floor so hard that the boy winced. The magician clung to his staff, beating his forehead against the polished wood.

"The Avatar—I thought it was the Avatar who came to me in the Flame. I believed. I did everything he said, but it was only another shadow tempting me to my own doom." He raised his face. "The sisters—what of the sisters at the temple? Did you see them? How are they?"

"Almost as surprised and disappointed as you seem to be," Drum shouted down the chimney. "Grab onto the belt. There's no time to waste."

Balthan's disdain for Erwald Ironhawk's household hadn't been strong enough to convince him to make friends among the artisans of the foregate. He didn't recognize the farrier's voice.

"Who's up there?" Balthan whispered. "Who brought you here?"

The boy whispered his reply, "Drum—he's a farrier from the foregate, and he's all mushy for Althea. Just like—"

"Jordan—where's your brother, Squirt?"

Drum bellowed before the boy could answer, "Stop whispering and climb up here! We haven't got all day!"

That struck a chord deep in Balthan's thoughts. "The harpies! How did you get past my three jailors?" Then suddenly the magician thought he could answer his earlier question. "Jordan. Is he— Did he—"

"We killed them yesterday. Me, Jordan, and Drum each killed one."

"And you all survived?"

"We'll all survive if you get yourself moving up this damn chimney! Althea's hurt bad—she's dying. You're our only hope."

Until that moment, Squirt would have sworn Balthan was as pale as a man could be without being a corpse, yet he grew paler before the echo of the farrier's words faded away completely. He thrust the gleaming staff into the boy's unwilling hand.

"I have nothing left," the magician muttered. "I used all the scrolls I had to make the time wall to sustain myself while I slept. If she's dying—I don't know what to do." He held out the ornate book so the boy could see that most of the pages were blank.

Darrel planted one fist on his hip. "You better do something for her," he said firmly, "and for Jordan, too."

"Jordan?" A pained expression settled over Balthan's features. "What about Jordan? You didn't say anything about Jordan, did you?" The spellbook fell from Balthan's hands. Before the magician retrieved it, his whole body contorted with a yawn.

"You weren't screaming—you were yawning!"

"I slept once after my mentor, Felespar, was taken—do you know about that? Did you understand my message?" The boy nodded and shrugged noncommittally and Balthan kept talking. "I haven't slept since. I don't think I've slept. I don't think I've actually fallen asleep yet. The time wall . . . everything. I can't think straight. Maybe if I *did* sleep—"

"You can sleep later! Now haul your worthless magician's hide up here!"

Twenty

W ith Drum ahead and Darrel behind, Balthan, his
spellbook, and his sack worked their way slowly
through the wormhole. Balthan was nearly as
blind as Jordan when he emerged into the late afternoon
sunlight. The magician sat on the flat rock where Jordan
had sat earlier in the day. He refused to move until his eyes
adjusted to the light, which they did quickly enough, though
Balthan reeled like a drunken tinker when he walked.

"I'm exhausted," Balthan explained, leaning against a
tall boulder. "It's twenty days at least since I slept—and
worse because I'd started to sleep within the spell." He
said he'd be himself again once the ginseng-and-garlic mixture he invoked against sleep took effect.

"I don't think it's doing what it's supposed to do," Squirt
confided after he faded back from Balthan to walk beside
the farrier. "He keeps saying the same things over and over
again—just like he did in the stairway. And that stuff he's

eating . . . ? Every time he opens his mouth to say something—the harpies didn't smell so rotten.''

Drum grunted. He didn't care how bad the magician's breath was, but he was concerned that Balthan couldn't seem to take three steps without stumbling over his own feet. "Stay with him, Squirt, I've got to think. There must be some way we can wake him up long enough to take care of Althea. Then he can sleep for a week if he wants to.''

Darrel wasn't happy to be Squirt again, and he was downright angry that both Balthan and the farrier seemed to forget that Jordan needed a magician's skills as much as Althea did. The boy understood that Althea's precipitous illness had to come first.

"But you can't leave my brother *blind* for a whole week! He's our leader. If anything happens—if more harpies come—you've got to heal Jordan's eyes before you go to sleep!'' Darrel whined when the magician lurched sideways.

"I won't sleep,'' Balthan slurred his words. "I can't sleep. The shadows'll find me again. They'll find you, too, and we'll all be doomed. I won't sleep.'' He shoved his hand into the sack he wore slung beneath his shoulder, then licked a greenish powder from his fingers. "*An Zu.*'' He invoked the spellcraft which banished sleep. "I won't sleep. I won't sleep.''

Balthan stumbled again and stayed upright only because Darrel had a firm grip on his belt. "Sure you won't. We'll drop a hot coal down your tunic. Maybe that will keep you awake long enough to heal Althea *and* Jordan.''

Where magic failed, the sight of three harpies—each of them broken, bloodied, and surrounded by a cloud of flies—succeeded. Balthan sought out a specific bird and stared at its dull eyes.

"This is the one *I* killed.'' The boy kicked the carcass as he bragged.

"It was the leader. You were lucky."

"I was not!"

The magician's back straightened and his shoulders rose. He would have pressed the argument if Drum had not clapped him on the back and turned him toward Jordan, who had not moved, and the heap of cloaks near Jordan's tree that marked Althea's bed.

Balthan deserved his reputation for sharp-tongued arrogance; he also deserved his reputation as one of the most promising young mages in Britannia. Though his formal training ascended only to the Second Circle, Balthan's hands wove above his sister's clothed and blanketed body with the deft assurance of a master. At length he sat on his heels with his hands folded in his lap.

"She reached too deeply for the skills she had. She drew the harpy's poison straight to her heart."

Drum turned away with a groan, leaving the boy to ask, "Can you heal her?"

"No," the mage said calmly, reaching into his sack. "Healing is the knitting up of torn flesh or bone, or— sometimes—the quelling of disease. I may *heal* Althea's leg injuries before I'm done here, but that's not what's killing her. Come here—hold your hand out flat."

Balthan poured pungent ginseng and garlic into Squirt's cupped hand. Then to the boy's abject dismay, Balthan spat on the powders and mixed them into a thick paste with the tip of his well-honed knife.

"Stop wiggling. *Your* blood won't help the reagents."

When the paste was smooth in the boy's hand, Balthan made a tiny cut in Althea's neck, earning himself a veiled threat from Drum who was, by that time, kneeling on the opposite side of the young woman. Only Jordan's curiosity was not roused by the incipient spellcraft; he remained where he was with his face pointed away from the activity. Balthan caught several drops of Althea's blood on the blade of his knife. These he mixed with the ginseng and garlic, then he smeared the paste over the cut and along the arch of his sister's neck, using his knife as a mason might use his trowel to spread mortar on a wall.

"Clean it." Balthan handed the knife to Squirt. "Carefully."

"Can't I watch?"

The magician closed his eyes dramatically. "If you must." His fingers surrounded the paste like the stone ring of a shrine. He invoked the power of the spell.

Darrel, and even Drum, expected something marvelous to happen, but nothing did. Balthan kept his eyes shut another moment more. The only indication that magic had occurred came from the weariness that showed in his eyes and the tremors that returned to his hands.

"When the paste's dry, the poison will be gone. If she hasn't recovered, I'll use healcraft." Balthan was talking to himself more than the two worried faces beside him. "She's young, healthy. The poison moved quickly. It hadn't had the time to cause much damage. She won't need healcraft." He was lightheaded and after trying to stand, decided he would stay on the ground where he was.

"Don't forget—you've got to fix Jordan, too," Squirt said, returning Balthan's immaculately clean knife.

Drum guided Darrel to the fire. "Leave him be. Help me get the fire rekindled."

"But Jordan—"

"We won't let him forget your brother. Tell me, would you truly want him working spellcraft on Jordan right now when he can't stand up or see straight himself."

The boy pouted, but conceded the point. He helped rig the spit over the fire again. His mood improved as soon as the venison was hot enough to release its particular magic.

The leeching paste was dry before the meat was ready. There was a red line where the cut had been and a faded bruise along the arch of Althea's neck. Her fever was gone and her eyes, when she opened them, were lively.

"Balthan!" Althea wrapped her arms around her brother's neck. "I'm so glad to see you. So glad you're well."

The magician returned her embrace. "I never meant for you to be the one to come after me."

His voice was so weak that Drum, who'd left the fire, could not tell how the statement was intended.

"When we learned that Lord Blackthorn had disbanded the Great Council, taken Councillor Felespar prisoner and then *tortured* him—all I could think of was how you fared. Then, when I saw the darkning in the talisman you gave me. There was no way I could not come after you."

"Darkning," Balthan repeated, reaching into his sack for another dose of sleep banishment. "What darkning?"

Drum returned to the fire and the roasting venison, taking the boy with him. The farrier would not presume to interrupt Althea as she told Balthan how they'd come to rescue him, or correct her version of the events she chose to reinterpret.

"But what about Jordan! He hasn't hardly moved since we got back. He says he's not going to eat anything." Darrel tugged on Drum's sleeve and danced from side to side as he tried, unsuccessfully, to enlist the farrier's help. "Jordie won't even come closer to the fire now that it's getting cold. Balthan's *got* to do something for my brother!"

The boy was scrappy and determined, but he had only a fraction of Drum's sheer strength. The farrier jerked his arm free. "Jordan was blinded by magic. It happened and that's the end of it. He's not sick; he's not injured; he's not dying the way Althea was. He's blind—simple as that. When Balthan's ready, he'll see what he can do. But there's no sense to rushing a magician, and Jordan's not getting any worse.''

"What do *you* know? I know what I'd do if I couldn't see, and I'm not the heir and I'm not a warrior like my brother is. I'd sit down, just like he's done, and I'd wait to die, 'cause life wouldn't be worth living.''

Argument wasn't going to improve the situation, besides, in his heart Drum suspected the boy was right about Jordan. Jordan Hawson without his bastard-sword was difficult to imagine; the thought of him tapping along with a blind man's staff was almost inconceivable. But the honest reason Drum turned his back on the boy was the terrifying image of a journeyman farrier barred forever from his forge by mid-night-blindness.

Althea concluded her narration of the quest to find, and free, Balthan with his apparition in the stairway. "The rest is obvious," she said, indicating the dead harpies and Jordan.

"*Kal Wis*—that's all you had to say. *Vas Wis; Kal Wis*,'' Balthan shook his head to answer the question his sister was about to ask. "No, it's not spellcraft, it's how we greet each other at the Lyceum. I wanted to leave everything I knew about Blackthorn and the evil around him in my legacy, but I was afraid at the same time. It was easy to modify the spell on the scroll. Any mage would complete the greeting, but Blackthorn or anyone they sent would not. Or so I hoped.''

"You expected another magician to search for you—not the Avatar, and certainly not me.''

Balthan did not say that the Avatar was the greatest of all magicians, nor did he offer to tell his sister those portions of his legacy they had not heard in the stairwell. That was all behind him now—a path not taken; Balthan looked to the future instead. "You should be a magician, Thea. The talent for spellcraft is in the blood, and we have the same blood. It was one thing for Lord Ironhawk to decree he would send me, but not you, to the Lyceum; he was within his rights as our guardian. But it was remiss of me not to send for you. Even a First Circle mage can support himself mixing apothecaries' potions. I've made several of those talismans. I'm not poor any longer. I'm not depending on Hawksnest charity, waiting for Lady Barbara to remember to send me my stipend.

"My thoughts were focused on acquiring land. I'd get for myself all those things Simon promised me. I'd make myself Lord Balthan without ever setting foot in a Virtue shrine.

"When I entered the Flame, I saw how hollow I'd become. I vowed to share my wealth with you—but even that is hollow. You have great potential, Thea. Drawing the poison to your heart was a terrible mistake—but it was a *magician's* mistake. I will take you to the Lyceum. I'll engage the best tutors. You'll claim the destiny that's rightly yours."

The spellcraft Balthan sent coursing through Althea's body left a sense of well-being in its wake. She was tired and weak, and filled with victory. Althea listened to her brother's impassioned plans without being swept along.

"I'm content at Hawksnest," she said truthfully. "I shall be content as the mistress of whatever small estate Lord Ironhawk arranges for me . . ." That was less than the truth: She'd be more content to remain at Hawksnest and most content to remain as the lady-wife of its next lord. "I don't want to *claim* my destiny—do battle for it like a warrior. You and Jordan, you're warriors—always proving yourselves and looking for new challenges. I'd rather live at the center of the life I have instead of the edge of the one I don't.''

Balthan was astonished by his sister's response to what he regarded as the first genuinely virtuous gesture of his life. ''You could be whatever you want to be,'' he sputtered.

''I want to be the person I already am.''

This was the exact dilemma Lord British himself faced when he exhorted the men and women of his realm to avail themselves of the liberties he gave them. All too often an intelligent, talented citizen, like Althea, would choose to ignore every opportunity.

''Destiny defines many paths,'' Althea recited. ''Watching you and Jordan take the High Path is all the excitement I need.''

Exhaustion robbed Balthan of the means to dispute Althea's determination not to become a magician, or, striking closer to his heart, her calm equation of himself and Jordan Hawson. If there were one person with whom Balthan wished no equality whatsoever, that person was the erstwhile heir of Hawksnest. ''Althea, you can't mean that,'' he said finally. ''Not Jordan. Don't turn your back on everything because of Jordan. Spellcraft is nothing like swordplay. Becoming a magician is nothing like becoming Jordan Hawson.''

Balthan looked at the morose young man leaning against his tree; Althea looked with him. Her mind's voice shrieked: *How could you forget?*

''Is there nothing you could do for him?'' Althea whispered, as if Jordan could overhear. ''You know he was blinded by your magic.''

Jordan had not been blinded by Balthan's magic; he'd been blinded by several scroll's-worth of his mentor's Eighth Circle magic which Balthan had desperately joined into a single invocation. The magical principles of conservation and symmetry prescribed that a counterspell *must* exist; but Felespar himself would be unlikely to uncover it—especially as the time wall was the product of scroll magic rather than spellcraft. This knowledge, plus Balthan's disdain for Jordan, blind or sighted, clamored for expression; and went unsaid.

The Flame of Virtue cast its purging light into every corner of the young magician's spirit. By itself, the Flame could not reform any man or woman's character. A determined mind could reconstruct its old subterfuges. Balthan did not lack determination; he lacked sleep. The most recent banishment was already losing its potency.

"When I bound the scrolls together to make the time wall, I never imagined how I would take them apart." Balthan assumed the Avatar could do it easily and hoped that Blackthorn and his allies could not. "I don't know where to begin with Jordan's eyes."

"But you'll try?"

The magician folded his hands into fists which did not tremble.

"For me? I swear I'll learn true magic—"

Balthan knew an empty promise when he heard one, he'd heard so many from Simon during the first decade of his life. He also knew better than to waste his precious strength arguing with Simon's daughter. "I'll do what I can for him in the morning, after I've slept. After *you've* slept, too."

Althea smiled and Balthan returned the smile. Drum, who'd been watching closely from the fire, sent the boy to tell them the venison was steaming hot and waiting to be eaten. Darrel gave his brother the same invitation, but Jordan grumbled that he'd done nothing to work up an appetite. Neither of Erwald Ironhawk's sons was a skilled dissembler. When Squirt tried to force a meaty rib into his brother's hand, Jordan used it as a club, then threw it clear across the glade. The boy's reply was a swift kick into Jordan's ribs and a swifter retreat to the fire.

The mood of the evening was set and Balthan quickly discovered the only thing that could halt the bickering between the boy, the farrier, and his sister was his own foolishness when he tried to mediate among them.

"You weren't with us," Althea scolded. "You don't know what we've all been through since we left Hawksnest. It's not your place to tell us what to do."

"I wasn't trying to. I merely said that this glade is an isolate of my mentor's Moonstone which lies buried here. He used it whenever he had to come to inspect the dungeon. I bound it with two scrolls to create the path that brought you here, but now it's free again. We can all use it to return to the moon gate nexus outside of Yew. It doesn't stay open very long—if the boy swears he didn't see it last night, then it must have opened during Jordan's watch—"

"Jordan would have told us," Drum decreed, brandishing a bone in the magician's direction.

"Aye, if my brother didn't say anything, he didn't see anything. It's as simple as that."

Balthan sighed and ate the rest of his meal in chastened silence, while his three companions moved further from any agreement about the next leg of their journey. At first the magician marvelled that they'd managed to settle on a direction outside Hawksnest foregate, then he remembered they'd had the *Kal Wis Por Mani* talisman, and Jordan.

The Peer's son was their leader. Jordan gave his cohort their direction, and a common foe. Balthan realized if he'd held his ground when the other three turned on him, he could have taken Jordan's place. This was not an idle or philosophical observation that Drum, Squirt, and Althea needed a Peer to lead them, but a personal understanding that he, Balthan Wanderson, could have been that Peer, had he so chosen. As his sister chose not to use her talent to become a magician, Balthan recognized that he had chosen not to become a Peer.

Balthan left the circle of firelight to avoid this mirror of his own devising. When instinct led the young magician to point directly opposite Jordan, he forced himself to find another place to sit. He stayed there, watching and thinking, until the sky was dark and Althea came over to bid him good night.

"Have you decided what you're going to do?" Balthan asked.

"We've agreed to wait until morning, after you've healed Jordan's eyes."

"What if I can't heal them?"

"You're doubtful because you're tired. Once you've gotten your rest, you'll feel better. You'll find a way. You will sleep, won't you? The boy says you swear you won't sleep and that you're using spellcraft to keep yourself awake. You said you'd sleep."

The magician committed himself to nothing. He found it easier to stay awake after the sun went down. Morning would be a different story, but he had enough ginseng and garlic in his sack to keep him awake for another month of ordinary time. He'd expected the reagents to last for years behind the time wall; the Avatar wouldn't be drawn to Britannia until and unless the situation got much worse.

Balthan watched Drum and the boy draw straws for the first watch. He couldn't tell who won, but Drum wrapped himself in his cloak and stretched out with his back to the fire. Darrel visited his brother, then came striding across the glade.

"You better go to sleep. You've got work to do once the sun comes up."

Balthan ignored the boy, much as Jordan had done. Squirt's confident facade crumbled.

"Jordie won't hardly talk to anyone. He says he doesn't care where we go tomorrow, 'cause he's not coming with us. And we can't go home without him. Even if you can't heal his eyes, you can talk to him—tell him that we'll find someone who can. Maybe Annon—"

"Go to sleep, Squirt," Balthan said flatly.

This wasn't the first time Squirt dropped Councillor Annon's name into the conversation. Both Althea and Drum emphatically believed the boy surprised the Eighth Circle mage in his bolthole. Balthan could not accept that, even though Squirt described the man accurately, from his favorite red robe to his absurdly thick spectacles; and the message—which Squirt swore he remembered word for word—sounded alarmingly sincere.

"You can't make me. I'm on watch."

"I'm staying awake. I'll take your watch. Now: *Go to sleep.*"

The common name for the linear spell was mother's-voice, and there was considerable debate in the Lyceum whether it was a manifestation of magic or nature because no reagents at all were needed to cast it. There was, however, no doubt that it worked best with children and when the spellcrafter appeared willing to reinforce magic with physical punishment. Squirt stifled a yawn before a third invocation sent him tottering toward his cloak.

Balthan meant to keep watch—he also meant to dig up the Felespar's Moonstone, and he didn't want an audience while he did. If his scroll-craft had damaged the stone, and its gate, in any way, Balthan had no better idea which direction led back to civilization than Althea, Drum, or the boy did. The magician had assured himself that the three by the fire were sound asleep and was about to start digging when he remembered Jordan.

"Decided to come over and gloat?"

Balthan leaped straight up. His heart was pounding when he landed. "No—how'd you know it was me?"

"I'm blind, not deaf. You have feet like lead. You always have and you always will. A corpse could hear you coming a furlong away."

There was some truth to the statement—Balthan had never had much success sneaking up on Jordan during the years they shared at Hawksnest. But the situation was not quite as bleak as Jordan painted it.

"I remember one afternoon after the hay was in. You were stalking the cow-herd's daughter, and had finally cornered her behind the barn. You thought you were alone . . . Is this starting to sound familiar?"

"I was listening. I did hear you—with those huge, heavy feet of yours, I thought you were her father."

"I was a lot closer than a furlong—you'll grant that?"

"Aye—I'll grant that." A nostalgic snicker slipped out with the words. "I was distracted. You never had a chance, Balthan, unless I was *very* distracted."

"Which you're not now."

The temperature between them plummeted. Jordan wrenched a chunk of bark from the tree behind him. He flung it at Balthan who gasped when it hit him in the chest and had no doubts that it struck precisely where it was aimed.

"Damn you and all magic," Jordan snarled.

"You never set a trap that caught the wrong prey?"

"I never set one to maim and cripple, not kill."

"If it's any consolation, Jordan—it *should* have killed you."

There was another long silence before Jordan said,

"Aye, that's a consolation. Everybody's luck goes sour eventually—and we'd had too much good luck finding you."

"Doesn't help you any. I made that time wall with Felespar's scrolls. I don't know how it worked or how to counterspell it. Honest."

"Since when have you sworn by a Peer's virtue?"

"I stayed in the Flame a long time. It—the Flame of the Avatar—didn't change me, but I can see things differently now."

"So can I, too bad we're both blind. It's lies, Balthan Wanderson. All lies. I don't think there ever was an Avatar. Even if there was, what difference does it make? No man or woman has ever received enlightenment at all eight shrines. There's never been an Avatar who stayed *here*, and there never will be. No one man or woman of us measures up to Lord British's standards—how could we, we're only human, and who knows what he and the rest of the Companions truly are."

"No one man or woman is supposed to." Countless memories came out of the corners of Balthan's mind. "That's what drove Simon to drink. He wanted to be *the* Avatar—the embodiment of *all* virtue—and he wanted to do it alone. But you can't do it alone. It's like making a spell—there are eight reagents and an infinity of spells to be crafted from them. Mix the pure reagents, invoke them with the proper word—and you get magic. There are eight virtues—but they are never pure, every man and woman has them all in different proportions—choose your cohort carefully, forge them together—and you all become the Avatar!"

Balthan wanted to share this sudden, unsought enlightenment. He tried to raise Jordan to his feet. The Peer's son shoved him forcefully away.

"I don't care. I'm not going to be any part of anyone's Virtue cohort."

The magician got a firmer grip on Jordan's arm. "You thick-skulled ox—you're the *Peer*; you're the leader! Drum, Squirt, my sister—you're the one who's forged them together."

Jordan would not listen. "Your hands are like ice."

"Forget my hands—I haven't slept in a month, my blood's like water. Listen to me! Don't you see it?"

"No—I don't." Jordan found a pressure point in Balthan's wrist and bore down with his thumb until he was free. "I'm blind!"

Balthan's fingers were numb, but he got them hooked under the cloth around Jordan's eyes just the same. "Take this off!"

Roaring like a wounded beast, Jordan surged at the magician.

"Leave me alone!"

It was not the first time the two fought each other, or the hundredth. Jordan had never had much of an advantage in size or speed; his usual advantage in strength was offset by Balthan's wild enthusiasm. They were as evenly matched as they'd ever been, and woke everyone else from a sound sleep. Drum made one futile attempt to separate them, then contented himself with keeping Squirt and Althea from joining in.

When the brawl was over neither Jordan nor Balthan could stand, and, in the faint moonlight, the other three could not tell who claimed the victory. One of them, however, was crawling toward the fire embers. Drum had almost reached Balthan when the magician wrapped his hand around a piece of half-burned wood and invoked the First Circle light-spell from its ashes. He swung it at the farrier who wisely retreated.

"How many fingers am I holding up?"

At that exact moment there were none. Balthan needed both hands to keep his grip on the gleaming torch while he limped over to Jordan. His fine damask shirt was torn down the front and the back. One sleeve had been ripped loose and dangled from his wrist. Dirt or blood, or both, was smeared across his face. Jordan looked a bit better when the steady light fell on his face. His bandage had become a necklace. His mail shirt had protected him, but both sleeves of his tunic were gone and somehow he'd managed to become separated from a buskin.

"How many fingers?" There were three—his thumb, index, and middle fingers.

Jordan raked the hair away from his eyes and squinted at the light, which was very near the source of Balthan's voice. Althea held her breath and Squirt called on the Eye of Destiny.

"Hythloth—I don't know. There're green and red blobs exploding everywhere. I can't see a damned thing, Balthan. I'm *blind*!"

"How many now?" Balthan tucked his hand behind his back.

This time Jordan didn't try. His head sagged forward. He braced his arms to keep from sinking further. "Leave me alone," he pleaded.

"Close your eyes. *Remember*. How many fingers am I holding up? Which ones?"

Jordan's hair touched the mossy ground. "I don't—" He stopped and raised his head. His eyes were wide open, and his mouth. "Three. On your left hand. The thumb and the next two."

The magician sank slowly to his knees. "I used three scrolls: An Tym, to slow time; Xen Corp, to kill; and Vas Lor, great light to bind them together and because it was the only scroll I had left. I don't know what happened to the Xen Corp—" The gleaming wood fell from Balthan's fingers"—but it's the other two that are blinding you."

"I can't *see*, but I can remember what I saw, like a stone skipping across water? Balthan, that's no better than being stone, midnight-blind."

"It is—trust me." Balthan coughed then moaned. "Anabarces—you busted my ribs."

"Why should I trust you? Can you unspell my eyes?"

The magician doubled over, clutching his side. "Feels like a damned knife."

"There's one around here somewhere." Jordan groped for it without immediate success. "I'll be glad to shove it between your ribs so you can tell the difference if you don't answer my question: Can you unspell my eyes?"

"No, but Councillor Annon can, when we find him, or it might just wear off. Time spells can't last forever."

That was all Darrel had asked of the Eye of Destiny. He slipped out of Drum's arms and, since his basic faith in his brother's indestructibility was restored, assaulted him.

"You're going to see again—you'll still be the heir!"

Jordan might well have crushed the life out of him if the air of the glade hadn't begun to crackle. He couldn't see the moon gate rise out of the ground like a spear then broaden into a shimmering wall, but he could smell and hear it.

Balthan rose painfully to his knees. "Hurry. It won't be open long. Get my sack and spellbook, and anything else that's important."

Althea and Drum gathered everything they could find in the sapphire light of the moon gate. Jordan probed the moss for his buskin and his boot-knife. Squirt raced from one harpy to the next tearing feathers from their wings. Balthan stood beside the gate, exorting them to hurry, before leading them into and through the moon gate to a glade that seemed, in the eerie light, identical to the one they'd left, but Balthan assured them, after tending his injuries with a mixture of ginseng and spider silk, that it was less than a mile from the city of Yew.

"We'll be there in time for breakfast," he mumbled as he fell asleep.